Smooth
PLAY

Smooth
PLAY

REGINA HART

KENSINGTON PUBLISHING CORP.
http://www.kensingtonbooks.com

DAFINA BOOKS are published by

Kensington Publishing Corp.
119 West 40th Street
New York, NY 10018

All Kensington titles, imprints, and distributed lines are available at special quantity discounts for bulk purchases for sales
promotions, premiums, fund-raising, and educational or in-
stitutional use.

Special book excerpts or customized printings can also be created to fit specific needs. For details, write or phone the office
of the Kensington Special Sales Manager: Kensington Publishing Corp., 119 West 40th Street, New York, NY 10018,
Attn: Special Sales Department, Phone: 1-800-221-2647.

ISBN-13: 978-0-7582-5882-3
ISBN-10: 0-7582-5882-8

First trade paperback printing: January 2012

10 9 8 7 6 5 4 3 2 1

Printed in the United States of America

To my dream team:

- My sister, Bernadette, for giving me the dream
- My husband, Michael, for supporting the dream
- My brother, Richard, for believing in the dream
- My brother, Gideon, for encouraging the dream
- My friend and critique partner, Marcia James, for sharing the dream

And to Mom and Dad always with love

Troy Marshall needed a plan. But when the Brooklyn Monarchs' vice president of media and marketing had read the Twitter message that the professional basketball team's captain was drinking heavily at this trendy Brooklyn nightclub, he hadn't stopped to think. He'd simply reacted.

He navigated the hot, smoky space past the sweaty, gyrating bodies in the darkened downtown club. The bass of a popular urban song pounded in his chest, echoing his heartbeat.

Memories of his own club-hopping years came back to him. Another lifetime, another world. Who had he been and what had he been hoping to prove? Trying to hold on to an image and a lifestyle he'd lost.

Troy mounted the stairs to the club's VIP floor. Two mountains masquerading as men secured the perimeter of the team captain's private section. Their stony stares dared him to approach them. Before Troy could introduce himself, Barron Douglas's voice defused the standoff.

"He's OK." The Monarchs' captain shouted his

grudging approval above the driving beat of the club music. His voice was slurred.

Troy's irritation rose. Shit. There were a lot of places he'd rather be at two o'clock on a weekday morning. Like home. In bed. Preferably with a warm and willing female. He'd leave that thought alone for now. He watched impatiently as Kilimanjaro on his left unhooked the purple velvet rope barrier to allow him into Barron's inner circle. He nodded to the large security guard as he walked through.

One of the women stood, separating herself from the pack. She moved toward him with practiced sensuality. Her stilettos' thin heels spotted her an extra five inches. The silver satin of her stingy dress wrapped her generous curves and shimmered against her brown skin. Even in the club's dim lights, Troy could see the avarice in her dark eyes.

"Who are you?" The groupie stood too close. She raised her voice above the club's entertainment.

"A friend of Bling's." Troy looked toward the NBA player. Hopefully using Barron's nickname would reassure him that Troy was there as a friend, not a representative of the franchise's front office.

"Are you a basketball player?"

The woman looked him over. Troy could hear the cash register in her head tallying the cost of his cream silk jersey, black pants, and Italian loafers. Did she think every tall, physically fit, and financially comfortable African American male played basketball?

"No." Troy started to move around her.

She shifted to block him, taking hold of his arm. "What do you do?"

Troy glanced from her to Barron and back. "I look after the players." As an NBA media and marketing executive, that wasn't part of his job. Then why was he here?

Her brown brow creased in confusion. "Like a babysitter or something?"

"Or something."

The groupie's greedy gaze considered him again. "You get paid a lot to do that?"

"Not enough."

"Do you want to babysit me?" She licked her lips as though her offer needed clarification.

In the past, it hadn't mattered whether a woman was interested in him or his wallet. But it mattered now. Troy removed her small hand from his arm. "No. Thank you."

Ignoring the groupie's disappointed pout, he continued toward Barron. He stopped beside the table. Barron scratched his scalp, bared between his thick cornrows. From the sheen in Barron's dark brown eyes, Troy feared alcohol wasn't the only contributor to the player's unnatural high. "Bling, let's talk."

Barron stared through Troy. His gaze wasn't quite focused. His movements were deliberate as he lifted a heavy crystal glass and took a healthy swallow of its brown contents. He put the drink down with a thud. "Talk."

Was the Monarchs' captain deliberately trying to antagonize him? It didn't matter. It had been a long day and Troy was short on patience. But he wasn't going away. "In private."

Barron's sigh was more tired than annoyed. He placed his hand on the shoulder of the big man beside him. "Move."

Barron stood with slow, unsteady movements. Troy tensed with worry. Getting drunk was bad enough, considering Barron was a professional athlete whose season hadn't ended. If drugs were involved, he wouldn't cover for the team captain any longer.

He followed the six-foot-five player past the velvet rope barrier and the human mountains guarding it. They came to the railed landing overlooking the dance floor. Shifting lights irritated him. What effect were they having on Barron in his intoxicated state?

Troy pitched his voice above the dance music. It seemed even louder up here. "What are you doing, Bling?"

The point guard's smile was too bright. "Partying!"

Troy wanted to shake him. "It's after two in the morning. Practice starts in nine hours. You need to bring your A game to the play-offs."

Barron's smile vanished. His glazed gaze hardened. "What do *I* have to do with whether the team does well in the play-offs?" Frustration tightened the other man's stance and strained his voice.

How could Troy reach the basketball player? "You're the team's captain. You represent the Monarchs to the public on and off the court."

Barron curled his lip. "That didn't stop the Mighty Guinn from benching me last night."

Troy should have expected that response. De-Marcus Guinn was the Monarchs' rookie head coach. The media had been stunned when DeMarcus led the perennially losing team to a postseason berth. But DeMarcus had done it with Barron riding the bench at the end of the last regular season game, the game that determined whether the team got into the play-offs.

Was there anything he could say to ease the other man's anger? His temper was probably worse because of his pride. Troy drew from his experience playing for a successful college basketball team. "This is the first time in four seasons the team's gotten to the play-offs. And it's the first time in your career you've made it to the postseason. Isn't that incentive enough for you to give one hundred and ten percent?"

Troy stepped back as Barron swept his arms in an emotional gesture.

"I gave one hundred and ten percent all season." Barron's expression twisted with pain and disappointment. "The Mighty Guinn still benched me in the final sixteen minutes of the game."

DeMarcus had been right to bench Barron. If he hadn't, the players would be preparing to watch the postseason games from their sofas. But Troy kept those thoughts to himself. He'd read somewhere you're supposed to humor drunks. "That's between you and Marc. My concern is that it's two in the morning. The team doesn't need headlines about your early-morning clubbing when the first play-off game is Saturday."

Barron swayed on his feet again. "It's only Wednesday. Well, Thursday. And what do I care about headlines?"

At least the point guard wasn't so drunk he'd forgotten what day it was. "Believe me, you'll care when your name is smeared in the press. So humor me. Let me take you home."

Barron jerked a thumb over his shoulder. "I came with Ten-speed."

Was he referring to the heavyset guy who'd sat beside him in the VIP lounge? "Ten-speed can find his own way home. You're coming with me. Now."

Barron frowned. Would the point guard continue to argue? Troy didn't have time for this.

Barron rested a heavy hand on Troy's shoulder.

"Yeah. I guess I'm ready to leave. Thanks, man. How'd you know where I was?"

Troy stared at Barron. "You sent a Twitter message about where you were and what you were doing. Don't you keep track of who's following you?"

Barron shrugged. "I have thousands of followers, man. How am I supposed to keep track of all of them?"

"Try. Andy Benson is following you."

Barron gave him a sloppy grin. "Oh, yeah? That *Sports* reporter? She's hot."

Why did the other man's observation rankle him? "She's a reporter. You need to know who's reading your messages. Do you want the press to report that you're getting plastered at a nightclub during the play-offs?"

Barron scowled. "They've turned against me, too."

"Stop giving them reasons to criticize you." He gestured toward the player. "Do you have everything you need?"

Barron slapped both pants pockets. "Yeah, I've got my wallet."

Troy followed Barron to the steps as a young male server approached. The large, circular tray the young man balanced was burdened with alcohol.

Barron stopped. "Yo, my man. If that tray is for Barron Douglas's private group, take it back. I'm leaving and taking my credit cards with me."

The server switched directions to carry the tray back downstairs.

Barron looked at Troy over his shoulder. "I don't mind their company, but their freeloading gets on my nerves."

Troy frowned. "Then why do you hang out with them?"

Barron started down the stairs. "They want a good

time. I want a good time. And *they* don't hassle me about basketball."

Troy caught the verbal jab. It didn't matter if Barron was annoyed with him. It mattered how he performed during the games. That's why he was pulling the team captain out of the club.

He followed the athlete across the club to the exit. Barron lost his balance several times, stumbling into the club's other patrons. Interesting that he subjected only women to his clumsiness. Troy braced himself, unhappy at the prospect of being dragged into a fight because of Barron's childish antics. He saw a headline in his mind: MONARCHS' CAPTAIN, MEDIA EXEC IN DRUNKEN BRAWL. Luckily, once the men recognized the klutz tripping into their dates was Barron "Bling" Douglas, they were more understanding.

Despite Barron's attempts to antagonize the clubgoers, his celebrity got them out of the establishment unscathed. Outside, the cool mid-April breeze seemed even colder after the heat generated by the crush of sweaty bodies in the club. Troy handed the valet the ticket to retrieve his Lexus.

He watched Barron take deep breaths of the early-morning air. "Your friends in the club don't have your back."

"And who does? My *teammates*?" Barron sneered the word.

Troy didn't react. "Yes."

"Those punks don't have my back. They let Coach bench me in the last sixteen minutes of the game." Barron didn't sound as drunk now. Was it the fresh air or his anger?

"You're stuck on those sixteen minutes. Where were you the other thirty-two?"

Barron's face twisted with temper. "I was leaving

everything I had on the court. I was busting my ass to make the plays no one else would."

"They couldn't. You wouldn't give up the ball." Troy held up his palm. "What happens on the court is between you and Marc. My concern is the media coverage. The team can't afford negative publicity, not when we're trying to rebuild our fan base and increase revenue."

Anger still sparked in Barron's eyes. "What do I care about that?"

Troy gave the belligerent baller a hard stare. "The negative coverage affects your money, too. Do you want an advertising contract? What company wants to have their product pushed by a drunk?"

The silence between them was tense. It continued when the valet pulled up to the curb with Troy's silver Lexus. He gave the young man a generous tip before getting behind the wheel. His irritation spiked when Barron sprawled unmoving in the passenger seat. "Buckle your seat belt."

The point guard complied, his movement jerky. "Why'd you come for me tonight, man?"

"You mean this morning?" Troy checked his rearview and side mirrors before merging into traffic. "It's my job to make sure the team gets only positive media. It would really help me out if you'd stop screwing around." He let Barron hear his frustration and disappointment.

"So you left your bed—and probably a honey—at two in the morning to make sure the team gets positive press?"

"I wasn't with a woman."

Barron chuckled. "Guys like you are *always* with a honey."

Troy ignored him. "I was working late at home."

Barron's voice was distant. "You think you're going to get some kind of recognition for your hard work? I'll give you some advice, man. Wake up. You think the front office cares that you care?"

Troy pulled up to a red light. He turned to Barron. "*I'm* in the front office."

"At the end of the day, your desk won't protect you. The front office isn't loyal."

"If I weren't loyal, I wouldn't be here."

Barron grunted. "You aren't here for me. You said yourself this is about the franchise."

"And you're part of the franchise."

"Am I?"

Of course he was. He was the Monarchs' starting point guard, their captain. He and the team were inseparable. To protect one, you had to protect the other. And that's exactly what Troy was going to do.

Troy strode into the *New York Sports* newspaper's weathered and worn reception area. The middle-aged woman behind the desk was simultaneously transferring phone calls, typing at a computer, and signing for packages. She stopped typing, transferred the call, and thanked the delivery woman before turning to Troy.

"May I help you?" The question was brisk and delivered with a hint of an Asian accent.

"Troy Marshall to see Andrea Benson."

Her dark eyes studied him as though trying to decide if he was trouble. "Do you have an appointment?"

Maybe he should have called before driving to the newspaper's office. But after reading Andrea's article in that Thursday morning's edition of the *Sports*, he hadn't stopped to think about it.

He tried to win the receptionist over with a smile. "No."

Her cheeks flushed. She lowered her eyelashes and picked up the phone. "I'll see if Andrea's available." She pressed a few buttons. "Andrea, Troy Marshall is here to see you." After a moment's silence, she slid her eyes back to him. "I'll let him know." She replaced the receiver and nodded toward a row of chairs. "She's on her way. Please have a seat."

Troy stepped toward the cracked and battered vinyl chairs. He chose one in direct line of sight of the newsroom. Before long, Andrea Benson walked through the doorway. Troy stood as she came closer. Her long, lithe body moved with a sexy confidence that defied her conservative black slacks, white blouse, and gray blazer. Her honey brown skin glowed. Her straight dark hair swung hypnotically behind her narrow shoulders as she advanced on him across the aging linoleum.

She stopped and offered her hand. The expression in her wide sherry eyes was more curious than welcoming.

"This is a surprise." Her melodic voice reminded him of satin sheets and summer nights. But with her distant manner, he'd never confuse fantasy with reality.

At five-foot-nine, she was almost a foot shorter than his six-foot-four inches. But her energy and assertiveness made her seem even taller.

Her hand was warm and delicate in his. Troy gave her the smile that had won over her receptionist. "Do you like surprises?"

Andrea ignored his question and drew her hand from his. "What can I do for you?"

He glanced behind her at the newsroom before meeting her gaze again. "Could we talk privately?"

She arched a winged brow. "A private conversation? What was wrong with the phone?"

Andrea was his challenge. He needed something more than a smile to charm her, but he still hadn't figured out what that was. "I wanted to talk with you in person."

Her perceptive eyes searched his. "All right." She led him to the newsroom.

Troy had never been to the *New York Sports* offices. He'd suspected the organization struggled financially. The worn gray carpeting, peeling paint, and battered furnishings confirmed his suspicions.

He was struck by the stench of newsprint and burned coffee, battered by the cacophony of ringing telephones and shouted conversations. The scene brought back memories of his days as a sports reporter. Part of him missed the adrenaline rush of chasing a story. But, on the whole, he'd rather be back on the court.

Andrea turned a corner, leading him around the newsroom's perimeter and into what appeared to be a combination conference and storage room. She turned on the light.

Troy looked around at the room's stained walls and scarred furniture. "Maybe you should turn the lights back off."

Her eyes sparkled with humor, but her manner remained cool. "What's on your mind, Troy?"

She shut the door, closing them into the musty space. Troy quashed the urge to step closer and inhale her soft scent instead. He'd better get this over with before he became even more distracted.

He rested a hip against the conference table and

slipped his hands into the pockets of his suit pants. "Let's talk about the article you wrote on Barron."

She remained near the door. "What about it?"

"You weren't fair to him, were you?" Troy tossed the words as a friendly question. But he was here to demand a retraction.

Andrea's eyes widened. "What makes you say that?"

"You accused him of being on drugs without giving him a chance to respond."

Andrea's smooth brow wrinkled. "I never mentioned drugs."

Troy shrugged. He hoped his smile would mask the frustration roiling in his gut. "The accusation was implied."

"Only if the idea of Barron using drugs is already on your mind." She tilted her head, causing her thick brown hair to sway behind her. "Is it?"

The muscles in Troy's shoulders bunched even as he strained to keep his tone light. "Come on, Andy. You know as well as I do that your article put that idea in readers' minds."

"I quoted people who know Barron. They're concerned about his increasingly irresponsible behavior. And don't call me Andy, Slick. You know I don't like it."

"Why didn't you interview Barron?"

She shrugged. "He refused to speak with me."

"Can you blame him? He knew your article could ruin his reputation. What gives you the right to do that?" He hadn't meant to ask that question.

Color dusted Andrea's high cheekbones. "I speak for the sports fans who want to see a competitive play-off series. I represent the ticket holders who want their money's worth. That gives me the right."

Troy met the challenge in her electric eyes. "Your

media credentials allow you into the press section with the other reporters for free. We all know reporters will write any sensational piece—fact or fiction—to get a headline."

Andrea's full red lips tightened. "You know the truth matters to me. That's why I came to you first when Gerry was planting lies about Marc's supposed drug addiction."

Her hard gaze forced Troy to face the facts. He remembered when Jaclyn Jones's franchise partner, Gerald Bimm, had tried to smear DeMarcus Guinn in the media. Gerald would have succeeded if Andrea hadn't warned him and Jaclyn of Gerald's plan. By her actions, Andrea had proven the truth did matter to her. Then what was behind her damaging story about Barron?

Troy leaned more heavily on the conference table and crossed his ankles. "We can't have negative stories about the team, Andy. They're a distraction. Instead of focusing on beating the Cleveland Cavaliers when the series starts Saturday, the players are wondering whether their captain has a drug problem. How does that help anyone?"

"If Barron's on drugs, you can't sweep that under the rug." Her voice was urgent.

"He's passed his drug tests. He's clean."

"Then what's causing his destructive behavior?"

He wished he knew. "That's Barron. That's just the way he is."

"But why?"

Troy dropped his arms to his sides and tried another persuasive smile. "Frankly, Andy, I'm not here to be interviewed. I want you to stop writing negative stories about the Monarchs."

2

Andrea considered the Monarchs' vice president of media and marketing. Was he serious? Should she be offended or amused?

Troy Marshall was a hazard to her mental health. He was handsome, charming, self-confident. His warm sienna skin, intense ebony eyes, and wicked goatee could make a woman stupid. Andrea had done stupid. She didn't intend to repeat the act. Now she carried her self-control like an American Express card. She wouldn't leave home without it.

She shifted her weight and crossed her arms. "I don't work for you, Troy. I'm not a member of the Monarchs' publicity team. I'm a reporter."

His heavy black brows knitted. "And you've had open access to the players and coaches. Until now."

Was he threatening her job? Andrea wouldn't be intimidated. She'd survived more dangerous challenges than this one. Barely. "I'm the only reporter who pays any attention to your team."

Troy shook his head. The room's dim lighting moved over his short, wavy black hair. "Not any more. We're getting more column inches in the

Times, the *Daily News,* and the *Post.* This morning, I had a call from the *Cleveland Plain Dealer.*"

"Will you cut them all off if they don't give the Monarchs positive coverage?"

Troy pushed his hands back into the front pockets of his gray suit. The gesture opened his jacket, exposing his burgundy shirt and calling more attention to his broad chest than seemed necessary. "I'll do whatever I need to do to protect the team."

Andrea blinked. His mask had fallen to reveal the steely determination beneath his calculated charm. "Does that include ignoring a player who's in crisis?"

Troy's gaze wavered. His square jaw tightened. "Barron's fine."

She studied his chiseled features. "What's changed, Troy? This isn't the first article I've written that hasn't been completely glowing about the Monarchs. Why are you jumping down my throat this time?"

"Nothing's changed."

That wasn't true. In the past, he'd flirted rather than fought with her. "You've never threatened my access to the team before."

"You've never attacked a player's character before."

Andrea's temper bristled. She hooked her hands on her hips. "That story wasn't an attack. It called attention to Barron's risky behavior, which, by the way, is getting worse."

"Barron's always been disruptive."

"This isn't 'Barron being Barron.' If you don't know what's wrong with him, you need to find out."

Troy cocked his head. "And then what? Should I schedule an interview with you?"

"I won't lie to you. I'd like to cover the story. But it's more important that someone find out what's wrong with him."

Troy tore his hands from his pockets. "Why are you so focused on Barron?"

"Why are you so determined to ignore him?"

"I'm not going to allow you to ruin a good person's reputation to sell a few papers."

"I don't do sensationalism. You've read enough of my work to know that."

Troy dragged his right hand over the glossy curls crowning his head. Andrea's palm tingled as though it were her hand touching his hair.

Troy seemed to regain his self-control. "You're right. I'm sorry. But I want you to stop writing negative stories about the team."

Andrea shook her head. "I don't take requests, Troy. You should know that as well."

He straightened from the conference table. "You have plenty of other things to write about. This is the first time the team has made the play-offs in four seasons. You don't have to write about Barron."

"You should be concerned about Barron, too. His attitude will infect the whole team."

Troy stared at her for several silent moments. He scratched his chin. Andrea visually traced his neatly trimmed moustache and goatee. She wasn't given to fantasies, but she could come up with several for Troy.

"I don't need your advice on taking care of the team." Troy started toward the door.

Andrea moved into his path. "You were a reporter. Are you holding me to the same standards you set for yourself?"

Troy stepped around her and opened the door. Air scented with burned coffee and newsprint rushed into the room. From over her shoulder, she watched him leave.

Why wouldn't the stubborn man believe this was

about more than a story? If Barron was struggling with the same personal demons from her past, she couldn't live with herself if she walked away. She had to help the NBA player for her peace of mind as well as his.

Andrea left the conference room, closing the door behind her. She'd barely sat down at her desk when her editor appeared.

"Is Marshall pissed over the Barron Douglas story?" Willis Priestly sounded almost disinterested.

He gulped his coffee. The dark liquid dribbled from a crack in the chubby, white mug. Not for the first time, Andrea wondered why her boss kept the aging cup. It leaked as much coffee as it contained.

"He wants only positive stories on the Monarchs."

Willis took another drink and nodded his head. He brushed his lank, gray hair from his forehead. He needed a haircut. He also needed more sleep. The bags under his dull green eyes carried bags. "What did you say?"

Andrea sat back in her worn, brown chair. It squeaked as she forced it to turn toward her editor. "I told him I'm a reporter not a publicist."

Willis nodded again. His questions seemed more like idle conversation. Had he even heard her answers?

"You know, Benson, the paper distributed almost double its usual number of copies when you wrote that piece exposing Bimm. I know when we take a count of the copies that circulated with this Douglas story, we'll have sold at least that many more copies of this issue as well."

She knew where this was going and she wouldn't let it get there. "I'm not going to write negative stories just to gain an audience, Will. You know that's not my style."

"That article on Bimm caught the attention of other papers. The story on Douglas will, too. Keep it up and pretty soon some big paper with deep pockets will make you an offer you'd be a fool to refuse."

"Are you suggesting I sell my soul to the devil?"

"You deserve much more money than I could ever pay you."

"And what would I do with these ill-gotten gains?"

Willis snorted. "Buy a car with an engine that doesn't fly south at the hint of cooler weather."

A sense of foreboding stirred the hairs on the back of her neck. "Are you trying to get rid of me?"

"You're better than this place." Willis inclined his head toward the other reporters in the newsroom. "Your coworkers are kids fresh out of school. And while you're trying to move up, you'll set the standard for these kids and help me build a name for *Sports.*"

Andrea studied the fresh-faced cub reporters with whom she worked. Their careers were just starting, while she felt every one of her twenty-eight years.

She lifted her pencil, bouncing its eraser against her desk. "I'd like more money and a bigger audience. But I'm not going to jump on the negativity bandwagon. The Jones family and the Monarchs have given a lot to this community." And to her. "I won't repay them that way."

Willis gulped more coffee. "You said you weren't the Monarchs' publicist."

She smiled. Her boss was trying to use her words against her. "Well played, Will. I'll report the news—good, bad, or indifferent—as long as it's relevant. But

I won't deliberately smear anyone's character." Not ever again.

"Sometimes you have to play hardball to get ahead."

That route hadn't worked for her in the past, and it wasn't the person she was trying to be. "At the end of the day, I need to be able to live with the decisions I've made."

He gestured toward the newsroom with his mug. "Look around you, Benson. Do you want to be working here in five years? Three years? Next year?"

She shrugged. "Worse things could happen." She'd already lived through some of them. Andrea bounced her pencil eraser against her desk again.

Willis scanned the room. "I had big dreams when I first started this paper. It's eight years later and they're still only dreams." He looked at her. "You're good, Benson. I don't want you to end up with stale dreams, too."

"Thanks, Will. But I'll take my chances and see what happens."

Willis's eyes were inscrutable as he held her gaze for a long silent moment. "Don't wait too long to see what happens. You'll never get that time back."

Andrea considered his drawn features and rounded shoulders. "What aren't you telling me, Will?"

Willis sighed. "Nothing. Keep up the good work."

Andrea watched him plod back to his office at the other end of the hall. What had that been about? She shifted her gaze to her coworkers. They were hard at work, unaware anything could be wrong.

She liked the other reporters. She enjoyed their drive and enthusiasm. But Willis was right. She'd had a much higher profile position in the industry just four years ago, and she wanted it back. Had enough time gone by to allow her to leave her past behind?

She didn't know if she could handle having the doors slammed in her face again.

"Why are we meeting in a conference room?" Kirk West, sports reporter from the *New York Horn*, settled into the black swivel chair.

Troy didn't like the reporter's tone or his dismissive expression as he took in the Monarchs' small meeting space. Kirk's blue gaze settled on him and Monarchs head coach DeMarcus Guinn.

DeMarcus's brown features were tight. He folded his hands on the rectangular mahogany table and leaned forward. "Where else would we meet?"

Troy winced at the chill in the coach's tone. The newspaper interview had barely begun and things had already taken a bad turn. A winning season and an NBA play-off spot had increased attention on the Monarchs, a team the media had all but forgotten the past three years. But with each interview, DeMarcus grew more annoyed.

The sports reporter lifted his nose and straightened the blue tie knotted under the collar of his white cotton shirt. "Byron Scott entertained me in his office."

Beside Troy, DeMarcus stiffened at the reference to the Cleveland Cavaliers head coach. "I'm not here to entertain you."

The truth was, DeMarcus didn't want the reporter anywhere near his players and assistant coaches. He hadn't even wanted Kirk in the Empire Arena, home of the Brooklyn Monarchs since the franchise's birth in 1956. Conducting the interview in one of the arena's conference rooms had been a compromise.

But if Kirk was baiting the coach, DeMarcus's image

was deteriorating faster than Troy had anticipated. He glanced at Kirk and swallowed a sigh. One crisis at a time.

Troy leaned into the table. "Coach Guinn has schemes and game plans in his office that aren't for public viewing. That's why we're holding this interview in our conference room."

He used a reasonable tone to counterbalance DeMarcus's impatience. He deserved a Most Valuable Player award for his performance, considering he'd had only three hours of sleep after driving Barron home from the club that morning. He also was still distracted by his less-than-successful meeting with Andrea earlier.

Kirk laid his reporter's notepad on the table and tapped his pen on the blank page. "Byron went over his game plans with me."

In Kirk's dreams. Troy looked away to keep from rolling his eyes.

DeMarcus didn't show such restraint. "He knew you wouldn't understand them."

"You're wrong." The reporter's voice was tight.

Troy rested his left hand on DeMarcus's shoulder. "Marc, let's stick to the interview."

DeMarcus's expression questioned Troy's intelligence at scheduling the reporter. "What interview?"

Good point. Troy shifted his attention to Kirk. "What did you want to ask us?"

Kirk glared his dislike at DeMarcus. "I wanted to ask what makes the Mighty Guinn think he won't be swept out of the play-offs in the first series."

Dammit. The interview was turning into a disaster. Did Kirk know DeMarcus hated that nickname? Probably. Like DeMarcus, Troy was beginning to question his intelligence at agreeing to this meeting.

DeMarcus sat back in the cushioned conference chair and ignored the reporter's hostility. He crossed his arms, covering the Monarchs logo centered in the chest area of his silver jersey. "Anything could happen. That's why we play the game."

Troy smothered a groan. That was the worst non-answer DeMarcus had given a reporter to date.

Kirk's pen hovered over his notepad as though waiting for the coach to elaborate. He moved on when DeMarcus remained silent. "Your first game is with the Cleveland Cavaliers. How do you think the Monarchs will match up with the Cavs? Your roster is a lot older and slower."

DeMarcus uncrossed his arms and sat straighter in his chair. "We split the regular season with the Cavs with one game a piece. The Cavs are a good team. They're fast, strong on defense, and quick on offense. But we've beaten them once. We can do it again."

Troy heard the relish in DeMarcus's voice and knew the head coach look forward to the best-of-seven series against the Cavaliers.

Kirk wrote a few lines in his notepad. "The Monarchs got to the play-offs despite your poor offense and lack of a defense. Do you think you'll make it to the second round?"

"We have a will to win." DeMarcus's response was curt.

Considering even he had been insulted by the reporter's question, Troy applauded the coach's control.

Kirk spread his hands. "'Will to win'? What does that even mean?"

Troy leaned forward, drawing the reporter's attention to try to prevent the explosion he sensed building in DeMarcus. "What Coach Guinn—"

DeMarcus interrupted. "Now we know why you *report* sports instead of *playing* them. The will to win is what separates winners from losers." The inflection in his words made it clear in which category DeMarcus considered the reporter.

Kirk heard the implication. His face flushed to magenta. He pushed to his feet. "I have everything I need for this article."

Troy stood as well. Thoughts sprinted across his mind as he sought a way to salvage the interview. "Are you sure that's all you need? We can give you more time."

"I can't."

Troy stiffened at DeMarcus's grumbled words. They couldn't continue now. "Thanks for coming, Kirk. Call me if you have any questions or need more information."

Kirk glared at DeMarcus. "I won't need anything else."

"Good." DeMarcus checked his watch. His temper appeared back under control.

Troy ground his teeth. As the head coach, DeMarcus should understand the need to have a good relationship with the media. In some ways, he was worse than the players.

Troy blocked his imaginary list of potential negative headlines and shook the reporter's hand. "Thanks for your time, Kirk."

Behind him, DeMarcus's voice was dry. "Yeah. Thanks."

Kirk released Troy's hand. He grabbed his notebook and marched toward the door. "Don't bother to show me out. I can find my own way."

Troy stood in the threshold, his back to DeMarcus, watching Kirk stomp down the hall. "Could you get through even one interview without antagonizing the press?"

DeMarcus snorted. "You heard his questions. *He* was antagonizing *me*."

Troy faced DeMarcus. "Do you know why I come to these interviews? Because you always piss off the reporters."

"That's not true. Andrea Benson and I get along fine. But you still come to *those* interviews."

Troy ignored the knowing glint in DeMarcus's eyes. He wouldn't admit he went to those interviews because he enjoyed looking at the *New York Sports* reporter. "The media have a job to do just like you. They help put the game in perspective for fans. It all comes back to the fans."

"I know."

Troy continued as though DeMarcus hadn't spoken. "The more fans we have, the better our chances of keeping our jobs. That's why it's important to project a positive image so people will actually like you."

DeMarcus rocked his chair on its back legs. "I'm out to win basketball games. People don't have to like me."

"Yes. They do." On this, Troy wouldn't accept an argument. "You're a reflection of the team. If the fans like you, they'll like the team and, hopefully, buy tickets."

DeMarcus scrubbed a hand over his face. "It always comes back to money."

"That *is* what I pay you with. Or are you offering to work for free?" Jaclyn Jones, co-owner of the Monarchs, spoke from the doorway. Her violet skirt suit warmed her golden brown skin and hugged the former Women's National Basketball Association player's tall, slender figure.

DeMarcus sent his boss and fiancée a wicked grin. "From the size of my paycheck, I thought I'd already made the offer."

Troy's neck muscles relaxed. The cavalry had arrived. "Good morning, Jackie."

"Maybe for some of us." Jaclyn moved farther into the room, carrying a newspaper in her right hand. She stopped beside DeMarcus's chair.

Troy doubted he could slip a piece of paper between the two of them. DeMarcus and Jaclyn were right for each other. They'd each achieved individual success. DeMarcus was a two-time NBA champion and gold medal Olympian. Jaclyn was a WNBA champion. She'd also been an associate at a prestigious New York law firm before assuming control of the franchise her grandfather had helped found. They were together because they wanted each other. Their need for each other had come later. Not everyone was that lucky. He hadn't been.

Jaclyn looked down at her head coach. "You know this franchise needs money, Marc. That's why it's so important we have at least three play-off games in a sold-out arena."

DeMarcus played with the fingers of Jaclyn's left hand. Her four-carat, Monarch-cut diamond engagement ring sparkled in the overhead light. "I'll make a deal with you. I'll play nicely with reporters if you tell me which one of the players has a personality similar to mine."

That comment surprised a laugh from Troy. "Are you still trying to figure that out?"

DeMarcus frowned at him. "If you know, why don't you just tell me?"

Jaclyn pulled her fingers from DeMarcus's hold. "No one's going to tell you. Get to know your players,

Marc." She patted his shoulder before turning her sharp brown eyes on Troy. "Was the angry man who marched out of here a reporter?"

"Kirk West from the *Horn*." Troy's gaze dipped to the newspaper in her hand. He'd lay odds she'd read the *New York Sports* article on Barron.

Jaclyn settled both fists on her hips. She gave De-Marcus a fierce frown. "If I see even a hint of a negative article about the Monarchs because of you, you and I will have some strong words."

"Yes, ma'am." DeMarcus sounded chastened, but laughter lit his eyes.

Jaclyn sighed. "Why do I waste my breath?" She held up the newspaper and looked from DeMarcus to Troy. "Have you read the *Sports* article on Barron?"

DeMarcus shook his head. "I don't read articles about the team while we're in season."

Troy tensed. "I did."

Jaclyn sat in a chair beside DeMarcus. "Is Barron abusing drugs?"

DeMarcus straightened in his seat. "Barron's not using."

An image of Barron weaving his way out of the nightclub at two o'clock this morning flashed across Troy's mind. Barron may be an alcoholic, but he wasn't abusing hard drugs. "I spoke with Andy this morning. I told her to stop attacking our players."

Jaclyn skimmed the article. "Andrea doesn't attack Barron. She quotes our players who describe his behavior as irresponsible and unpredictable."

Troy looked at DeMarcus. "The players should be reminded not to air their grievances in public."

DeMarcus nodded. "I'll talk to them at today's practice."

Jaclyn laid the paper on the table. "That's not the point. I'm concerned Barron may be in trouble."

Troy crossed his arms over his chest and feigned a confidence he didn't feel. "Andy's trying to advance her career with sensational stories."

Jaclyn's brows knitted. "That's not like her."

Troy wasn't as sure about Andrea. But he did know the Monarchs' playbook centered around its captain. How far would the team advance in the play-offs without him? "Barron's fine."

Jaclyn pinned him with a look. "How do you know that? How often do you talk to him?"

Not that often. But for the good of the team, he had to find a way to minimize the damage Andrea's article was causing internally as well as externally. "Often enough to know Barron's behavior has always been aggressive and erratic. Andy's exaggerating his actions to sell papers."

Jaclyn's eyes were clouded with concern. "Andrea has always been more than balanced in her coverage of us."

Troy's attention bounced from the newspaper back to Jaclyn's gaze. "She shouldn't be writing articles like that one."

Jaclyn looked up at him. "We can't tell the media what to write as long as they're writing the truth. That's what I'm trying to find out." She turned to De-Marcus. "How has Barron seemed to you?"

DeMarcus shrugged. "The same. A couple of times, he's come to practice with hangovers, but he's passed the drug tests."

Jaclyn nodded. "Keep an eye on him."

DeMarcus checked his watch. "I'd better go. Practice starts soon." He kissed Jaclyn's cheek before leaving.

Troy uncrossed his arms. "The only reason we're putting Barron under a microscope is because of Andy's article."

Jaclyn gathered the newspaper and stood. "Her article raises an important question."

"If that's what she wanted, she could have picked up the phone."

Jaclyn's gaze scrutinized him. "I know you're under a lot of pressure since we made the play-offs, but let's not lose sight of what's really important—our players."

Was she saying he couldn't handle his job? "I know the players are important. That's why I want to make sure the papers treat them fairly."

Jaclyn's stare seemed to reach into his mind. "I've heard that some reporters are complaining about you."

His brows shot up his forehead. "Why?"

"They're saying you're limiting their access to the players and trying to direct their stories."

Troy couldn't deny the charges. He wouldn't apologize, either. He gestured toward the newspaper in Jaclyn's hand. "I don't want them distracting the team with stories like that."

Jaclyn lifted the paper. "Bad press hurts our revenue, and I'm depending on you to minimize the damage. But we're still obligated to address any problem we may have with the franchise and our employees. Not bury them."

Troy watched Jaclyn exit the conference room. His boss was right. He had to find a way to protect the team—and his job. But how do you keep thirteen hard-working, hard-playing athletes out of the media spotlight, especially when they had targets on their backs?

3

"Tell me your secret." Vella Wong whispered into the phone.

Andrea frowned at the *New York Sports* receptionist's command. "Why are you whispering?"

Vella continued in hushed tones. "Another wealthy, handsome man is asking for you. This one's a little older, though. His name's Gerald Bimm."

Andrea's mind went blank. "Gerald Bimm?" She needed confirmation that the Monarchs' co-owner actually was here.

Vella's voice returned to normal. "Gerald Bimm is at the front desk for you."

This couldn't be good. "I'll be right there."

Andrea pushed away from her desk and set off for the reception area. The last time she'd spoken to the Monarchs' co-owner, he'd been furious that her story had exposed his attempts to move the Brooklyn Monarchs to Nevada, despite the fact the National Basketball Association still had reservations about allowing a franchise in the country's gambling capital.

Gerald stood watching her enter the waiting area. He looked like Hollywood's casting of a wealthy, pampered executive with delusions of entitlement. His pinstriped navy suit was custom fit to his tall, lean frame. His pink and blue tie probably cost more than her pantsuit and pumps combined.

Andrea extended her hand. "Good morning, Gerry." She bit her tongue to keep from asking why he was here. She didn't want him to know she was uneasy with his surprise visit. Strange. She hadn't been uncomfortable with Troy's unexpected appearance. At least not until he'd started telling her how to do her job.

Gerald held her hand too long. "Forgive me for not calling first. Can we talk privately?"

Another man who wanted to speak with her in private? What was going on?

"Sure." Andrea pulled her hand free and turned to lead him to the newspaper's conference room. The same room in which she'd spoken with Troy. The similarities were unnerving.

His hold on her shoulder stopped her.

Gerald wrinkled his nose and looked around the worn-and-tattered waiting area. "I noticed a coffee shop around the corner. Could we go there?"

Andrea looked around the room. During the three years she'd worked for *New York Sports,* she'd become oblivious to the office's shabby appearance. It hadn't seemed to disturb Troy this morning, either. Now she tried to see it through a stranger's eyes, through a wealthy, pampered stranger's eyes.

There wasn't any point in mentioning the neighborhood coffee shop wasn't much better. "I'll get my purse."

* * *

The screech of athletic shoes across the Monarchs' practice facility almost drowned the echo of Troy's dress shoes against the high-gloss hardwood floor. He paused beside the black wire carts of NBA-regulation basketballs and the counters on which stood about a dozen water bottles. A deep breath brought with it the scent of floor wax. Above the floor, following the ceiling's perimeter, were twelve baskets.

Troy took a moment to watch as players in baggy black shorts and either black or white T-shirts used the baskets for shooting drills. The starters were in black T-shirts. The bench players wore the white ones. From the center of the rectangular room came the rhythmic smacking of jump ropes against the court as other players did their cardio warm-ups. The remaining members of the thirteen-man roster sat on the floor, stretching their legs, hips, and hamstrings with oversized purple exercise bands.

Dressed in Monarchs-logo silver warm-up pants and black T-shirts, the head athletic trainer and three of the four assistant coaches were on the court working with the athletes. The scene brought back bittersweet memories of his college basketball career at Georgetown University. It had ended abruptly.

DeMarcus Guinn had his back to Troy as he spoke to Oscar Clemente, one of his assistant coaches.

Troy's approach drew the men's attention. "Can I speak with the team?"

DeMarcus lowered his clipboard. "About what?"

"Keeping their grievances inside the organization."

Oscar scratched the scalp beneath his thinning gray hair. "We covered that."

Troy heard the resentment in the older man's

tone. "Hearing the message from someone else will emphasize its importance."

Oscar narrowed his dark eyes. "You mean from the front office."

Troy took the comment the way it was meant. Oscar was marking his territory. "That's right."

"It couldn't hurt." DeMarcus stepped around Troy. He blew the whistle suspended from a cord around his neck. The noise bounced across the practice facility. "Bring it in."

The thirteen players looked over in surprise before grabbing their exercise bands and basketballs and jogging toward DeMarcus. Their sneakers squeaked against the court. Most of the men were NBA veterans facing the sunset of their glory days. The one exception was Jamal Ward, a nineteen-year-old rookie picked in one of the last rounds of the 2010 draft.

Barron Douglas gave Troy a cautious look as he sauntered past him. The point guard's baggy, black nylon shorts, a match to his teammates', skimmed his knees. His oversized black T-shirt hung past his hips and bared tattoos that extended like sleeves down his dark brown arms to his wrists.

Troy made eye contact with each of the players. Most seemed curious about his presence. A couple seemed disinterested. Troy understood. Players would rather the front office remained upstairs and left them alone. Over the years, he'd made a point of getting to know all of the players, though. That familiarity was especially helpful in pitching human interest stories to the media. But he also wanted to know the members of the franchise's family.

"Monarchs." DeMarcus paused while the players stilled to give him their attention. "Troy Marshall, our media exec, wants to talk to you."

"Thanks, Coach." Troy stepped forward. "Even before the season started, we were the target of a lot of bad press, more than usual."

Jamal, the rookie shooting guard, raised his voice to interrupt Troy. "That's Gerry Bimm's fault, not ours." A sheen of perspiration covered the wiry, six-foot-four-inch shooting guard from his clean-shaven head to his tattooed arms.

Troy held up his hand. "Gerry was the source of most of the negative stories, but not all of them. Coach asked you to keep whatever issues or concerns you have about each other within the team. Those complaints can't leave the locker room. Definitely, don't discuss it in the press."

Jamal's grin was sheepish. "But that *Sports* reporter is hot. You can't have all the honeys, Trademark."

Trademark. TM. Troy Marshall. He didn't mind the nickname. He actually liked it. It made him feel like one of the players again.

Anthony Chambers's dark olive eyes gleamed in his fair skin. The starting forward's rounded natural was a 1970s throwback. "Yeah. She's hot. In a touch-me-and-I'll-rip-out-your-spleen way."

Vincent Jardine, the team's center, spoke with fake concern. "Does she scare you, St. Anthony?"

Anthony wasn't amused. "Shut up, Vinny."

"Jamal's right." The six-foot-ten-inch forward, Serge Gateau, cut through the bickering. The Frenchman's shoulder-length, blond ponytail was pulled back from his lean, square features. "When a beautiful woman asks me a question, I must answer her. I cannot help myself."

"Try." Troy ignored the bite of jealousy. "None of you is new to this aspect of the sport. Even you, Jamal. The media's followed you since high school."

Jamal puffed out his chest. "Yeah, but no one's ever told me not to talk to them before."

Troy arched a brow. "They should have. The media are enough of a distraction throughout the season. Negative stories make it worse."

"You're right, Troy." Warrick Evans's expression was solemn. The six-foot-seven-inch shooting guard passed a large hand over his bald, brown head. "This is the first time some of us have ever been to the play-offs, and it may be the last chance some of us will ever have. We can't afford distractions."

Troy swallowed a sigh of relief. Finally, someone understood. "Right. It doesn't help anyone to complain about the team in public. But it hurts everyone to argue in the press."

Barron shouted his question. "So if reporters ask me how everything's going, what am I supposed to say?"

Troy faced Barron. The other man's tension beat at him like a club. "Tell them everything's fine."

Barron snickered. "You want me to lie?"

Troy ignored the baiting tone. "If you have a problem, talk to Coach."

Barron gave DeMarcus a scathing look. "What's he going to do?"

Oscar stepped forward. "Coach got you to the play-offs."

Troy almost did a double take. Oscar hadn't accepted DeMarcus as the team's head coach at first. But now the grumpy older man was DeMarcus's greatest supporter, second only to Jaclyn.

But Barron wouldn't back down. "He turned the team against me."

DeMarcus's tone was level. "You did that by putting yourself above the team."

Barron ignored DeMarcus and turned to Anthony. "And if you punks have something to say, tell me to my face instead of talking to the reporters."

Troy's attention bounced from Barron to Anthony. Andrea's article had quoted the forward, Jamal, and Serge complaining about Barron's undisciplined behavior.

"We tried that, too." Anthony spread his hands. "'Where two or more are gathered in my name, there will I be also.' Matthew eighteen, twenty."

Barron clenched his fists. "Stop quoting the Bible and face me like a man."

Troy raised his hands, palms out. The situation was getting out of control. "Barron, the point is, your behavior's hurting the team."

Instead of calming him, Troy's words seemed to push Barron over the line. He shoved his way past his teammates to the door. "Man, forget this. I'm not some head case on *The Tyra Banks Show.*"

DeMarcus called after him. "Barron, my office."

Barron didn't acknowledge his coach. He pushed through the exit. The heavy metal doors slammed behind him.

Oscar turned to Troy. "Good job."

Troy braced his shoulders against the weight of defeat. The remaining twelve players stared at the metal exit with varying degrees of surprise and disappointment. All except for Warrick. The point guard studied the doors with a distant, impassive expression.

DeMarcus broke the silence. "Let's get back to work."

The players muttered to each other as they returned to practice.

Troy turned to DeMarcus. "I made things worse. I'm sorry."

DeMarcus gave him a narrow-eyed stare. "Do you still think Barron's not using?"

Troy held the other man's gaze. "I know he's not."

DeMarcus's expression didn't change. "Why do I have the feeling you know more than you're saying?"

"I don't."

Oscar grunted. "You're lying."

Troy gave the older man an annoyed look. "Why would I?"

Oscar surveyed the action on the court before turning back to Troy. "This team is your family just like it's mine. Brothers don't betray brothers. But you can't ignore when one has a problem."

"I don't know what's bothering Barron. He won't tell me." Troy turned again to DeMarcus. "What are you going to do?"

DeMarcus shrugged. "Fine him for skipping practice, for all the good that does. He just writes the check. I'm sure Morning Glory appreciates his generosity."

Troy knew Morning Glory Chapel's food bank and homeless shelter could use the money generated by the team's fines. Still, the Monarchs needed their captain. "What about his playing time?"

DeMarcus rubbed his forehead. "That depends on how he plays. I won't risk the play-offs to spare his feelings."

The coach was right. They had to protect the team. But Barron was part of that team. Troy would make sure it stayed that way.

Andrea chose one of the tables in the front section of the coffee shop. Gerald settled into the cracked, red vinyl chair across from her. The display of fresh pastries whispered her name. Andrea forced her gaze away, resisting temptation. She was getting better at that.

She sipped her coffee. It was strong, but anything was better than that battery acid that passed for coffee in the newspaper's community kitchen.

Gerald lowered his mug. He seemed even less comfortable with these surroundings than the *New York Sports* office. "I enjoyed your article on Barron Douglas."

What is he up to? It didn't bode well for the franchise that Gerald and Troy had very different reactions to the same story. "What did you like about it?"

"It's about time someone held Barron accountable for his actions." Gerald sounded ready to do a campaign stump speech on morality.

Andrea angled her head. "What's stopping you?"

"What do you mean?"

"You co-own the team. Why don't *you* hold Barron accountable?"

Gerald's gaze slid away from hers. "Jackie protects him."

Andrea didn't buy that, and not just because Gerald couldn't look at her as he made the claim. "You were the one who arranged the Monarchs' trade for Barron."

Gerald shrugged. "I thought the coach at the time could handle him."

Andrea remembered the Monarchs' former coach. Everyone had liked and respected him. Gerald had fired him after one season. Barron had stayed. "You made Barron captain, although that had been Warrick Evans's role for almost ten years."

"I thought the responsibility would mature him."

"You have an answer for everything." Andrea sipped more coffee as she tried to discern truth from lie in Gerald's eyes.

"That's usually the case when you're telling the truth."

Was he telling the truth? Probably not.

Gerald's expression was earnest. "I want you to keep the pressure on Barron and the rest of the team."

Andrea blinked. Troy had demanded she write only glowing articles about the Monarchs. Gerald wanted her to expose the players' failings. It was as though they represented rival teams. The only thing both men shared was the mistaken idea they could tell her how to do her job.

She lowered her mug. The table rocked on uneven legs as she braced her forearms on its black-and-white tile surface. "What are you doing, Gerry?"

"As general manager, everything has to go through Jackie. But she's too soft on the players." He leaned toward her. "I want you to help me improve the team's reputation."

"Why the sudden concern for the team's image? You never cared before."

He gave her a sincere look she didn't buy for a New York minute. "I want to polish the team's image. I don't want to be associated with the bad boys of Brooklyn anymore."

Andrea stilled. Gerald had quoted a headline from an article about the Monarchs that had appeared in this morning's *New York Horn*. Had he planted the story? "You tried to keep the Monarchs out of the play-offs and were campaigning to move the team out of Brooklyn. I have a hard time believing you're this upset over the team's bad image."

Gerald's features tightened. "The Monarchs are in the play-offs, and they're staying in Brooklyn."

Andrea suppressed a grin. "Not by your choice. Jackie Jones co-owns the Empire Arena now. She won't let you break the Monarchs' lifetime contract to play there."

"Believe what you like."

She'd hit a nerve. Andrea ignored his spark of temper. "Why would you want to work with me? Did you forget the article I wrote exposing your plan to move the team?"

Gerald's grunt of laughter sounded forced. "Hardly. But I'm willing to put that behind us if you'll help me monitor the team."

He was the second person in less than an hour who wanted her to grab a seat on the Bash the Brooklyn Monarchs train. Willis said the negative coverage would increase sales. What was Gerald's true motivation?

Andrea picked up her mug and sipped her coffee. The scalding liquid had cooled. "You expect me to believe you want my help improving the team's reputation? I didn't come down with the last rain, Gerry."

Gerald leaned back in his red chair. "You should consider my offer. I doubt you want to spend the rest of your professional career with *Sports*. Let me use my contacts to get you a better job."

Maybe it was in Gerald's power to get her a better paying position with a higher profile newspaper or magazine—like the job she'd lost four years ago. But she wouldn't accept his help. Her soul was too high a price to pay for a better career.

Andrea stood, adjusting her brown purse strap on her shoulder. "No, thank you."

She turned to leave. Once bitten, twice shy. Andrea

had forgotten her integrity four years ago, and she was still working hard to get it back.

Gerald rose to accompany her. "Think about it." His tone was urgent, persuasive. "We'd be doing each other a favor."

"There's nothing to think about." She walked faster, anxious to return to the *Sports*'s building so she could get away from Gerald. He easily kept pace with her.

They were almost to the corner of the block when Gerald broke the silence. "I'd hate to give this opportunity to another reporter."

Andrea stopped to turn on him. "You're not going to find anyone unscrupulous enough to help you."

Gerald laughed. "Do you really believe that?"

No, she didn't.

She watched Gerald continue a few feet farther down the street to a red Lexus coupe. He climbed into the car and pulled away from the curb. To go where? Home? The Empire Arena? Another newspaper's office?

Andrea glanced at her navy Ford Escort. Little did her editor know her twenty-one-year-old compact wasn't temperamental only in cold weather. Andrea walked across the street to the bus stop to wait for the line that would deliver her two blocks from the Empire Arena. She crossed her arms and scowled. Troy had been judgmental and rude to her earlier. Why was she making a personal visit to tell him about Gerald's latest scheme? Was it professional courtesy— or an excuse to see the media executive again?

* * *

Serge Gateau's broad back blocked Andrea's view of Troy's administrative assistant. The Monarchs forward towered over the desk.

Andrea stopped beside the giant Frenchman. "I'm sorry to interrupt."

"Non. Non." Serge's blue eyes twinkled with humor. His golden locks grew in sexy waves to his broad shoulders. "I was welcoming the newest member of our team." He swung his large hand between Andrea and the slender woman seated behind the desk. "Andrea Benson, may I present Troy's new administrative assistant, Constance Street. Connie, Andrea is a reporter with the *New York Sports.*"

Andrea offered the smiling blonde her hand. "It's a pleasure to meet you."

Constance blinked her wide, grass green eyes. "It's nice to meet you."

Serge stepped back from the desk. "I'll leave you ladies to your work." He gave Constance a warm smile, the kind Andrea had seen on the Turner Classic Movies channel. "Let me know if there's anything I can do to help you get settled here."

Constance lowered her gaze. "Thank you."

Andrea waited for Serge to leave before turning back to the slender blonde. "Have we met before?"

A vague discomfort clouded Constance's expression. She set aside the newspaper she'd folded open to the Apartments for Rent section. "We met at the Morning Glory Chapel. You helped sort the clothes donated to the shelter."

Andrea still couldn't make the connection. "Are you a volunteer, too?"

"I'm one of the homeless." Her warm Midwestern accent tensed.

The image of a pale, stressed woman bundled in layers of thin clothing and holding firmly to a toddler superimposed itself over the more relaxed woman in a too-large, lavender sweater. Andrea also remembered her bruises. "You have a little girl."

Constance's smile returned. "Tiffany."

Andrea nodded. "How long have you worked for the Monarchs?"

Constance's eyes sparkled. "Jackie told me about the job opening last week. I started Monday, four days ago. Now I just need to find a place to live."

Andrea's gaze dipped to the newspaper on Constance's desk. Finding an affordable apartment was harder than it sounded. Although Andrea guessed Constance made more than she did—part-time seasonal workers probably made more than she did—which would make it easier to find decent accommodations for her and her little girl. "Good luck."

"Thank you. Are you here to see Mr. Marshall?"

She'd never heard Troy referred to so formally. His previous administrative assistant had used his first name in a proprietary tone. "Is he available?"

"He's working through lunch." Constance lifted her telephone receiver and pressed four keys. "Andrea Benson of the *New York Sports* is here." She thanked Troy, then ended the call. "He'll be right out."

Seconds later, Troy appeared in his office threshold. Andrea's pulse jumped.

4

Excitement swept through Troy at the sight of Andrea waiting for him. It was always this way when he saw her. Like the anticipation of a new NBA season or the euphoria of a winning game.

"Come in." He stood aside so she could enter his office.

Andrea tossed a smile to Constance before approaching him. Troy felt a sharp slap of envy. Her expression was so different from the guarded looks she gave him. On occasion he'd surprised a laugh from her. But the moments never lasted.

She walked past him. Troy inhaled her powder-soft scent and the morning's tensions eased. Her long, efficient strides carried her to the three black-cushioned guest chairs in front of his mahogany desk. She chose one, then surveyed his office—the framed community commendations, advertisements and news articles covering the cream walls—as though she hadn't been here a score of times before. Did his office tell her anything about him? What would her desk at the newsroom reveal about her? Andrea was as much a mystery today as when they'd first met three years ago. That fact bothered him more than it should.

Troy circled his desk and settled into his seat. "I didn't think I'd hear from you again so soon much less see you."

"Neither did I. I'm sorry to interrupt your lunch." Andrea avoided his eyes. She seemed uncertain. Why?

"Don't worry about it. Have you eaten?" Troy pulled the lid from his plastic soup container. The savory scent of beef and vegetables floated into the room.

Andrea tucked her brown purse beside her. "I'll eat later."

He pulled a plastic-wrapped sandwich close to him. "Do you like PB and J?"

She dragged her suspicious, sherry-brown gaze from the thick peanut butter and jelly sandwich on wheat bread to his face. "Are you offering me food to make amends for your comments this morning?"

A corner of Troy's mouth kicked up as he struggled with a smile. "I don't need to apologize for what I said. But I'm sorry for the way I said it. My temper got the best of me."

"Your accusations were untrue and unfair."

Troy unwrapped his sandwich. He slid it just a little closer to Andrea. "So was your article."

"We'll have to agree to disagree." Her voice cooled.

He released his smile. "You sound as though you're chewing nails. Wouldn't you rather have PB and J?" He took half of the sandwich and slid the other half, still on its wrapper, toward her.

"No, thank you. I'll eat later." Andrea's stomach growled, betraying just how much she wanted that sandwich. Her right hand flew to her flat abdomen, pressing against it.

Troy watched a blush sweep under the honey tones of her skin. He'd never seen her composure slip. She was usually so controlled. The unsuspected vulnerability triggered buried needs inside him. The need to protect, to provide, and to possess.

Troy cleared his throat. "It's PB and J. Who doesn't like PB and J?" The words were rougher than he'd intended.

Andrea hesitated before leaning forward to accept his offering. Her voice was warmer. "Thank you."

"You're welcome." It was like having the most popular girl in high school agree to be his date for the prom. He crossed to the mini-refrigerator in a corner of his office. "Milk or soda?"

"Milk, please."

She sounded surprised. Had she come to continue their argument? Instead, he was giving her a meal. Could half a PB and J sandwich and a pint of milk count as a first date? Perhaps in another life, one in which her newspaper didn't come between them.

Troy carried the milk and some extra napkins to her and accepted her thanks in exchange. He picked up his half of the sandwich. "Are you here to continue our discussion?"

"Gerry's up to his old tricks." Andrea tipped back her head to drink the milk.

Troy's attention shifted from Andrea's long, graceful neck to her face. "What do you mean?"

Andrea lowered the sandwich to the napkin on her knee. "He offered to use his connections to get me a better paying job provided I agreed to write negative stories about the Monarchs."

Troy clenched his jaw. "What did you say?"

Andrea looked offended. "I said no, of course. Would I be here otherwise?"

"Thank you."

"It doesn't end there. Gerry said he'll find someone else to write the articles."

Troy stood, turning away from what was left of his lunch. He massaged the back of his neck as he paced to his black mini-fridge and back. "Just like last time when he tried to use you to plant a fake story about Marc."

"And when I refused to help him, he went to another paper."

Thinking about it, Troy ground his teeth. If Gerald had succeeded, the Monarchs would have lost respect for DeMarcus and his leadership. The team would have had a hard time finishing the season much less making it to the play-offs.

He sank back into his chair and stared at his half-eaten sandwich and cooling soup. "I have to find a way to stop him."

"Let Jackie handle Gerry. You have to get in front of this like we did last time."

Warning whispers stirred the hairs on the back of Troy's neck. "Are you using Gerry's threat to convince me to let you write another damaging story on the team?"

A flicker of anger moved across her heart-shaped features before her impressive control steadied her emotions. "It doesn't benefit me to attack the Monarchs."

Troy cocked a brow. "Do you expect me to believe your newspaper's sales didn't go up when you wrote about Gerry's attempts to move the team out of Brooklyn?"

Andrea ignored him. "Many of the players are

going to the play-offs for the first time. There's a story here about how they're handling the pressure."

Troy drummed his fingertips on his desk. "Do you want to paint a picture of the players crumbling under postseason stress?"

"Only if it's true. Their first trip to the postseason in four years is a subject that will interest my readers, who, by the way, are also your fans."

"And I'd like them to stay that way. I'm not sure your article will help us."

"Why are you treating me like the enemy? You know I never take a position with my articles. Readers will decide whether the Monarchs are handling the postseason well. I only report what the players tell me."

Troy stopped drumming his fingers. "How can I be sure of that?"

Andrea narrowed her eyes. She'd worked too hard rebuilding her career to allow anyone to question her integrity. She especially resented that attitude coming from Troy, who'd probably never known failure in his life.

She took a slow, deep breath. "I've covered the Monarchs for three years. In that time, I've written scores of articles about the team. Not one of them gives you the right to question my motives."

"You've been better than most." Troy's grudging words stoked her temper.

She dug her nails into her chair's padded arms. "You were a reporter. Were your stories always complimentary to the teams?"

"I'm not a reporter anymore." Troy settled back into his chair, crossing his arms over his broad chest. "How can I be sure you won't spice up your story?"

Andrea's cheeks stung as the blood drained from

her face. "My job is to give my readers context for the game, not to make up information."

"And my job is to make sure the Monarchs aren't tarnished in the press. Who do you think will get their way?"

She forced her fingers to relax against the chair's arms. "I could speak to the players without your permission."

Troy spread his arms. "You could try. But Marc and I told them not to speak to reporters, including you."

Andrea sucked in a breath. He was denying her access. "Why won't you trust me?"

"I can't shut out every reporter but you. That wouldn't be fair."

Andrea wrapped her half-eaten sandwich in the napkin Troy had given her and stuffed it into her bag. She stood, jerking her purse strap onto her shoulder. "I covered the Monarchs when Brooklyn tried to forget you were here. I come to you for answers when other reporters print speculation. And now you're going to treat me the same way you treat them. Who's not being fair?"

Bitter disappointment soured in her stomach as she stalked out of Troy's office. He'd implemented a gag order, preventing the team from talking to her. How was she supposed to advance her career if she couldn't do her job?

Minutes after Andrea left, Troy strode into Jaclyn's office. He stopped behind her guest chairs. "Gerry's trying to get the media to smear the team again."

Jaclyn tossed her pen onto her desk and sank back into her chair. "The man's a one-trick pony."

Troy glanced at the silver and black Monarchs pin fastened near the left shoulder of Jaclyn's violet skirt suit. "Why is he doing this?"

"I wish I knew." Her expression was tight with an anger Troy understood.

He rubbed the back of his neck as he paced Jaclyn's office. His gaze circled the room. It was decorated in the team's colors, silver and black. Like his office, Jaclyn's beige walls displayed accolades from the Monarchs' past, including team awards, commendations, and photographs of her grandfather—one of the franchise's four founding members—with community leaders.

He strode back toward his boss. His shoes sank into the plush silver carpet. "How do we make him stop?"

"You mean, how do *I* make him stop." Her voice was dry enough for kindling. "I offered to buy Gerry's shares at more than fair market value. He refused to sell."

"How do we change his mind?" Troy didn't want to hear about what wouldn't work. He needed a solution. His job was to get positive press for the team. Gerald was threatening that goal.

Jaclyn arched a brow. "Short of threatening him?"

Troy tossed Jaclyn a look as he settled into one of her visitors' chairs. "I'm serious. We can't afford another article like the one Andy wrote on Barron."

She angled her head. "Why do you call her Andy? You know she doesn't like it."

"It suits her." It goaded her. Sparks flew from the reporter's startling brown eyes every time he used the nickname. It was a childish tactic, but the reaction let him know she was at least paying attention to him. Like tugging on the cute girl's pigtails in the elementary school playground.

"Andrea did a good job on the article."

Troy drummed his fingers on the chair's arm. "No, she didn't."

"It was fair. That's all we can expect from the media. We can't tell them what stories to cover or how to write them. But we should at least expect them to be fair."

"Fair? It shows Barron in a bad light and quotes the other players complaining about him. Another story like that could disrupt the locker room."

Jaclyn raised one hand palm out. "Andrea didn't make the team look bad. They did that themselves. You've told the players to keep their complaints in house. The next time Andrea interviews them, they won't have anything negative to say."

Troy's fingers stilled. "I didn't only tell the players not to complain to the press. I've denied reporters access to the team."

Jaclyn's brows knitted. "Was that a good idea? The press is already complaining about you."

Tension tightened his muscles. "My priority is the Monarchs. I'm not going to let the media distract the team."

Jaclyn didn't look convinced. "Are you including Andrea in your media ban?"

He gave her a sharp look. "Yes. I have to treat all of the reporters the same. Either they all have access or they don't."

"Says who?"

"It wouldn't be fair to give Andy preferential treatment."

"Why not? Who gets access to our team is our decision."

Troy recognized a hint of reason in Jaclyn's point. "If we play favorites, we'll make the situation worse."

Jaclyn leaned into her desk. "Andrea has proven

herself to be a good ally. We're going to need one or two of those when Gerry shops his stories."

"Considering Gerry's track record with planting fake stories, I don't think a lot of newspapers will jump at his bait."

"I hope you're right."

Troy's stomach muscles knotted. Was his boss losing confidence in him? "I have ten years' experience working with the media. Four of those years are with this organization. My decision to deny reporters unofficial access to the team is based on that experience."

Jaclyn held his gaze for a long moment. Troy could feel her mulling over his words. He returned her regard without expression. But inside, he worried. What would he do, what would it mean, if she challenged his decision?

Finally, she nodded. "All right. My grandfather made you our V.P. of media and marketing for a reason. I'll support your decision."

Troy relaxed. "Thank you."

Jaclyn lifted her pen, rolling it between the thumb and index finger of her right hand. "But I hope your decision is based on your professional concern for the team and not because you're trying to protect a specific player."

His relief hadn't lasted long. "What do you mean?"

Jaclyn lowered her pen. "Marc told me Barron stormed out of practice this morning in the middle of your speech to the team. You're angry with Andrea because of her article in today's paper. Am I reading too much into the situation or not enough?"

Troy held Jaclyn's gaze. "This is about the team, not just Barron."

At least that's what he kept telling himself. Barron

was a Monarch. He had to protect Barron to protect the team.

Jaclyn searched his eyes. "I hope so. We both know that no one player is more important than the team."

Troy walked to the door. Jaclyn was right. Every athlete knew no player was above the team. But the Monarchs were more than a team. They were a family. And when one family member was in trouble, everyone stuck together. Just because his family hadn't stood with him when he'd been in trouble doesn't mean it wasn't supposed to be that way.

Later Thursday afternoon, Troy strode into the Monarchs' practice facility, slapping a computer printout against his right thigh. It was almost two o'clock. Practice had officially ended about twenty minutes ago. But Troy knew players stayed hours later for additional practice and training.

He found Jamal, his target, taking shots at one of the twelve nets suspended around the facility's perimeter. The rookie stole frequent looks at Warrick, who practiced a couple of baskets away.

Troy stopped almost on top of the young shooting guard. "I asked the team not to talk to the press."

Jamal adjusted his focus from the net to Troy. "I know. I was there."

"Then why did you talk to a *Horn* columnist?"

Jamal turned away from the basket and gave Troy his full attention. "I never spoke to any reporters or columnists or whatever. Who said I did?"

Troy sensed the other man's confusion. Had Jamal thought Troy wouldn't find out? He gave the rookie the folded printout of the *Monarchs Insider*, the *New York Horn*'s new online blog.

Jamal scanned the sheet of paper. His eyes widened. "Who the hell is the Monarchs Insider? The guy doesn't even use a name."

"You tell me." Troy hooked his hands on his hips. Jamal seemed genuinely surprised. But how could he be? The blogger had quoted him in the debut post.

"I've never met the guy." As irritated as Jamal sounded, he had a long way to go to match Troy's anger.

"You wouldn't have to meet him to speak with him."

Jamal narrowed his gaze. "I've never spoken to him, either. I don't know this guy."

Troy gestured toward the sheet Jamal was crumpling in his fist. "He quotes you in his article."

"Listen, man, you told us not to talk to the press. I don't know where this dude gets off saying I spoke to him. I didn't." Jamal was almost shouting.

"What's the problem?" Warrick's question interrupted their exchange.

Troy turned to the veteran shooting guard. "I got a Google Alert on an interview Jamal gave to a new online sports blogger with the *Horn*."

Warrick's brows came together. "A recent interview?"

"Yeah." Jamal shoved the nearly ruined printout at his teammate. "The only thing is, I keep telling Troy I didn't talk to the guy."

Warrick took the sheet from Jamal. Troy watched as the seasoned player smoothed the paper and started to read the column. A muscle flexed in Warrick's jaw. He must have come to the part where the columnist quoted the rookie denigrating Warrick's skills. Or maybe it was the part where Jamal declared it was time for the veteran to retire.

Troy rubbed his gritty eyes, then rubbed the back

of his neck. This was one of the longest Thursdays ever, starting with his taking Barron home from the club. He hadn't meant for Warrick to read that trash. The interview was with a brash baller masquerading as a teammate and reported by an irresponsible gossip pretending to be a legitimate journalist.

The smack of basketballs against the gleaming hardwood court and the chatter of conversations spoken above normal decibels faded into the background, becoming an annoying buzz.

Warrick finished the column. He looked first to Jamal. The younger man returned his study with a mixture of defiance and dismay. Silence lengthened as they held each other's gaze.

Finally, Warrick handed Troy the printout. "Jamal didn't talk with this columnist."

"See? I told you." Jamal vibrated with righteous indignation.

Troy ignored the rookie, keeping his attention on Warrick. "How do you know?"

Warrick also ignored the younger player. "Jamal is arrogant, obnoxious, and juvenile, but he's not a liar."

"I'm not juvenile." Jamal sounded annoyed.

Warrick held Troy's gaze. "If he said he didn't talk to this columnist, he didn't."

"I'm not arrogant, either." Jamal seemed offended.

Warrick was probably right. Troy didn't have any personal history on which to base his suspicions of Jamal. All he had was that column. "Then how did the blogger get that interview?"

Warrick shrugged. "He didn't. The blogger is the liar. He says he interviewed Jamal, but he didn't."

Why was the veteran point guard defending the rookie who took his spot, especially after all the aggravation the younger player had caused him? That was beyond Troy's comprehension.

He inclined his head toward Jamal. "You really believe him?"

Jamal bounced on his toes. "Why shouldn't he? I'm not a liar."

Troy still had some doubts. "Those quotes sound just like you. That blogger couldn't have made them up."

Warrick nodded. "He probably lifted them from articles that ran earlier in the season."

Troy scowled at Jamal, letting the younger man see his irritation. "Or heard the comments you made from the court."

Jamal dropped his gaze. "I didn't mean them."

Warrick's chuckle was dry and unamused. "Yes, you did." He checked his watch. "Are we good here? I want to get some weights in before I leave."

Jamal's eyes stretched wide. "No, we're not good. This needs to be fixed. It's bad enough having my teammates think I'm arrogant, obnoxious and . . ."

"Juvenile," Troy prompted.

"Right." Jamal gave him a sour look. "I don't need them thinking I'm a liar, too."

Troy nodded toward Warrick. "We believe you."

Jamal set his jaw. "Rick isn't the whole team."

Troy saw his point. "I'll tell them to take it down and threaten them with legal action if they continue to harass our players." He'd consult with Jaclyn to make sure he had her support before he made those threats.

Jamal crossed his arms. "I want an apology."

Troy arched a brow. "I know you're upset that the columnist pretended to interview you. But if anyone deserves an apology, it's Rick. Your comments insulted him and damaged his reputation. I don't care when you made them."

Jamal dropped his gaze again. "I'm sorry."

Warrick looked at the rookie, who still couldn't meet his eyes. "Help me get this championship and we'll call it done." He nodded at Troy. "Good luck with that blogger."

Troy watched as Jamal followed Warrick to the weight room. Warrick impressed Troy. Whether he was on the court or the bench, for the veteran NBA player, it was all about the team and the win. Jamal took his starting spot and attacked him in the media. Still, Warrick didn't hold a grudge. Troy couldn't understand how the other man did it.

He turned to leave the facility. Identifying the Monarchs Insider was Troy's priority for what remained of the day. He already had an idea who was behind this latest harassment. Getting Gerald to admit his role was another matter.

"Man, don't you have a life? Why are you trying to live mine?" Barron turned away from his front entrance, leaving Troy to follow him—or not—into his Prospect Park condominium. At least Barron hadn't slammed the door in his face, as Troy had half expected.

He locked the door before finding his reluctant host in the entertainment room. Barron stood behind the oak bar, pouring dark liquid—Scotch?—into a highball glass. The black carpet swallowed the sound of his approach.

Troy stopped on the other side of the bar. He looked from the glass to Barron. "What are you doing?"

"What does it look like?" Barron's tone snapped with impatience.

"Like you're getting drunk at six o'clock in the evening."

"It's almost six-thirty."

"And you're sitting here by yourself." He raised his BlackBerry toward Barron. "I got your tweet asking for friends to go clubbing with you tonight."

"I knew I should have blocked you."

Why hadn't he?

Troy shoved his BlackBerry back into his front pocket. "We're going into the postseason. Put your clubbing on hold."

"You're not my mother, man. You're not even my coach. Go back to the front office where you belong." Barron corked the bottle of liquor and took a deep drink from his glass.

Troy didn't react to the anger hardening Barron's eyes or the liquor he was pouring down his throat. The point guard was searching for buttons to push. Troy wouldn't let him know he'd found one of his. "I'm not in the locker room with you, but we work for the same team."

"What are you doing here, man?"

"What are *you* doing? You read the *Sports* article about you. Don't you care that you're letting your teammates down?"

Barron raised his chin and his voice. "*They* let *me* down."

Troy wandered over to sit on the arm of Barron's red leather sofa. Matching armchairs circled an oak center table. An enormous plasma screen television hung on the off-white wall across the room. It was almost the size of the Empire Arena's JumboTron. The TV played ESPN's *SportsCenter*. The sound was muted.

He watched Barron lean against the bar. "Marc benched you for the final game of the regular season.

Are you going to make them pay by throwing away the play-offs?"

Barron jabbed a thumb against his chest. "*I'm* the team captain. *I* should have been on the court."

Troy smelled the liquor on the other man's breath from more than an arm's length away. "And you would have been if you'd been playing well. But you weren't. Marc made the decision. He was right. The Monarchs made the play-offs."

"I would've taken the team to the play-offs."

Troy watched him sway on his feet. Why was Barron doing this? "No, Bling. You wouldn't have."

Barron's gaze wavered. He took another gulp of Scotch. "You don't know that."

"No, I don't." He nodded toward the bottle still within Barron's reach. "But I'm sure we won't make it past the Cavs if you drink yourself into a stupor every night."

"I can share." Barron lifted the bottle. "Do you want some?"

Troy had to believe he wasn't wasting his time here. When Barron had his act together, he was a vital part of the team. Troy just needed to convince the team captain to pull himself together. "Are you going to stand here drinking all night?"

Barron set the bottle on the surface of the bar. "I'll probably sit after a while. Then, once I get my second wind, I'll go to the club."

"What about practice in the morning?"

Barron shrugged again. "It starts at eleven."

Troy held on to his patience. "Will you be there?"

Barron arched a brow. "Why? Are you going to talk to us again?"

His temper was starting to fray. What made him think he could reason with the point guard? "This isn't a joke. It's the play-offs. Doesn't that mean anything to you?"

Barron leaned across the bar toward him. His voice was low and throbbing with anger. "Only if I'm going to play."

"Marc won't let you play if you don't practice. You know that."

"I guess I'll just keep drinking then." Barron pulled the bottle toward him.

Troy fisted his hands in his pockets. "Meanwhile, you'll give Gerry plenty of material to hurt the team."

Barron scowled his disbelief. "The team he owns? Why would he do that?"

"Co-owns. He doesn't want us to contend in the play-offs."

Barron barked a laugh. "You think I'll stay home if you tell me Gerry's going to use me to hurt the team? Nice try. You told us not to talk to reporters outside of the media sessions."

Troy let his anger show. "You won't have to talk to reporters. Your teammates will see that while they're taking care of their bodies and showing up for the team, you're coming to practice with a hangover. Think they'll want you around?"

Barron glowered at him. "Screw them and screw you."

"You already have." Troy turned to leave.

Nothing had changed with Barron tonight. He may never get through to him. All right. If he couldn't stop Barron, could he stop Gerry?

5

"I think I've found our new roommate." Andrea spoke over her shoulder to Faith Wilcox as she loaded the dishwasher. She and her roommate had finished dinner and were tidying the cozy confines of their kitchen.

"Who?" Faith scrubbed the pots and pans by hand. The rhythm of her movements was in time with the pop song she hummed under her breath.

"Connie Street. She's the Monarchs' new administrative assistant." Andrea added detergent to the dishwasher's well. "And she has a three-year-old daughter."

"I don't remember you mentioning her. How long have you known each other?" Faith rinsed the pots and pans, placing them on the drain board.

Andrea drew a deep breath as she straightened from the dishwasher. The savory scents of their chicken stew dinner lingered in the air. "We met her at the Morning Glory homeless shelter a couple of weeks ago. Do you remember a tall blonde with a toddler daughter?"

"No." Faith dried her brown hands on the white

and blue dish towel hanging from the refrigerator's door handle. "She's a stranger."

"I was, too. When I answered your ad for a roommate, I didn't know you or Keisha. Still, you let me move in with you."

Faith's dark brown gaze was speculative. "Our first roommate got married and left just like Keisha. I see a pattern here."

"And I came from the shelter just like Connie and her daughter." Andrea remembered who and where she'd been when they'd first met.

"A little girl could cramp our love lives." Faith led them from the kitchen.

Andrea chuckled. "When was the last time either of us brought a man home?"

Faith tossed Andrea a smile. "*Your* dry spell has been longer."

"Thanks for reminding me. I might have forgotten." Andrea grabbed the television remote control and collapsed onto the faded tan armchair across from the small, aging television. It had been a long and mentally exhausting day. "Let's invite Connie and her daughter for dinner tomorrow so we can get to know them."

Faith curled up on the fat brown sofa on Andrea's right. "Is she going to be another one of your good deeds?"

Andrea avoided Faith's gaze. "She needs a home. We need a roommate. Why do you think it's more complicated than that?"

Faith let out an exasperated sigh. "You've been doing penance for your mistake for as long as I've known you. When is it going to be enough?"

"I haven't been keeping track." The truth was she didn't know. It may never be enough.

Faith's expression clouded with concern. "Are you doing this because you want to or because you think you have to? Do you even know?"

"She seems nice and, if she moves in, everyone gets what they need. She gets a home for her and her daughter. We get someone to help with expenses. I don't think that's a bad thing."

Her friend studied her a moment longer. "All right. Invite them to dinner. We'll see how it goes."

Andrea's shoulders relaxed. "Thank you."

"Is that the reason you've been moping around all evening like someone stole your superpowers?"

Andrea scowled. "It's worse. Troy pulled my access to the team."

"What? Why?" Faith sounded ready to pummel Troy.

"He says he's trying to protect the team from bad press."

Faith's brows knitted. "Then why is he blocking *you* from the team? New York would have forgotten about the Monarchs if it wasn't for you."

Andrea's gaze slid to the remote in her hands. She looked at the buttons without really seeing them. She'd rebuilt her confidence with the Monarchs. She could thank Jaclyn Jones for that. "Troy thinks he's doing the right thing. I don't agree, but how do I change his mind?"

"By working for another paper." Faith uncurled her legs, planting her feet on the floor. "Troy thinks he can get away with treating you unfairly because you write for *Sports*. He wouldn't treat the *Times* or the *Daily News* this way."

Andrea wasn't as certain. "He said he will."

Faith snorted. "No, he won't. Face it, Andrea. You need to work for a newspaper with more clout."

Faith was a good friend and the closest thing to

family she had since her mother died. But Faith's expectations for Andrea's career advancement were sometimes more stressful than encouraging. "I enjoy working for *Sports*. The pay is horrible. Resources are slim to none. And technology is decades behind industry standards. But Will is a good boss. He gave me an opportunity when no one else would."

"And you're afraid they'll reject you again when you start looking for a new job."

Andrea lifted her worried gaze to Faith. "It's too soon to expect they've forgotten my past."

Faith crossed her arms. "*You're* the one who won't let go of the past. It's been four years. How long are you going to punish yourself for your mistakes?"

"We've had this conversation before. You don't understand what it was like."

"No, I don't. But I do know that you're the only thing holding you back. You're a great writer. Even I can see that and I don't like sports."

Andrea stared at the floor. Instead of the red and orange Oriental-style rug, she saw broken dreams and unfulfilled goals. "I want to write for a major paper again. I want a wider audience."

"A bigger paycheck wouldn't hurt, either."

"But just because I want it doesn't mean I'll get it." *Or that I deserve it.*

"The role of Eternal Penitent doesn't suit you." Faith leaned toward Andrea. "Get off your backside, pack up your fears, and go for it."

"I would—if I had somewhere to go. The industry has a long memory." Andrea pointed the remote control at the television screen and pressed the on button, signaling the end of the discussion.

The cable news came to life on the screen. Andrea set the remote on the coffee table. She pulled her cell phone from the pocket of her warm-up jacket and checked her Twitter account. She bit her lower lip when she read Barron's latest message.

"What's wrong?"

She looked up at Faith's question. "Barron Douglas is going clubbing again tonight."

Faith shrugged. "So?"

"That's two nights in a row, and practice is eleven o'clock in the morning."

"I guess that's a bad thing."

Andrea lowered her cell phone. "His team has made it to the postseason. Barron should be focused on the play-offs, not the clubs. His behavior is out of control—just like mine was."

"If you're worried about him, talk to Troy."

Andrea returned her gaze to her phone. "I tried. He won't listen to me."

"And you said he won't let you talk to the players, either."

Andrea's hand tightened around her cellular. "I have to at least try to help Barron." She shrugged. "I can always apologize to Troy later."

The next morning, Andrea got out of her Escort as Barron pulled his liquid silver BMW sports car into a parking space about five rows ahead of hers. The Monarchs' captain was cutting his schedule pretty close. Friday's practice would start in a few minutes. Then the team would leave for Cleveland and its best-of-seven series against the Cavaliers.

"Barron." She shouted his name to detain him as she jogged across the Empire Arena's parking lot.

Barron stopped, lowering his wraparound black sunglasses to scan the lot. In seconds, his gaze landed on Andrea. His features twisted into an irritated scowl before he turned and continued toward the arena. Too late. His momentary hesitation bought Andrea enough time to catch up with the NBA star as he was halfway across the lot.

"Barron." She was slightly out of breath. Little had she known her morning jogs would help her chase down professional athletes. "May I speak with you?"

"No." He didn't slow down.

Andrea tried to match his long strides. She angled her head to search his features about eight inches above her. Strain lines bracketed his tense lips. His jaw flexed as he gritted his teeth.

"You have a hangover." She made it a statement.

A light breeze carried the scents of nearby cut grass, spring blossoms, and the marina. It ruffled her hair. She brushed the loose strands away from her face.

Barron dragged a hand over his thick cornrows. He didn't look at her. "Find someone else to screw with for your paper."

Andrea winced but still managed to keep pace with the point guard. He'd probably move faster if he weren't afraid his head would shatter.

The front entrance was in sight. "I'm not screwing with you. I'm trying to help you."

Barron came to an abrupt halt. He moved in, crowding Andrea. "Are you kidding me? How is that piece of crap you wrote about me supposed to help me?"

Andrea stood her ground. "You're staying out late clubbing every single night. You're getting to practice late and not giving a hundred percent when you're there. Your behavior is a cry for help."

His expression darkened. "This ain't no soap opera. I'm not some teenage girl losing her mind."

"No, you're not." Andrea held his gaze behind his sunglasses. "You're an NBA player under a lot of pressure."

Barron rocked back as though she'd slapped him. "What the hell are you talking about?"

Andrea stepped forward. "This is the first time you've been on a play-off team—"

"So?"

Andrea ignored Barron's interruption, concentrating instead on his labored breathing and the familiar stench of fear. She'd worn it herself four years ago. Behind his sunglasses, she thought she saw his eyes flick left, then right. "You're the starting point guard and the team captain. You're supposed to lead the team. Instead, you sat on the bench watching them win the game that decided if they'd get to the play-offs."

Anger curled Barron's lips. "Mind your damn business." He spun on his heel and marched toward the arena.

Andrea rushed to keep up with him. "Your teammates and coaches think you're being selfish and irresponsible. But that's not it at all."

"I said mind your business." Barron sounded desperate. Afraid.

Andrea took heart from the player's agitation. It meant he was almost ready to listen. She remembered that feeling. "I know what you're running from. Talk to me. I can help you."

Barron stopped again. He spun to face her. "I'm not running away from anything." He growled the denial.

"OK. We'll use the term *avoidance.*"

Barron snatched the wraparound sunglasses from his face with his right hand and rubbed his bloodshot eyes with his left. "What do you want from me?"

"Nothing. I want to help you."

His pained dark gaze searched hers. Andrea saw the hope warring with suspicion in his eyes. "How?"

"Talk to me. Tell me what you're thinking, how you're feeling, what's on your mind."

"You're going to help me by interviewing me for your newspaper?"

Andrea shook her head. "This isn't about *Sports*. I just want to help you."

"Help me do what?"

"Face whatever's bothering you. That's the first step toward your recovery, being able to admit you have a problem."

Barron shoved his sunglasses back onto his face. "Yeah. Sure. And if you happen to get your story while you're *helping* me, it's all good. Right? Wrong. I don't trust you."

"I know what's bothering you, but you have to admit it to yourself."

Barron barked a laugh, shaking his head. "Oh, you're good. You pretend something's wrong with me. Then you try to sucker me into telling you exactly what it is so you can slap your byline on the story."

Andrea moved closer to him, taking hold of Barron's forearm to prevent him from moving away from her. "I'm not trying to trick you. I promise."

Barron looked from her hand on his forearm to her face. "You expect me to believe you're doing this for my sake?"

"No." Andrea held onto his gaze, willing him to believe her. "I'm doing this for *my* sake."

Uncertainty flashed across Barron's dark face before his features hardened. "Nobody does anything for anyone for free." He shook off her hand and marched into the arena. This time, Andrea let him go. What could she do to get through to him? He wasn't ready to talk about the reason for his erratic behavior.

Andrea checked her wristwatch. Barron may not want her help, at least not yet. But there was another Monarchs employee who might.

Minutes later, Andrea stood in front of Constance Street's desk. "Are you free for dinner tonight?"

Constance stopped typing. Her green eyes filled with suspicion. "Why?"

Andrea spied the *New York Daily News*'s Apartments for Rent section neatly folded in a corner. "My friend, Faith, and I are looking for a roommate to help with the rent. Our last roommate just got married and moved out."

Suspicion became uncertainty. "I have a three-year-old daughter. I can't see two young, single women welcoming a toddler who isn't theirs into their apartment."

Andrea quirked a brow. "You make us sound like swingers. We're actually pretty boring. But it's just a dinner invitation to get to know each other. No commitments."

Constance stared at her keyboard. "I don't know."

Andrea stepped closer to her desk, needing to persuade this single mother of modest means to accept her help. "It's just dinner. Faith is a great cook. I'll pick you and Tiffany up at the shelter after work."

Constance picked at the cuff of her long-sleeved white blouse. It was pretty and professional but too large for the slender woman. She probably was looking forward to buying some new clothes—after all of her bills were paid. "I don't know if we should become friends."

Andrea laughed her surprise. "Why not?"

Constance's eyes were wide and worried. She knotted her fingers together. "You're a reporter. I work for the Monarchs. I can't give you insider information. I'd lose my job."

Andrea sobered. "I know. That's why I wouldn't ask that of you. If we all agree to give this a try, we'll just be roommates. And, hopefully, friends."

"My husband beat me." Constance's admission rushed out at Andrea. Her cheeks were red with shame. Her gaze remained glued to her knotted fingers.

"I know."

Constance's eyes darted up to her. "You know?"

"Your makeup didn't conceal everything. I'm glad the bruises have faded." At least the ones that were visible.

Constance brushed away tears with her fingertips. "When he hit Tiff, I had to leave. She's just a baby."

"I understand." Sometimes it was easier to find courage for someone you love than it was to be brave for yourself. Andrea clenched her hands inside the front pockets of her pants. She imagined using her fists against the man who would beat his wife and child.

Constance's voice shook. Her eyes filled with panic. "What if he finds out where I work or where I live? I don't want to involve anyone else in my problems."

Andrea reached into her purse. She pulled a business card from her wallet and handed it to Constance. "One step at a time. Come for dinner. Don't expect anything fancy. But we'd really like for you and Tiff to join us."

She smiled encouragingly while Constance's frightened gaze skipped from her business card to her face, then back. The struggle between her timidity and temptation was palpable.

Constance reached for the card. "I'll think about it. I promise."

"Fair enough." Andrea turned to leave.

Constance's voice halted her. "Didn't you want to see Mr. Marshall? He should be back soon."

Andrea shook her head. "I came to speak with you."

Suspicion returned to Constance's eyes. "You came all this way to invite me to dinner?"

Andrea hesitated. "And to check on a player."

"Mr. Marshall doesn't want the media talking to the players or the coaches."

"This wasn't for a story." She sensed Constance's curiosity, but she wasn't ready to satisfy her. "If we become roommates, I wouldn't ask you to jeopardize your job to help advance mine."

Andrea made it out of the office. She pushed through the double glass doors that led to the elevators and pressed the down button. The black laminate walls gleamed in the fluorescent light. The silver metal elevator doors captured her reflection.

She'd been prepared for Constance's reservations about raising her daughter in an apartment with two single women. She'd also anticipated her fear that her abusive ex-husband would find her. But she'd never considered Constance would think Andrea wanted to room with her to get insider information on the Monarchs.

Troy would believe that also. Would he try to prevent Constance from moving in with her? Would the other woman let him? Perhaps she could win Troy's trust if he got to know her. But a closer relationship with Troy was too great a risk.

6

Gerald's administrative assistant had told Troy he'd find her boss having brunch in this trendy Brooklyn café.

Troy took the empty seat at the table for two. "Mind if I join you?" His calm tone surprised even him, considering the turmoil building inside him.

Gerald lowered his copy of the *Wall Street Journal.* "As a matter of fact, I do."

The other man looked surprised to see him. Had Gerald really thought Troy would sit back and allow him to attack the team? It didn't matter that Gerald was the Monarchs' co-owner and, therefore, his boss. He wouldn't allow anyone to jeopardize the Monarchs' reputation.

Troy folded his hands on the table. "Then let's make this quick. Call off your dog, Gerry."

"What dog would that be?"

A slender young woman dressed in the café's red and white uniform paused beside Troy. "Sir, can I get you something to drink?"

He'd ask for a beer if he weren't returning to the office. "Ice water, please." He waited for the young woman to leave before continuing. "I saw the *Insider* blog on the *Horn*'s website, Gerry. Tell the paper to take it down."

Gerald picked up his own glass of ice water. Idle curiosity marked his manner. "Are you ordering me?"

It was hard to remember Gerald was the boss when Troy had more loyalty to the company. "I'm *asking* you."

"Maybe Jackie lets you get away with that tone, but I don't take orders from staff."

Troy narrowed his gaze. "Why are you doing this? The only ones who benefit from your attacks against your own team are your competitors."

The server returned with Troy's water. "Are you gentlemen ready to order?"

Troy declined food but waited while Gerald placed his brunch request. He gave Troy a sly look when the young woman left. "What exactly do you think I'm doing?"

The throbbing started in Troy's temples. He took a sip of water. "You're paying the Insider to harass the team. Jamal didn't give the guy an interview. The blogger made it up, probably with your help."

"What makes you think I have anything to do with this blog?"

Troy almost choked on another sip of water. "It's your M.O., Gerry. You did the same thing with Marc."

Gerald shrugged. "Actually, I didn't."

"You're right. Andy Benson exposed you first."

Gerald gave him a smug smile. "So you say."

Troy drained his glass of water. "Stop trashing the team, Gerry. With all due respect, you should have let go of whatever grudge you held against Jackie's grandfather when he died. These players shouldn't have to suffer for it."

Gerald spread his hands above the table. "I don't have any knowledge of the blogger or the blog you're talking about."

Troy stood and parroted Gerald's earlier response. "So you say."

He strode from the restaurant, disappointed but not surprised. It was Gerald, after all. His whole reason for being was to bedevil the Jones family, and his weapon of choice was the Monarchs.

Reasoning with Gerald hadn't worked. He'd move on to Plan B. Whatever that was.

"You convinced the *Horn* to take down the *Monarchs Insider* post about Jamal." Jaclyn's terse words were more warning than praise.

Troy stood as his boss strode into his office Friday afternoon. He'd told Jaclyn about the blog yesterday. She hadn't seemed worried at the time. But today, her features were tight with anger.

His gaze fell to the printout in her right hand. He had a premonition of disaster. "They took it down yesterday."

"And replaced it with this." Jaclyn thrust a computer printout at him.

The new blog entry was a popular topic. There were almost three hundred comments posted to it. The title was "Mrs. and Mr. Jones." Troy gripped the sheet. He hadn't received this latest Google Alert, nor had he checked the online column. He should have.

Troy skimmed the brief blog. The Insider called Jaclyn a fool for believing DeMarcus Guinn was in love with her when he could have any woman he wanted. It offered a David Letterman–style list of the top ten reasons DeMarcus would fake a relationship with the Monarchs' co-owner. Each reason was more insulting than the last.

He looked into his boss's flashing brown eyes. Even her long, black curls quivered with fury. "This is trash." What else could he say?

"If this blogger wanted to distract the team, he's succeeded beyond his wildest dreams. I'm furious. Marc will be livid." Jaclyn's normally smooth voice was rough as sandpaper.

Troy dropped the printout to his desk. "Don't let them get to you."

"Too. Late." She clenched and unclenched her fists.

"It's a gossip blog. Don't waste your time worrying about it." Troy knew he'd said the wrong thing when Jaclyn's posture stiffened.

"That's easy for you to say. Your personal life isn't being derided and dissected on the World Wide Web."

"Everyone who knows you and Marc knows this stuff isn't true. It's obvious you love each other." Troy stopped talking. Jaclyn wasn't listening anyway.

She stabbed a finger toward the printout. "Who is the Monarchs Insider?"

Troy massaged the back of his neck. "I spent more than an hour on the phone with the newspaper yesterday asking that question. They bounced me around, refusing to reveal their sources. The best I could get was their taking down the post about Jamal."

"But they just replaced yesterday's trash with today's garbage." Jaclyn slammed her hands onto her hips. She stood frozen for several silent moments. "Do you think the Insider is an employee?"

Troy felt the pain he heard in Jaclyn's voice. "Gerry denied having anything to do with it."

Jaclyn's eyes widened. "You spoke to him?"

"Earlier today."

Jaclyn closed her eyes and rubbed her forehead. "I told you that I'd handle Gerry. You have to be careful in your dealings with him. He's your boss, too."

"I'm not worried about Gerry."

"You should be. But besides Gerry, is there anyone else who might be involved with this blog?"

Troy shook his head, as he considered all of his coworkers. "With the exception of Gerry, everyone's loyal to the franchise."

Jaclyn paced his office, which was almost as spacious as her own. Her anger spread across the room. "I want the entire blog taken down."

Troy tracked her movements. He wanted to take down the blog, too. But it wasn't that simple. "If we keep complaining about their posts, we'll only draw more attention—and traffic—to their website."

"They took down the post about Rick and Jamal."

"Because the blogger lied about interviewing Jamal." Troy sighed. "Jackie, we don't want them to know they can rattle us."

Jaclyn glared at Troy over her shoulder as she strode to the opposite side of the room. "I'm not rattled. I'm angry."

No kidding. But as long as she focused her anger on the blogger and not him, Troy felt relatively job secure. "I'm sure Gerry's behind the blog."

"Do you think *he's* the actual Insider?"

"I doubt he's writing the posts, but I'm sure he's feeding the blogger information."

Jaclyn expelled a breath. "But we don't have proof."

Troy shoved his hands into his pants pockets. "The blog appeared the same day Gerry asked Andy to write negative stories about the team. That can't be a coincidence."

Jaclyn paused before the window. She appeared deep in thought. "I wish I could figure out how to force him out of the franchise."

"So do I." Troy freed his hands from his pockets and crossed his arms. "I'll keep trying to find out who Gerry's working with on the blog."

Jaclyn looked over her shoulder. "How long will that take?"

"I don't know." He wished he did.

She turned to face him. "This is serious, Troy. Whoever this blogger is, he's picking the team apart. He's lied about Jamal, shredded Rick's reputation, and attacked Marc and me. Who's his next target? The play-offs start tomorrow. We need to stop this sooner rather than later."

Troy held her gaze. "I won't give up until I find the coward behind these attacks."

"Work fast." Jaclyn strode from his office.

She was counting on him. The whole team was counting on him. Troy returned to his seat. He'd do whatever it took to protect the franchise.

Andrea grabbed her office phone to make the ringing stop. But she continued reading the Cleveland Cavaliers stats in preparation for Saturday's game. "*New York Sports*. Andrea Benson."

"Hi, Andy." At the sound of Troy's sexy baritone, Andrea's vision blurred.

"Hello, Slick. Aren't you supposed to be on a plane to Cleveland for tomorrow's game?" Game one of the

Monarchs versus Cavaliers series was scheduled for Saturday in Quicken Loans Arena.

"I have a couple of hours. How's my favorite sports reporter today?"

Andrea's suspicion stirred. Why was he being nice to her? "I'd be a lot better if you hadn't blocked my access to your players. Have you come to your senses?"

His low chuckle strummed the muscles in her abdomen. "I came to my senses the day I blocked access. But it looks like you've found a way around that."

Andrea was confused. "What do you mean?"

"Connie told me you invited her to move in with you. You're not looking for a back door to the team, are you?" His accusation stung.

"This has nothing to do with the Monarchs. Connie and her daughter need a place to live, and my friend and I need another roommate."

"Then put an ad in the paper."

Andrea gripped the receiver. "Why?"

Troy's tone sobered. "It's not a good idea for you and Connie to room together."

"Why not?" She would make him say it. Troy would have to state the reason for his objection to Constance living with her. She wouldn't let him dance around his apparent discomfort when he was the one who'd made the call.

The line went silent. Could he have realized the idiocy of his position? No such luck.

"If you live with a Monarchs employee, you're going to have access to sensitive information."

He'd already blocked her access to Barron, making it difficult for her to help the shooting guard. She wouldn't let him stand in the way of helping Constance get herself and her daughter back on their feet. This was as much for the mother and daughter as it was for her.

Andrea glanced around the newspaper's office. Its open floor plan made privacy impossible. She wasn't anxious for her coworkers to overhear her arguing with one of her sources. She lowered her voice. "Don't worry, Troy. If Connie confesses that you're a jerk of a boss or you never miss an opportunity to admire your own reflection, I won't put that in the paper."

"I'm serious." He didn't sound offended, either. Too bad.

"That's what's so irritating." Andrea's gaze dropped to the surface of her dented metal desk. It was piled high with folders and research printouts. "What do you think I'm going to do? Withhold the TV remote until Connie tells me all of the office gossip?"

"Something like that." His tone was dry.

Andrea checked the clock at the bottom of her computer screen. It was minutes after five in the evening. She'd have to leave soon to get Constance and Tiffany. Nothing Troy said was going to change her mind about inviting them to live with her. They represented another act of atonement, another attempt to make amends for past mistakes. Hopefully.

She recalled Constance's comment about her talking to one of the players despite the media block. "Connie's loyal to the team. She won't give up any company secrets."

"I know."

Andrea inhaled the dusty air, heavy with the scent of newsprint. "I've proven I'm trustworthy as well."

"You're also ambitious and determined. That

makes you dangerous. You'll do anything to get ahead."

That was her past. The memory of that mistake still made her face burn. Luckily, Troy couldn't see her over the phone. "Why won't you trust me?"

"We're on opposite sides, Andy. Positive press sells tickets, but negative news sells papers. My job is to fill the arena. Your job is to sell the news."

She could hear the door of reason locking behind Troy. Her heart weighed heavy in her chest. "I guess it's lucky that Connie and I don't need your permission to room together." Andrea recradled her telephone receiver.

Troy trusted Constance. Why wouldn't he trust her? And why did it bother her so much?

"We're glad you came." An hour later, Andrea's roommate shook Constance's hand as the young mother stood in the entryway of their three-bedroom apartment. Faith then bent to cup Tiffany's tiny right shoulder. "Hi, Tiffany. I'm Faith. I'm happy to meet you."

The three-year-old stepped back. She regarded Faith with healthy suspicion, a look that reminded Andrea of the toddler's mother. Constance stroked her daughter's fine, honey-blond hair. "Can you say 'hi' to Miss Faith?"

Tiffany responded with a barely audible whisper.

Andrea extended her hand. "Let me take your jackets. Then I'll show you where you can freshen up before dinner."

Constance smiled at Faith as she helped Tiffany pull off her jacket. "Something smells wonderful."

Faith glanced at the kitchen to their right. "I made

spaghetti for us. But I thought Tiffany would prefer chicken nuggets and French fries."

Constance chuckled. "Finger foods. Perfect."

More than an hour later, the dining room table was cleared and the dishwasher was loaded. Even better, Tiffany had lost most of her shyness. Constance helped her small daughter onto the thick, brown sofa, settling Tiffany between her and Andrea. Faith sat on the tan love seat facing them.

Tiffany angled her head to look up at Andrea. "My mommy goes to work." When the little girl had found her voice, she'd pumped up its volume. Still, her wide green eyes, so like her mother's, appeared drowsy.

Andrea responded to her young companion in a serious tone. "I know. I've seen your mommy at work."

Tiffany studied Andrea for a moment before relaxing against her mother's side.

Constance glanced from Andrea to Faith. "Dinner was delicious. Thank you for inviting us."

Faith crossed her jeans-clad legs. "You're welcome."

Andrea shifted her attention from daughter to mother. "Now that you're working, how long will the shelter allow you to stay with them?"

The pleasure in Constance's expression dimmed. "They aren't pressuring us to leave, but I know they'd like to make room for people who are in worse trouble than Tiff and me."

Tiffany again spoke up. "When my mommy is at work, I stay with Sister Julie."

Constance wrapped her arm around Tiffany's tiny torso. "Sister Julianne is in charge of Morning Glory's day care. They accept donations."

Andrea brushed a gentle finger across Tiffany's tiny hand. It was coming up on seven o'clock in the evening. The little girl was growing tired. "Do you like Sister Julianne?"

Tiffany nodded groggily. "But I like my mommy better."

Andrea grinned. "That's nice." She laid her hand back in her lap. "Can she stay at day care even when you move out of the shelter?"

"As long as I can show a financial need." Constance tucked her hair behind her ears. "My salary is good. But it will be a while before I get on my feet."

Andrea glanced down at Tiffany. The little girl's eyes were closed and her lips were parted. Her breathing was deep and even in sleep. She looked at Faith. Her friend nodded. "Faith and I would like you and Tiff to move in with us."

Constance's shaky laughter betrayed her nerves. "We don't really know each other."

Faith tilted her head to the side. "Do you know anyone else better who has an apartment in Brooklyn?"

Constance's cheeks flushed. "I guess not. But I have to be extra careful because of Tiff."

Andrea looked from mother to daughter. "We understand. You don't have to worry about a long-term commitment. If things don't work out, just give Faith and me thirty days' notice, then you can move out. No hard feelings."

Constance's gaze remained on her sleeping daughter. She was silent for such a long time Andrea began to wonder at her thoughts.

The young mother looked first at Andrea, then Faith. "What about my ex-husband?"

"What about him?" Faith's voice held more than bravado. There was a warning for any man foolish enough to raise his hand against a woman or child.

Constance must have heard the warning. She hesitated before explaining, "Suppose he finds out where I live and he comes here?"

Faith sat straighter in the armchair. "I wish he would. I'd—"

Andrea interrupted her friend's tirade. "Wouldn't you feel safer knowing you weren't alone?"

Constance's eyes were wide and haunted. "I'd feel better knowing I wasn't putting other people in danger."

"There's strength in numbers." Faith sounded confident.

Constance looked again to her daughter. "I don't know."

Faith crossed her arms. "We do."

Andrea gave Constance an encouraging smile. "When can you both move in?"

Another nervous laugh escaped Constance's lips. "We don't have much to move."

"Tomorrow it is, then." Faith sat forward. "Would you like some tea?"

Constance seemed overwhelmed. "Yes, please."

Andrea watched her roommate walk to the kitchen. She arched a brow at Constance. "I probably should have warned you that Faith can be pushy. And you'll be on your own with her until Tuesday. I'm leaving for Cleveland to cover the first two Monarchs games tomorrow."

Constance tucked her little girl closer to her. "Why are you two doing this?"

Andrea ran her hand over the orange and yellow afghan that covered the sofa's fraying back. "I lived at the shelter once, too."

Constance's jaw dropped. She searched Andrea's face. "*You* did?"

Andrea nodded. "My problem wasn't an abusive husband. It was something else. Faith and her friend took me in when I was trying to get back on my feet."

Constance sighed. "I just hope you don't regret this."

"We won't." Andrea settled back into the lumpy sofa. A couple of years ago, she'd been in a similar situation to Constance. It felt good to now be in a position to help the other woman. Pay it forward.

It also was becoming easier to face her past. Was she finally getting to the point where she could forgive herself for her mistakes? When would she be certain she wouldn't ever repeat them?

7

"Barron Douglas is going drinking again tonight." Faith's announcement startled Andrea. Her room-mate curled up onto the sofa and settled her sketch-book on her lap

She gaped at Faith from the tan love seat. "How did you know?"

Faith drew a circle in the air with her index finger as though tracing Andrea's face. "You're gnawing on your lower lip and staring at your cell phone. That's what you usually do when Barron tweets that he's going clubbing."

Disappointed by the mundane explanation, Andrea returned her attention to her cell phone.

She'd driven Constance and Tiffany back to the shelter hours ago. But the tiny apartment still smelled of their pasta dinner with a hint of Tiffany's French fries. It also was almost surprisingly quiet without the chatty toddler.

Andrea glanced up from her phone. "The team's settled into their hotel in Cleveland. Barron sent a

Twitter message asking for nightclub recommendations."

Faith crossed her right leg over her left. "There's nothing you can do about that. He's in Cleveland. You aren't flying out until tomorrow."

Andrea heard the concern in Faith's voice. She set her cell phone beside her on the love seat and met her friend's troubled gaze. "Barron's in trouble."

"You've been saying that for months. I know you're worried, but he doesn't want your help. Besides, he has his teammates around him. You can ease up on the Barron Douglas Watch."

Andrea considered her recent interviews with the Monarchs and the players' comments. "Barron's teammates don't realize he's in trouble. They think he's being himself."

Faith opened her sketchbook. "If his teammates don't think his behavior is unusual, what makes you think something's wrong?"

How could she put her instincts into words? As she gathered her thoughts, Andrea glanced around the worn living room. Her gaze bounced off the simple neutral furnishings and lingered on the vibrant accent colors.

"It's as I explained before, I recognize Barron's behavior because I've been there." Andrea's words came faster as she struggled with remembered emotions. "The expectations on you are so high. Fear of failure overwhelms you. Your behavior becomes riskier as you try to compensate for your insecurity and numb your panic."

Faith looked up from her sketchbook. "But that was *your* experience. It's not necessarily what Barron's going through."

Andrea couldn't allow the memories to overwhelm her. "I think it is."

Faith put down her sketchbook and circled the laminate coffee table to sit beside Andrea on the tan love seat. "Tonight, you convinced a homeless mother running from an abusive ex-husband to move in with you."

Andrea couldn't escape Faith's steady gaze. "*We* did."

"Isn't that one good deed enough? You can't save everyone, Andrea."

"I'm not trying to save everyone. I'm trying to help Barron avoid the mistakes I've made. You would do the same."

Faith took hold of her forearm. "Yes, I would. But how are you going to help Barron when he won't listen to you?"

Andrea sighed. Troy's distrust echoed in her ears. "He thinks I'm trying to trick him into doing an interview for *Sports*."

"Let the team handle Barron."

"He won't listen to them, either. They've done interviews criticizing him. I have to find a way to earn his trust and talk to him without Troy knowing."

"And what will you say to Troy when your article is published? 'Oops'?" Faith's tone was dry.

"I can't walk away from Barron." After her mother died, she'd been alone and afraid, a dangerous combination. Barron seemed to be in a similar situation.

"How many people do you have to help before you can forgive yourself?"

A blush burned Andrea's skin. "That's not what this is about."

"That's *exactly* what this is about." Faith released Andrea's forearm. "You made a mistake. You've paid for it and you've learned from it. Stop punishing yourself and move on."

Andrea thought of the reporters who ignored her during the games. And Troy. He wasn't aware of her mistakes. But he still challenged her integrity. "I want to. But it's hard to let go of the past."

Troy looked away from ESPN's Saturday morning *SportsCenter* to answer his cell phone. He recognized the number. "Hey, Rick."

"Mary left me." The Monarchs point guard sounded as though he were chewing glass.

Troy scrambled to gather his thoughts. "When?"

"This morning. After she read the latest *Insider.*"

Troy squeezed his eyes shut and pinched the bridge of his nose. He spun on his heel and marched across the hotel room to his laptop. "What did she say?"

He hadn't given the malicious gossiper any thought this morning. He'd been too anxious to hear what the sports pundits were saying about the Monarchs' chances of winning their first play-off game in four years. He was pleased the anchors had used the franchise's new marketing slogan, "We're back," in their coverage, but his priorities had been wrong.

"She accused me of flirting with other women."

Troy froze with his hands above the keyboard. "What?"

"Last night—I mean, this morning—we went to some clubs looking for Barron."

"Who's we?"

Warrick's sigh was impatient. "Jamal, Serge, Anthony, Vincent, and me."

"Barron went clubbing the night before a game? Why didn't anyone call me?"

Warrick's voice tightened. "This isn't about Barron now. It's about Mary."

Troy hit the space bar to wake his computer. "Sorry."

"That blogger must have been there. He wrote a column about us going to the club where we found Bling. He made it seem as though we were there to get laid."

Troy felt a surge of anger. He stared at his monitor. "Did anyone approach you?"

"Of course people approached us." The shooting guard was rapidly losing his patience. "Men and women. Some wanted autographs or pictures. Others wanted to talk about the game. But no one who seemed as though they were going to do a piss piece about us."

Troy kept his tone balanced. "Give me a second to call up the website."

"Why?" There was a snap in Warrick's tone.

"I want to read what the blogger wrote."

"You can do that later. What are you going to do to make this right?"

The website loaded on Troy's computer screen. He scanned the copy. The post made it seem as though the Monarchs were sex-starved adolescents gone wild at a legal brothel. The blogger went on to make the shooting guard's wife the target of his latest electronic assault. The post was an affront to fairness and propriety.

Doctor Marilyn Devry-Evans wasn't resting on her husband's NBA laurels. She had an established career as an obstetrician/gynecologist. She also happened to be a beautiful woman, although the blogger disagreed. According to him, Marilyn wasn't worthy to be seen on the arm of a professional athlete. What made it even worse was that, at a glance, there were hundreds of comments to the site and most agreed with the blogger.

Later today, the Monarchs would face the Cleveland Cavaliers in the Quicken Loans Arena in their first game of the best-of-seven-games series. This column couldn't have come at a worse time. But then, that was probably Gerald's intent. The team—Warrick—didn't need this distraction, especially not now.

Troy wanted to punch the gossip. He could only imagine how Warrick felt. "How did you find this post?"

"One of Mary's friend's sent her the link this morning." Warrick sounded tense and tired. "Mary sent it to me."

Troy clenched his teeth. Marilyn had read the column before he'd even seen it. The situation was going from bad to worse to horrific. "I'm sorry. I should have stayed on top of this."

"What are you going to do about it?" Warrick asked the question with controlled fury.

Facing a furious husband was harder than trying to diffuse his boss's anger. "I'll threaten the paper with a lawsuit if they don't stop libeling our players and our staff. I'll also demand they take the post down."

"That's it?" Warrick's tone was incredulous.

Troy frowned. What did Warrick mean? "I'll force them to take the post off the Internet."

"This is bullshit. What good is getting rid of the post *now*? Mary's gone. I want her back. What are you going to do about that?"

What could he do? "Rick, right now Mary's angry

and embarrassed. Once this blows over, she'll come back." In the silence, Troy felt the waves of Warrick's tension crashing down the phone line.

"When will this 'blow over'?"

Troy kneaded the back of his neck where the tension tightened his muscles. "I don't know." Everyone was losing patience with the blog—Jaclyn, Warrick, most of all him. He had to end it.

"I want that blogger fired." Warrick bit the words. "Then I want the publisher to apologize to my wife. Publicly."

"Rick, I'll do—"

"She cried." Those two small words revealed the athlete's torment.

Troy couldn't feel any worse. "I'm sorry."

Warrick's words sped up as he transitioned from sorrow to anger. "If this guy wants to take cheap shots at me, I'm up for that. *I'm* the one who plays for the Monarchs. My wife isn't Mrs. Warrick Evans. She's Dr. Marilyn Devry-Evans. She deserves respect."

"I'll demand an apology for Mary." Troy spoke gingerly. "But the next headline could read 'Mrs. Evans Cries Foul.' Are you willing to risk that?"

Warrick spoke through clenched teeth. "If you don't have the stones to tell the paper to take down that crap, I'll do it myself."

A quick ten count reminded Troy that Warrick didn't mean to threaten his job. He was a husband reacting to his wife being publicly embarrassed. "You can do that. It might even work. But keep in mind the previous *Insider* post claimed Marc was only with Jackie for her money."

Stunned silence dropped down the line. "Are you kidding me?"

"No. Jackie and I agreed to ignore it." After Troy

exerted all of his powers of persuasion. "The Insider's goal, obviously, is to post as much cheap and hurtful gossip as he can. We have to be careful how we respond. We don't want to encourage him."

Warrick grunted. "Your strategy to ignore him didn't work. He followed his post about Jackie and Marc with this crap about my wife. You should have threatened him with a lawsuit *then*. If you had, Mary would still be with me."

Guilt pulled on Troy's shoulders. Was Warrick right? Troy hadn't insisted the *Horn* take down the post about Jaclyn and DeMarcus because he'd been afraid it would seem as though the Monarchs considered the blogger important. Well, he considered the malicious gossip important now.

Troy dragged a hand over his hair. "Even if the *Horn* had taken down the post about Jackie and Marc, they still would have posted this one. This sort of malice draws readers. And readers bring in revenue."

"You need to fix this, Troy."

He'd never seen this side of Warrick before. The Monarchs shooting guard could keep his cool even in the face of verbal abuse and physical assaults on the court. Nothing seemed to faze him. But this morning, Warrick was angry and desperate. His desperation was shutting out reason. What was Troy supposed to say to reassure him? "I'll get them to take down the post, Rick."

"That's not good enough. I want them to admit that they made up the story. We were there to get Barron, not to get laid. They lied."

Troy's tone was tentative. "Taking down the post won't magically bring Mary back. If she doesn't trust you, she's going to need some time."

"Why wouldn't she trust me?" There was pain in

the other man's voice. "We've been married for two years. I've never cheated on her. I never would."

"Ballers have a reputation."

Warrick's tone hardened. "I'm not some baller. I'm her husband." He took a breath. "Make the call, man."

"I will." Troy tried to sound confident.

Warrick exhaled. "Thanks."

Troy gripped his cell phone even after ending the call. The blog was becoming more destructive. He needed to find a way to stop them. But how?

8

"I love hearing about your job, Troy. But when are you going to call me because you're depressed over a woman?" Troy's sister sounded more irritated than concerned. He was three years older than her, but Michelle Marshall-Redding's superior attitude often made him feel like the younger sibling.

"Today's not that day." Troy stood from the sofa and wandered his hotel room's sitting area.

The room's royal blue carpeting was soft beneath his bare feet. He circled the wood and glass coffee table and muted the ESPN sports program rerunning from this morning. He could hear his five-year-old nephew and three-year-old niece arguing in the background. Did Michelle see their history repeating itself with her children?

His sister gave his nephew and niece a few sharp words and the noise level decreased. She returned her attention to their conversation. "Look, I'm sorry that your friend's wife left him, but how is that *your* fault?"

"I didn't say it was." But that's how it felt.

"You sound as though you blame yourself."

He started pacing again—long, angry strides. "Gerry's the one to blame. He's gone too far this time."

The clinking of metal on metal jarred the telephone line. Michelle was loading her dishwasher. "How do you know it's your boss?"

Troy pressed the silver cell phone against his ear. Jaclyn was his boss. Gerald was a snake in the grass who needed to be removed. "It's his M.O. He's using rumors and innuendo to turn our fans against us."

"What does Jackie say?"

Troy was impatient with Michelle's interrogation. He needed a solution, not an oral questionnaire. "She wants me to get rid of the blog."

"What's she doing to get rid of Gerry?" His sister's questions continued.

"Gerry won't sell his shares, and she doesn't have a contractual reason to drop him."

"Jackie's a lawyer as well as the franchise owner. If *she* can't get rid of her partner, what do you think *you're* going to be able to do?"

Troy stopped pacing. Through his hotel window, he stared at downtown Cleveland's tall, older buildings and narrow, hilly streets. "I don't know. But I've got to do something."

"Handle the publicity for the team. That's your job. Not babysitting the players. You're dealing with adults, not children."

Considering the recruiting age of many of today's players, Michelle's pronouncement wasn't strictly true. "I'm trying to manage the media. But it's damn hard when someone inside the franchise is feeding bloggers gossip about the team."

Michelle broke the pensive silence. "Gerry's your boss. In this economy, I wouldn't push him, if I were you. You might find yourself out of a job."

Troy dragged his hand over his hair. "*He's* the one who needs to be out of a job."

"*That's* what I'm talking about."

"What?" He prowled past the beige tweed sofa. Another segment of ESPN's *SportsCenter* was starting.

Michelle's laughter was incredulous. "I know you, Troy. You rush into situations without a plan. You've been lucky so far, but your luck's not going to hold forever."

He hadn't always been lucky. But some things were worth the risk, and the Monarchs was one of them. "I know what I'm doing, Shelley."

"And what's that?"

"Protecting the team. It's what they pay me to do." Troy strode back to the window and stared down at the pedestrian traffic along Carnegie Avenue.

"What's more important? Your job or the team?"

Troy hesitated. "The players are like brothers to me. I can't separate the two."

"I hope Gerry can. Otherwise, if you put your neck out to protect the team's image, you may find yourself unemployed."

Troy sighed, turning away from his view of spring in Cleveland. "It won't come to that. I just need a plan."

Saturday evening, less than an hour before the first Brooklyn Monarchs versus Cleveland Cavaliers game, Andrea made her way to the media section in the Quicken Loans Arena. Her stomach muscles knotted.

The section started about six rows up from the court to the right of the far basket. There were five rows of tables and chairs arranged for national and international print and Internet reporters. And all of them remembered the newspaper scandal she'd been involved in four years before. They weren't as openly hostile since she'd caught the story of Gerald trying to move the Monarchs. Still, she felt the cold slap of their disdain as she forced her way past them to an empty seat in the third row. They behaved as though they didn't hear when she asked them to excuse her. They pretended not to see as she struggled around them with her purse and laptop. But she always acted as though their scorn didn't affect her.

Andrea chose the first open chair in the row, refusing to isolate herself from the other journalists. She set up her laptop, then consulted the teams' stats, which were uploaded to a computer mounted to the table. The excitement in the Empire was palpable. Against her better judgment, Andrea was caught up in it, too. She shifted in her seat to gaze around the arena.

A series of pop songs played at near-deafening levels, but she still heard Sean Wolf, a *New York Post* sports reporter, hail her from two seats away. The middle-aged reporter with the lank brown hair was the biggest bully in the bunch. "Hey, Benson. I'm surprised that rag you work for could afford to send you to the play-offs."

She braced herself before turning to meet Sean's hazel-brown eyes. "Are you sure your publisher bought you a round-trip ticket?"

The responding laughter from the reporters who'd heard her surprised Andrea. She glanced at the two seated between her and Sean, Jenna Madison with *The New York Times* and Frederick Pritchard of the *New York Daily News*. Neither met her gaze.

Andrea returned her attention to the court. The Cavaliers cheerleaders concluded their dance routine for "Yeah!" by Usher and began dancing to "Let's Get It Started" by The Black Eyed Peas. The Cavs mascot, Moondog, helped young Cavaliers shoot baskets from the free throw line. Action photos and posed images of the Cleveland players moved on and off the Sony JumboTron above the crowd.

The players took the court for warm-ups. Andrea sat forward, trying to read their body language. The Cavaliers appeared confident and full of energy. The Monarchs looked tight. Not a good sign. She typed some notes into the open document on her laptop.

"Hello, Andy." Troy's baritone came from somewhere above her left shoulder and shivered down her spine.

Why wouldn't he stop calling her by that ridiculous nickname?

"Hello, Slick." Andrea's gaze traveled up his black European-style suit, white dress shirt, and silver tie. Her breath stopped.

He circled her chair to half lean, half sit on the table. She wished Troy had taken the empty seat beside her instead. He was too close. She could feel the heat from his body.

Troy crossed his arms. The pose emphasized the width of his shoulders. "Have Connie and her daughter moved in?"

Andrea nodded. "My roommate helped them get settled this morning. I called them after my plane landed this afternoon."

Troy's smile stiffened. "I look forward to reading your articles. I may learn something new."

Andrea thought of Constance, and her muscles tightened with temper. "You said you trusted Connie."

"I do. She's reliable and trustworthy."

Meaning *she* wasn't? Would it even be worth the effort to change his mind?

Troy's gaze shifted to the reporters behind her, moving up and down the row. His attention returned to her with a question in his eyes. Could he tell she was an outcast in this group? She didn't want to know.

Andrea hurried to speak first. "I'm not the one you need to worry about. Did you read the *Insider* blog this morning?"

Troy's well-formed lips tightened. "What about it?"

She was glad to have distracted him, but she hadn't intended to make him angry. "Are you going to respond to it?"

"I'm not getting into a dialogue with that blogger. I'm going to stop the person behind it."

Andrea blinked. "You know who the Insider is?"

"Yes. And once I expose him, the *Horn* will take the post down."

"Him? Who is it?"

Troy's gaze bounced from her reporter's notebook to her eyes. "You'll see." He straightened and checked his watch. "The game's starting soon. I'll see you at the press conference later."

How had Troy identified the Monarchs Insider? And how did he intend to expose the blogger?

"Benson rates a whole conversation with the guy, but he won't even return my calls." Sean's sulky comment wasn't addressed to her, and Andrea didn't respond.

"She did write that piece exposing Gerald Bimm's plans. Maybe Marshall thinks he owes her." Jenna's tone was pensive. With her flawless peaches-and-cream skin and the perpetual twinkle in her almond-shaped hazel eyes, the other woman seemed more suited for broadcast news than print journalism.

Should she consider it progress that they were talking *about* her although they still weren't talking *to* her? She'd brought their treatment on herself. But how much longer would it last?

"How did the Monarchs make it to the play-offs?" Jenna Madison sounded as stunned as Andrea felt.

Andrea studied the Monarchs as the game clock counted down the final two minutes of the first half. The players looked like they were sleepwalking through this first twenty-four minutes of the game. Their sloppy passes and flat-footed defense had made the Cavaliers look like legends. As a reporter, Andrea had to remain objective. But more than once, she'd wanted to jump to her feet and scream, "Wake up!"

"Cleveland owes their double-digit lead more to the Monarchs' mistakes than their own skills." Frederick Pritchard of the *Daily News* was more interested in the numbers of the game than the emotions. He was a human calculator with a sports media pass.

The half-time score was careening toward an embarrassing 55 to 35, Cavaliers. Those 35 points were mainly courtesy of forward Serge Gateau and center Vincent Jardine. The team hadn't even completed the first quarter before head coach DeMarcus Guinn had used all but one twenty-second time-out.

Jenna glanced around. "Cavs fans don't care how their team got their lead. They just love the score."

The *Times* reporter was right. Early in the second quarter, the Cavaliers' fans were so loud, Andrea feared the roof would collapse.

"Fan frenzy's never a good thing for the visiting team." Sean Wolf studied the crowd. "It'll be hard for the Monarchs to get into the game. They'll probably be swept out of the series."

Andrea was desperate to join the debate. But she knew the other reporters wouldn't welcome her contributions. Instead she listened, agreeing with most comments and disagreeing with a few. For example, she didn't think the Monarchs would be swept as Sean predicted. DeMarcus Guinn wouldn't allow that.

The coach looked furious. The Monarchs had more turnovers than possessions and more fouls than scores. They'd sent Cleveland to the free throw line so often that Andrea thought Cleveland's power forward, Antawn Jamison, should just stand at the line for the rest of the half.

Andrea's scrutiny shifted to Warrick Evans. The shooting guard had been riding the bench for the whole game. That wasn't like him. Usually, he ran up and down the sideline, calling encouragement to his teammates. Tonight, he looked as though he'd lost his best friend. The *Monarchs Insider*'s attack on Warrick's wife was responsible for that. She was certain of it.

With seconds remaining to the first half, Andrea hustled down the eight rows to the court level, hoping to intercept DeMarcus on his way to the locker room at halftime. She'd normally wait for the postgame news conference. But Andrea thought she'd have a better chance of getting a candid response from him away from other reporters. She wove through the crowds on their way to the restrooms or the food courts. Several traveling Monarchs fans groused about returning to their hotels. They'd rather leave at the half than watch their team embarrass them.

Andrea arrived near the entrance to the locker

room tunnel just as the buzzer sounded the start of the halftime break. She looked up and saw Troy approaching her. The Monarchs' ever-vigilant protector. She wished she'd waited for the postgame conference after all.

Troy ignored the groupies vying for his attention. Curious stares and a few daggers were aimed her way. His wicked smile had the power to distract and disarm. Andrea fought to stay focused.

"Looking for me?" This playful side was another weapon in his arsenal.

"You know I'm not."

"My loss." His eyes danced with humor.

Their exchange set off a chorus of pleas from the other women who promised they'd treat him better. Andrea ignored them. She scanned the crowd for DeMarcus.

Troy moved closer to her. "What are you going to ask him?"

What was the point in asking, "Him who?" They both knew she was waiting for DeMarcus.

"You'll see." She echoed his response to her question about his unmasking the Monarchs Insider.

Troy's bedroom eyes twinkled. By the time Andrea pulled away from his gaze, DeMarcus had appeared. She stepped into his path. "Coach, Barron Douglas looked tired and sluggish during the first half. Are you going to bench him and put Rick Evans in?"

DeMarcus looked frustrated. "I'll have to see how Barron starts the first half."

"What are you going to do about the rumors of his late-nightclubbing?"

Anger snapped in DeMarcus's eyes. He looked at Troy before responding to Andrea's question. "You mean that blogger? I'm not going to let a gossip columnist tell me how to coach my team. Excuse me."

Andrea stepped aside so DeMarcus could join his players. The former NBA superstar-turned-head-coach disappeared into Vom Two, the tunnel leading to the visiting team's locker room.

"Probably not the quote you were looking for." Troy's tone was dry.

Andrea studied his features. "I don't think it was the response you wanted, either."

Troy shrugged. "What else could he say? His job is to coach the team. Media is my job."

Andrea briefly closed her eyes, almost weary with frustration. Everyone was in denial. "Locking the players away from the media isn't going to stop Barron's drinking. And now he's taking other players with him."

"They went to that club to get Barron."

Andrea had thought as much. "Is that going to be the pattern for the rest of the play-off series? Players scouring clubs the night before every game looking for Barron?"

"Barron is a Monarch. We'll worry about how many clubs we have to search to find him." There was tension in Troy's voice. How much pressure was he under because of the *Monarchs Insider* blog, and how was he dealing with the stress?

"And when will you start helping him?" She didn't wait for a response. What was the point?

Andrea dove back into the arena crowd. The smell of French fries, chicken nuggets, and hot dogs soaking the arena made her mouth water. Reaching the media section, Andrea pulled up short at the sight of a familiar face. "Mindy?"

"Hello, Andy." Troy's former secretary didn't seem surprised to see her.

"It's Andrea." She stepped closer to the tall, slender woman to get out of the crowd's way.

Mindy Sneal pulled her well-manicured, black-tipped nails through her thick auburn hair. "Oh. Is Troy the only one who can call you that?"

Andrea narrowed her gaze. Was the other woman deliberately antagonizing her? "He's the only one who won't *stop* calling me that. I thought you no longer worked for the Monarchs."

Mindy shrugged. Her manner seemed sulky. "I left a couple of weeks ago."

"Where are you now?" It seemed polite to ask.

"I'm between jobs."

Andrea's eyebrows jumped. "You left the Monarchs without having another offer?" In this economy? Had she left voluntarily or had Troy asked her to go?

"I was ready for a new challenge." Mindy's expression dared Andrea to call her a liar.

"A new challenge." That was one way to describe being unemployed. Andrea glanced around the arena. "I take it the Monarchs let you keep the playoff tickets."

Mindy folded her arms. "Why shouldn't they? It's not as though I left on bad terms." Was her tone just a little defensive?

Andrea glanced at her watch. Less than ten minutes remained to the break, but she didn't want to talk to Mindy for that long. The other woman's subtle hostility always made her uncomfortable.

She started to turn away. "I hope you enjoy the game."

Mindy reached out to stop her, then let her hand

drop from Andrea's forearm. "I saw Troy speaking to you earlier. He isn't usually so friendly with reporters. He must consider you special."

Andrea's brows knitted. Nothing could be further from the truth. "We were discussing Troy's new secretary."

The other woman flinched at the mention of her replacement. "It's probably a matter of time before you're watching the games with Troy in the owners' booth."

Was that hatred in Mindy's cool blue eyes? What could Andrea have done to cause such a reaction? "I have my own seat in the media section."

Troy's former assistant gave her a condescending smile. "Do you still have a crush on him?"

Andrea's lips parted. "I've never had a crush on him." In fact, it seemed to her Mindy had been unusually possessive of her former boss and his attentions.

"I had access to his personal communications. I know a great deal about our Troy."

Had Mindy been eavesdropping on Troy? Is that why she had to leave? "He's not 'our Troy.'"

Mindy drew her nails through her auburn locks again. "Be careful around him. He's a heartbreaker. Just ask his ex-wife."

Troy had been married? Why was she surprised? Why did she care? "There's nothing for you to worry about, Mindy. I don't have a personal interest in Troy." She spoke with finality and turned to leave.

Mindy's warning about Troy has been completely unnecessary. Troy may look like every woman's fantasy, but she found his aversion to reporters a turnoff. It also had seemed as though Mindy had wanted information. About what? Or who? And why?

* * *

Andrea slapped the steering wheel of the rental car as she drove back to the hotel Monday night. Sports reporter or not, she was upset over the Monarchs' second straight loss to the Cleveland Cavaliers in their best-of-seven-games series. At 105 to 78, it hadn't even been close. Most of the Monarchs fans had left Quicken Loans Arena midway through the fourth quarter. She'd lead with that for her story.

It was almost eleven-thirty by the time she'd parked in the hotel's garage and returned to her room. Her cell phone started ringing as she logged on to her computer.

Her caller identification displayed her editor's home phone number. "Why are you still up, Will?"

"Turn to ESPN." Willis sounded as excited as a kid with a favorite toy—or a newspaper publisher with a hot lead story.

Andrea found the television remote control and tuned into the station. "OK. What am I supposed to—" She broke off when the camera framed the female sports reporter sitting beside Troy Marshall.

The young woman smiled into the camera. ". . . here with Troy Marshall, the vice president of media and marketing for the Brooklyn Monarchs." She turned toward her guest. "Troy, you said you had an announcement for us tonight. I'm sure our viewers would agree that the suspense is killing us. What's your announcement?"

Troy wore the suit she'd seen him in earlier. This piece must have been taped right after the game. She recognized the Quicken Loans Arena's press room.

The Monarchs executive looked at the anchor-woman rather than the camera. "I know the identity of the blogger who posts as the *New York Horn*'s Monarchs Insider."

The anchorwoman's perfectly shaped eyebrows rose. "Really? Who is it?"

Troy didn't blink. "Gerald Bimm, the Monarchs' co-owner."

The remote fell from Andrea's hand. "Oh, my God. What has he done?"

9

The raging cell phone beside his bed jerked Troy
awake. He grabbed the cellular in the dark and
blinked at the red liquid crystal display numbers on
his radio alarm clock. Who the hell would be calling
him at one-thirty in the morning?

"Hello?"

"You're fired!"

Gerald's bellow of fury slapped the cobwebs from
Troy's mind. He sat up, turned on the lamp beside
his bed, and blinked to clear his vision. Troy looked
away from his bare-chested reflection in the oak-
framed mirror on the wall across the room. "Gerry?"

"You'll have a security escort when you arrive at
the arena Tuesday. I'll be waiting to watch you pack
your belongings, then vacate the building."

Troy clenched the phone with his right hand and
clutched the lightweight green quilt pooling around
his hips with his left. "On what grounds are you
firing me?"

"Are you kidding me!? Was that your witless twin
being interviewed on ESPN or were you having an
out-of-body experience?"

"I know you're the Insider."

"Two words, Troy. Prove. It. You can't, can you?"

Troy's anger outpaced his nerves. "Can you deny encouraging the media to write damaging stories about the Monarchs?"

Gerald sneered down the phone line. "Despite your playing on a championship college team, I see I need to use simple concepts. I'm the boss. That means I don't have to answer your questions."

The fact that Gerald was familiar with any part of his resume took Troy off guard. He recovered quickly. "Your smear campaign against the team makes my job harder."

"You don't have any proof that I'm the Insider. But that didn't stop you from going on television and accusing me of being the blogger. Your actions make *my* job harder."

Troy frowned. "What job?"

"The job of being your boss. No employer wants a disloyal employee."

Troy felt the sting of Gerald's words. "You're calling *me* disloyal? I'm working my ass off to protect the team. What do you gain by continuing to trash them?"

Silence was heavy on the other end of the line. "I'll be waiting for you Tuesday. Enjoy the rest of your night."

The line went dead. Troy's body heated with fury beneath the quilt. He slammed the phone onto the table and scrubbed both hands over his face.

Gerald could deny his connection with the *Monarchs Insider* forever. But Troy wouldn't buy it. If he wasn't the blogger, he knew who was.

After almost four hours of tossing and turning, channel surfing, and working on the Monarchs' ad campaign, Troy climbed out of bed. Around five in the morning, he got dressed and went for a run through downtown Cleveland. The chill mid-April air slapped the remaining fatigue from his mind. He ran until the sun came up around seven o'clock. He circled the same blocks over and over, chasing his own thoughts. He ran until his lungs hurt, his muscles screamed, and his body dripped with sweat.

Troy listened to his footsteps slapping against the asphalt as he turned toward the hotel. The echo of sound didn't drown the questions chasing each other across his mind. Had Jaclyn done everything she could to get rid of Gerald? Why wouldn't Gerald sell his shares in the franchise? What did the Monarchs Insider really want?

Why had he asked for the ESPN interview?

He raced back to the Hilton Hotel on Carnegie Avenue, showered, and changed. Troy tried to distract himself during the half-hour wait until eight o'clock. By then, Jaclyn should be awake. She was his last hope to get his job back. His only hope.

Troy checked his wristwatch for the hundredth time, then glanced at the clock on the hotel room's wall. Both read minutes after eight a.m. Jaclyn and DeMarcus were early risers, and the Monarchs were scheduled to return to Brooklyn this afternoon. Still, he called Jaclyn's cell phone instead of their hotel room. He didn't want to disturb DeMarcus. The head coach may have decided to sleep in after the team's second loss last night. The call connected after two rings.

"What were you thinking?" Jaclyn sounded wide awake. Her question as well as her tone told Troy she'd seen the interview.

He straightened his shoulders and jumped into his defense. "If Gerry isn't the Insider, he knows who is."

"And you know that how?" Jaclyn's speech was precise. Her tone was clipped.

This interrogation was worse than Troy's clash with Gerald. Jaclyn's experience practicing law before assuming her role with her family's franchise was probably the reason Troy felt as though he were on trial. "Gerry's tried to get reporters to write stories criticizing the Monarchs before."

"But you don't have any proof that he's behind the blog, do you? You don't have anything connecting him to those posts."

Troy balanced his right elbow on his thigh and braced his forehead in his right palm. "No, I don't."

"I'll ask you again. What were you thinking? No. Wait. I have a better question. *Were* you thinking?"

Troy tightened his grip on his cell phone. "I wanted to stop Gerry's attacks against the team."

There was a beat of silence before Jaclyn spoke. "Troy, with that one interview, you've done more damage than the Insider, whoever that may be."

Troy straightened in his armchair. Her accusation seemed unfair. How did he respond to that? "What are you saying?"

"You went on television with a baseless accusation that your boss was trying to destroy the team." Jaclyn's voice was taut with anger. "In a best-case scenario, you're being disloyal to your employer. In a worst-case scenario, you're committing slander."

Troy switched his phone to his right hand and flexed his left to relax his fist. "But I'm right."

"Without proof, you're just reckless."

Troy paced his hotel room. His bare feet sank into the soft carpet. He didn't want to believe she was right. "What can I do now?"

"I don't know. If you'd talked to *me* before talking

to ESPN, I'd have stopped you." The anger had drained from Jaclyn's tone. "Why is it that the men in my life don't discuss their plans with me first?"

Troy's face heated. Jaclyn was talking about him. She was also speaking of DeMarcus, who hadn't told her about Gerald's attempts to blackmail him several months ago. DeMarcus intended to deal with Gerald on his own. Luckily, Jaclyn found out about Gerald's scheme in time.

Just as DeMarcus's strategy had almost backfired on him, Troy was now dealing with the ramifications of his impetuous act. "I should have talked with you first."

"He could sue you for slander."

Troy heard the concern in Jaclyn's somber tone. He massaged the back of his neck. "That might be next. He fired me this morning."

"What? He can't fire you without consulting me. Not only am I his partner, I'm the general manager."

Troy stilled, gripping the back of the hotel's desk chair. The muscles in his neck slowly unknotted. "Good. Then I've still got my job."

Jaclyn's hesitation didn't bode well. "It's not that easy, Troy."

"Why not?"

"Gerry's your boss. We both own fifty percent of the Monarchs."

"Yes, but—"

"He fired you because you went on the news and embarrassed him. Frankly, if you'd done that to me, I'd have fired you."

Troy turned away from the window, rubbing his eyes. "I wouldn't do that to you."

"That's good to know." Jaclyn's tone was dry.

Troy rested his hips against the desk chair. "I have to keep my job, Jackie."

"I want you to keep your job, too. That's why I told you to leave Gerry to me."

Dread grew like a cold front from Troy's abdomen. "So there's nothing you can do?" He forced the question from his throat.

"I didn't say that. I'll arrange a meeting with Gerry. I'll do my best to change his mind, but I can't make any promises."

"I understand." His words rushed out on a relieved breath. "Thank you."

"Don't thank me. You'd better decide what you're willing to do to keep your job. Gerry won't change his mind easily."

They ended the call, and Troy pocketed his cell phone. Jaclyn was right. Gerald was going to ask for a pound of flesh and more.

Troy's gaze drifted across the hotel room toward the windows. Jaclyn's question replayed on a loop in his head. What would he do to get his job back? He'd do whatever it took to prove Gerald was the Monarchs Insider.

"You fired Troy?" Andrea sat across the table from Gerald in the trendy coffee house where he'd agreed to meet her Tuesday afternoon. She'd been amazed that he'd been willing to talk with her on such short notice. He'd also surprised her by agreeing to let her tape record their conversation.

Gerald nodded once. "Last night. Well, this morning, after I'd seen clips of his ESPN interview on the local stations."

Andrea swung her gaze around the coffee house trying to gather her thoughts. What would the Monarchs Insider make of this development? She couldn't imagine it being worse than what the blogger had posted about her and Troy just that morning.

She took a deep breath, releasing her temper before it got the better of her. The scent of baking pastries was almost overwhelming. She looked at Gerald. Had he read that morning's *Monarchs Insider* post? Had he written it? "What was Troy's reaction?"

Gerald shrugged his shoulders under the ruby-red shirt and tan blazer. "He kept accusing me of being the Insider. But, of course, he doesn't have proof."

Andrea arched a brow. "You haven't denied Troy's accusation."

Gerald sipped his latte. "And he hasn't proven it."

Andrea tried to read his brown eyes. "*Are* you the Insider?"

He glanced at the mini-recorder sitting on the table between them, then raised his gaze to hers. "No, I'm not."

Andrea had expected Gerald to deny it. "Do you know who the blogger is?"

His stare never wavered. "No, I don't."

She studied Gerald's fair skin and aquiline features. At close to sixty years of age, he remained fit and attractive. His wavy black hair showed very little gray. Gerald had model good looks and a wealth of self-confidence, just like Troy. But, unlike Troy, the interest lighting Gerald's features and gleaming in his eyes was all self-directed. Gerald Bimm cared a great deal for himself. Troy's passion was for the team. That's what drove him—perhaps too far?

She picked up her mug of coffee. Wrapping her

fingers around its warmth, she sipped the hazelnut-flavored brew. "Why do you think Troy believes *you're* the blogger?"

Gerald seemed to tense in his chair. He drank more of his latte. "I have no idea."

She pushed at him. "He wouldn't have gone on television unless he was certain you were the blogger."

"Maybe he's lost his mind." Gerald's response was testy.

"He looked sane on camera."

"Look, I can't control what Troy thinks." Gerald's voice and eyes hardened. "But I can't allow him to destroy my reputation by spreading lies, either."

Andrea arched a brow. "Isn't that what you tried to do to Marc Guinn two months ago?"

Gerald leaned back in his chair. "It's Guinn's word against mine."

She was beginning to believe Gerald. That scared her. *What had Troy done?*

Andrea turned away, hoping to hide her consternation. She looked around the coffee shop. The sleek, modern interior was a world away from the coffee shop near the *Sports*'s building. This one was three blocks from the Empire Arena. So why weren't they meeting in Gerald's office?

She picked up her mug. "Did Jackie Jones agree with your firing Troy?"

"I didn't consult her."

Andrea's brows knitted. "Why not?"

Gerald leaned toward the recorder and spoke a little louder. "A franchise employee publicly—and falsely—accused me of attacking the team. I made the decision to dismiss the employee. End of story."

Andrea knew Jaclyn Jones. Gerald was deluding

himself if he thought this was the end of the story. "But Jackie is the general manager in charge of personnel."

"And I'm an equal partner." Gerald gave her another shrug. "In any case, she knows now."

What wasn't Gerald telling her? "What are you going to do about the Insider?"

"What do you mean?"

She lowered her mug. "The Insider's posts have been a nuisance to your team. Aren't you curious about the blogger's identity?"

Gerald's eyes danced with humor. "Not really. You know I've wanted the media to help me keep the team in line."

"Then maybe you should thank the Insider."

"I'll leave a comment on his blog."

"Those posts don't just target your players. They've also attacked your coach and your business partner."

"Marc and Jackie can take care of themselves." He raised his mug to his smiling lips.

She watched him closely. "I've noticed that none of the posts have been about you."

Gerald chuckled. "What could he possibly find about me to criticize?"

Andrea could make a list. "What about Troy's position? Are you going to start an executive search to replace him now or wait until you've relocated the team to Nevada?"

Gerald's smile turned sardonic. "Why? Are you interested in the job?"

Startled laughter escaped Andrea. "I'm comfortable where I am."

"Are you?"

Andrea sobered. She forced herself to remain still under Gerald's mocking gaze. "I don't want to move out of Brooklyn, and you've made it clear you want to relocate the Monarchs."

Gerald's brow cleared. "I don't know why people think I'm out to ruin the team."

"Go figure."

He glanced at his Rolex. "If we're done here, there's another meeting I have to attend."

Andrea stood, collecting her recorder and empty coffee mug. "Mind if I ask with whom?"

"As a matter of fact, I do." Gerald stood with her.

She nodded and turned off the mini-recorder. Andrea dropped the device into her oversized brown purse. "I have what I need for now. Thanks for your time, Gerry."

"You're welcome. Call me if you have any other questions. Or change your mind about the job."

They parted company outside of the coffee house. Andrea watched Gerald cross the street, walking toward the Empire Arena. She'd bet money his meeting was with Jaclyn Jones. Oh, to be a fly on that wall.

She turned toward the public parking lot two blocks in the opposite direction to collect her temperamental Ford. The sky was a vivid blue with thin streaks of white clouds. But the bite in the air said Mother Nature wasn't ready for spring. Andrea was. She stuffed her hands into the pockets of her tan overcoat and quickened her pace.

After buckling into her driver's seat, Andrea dug through her purse for her cell phone. She selected Troy's mobile number, but the call went directly to voice mail. His rich baritone made her toes curl in her shoes.

The recording ended and she left a message at the signal as directed. "Troy, it's Andrea." She hesitated. "I'm sorry you're no longer with the Monarchs. There's something else we need to talk about. Could you call me as soon as you can?" She left her cell phone number and ended the call.

Andrea had thought Barron was the Monarchs' employee who'd needed her help. She'd seen herself in the point guard's increasingly destructive behavior. In contrast, Troy had seemed confident and in control. Was it just a pretense? She was beginning to think it was.

She started her car. It took a couple of attempts before her engine turned over. Andrea pulled out of the parking lot and headed toward home.

Troy's ESPN interview had been a desperate, reckless act. It was exactly the type of impulsive behavior that had cost Andrea her career. Perhaps Troy was the Monarch more in need of her help. But getting him to accept her offer would be easier if he trusted her.

The situation was surreal—and unfair. Troy was grateful Jaclyn had arranged their meeting with Gerald. But why was he the one fighting for his job when Gerald was the one trying to destroy the franchise?

He'd taken the chair to the right of Jaclyn, who sat at the head of the small conference table. Gerald had the seat at the opposite end. Troy kept his expression blank as he held the other man's triumphant gaze.

Jaclyn folded her hands on the table. "You were wrong to fire Troy without consulting me, Gerry. I'm the general manager. Personnel matters are in my purview."

Gerald looked at Troy. "Are you hiding behind Jackie now?"

Troy spread his arms. "I'm right here."

Jaclyn's voice hardened. "According to our partnership agreement, you're obligated to discuss personnel issues with me *prior* to acting. You failed to do so."

Gerald gestured toward Troy. "Did he discuss his television interview with you?"

When Jaclyn hesitated, Troy spoke up. "No, I didn't."

Gerald looked from Troy back to Jaclyn. "Then you should thank me for firing him. Now you can hire someone you can trust."

Jaclyn's expression tightened. "I trust Troy."

Gerald's hard brown eyes glinted with challenge. "Do you agree with what he said during his ESPN interview?"

Jaclyn crossed her arms, leaning back in her chair. "I didn't say that."

Troy interrupted again. "Jackie didn't know I was going to do that interview. She's made it clear she wasn't happy about it, either." How far was he willing to go to get his job back? Troy squared his shoulders. "I regret doing the interview and the things I said. I apologize."

Gerald gave him a long, hard stare. Every muscle in Troy's body tensed. His future—personal and professional—was on the line. Would he remain with the Monarchs? He couldn't imagine working anywhere else. Troy held his breath, waiting.

"Good." Gerald stood. "Since you're here now, you can pack up your office."

Shock punched him in his gut. Troy couldn't move. He searched for words that would end this nightmare. But the other man's gleaming brown gaze told him there was nothing he could say, nothing he could do to change Gerald's mind.

Jaclyn pushed away from the table and rose. "We're not done."

Gerald turned to her. "Tell me, Jackie, what would you do if one of our employees disparaged you during an interview? Would you keep that employee on the payroll?"

"Troy has apologized."

Gerald put his right hand on his chest. "And the words have warmed my heart. But I'm not obligated to accept them."

Troy pushed himself to his feet. "You've spent years trying to destroy the team. We have evidence you were negotiating with that real estate investor in Nevada."

Gerald shrugged. "So I'm interested in property in Nevada. That's not a crime."

Anger was edging out shock. "You tried to get Andy Benson to write a story you fabricated to damage Marc's reputation. You also tried to get her to write negative stories about the players."

Gerald crossed his arms and gave Troy a speculative look. "Most of your evidence is hearsay from Andrea. That makes me wonder if today's *Insider* blog's true."

Troy frowned. "What are you talking about?"

"You haven't seen today's blog post?" Gerald barked a laugh. "Well, I won't ruin it for you."

Jaclyn's words stopped Gerald as he tried to make his way out of the conference room. "We're rolling out a new marketing campaign. We need Troy to coordinate that. We're also in the postseason. We need him to handle the increased interview requests."

Gerald met Troy's gaze over his shoulder. "I'll supervise Troy's staff until we find a replacement."

Troy fisted his palms. "Gerry, the blog has to come down."

Gerald shrugged. "Maybe it does. But I can't make that decision." He turned back around. "You accused me of trying to destroy the team. In the end, you're the one who caused it the greatest harm because of that interview. Isn't that ironic?" Gerald shook his head as he left the room.

The parting comment weighed like a stone in Troy's chest. He was right. In trying to protect the team, Troy had done more damage than Gerald ever had. He'd created a huge distraction while the team was already struggling with its first postseason appearance in four years. Why hadn't he considered that before he'd asked to do the ESPN interview?

Then something else Gerald said returned to him. Troy frowned at Jaclyn. "Why did Gerry ask me about today's blog? What has he posted now?"

Jaclyn circled the table and walked toward the door. "You can read the post later."

His skin grew cold. He beat Jaclyn to the exit and stood barring her way. "Just tell me."

She met his eyes. "The Insider said you gave Andrea exclusive coverage with the Monarchs because you're sleeping with her."

10

Troy saw a different Andrea Benson when she opened the door to her apartment Tuesday evening. The normally buttoned-up reporter wore hot pink Capri pants, exposing her trim calves and slender ankles. Superman's logo dominated a powder blue T-shirt that molded her small breasts. But her toes were the greatest surprise. Who would have thought her conservative black pumps hid sparkly pink toenails?

"I asked you to *call* me." Andrea stood with one hand braced on the doorjamb. The other gripped the doorknob.

He dragged his gaze back to her eyes. "I wanted to talk with you in person. May I come in?"

He sensed a "no" hovering between them. Andrea considered him for a silent moment. She seemed uncertain. Troy braced for the rejection. He'd lost his job. Disappointed a boss he admired and was the source of distraction for the team he'd tried to protect. He couldn't handle being turned away now. Troy opened his mouth to plead his case just as Andrea stepped aside.

She gave him a curious look. "How did you know where I lived?"

Troy crossed her threshold. "Connie's change of address form. Jackie gave it to me since I no longer have access to employee records."

He followed her down a short entryway, past a modest kitchen. She took him to an eclectic living room that held a collection of mismatched furnishings and even more surprises. "Serge?"

The Monarchs forward looked up from his position sprawled on the beige carpet. He was propped on his elbow. A coloring book lay in front of him. He gripped a small crayon in his large hand. "Troy."

Troy shifted his attention to his former secretary. He hadn't had a chance to call her. Had Andrea already told Constance she didn't work for him anymore? "Hi, Connie."

Constance smiled at him. She was sitting on the floor with her legs folded. "Hi, Mr. Marshall."

"Troy," he urged her, not for the first time.

Constance laid her hand on the fine blond hair of the little girl lying belly down on the carpet between her and Serge. "This is my daughter, Tiffany. Tiff, can you say hello to Mr. Marshall?"

The little girl looked up from her coloring book. "Hi." The word came out on a long, soft breath.

Troy smiled. "Hi, Tiffany. You look just like your mother."

Tiffany glanced at her mother before returning to her coloring.

What surprised Troy more? The presence of the Monarchs forward in the women's apartment or the fact Serge was coloring with Constance and her toddler? How long had this relationship been developing?

Andrea gestured toward an attractive woman curled up in an armchair. "Faith, this is Troy Marshall."

Faith set aside her sketchbook and stood to accept Troy's hand. "It's nice to meet you."

"You, too." Troy saw the speculation in Faith's eyes. What, if anything, had Andrea told her roommate about him?

Troy returned his attention to Andrea. "Can I speak with you privately?"

"Sure." Andrea led him across the living room.

She opened the left rear window and climbed out onto a deep red metal fire escape. Troy hesitated before clenching his teeth and stepping out after her. Andrea closed the window partway, probably to minimize the amount of crisp spring air that blew into her apartment.

Troy watched her cross to the opposite railing. He folded his arms over his chest and stepped back against the building's red brick facade. A network of metal fire escapes crisscrossed up and down the building. The congested sidewalk waited a long twelve stories below. He hated heights. "This isn't exactly private."

Her tone was droll. "Did you expect me to take you to my bedroom?"

At least they would have been indoors. Troy smiled to mask his nerves. "You're right. I wouldn't want you to be tempted to take advantage of me."

Andrea's sherry eyes sparkled with humor. Her full, bare lips curved ever so slightly. "I wouldn't have been able to help myself."

Troy was running on maybe an hour's sleep. He'd been angry and anxious since receiving Gerald's call in the predawn hours. And he'd been wound too tight to rest. But her smile gave him a surge of energy and a sense of hope.

He glanced over his shoulder toward the group in the living room. "Do they know Gerry fired me?"

He felt naked and vulnerable as he waited for her reply. Had they been talking about him before he'd shown up? Did they think he was a fool for calling Gerald out without proof to support his claim?

Troy looked again at Andrea. She leaned against the railing of the suspended fire escape. The evening breeze teased her long dark hair. What did she think of him? Did she hate him because of the latest *Monarchs Insider* blog?

Andrea shook her head. "It's not my place to tell Connie or Serge. And I didn't want to tell Faith until Connie knew." She offered him a smile. "I did mention it to Tiff over coffee this morning, but she won't tell her mother."

He smiled at her joke. Why was she being nice to him after the trouble he'd caused her? He gave her a grateful look. "Thank you."

"Are you going to tell them now?"

"I don't know." He dragged his hand over his hair.

"Don't wait too long. The media will break the news tomorrow if not later today."

Dammit. "You're probably right. But that's not what I came here to say."

Andrea seemed to stiffen. He sensed her suspicion. "What is it?"

Troy drew a breath. "I owe you an apology. I never meant to bring you into the line of fire when I gave that interview against the Insider."

She tilted her head. "You called the blogger a

small-minded, petty hack. What did you think would happen?"

Troy had withstood Gerald's fury and Jaclyn's disappointment. But he struggled in the face of Andrea's concern. The crisp breeze chilled him. Or maybe it was self-doubt. "I didn't think he'd take his anger out on you. After I exposed him, I expected Gerry to take down the blog."

"But Gerry's not the Insider."

Troy's impatience spiked despite Andrea's reasonable tone. "How do you know that?"

She crossed her arms over the Superman logo. "Well, first of all, the Insider's a woman."

Surprise chased away his irritation. "Do you know who she is?"

"No. And, before you ask, it's not me." Andrea shifted her body weight from one leg to the other.

Troy could swear the fire escape moved. He gripped the railing beside him. "I never thought you were the blogger. Why would you post a blog entry attacking yourself?"

Andrea blinked her bright eyes. "Is that the only reason you think I'm not the Insider?"

"Why would I think you were the blogger?" Her question confused him. She was straying from their topic.

"Never mind." She sounded exasperated.

Troy let it go. "What makes you think the blogger is a woman?"

"Her writing style and the subjects of her posts." Andrea counted her reasons on her fingers. "She writes with a lot of emotion. And, as you pointed out, she seems jealous."

Andrea's face glowed as she stated her arguments.

She was more animated than Troy had ever seen her. He couldn't take his eyes from her. "Petty and jealous describe Gerry."

"But look at who the Insider attacks. Jackie Jones and Mary Devry-Evans. In those posts, she tells both women they can't hold on to their men. Does that sound like Gerry?"

She scored some points there. Still, Troy wasn't convinced. "But in his first post, *he* attacked Jamal and Rick."

Andrea raised her index finger, a smug expression on her heart-shaped face. "No, *she* used Jamal's words to attack Rick. That first post was an anomaly."

"I'd noticed the difference between the posts, too." Could Andrea be correct? Was the Insider a woman?

Andrea stepped toward him. She moved as confidently as though they stood in her living room. Troy kept a close watch, ready to save her if she fell. She leaned against the rail, and this time he was certain the fire escape swayed.

"Then, this morning, she attacked me." Andrea rested an elbow on the railing beside her. "My name never came up in your interview. Still, she said the only reason I was able to cover the Monarchs is that you and I are having an affair."

Once again, regret pressed heavily on Troy's shoulders. "I'm really sorry about that."

Andrea shrugged. "*You* don't need to apologize. *She's* the one who attacked me."

"But I feel responsible." He hesitated. "Do you want me to speak with your editor?"

Andrea blinked her pretty eyes. "And tell him what? That you and I *aren't* sleeping together? I think I can handle that."

"Is her accusation going to cause you any trouble in the press section?"

Andrea looked away. "Do you mean *more* trouble?"

Troy traced her delicate profile with his gaze. He'd be lying if he said he'd never noticed the tension between Andrea and her colleagues or that he'd never wondered about it. But he'd save that discussion for another time. Right now, he wasn't ready to give up the idea of Gerald being somehow responsible for the *Monarchs Insider* blog.

"Even if the Insider is a woman, that doesn't mean Gerry isn't somehow involved."

Andrea started to move away from him. Troy stepped from the wall and reached for her shoulders. The warmth of her skin through her thin T-shirt carried through his palms, up his arms, and to his chest. He didn't want her to walk away from him. If she did, somehow he knew he'd be lost.

Troy searched Andrea's startled eyes. "What do we do now?"

Was he talking about the blog or the attraction growing between them? His heart beat slow and hard against his chest. Her lips parted, drawing him even closer to her.

The window opened behind them. Faith interrupted the moment. "Troy, would you like to stay for dinner? I'm making spaghetti. Serge is joining us."

Troy couldn't look away from Andrea's sherry brown eyes. "I don't want to impose."

Faith chuckled. "You're not any trouble. I'll set another place."

The window slid closed behind him. "Will you help me?"

Andrea stepped back. Troy's hands dropped from her shoulders. "Right now, I need to help Faith."

Troy watched her hurry to the window, then climb back inside. An electric awareness had arced between them. He couldn't have been the only one to feel it. He'd seen the reaction in Andrea's eyes. Troy frowned. He wasn't the Monarchs' vice president of media and marketing anymore. What was standing in the way of his acting on the attraction he'd felt since they'd first met?

Nothing.

Andrea hadn't wanted to let Troy into her modest apartment. She'd caught the look Faith had flashed at her after she'd introduced Troy. It screamed, "What are these millionaires doing here?" Andrea shared her friend's horror. Serge and Troy could probably buy everything the women owned with the cash in their wallets. Troy may have traded his fashionable business suits for expensive casual clothes, but the simple lifestyle she and her roommates enjoyed still didn't fit his image.

Or so she'd thought.

She took in the crowd seated at the rectangular, dark wood dining table. The camaraderie made it seem as though the motley crew—the professional basketball player, the NBA executive, the single mother and her toddler daughter, the cartoonist moonlighting as an accountant, and the sports reporter—had been together for years. Constance had even stopped calling Troy "Mr. Marshall."

Andrea stood to clear the table. "Does anyone want seconds?" She grinned at Serge. "Or thirds?"

The forward patted his flat stomach. "No, thank you. Everything was delicious."

Troy stood as well. "I'll help with the dishes."

Andrea's smile wavered just a bit. "Thank you."

She felt awkward as he followed her into the kitchen. Her shoulders still tingled from his earlier touch more than an hour ago.

Troy made subsequent return trips to the dining room to clear the table. He stacked the dishes, serving bowl, platter, and utensils in the sink. Andrea arranged them in the dishwasher.

After carrying in the last of the dishes, he leaned his hips against the white-tiled kitchen counter. "Will you help me expose the Insider?"

Andrea looked away from his long, lean body and model good looks. "Why are you still concerned about her? You don't work for the Monarchs anymore."

"I'll always care about the team." Troy's voice was tight. "I want them to be successful. They can't do that if this gossip keeps hounding them."

The conviction deepening his baritone didn't surprise her. Troy was passionate about the Monarchs. Devotion like that didn't turn on and off like a faucet. What would it feel like to be the recipient of that focus, that kind of passion?

She took her time packing the dishwasher. "The players can take care of themselves. Tell them to stop reading the blog."

"You sound like my sister."

He had a sister? She'd learned about Troy's ex-wife from Mindy Sneal, his former secretary. Now he was telling her about a sibling. Andrea had learned more about Troy as a person in four days than she had in three years. "Your sister sounds like an intelligent person. You should listen to her."

"Rick Evans isn't reading the blog, but his wife is. She left him Saturday—after reading it."

She looked up in surprise. The news saddened her. "I'm sorry to hear that."

Troy continued as though he hadn't heard her. "From the questions during the postgame conference, you know the media's reading it. *You're* reading it."

She wasn't proud of that. "Finding the blogger isn't going to get your job back."

"I want my job back. But my priority is protecting the team." He straightened from the counter. "And if I can prove Gerry is somehow involved with the blog, it would show I'm right and he's lying. Maybe then I can return to the Monarchs and force the *Horn* to drop Gerry's blog."

Andrea straightened, resting her hands on her hips. "Which is more important to you, the team or your job?"

Troy set his jaw. "Both."

"What if Gerry's not involved with the *Insider*?"

He looked away. "Then I'll move on to another job."

"It's not always that easy." She knew that from bitter experience. She hoped he wouldn't have to go through it.

"I know." He met her gaze. "Will you help me?"

Andrea bent to pour the dishwashing detergent into the machine's reservoir and locked its door. "We're friends now?"

Troy looked confused. "What do you mean?"

Resentment stirred inside her. "Even though my coverage of the Monarchs has always been impartial, you cut off my access to the team. You didn't trust me. Do you trust me now?"

"I had to block your access. If I'd treated you differently from the other reporters, they'd think you had a special relationship with the organization."

Andrea smiled without humor. "And now, thanks to

the Insider, they think I have a special relationship with *you*. I'd earned that access because I treated the team fairly."

Troy shifted against the counter. "You're right. I'm sorry."

Andrea crossed her arms. "Is it true the only reason you don't think I'm the Insider is that I wouldn't have written that damaging post about myself?"

He frowned. "Why do you keep asking me that?"

She thought her eyes would cross. Stubborn man. "Because I need an answer."

"No, that's not the only reason. The blog isn't your style. You're too confrontational to sneak around and post anonymous messages."

Not good enough. If he wanted her to help him, he needed to trust her. "Is *that* the reason? I'm too confrontational to be an anonymous blogger?"

He spread his arms. "What do you want from me?"

"Your trust. But I don't think you're ready to give it." She pressed the power button on the dishwasher. "It's time you told Connie and Serge what's going on."

Troy caught her arm and pulled her to him. "Will you help me find the blogger?"

His heat. She could grow addicted to his touch. But like the moth and the flame, theirs would be a relationship that wouldn't last.

Andrea stepped back. "I'll find the Insider. But I won't do it for you. It's the hottest story in New York sports since the question of whether A-Rod was taking performance-enhancing drugs. I want this story. I'm sure every other sports reporter wants it, too." She left the kitchen.

Troy closed his palm to hold onto her touch.

She'd been toying with him. Andrea had intended to investigate the *Monarchs Insider* all along. She'd apparently also decided to make Troy sweat. Stubborn woman. Troy pushed away from the counter. It was time to face the music. When would this nightmare end?

Faith, Constance, Tiffany, and Serge had returned to the living room. Andrea took a position beside Faith's armchair and gave him a pointed look.

This is it. No more stalling. He looked from Serge to Constance. "I have something to tell you." He took a steadying breath. "I'm no longer with the Monarchs."

"What?" Constance's fair brows flew toward her blond hairline.

Serge held Troy's gaze. "This has to do with the interview you gave ESPN, doesn't it?"

Troy nodded, then tried a wry smile. "It seemed like a good idea at the time."

Serge shook his head. "That took—" He cut himself off and glanced down at Tiffany. The little girl gave him a curious look. Serge returned his attention to Troy. "Courage. That took a lot of courage."

Constance's gaze swept from Serge to Troy. "What happened?"

Troy made himself meet Constance's puzzled green gaze. "I accused Gerry of being the Insider."

Constance gaped. "That blogger? What makes you think that?"

Serge answered her. "Gerry may be part owner, but he doesn't want the team to be a success."

Andrea continued the explanation. "He's contacted the media about printing negative stories about the team before. And he doesn't care whether the stories are true."

Constance's jaw dropped. "But that's crazy."

Tiffany giggled. "My mommy said 'That's crazy.'"

"No one said Gerry was sane." Troy smiled at the little girl's levity.

Constance's gaze swung to Troy. "But if the team isn't successful, he loses money."

Troy shrugged. "He doesn't care. Destroying the franchise is more important to him."

Constance scowled. "It must be nice to have so much money that you don't care whether you lose some of it."

"No kidding." Andrea's tone was dry.

He saw amusement rather than resentment in her eyes.

What was behind her question in the kitchen? She'd repeatedly asked why he didn't believe she was the Monarchs Insider. Why was that so important to her? He knew she had too much integrity to attack someone anonymously. But his answer had upset her. What was she looking for? She said she wanted his trust. Could he trust her?

Troy refocused on the conversation. "I wanted you to hear the news from me rather than the media."

Faith shifted in her armchair. "I'm so sorry about your job. What will you do now?"

Troy shrugged, more to ease the pressure in his chest than to pretend a casual attitude. He'd loved his job. He loved being a part of a team, even if he wasn't on the court anymore. "I'm going to prove Gerry's involvement with the blog."

"Are you sure you should do that?" Constance looked around the room as though searching for someone to support her. "I mean, trying to identify the Insider's already gotten you into trouble."

Troy chuckled without humor. "So what more do I have to lose?"

"And I'm going to help him." Andrea's eyes sparkled.

"At the very least, maybe I can talk him out of appearing on TV again."

Troy smiled. "I appreciate that."

"The team will help, too." Serge rested his forearms on his lap. "After all, you took the risk trying to help us."

Constance wrung her hands. "I'll do whatever I can. Maybe I'll see something or hear something that will give us a clue."

Tiffany put her small palm over her mother's nervous hands. The little girl looked worried as she leaned closer to capture Constance's attention. Her smile shook a little. "My mommy said that's crazy."

Troy swallowed the lump in his throat. He hadn't expected their offers to help him. He was used to dealing with problems on his own.

He watched Constance smooth her daughter's hair. "Thank you both. But please don't do anything that will jeopardize your job."

Constance lifted Tiffany onto her lap. "I'll be careful. Do you know who my new boss will be?"

Troy hesitated. The words didn't come easily. "Gerry's going to fill in until they hire someone else."

Serge snorted. "Gerry? We're doomed."

Troy agreed. It seemed the Monarchs co-owner was right where he'd wanted to be. Had Gerald been lucky or had this been part of his plan?

11

"They *fired* you?"

Troy winced. He held the telephone receiver away from his head. Still, his sister's shriek reverberated against his eardrum. "Careful, sis. I think all the dogs in the neighborhood heard you."

"Don't take that irritated tone with me. I told you to let Jackie handle this."

Judging by Michelle's autocratic tone, she'd forgotten—again—that she was the younger sibling. Troy slumped back into the black leather armchair in his living room but kept a safe distance between his ear and his cordless phone. "Shelley, no one likes to hear 'I told you so.'"

She harrumphed into the phone. "You *need* to hear it. What are you going to do now?"

"Look for another job." No way was Troy going to tell his bossy younger sibling he was going to continue looking for the Monarchs Insider. She wouldn't understand.

Troy's television was on mute. ESPN's *Sports-Center* was replaying clips from his interview. Again. They also announced that he'd been fired after his "outburst." Great. He looked away from the TV and focused on his sister's words.

"Why don't you come home to D.C.? The Wizards are here. And the Redskins, the Nationals, the Capitals—"

"We have a lot of sports teams here, too, Shel." Troy stared out the picture window of his twentieth-floor condominium. He absently noted the nighttime view. The lights from other buildings in the background. The streetlights glowing on the billboards.

"You have family here." Michelle tried a cajoling tone.

Return home to lick his wounds? He couldn't do that. Besides, he had unfinished business in New York.

He wasn't looking forward to telling his parents he'd been fired, either. He'd collected three straight failures: basketball, his marriage, and now his job. It didn't matter that none of these failures was his fault. His parents would still count them against him.

"I'm going to look for another job here first." Troy sensed the wheels of Michelle's mind turning. He was uneasy with her silence. His sister always knew when he wasn't telling her everything. What was she piecing together now?

"Does this need to stay in New York have anything to do with that reporter you're supposed to be sleeping with?"

Shock and disappointment swamped him. "Are you reading the *Insider*?"

"I wanted to know more about the blog that's making you crazy. So? Are you sleeping with her?"

Troy closed his eyes. Why was he having this conversation? "First, that's none of your business. Second, don't believe everything you read in anonymous, gossip blogs."

"That means no." His sister's sigh was heavy. "She must be pretty ticked off at you about that blog then. Have you apologized?"

"Yes, and she—" Troy's security phone rang. Saved by the bell. He stood. "And she accepted my apology. Shel, I've got to go. Someone's at my door."

She sighed again. "Call me back. We aren't done with this."

"Sure." He'd say anything to get his sister off the line.

Troy replaced the phone receiver and glanced at the clock on the cable box beneath his television. It was after nine o'clock in the evening. He'd only recently returned from Andrea's apartment. His security phone rang again.

Troy strode to his hallway and picked up the phone. "Marshall."

"Good evening, Mr. Marshall. Barron Douglas is at the security desk for you, sir." Beneath the guard's smooth delivery, Troy heard a hint of disapproval.

He rubbed the back of his neck. Was Barron drunk again? "I'll be right down."

He grabbed his keys and rode the elevator to the marble and mirrored lobby. Waiting with the young guard beside the security desk, Barron gave Troy the wide, blurry grin of the happy drunk.

The NBA player flung his arms wide, causing the wiry security officer to lurch back. "Troy, I'm here to cheer you up, buddy. Sorry to hear about your job."

Troy winced. Serge must have called Barron. Who else had he told? Luckily, the lobby was empty except for him, Barron, and the hapless guard. He wasn't eager to share his unemployment status with his neighbors.

He grabbed one of Barron's outstretched arms, then glanced at the guard. "Thanks, Ted."

Ted nodded stoically, but Troy saw the relief in his eyes. "You're welcome, Mr. Marshall."

Troy guided Barron back to his condo. Once inside, he poured a glass of cold water for the Monarchs captain.

Barron curled his lip as he took the glass. "What am I supposed to do with this?"

"Drink it." Troy turned away. "I'll make coffee."

"Don't you have anything else to drink?"

"Not for you." Troy spoke with his back to the player as he filled the coffee carafe with water from his sink's filtered faucet. "What the hell's wrong with you, Barron? You're already drunk and it's only nine o'clock. When did you start drinking today?"

"What are you, a priest? I don't have any confessions for you. I'm trying to cheer you up and you're bringing me down." Barron sounded like a petulant child.

Troy squelched the urge to pop the other man in the mouth. Instead he concentrated on measuring coffee into the filter. "You played like shit last night. Are you planning on repeating that Thursday night? Do you *want* the Monarchs to be swept out of the play-offs because of you?"

"You're blaming *me* for Monday's loss?" Gone was the sulky child. Barron sounded angry and defensive.

Troy wasn't impressed. He turned on the coffeemaker and poured the water into the machine. "I'm blaming you for not being ready for the game.

You looked like a man playing with a hangover, probably because you were."

"At least I didn't go on TV to call my boss a liar. Yesterday wasn't a good day for either of us, cuz."

Troy turned away from his kitchen counter. The player was right. "No, it wasn't."

The security phone rang again. Troy crossed to the entrance way to answer it. "Marshall."

"Good evening, Mr. Marshall. There are several other Monarchs players here to see you, sir." The usually unflappable Ted sounded starstruck.

What were they doing here? Serge must have told the whole team. He gritted his teeth. "Thanks, Ted. I'll be right down."

"You're welcome, Mr. Marshall."

Troy recradled the security phone and collected his keys. "A couple of the other guys are here. I'm going down to meet them. Drink the water."

"You're not my mother." Barron brought the glass to his lips.

Troy locked his condo and took the elevator back downstairs. At the lobby, Serge, Warrick, Anthony, Vincent, and Jamal stood around the security desk looking as grim as the Monarchs fans who'd attended the first two play-off games.

Troy caught Serge's eyes. "You told them?"

The Frenchman looked defiant. "Yes."

Anthony stepped forward. "*You* should have told us. 'Greater love has no one than this, that he lay down his life for his friends.'"

Vincent tapped Anthony's shoulder. "Hey, St. Anthony. Troy's not asking us to lay down our lives, man. He just needs a friend."

"Come upstairs." Troy interrupted before the scowl on Anthony's face turned into a heated exchange in the posh lobby of the upscale building.

He nodded toward Ted before leading the Monarchs upstairs. When he let them into his condo, Troy found Barron searching his kitchen.

The point guard glared at him. "Where do you keep the liquor?"

Serge entered Troy's home, followed by his teammates. "It looks as if you've had enough."

Barron turned his glare on the Frenchman. "Who asked you, man?"

Troy went to the coffeemaker. "I'll pour you some coffee. Does anyone else want some?"

Warrick accepted Troy's offer, but Serge, Anthony, and Vincent requested ice water. Jamal wanted orange juice. After filling everyone's request, Troy moved the players into his living room.

Warrick lowered himself beside Troy on the sofa. "I'm sorry about what I said yesterday. I know it's not your fault Mary left. I was angry and being stupid."

Troy nodded. "You had a right to be upset. Have you heard from her?"

Warrick stared into the mug of coffee. "No. I've left messages, but she hasn't returned any of them."

The other man was hurting. "Give her time, Rick. She knows you'd never cheat on her."

Warrick searched Troy's gaze. "I keep telling myself the same thing every night before I go to bed—alone."

Serge joined them on the sofa. He glanced at Warrick's coffee mug. "All that cream? And sugar, too?" He feigned a shiver of revulsion. "Is there any coffee in there?"

Troy smiled. Warrick took a long drink of the coffee, then smacked his lips. Serge shook his head.

Jamal examined Troy's home entertainment system. "What does Gerry know about handling the media?"

"Not a damn thing." Vincent sat in one of the armchairs near the picture window, drinking his water.

Troy tensed. Gerald could break the fragile foundation of the Monarchs' rebuilding season in one day. "Just don't give the media any reason to attack you. Whatever happens in the locker room stays in the locker room."

Warrick jerked his head toward Barron, who sat across the room. He pitched his voice low. "In other words, keep Bling away from the press."

Serge sent Barron a dubious look. "Who's going to take him home?"

Troy watched the Monarchs team captain sway slightly in the chair. "He might as well stay here. If he goes home, he'll just keep drinking."

Keeping the players below the media's radar should prevent further distractions. Unless Gerald had other plans.

Andrea could hear a pin drop in the Empire Arena Thursday night. She was baffled by the debacle on the court as the Monarchs struggled against the Cleveland Cavaliers in game three of the series. Their performance wasn't much better than it had been during the first two games. What had become of the Monarchs who'd defied the odds to attain a play-off berth?

Barron's cautious movements made Andrea think the player had yet another hangover. Jamal, Anthony,

Serge, and Vincent tried to cover for him, but their movements were tentative as well. The younger Cavaliers were forcing the aging Monarchs to play faster than they were accustomed. By halftime, the Cavaliers led the Monarchs 58 to 36.

"Andy, you look like you're about to cry." Jenna Madison, from *The New York Times*, leaned back in her chair.

Jenna had pitched her voice to be heard above the song, "I've Got the Magic in Me" by B.o.B. and featuring Rivers Cuomo. The Empire Arena was playing the single to entertain their fans during the break.

"There's no cheering in the press box. There's no crying, either," the *New York Daily News*'s Frederick Pritchard threw out the modified adage in a distracted voice.

As soon as halftime started, Frederick had settled into his default pose of squinting through his rimless glasses at his computer monitor. Frederick didn't have much time for human interaction. However, his mind housed an encyclopedia's breath of knowledge—names, stats, and quotes—on all the NBA teams.

"We're not in a press box." Andrea turned back to the table and her laptop. She'd typed a few more observations about the game's second quarter into her news draft, including the Monarchs' criminally low points percentage and their missing-in-action defense.

This was the team's first of two consecutive home appearances in their best-of-seven-games series against the Cavaliers. Would the Cinderella team be able to win at least one? Or would they be swept out of the play-offs on their home court?

On Andrea's other side, the *New York Post* reporter, Sean Wolf, nudged her with a bony elbow. "Hey, Benson. What are you going to do now that the Monarchs fired your confidential source?"

Andrea turned a cold look on the *Post*'s tall, thin reporter. She raised her voice so their colleagues around them could hear. "Do you get your information from the *Insider* blog, Sean? Or maybe you *are* the Insider."

Startled amusement from the journalists around them brought a blush to the young man's cheeks. Sean's hazel eyes hardened. He scraped his lank brown hair back from his forehead "If anyone has insider information, it would be you, Benson."

Jenna tut-tutted at the arrogant sports reporter. "Now, Sean. Don't dish it if you can't take it."

Andrea blinked at Jenna's defense of her. For three years, the other reporters had treated her like a leper. Her article on Gerald's attempts to move the Monarchs out of Brooklyn must have cured her. Her colleagues were speaking to her again. Was this a sign that the higher profile news outlets were willing to take her back?

Andrea turned to Jenna. "Who do you think the Insider is?"

Sean offered his thoughts. "That's obvious. It's one of the bench players who wants more game time."

Jenna chuckled. "Spoken like a true armchair athlete, Sean. Still bitter you weren't picked for varsity?"

Sean glared at the glamorous journalist. "Do you still wish you'd been born a man?"

Jenna's smile stretched into a cold grin. "No. Do you?"

Andrea covered her laughter with a cough. She

leaned forward to better see Jenna seated on the other side of Frederick. "Do you have another theory?"

Jenna shrugged. "I always disagree with Sean. I believe the blogger's a woman."

Andrea was surprised. "So do I."

Jenna scanned the seats on the other side of the court. It included a section reserved for Monarchs players' families. Many teams offered seating in the special section only to the relatives of their five starters. But the Monarchs offered the seats to all players' families. It was usually filled with wives, children, and girlfriends.

Jenna continued. "It could be an ex-girlfriend or ex-wife."

Andrea followed the other woman's gaze. "That would be hard to narrow down. Some of the players change girlfriends several times during the season."

Sean's chuckle seemed admiring. "That's true. But for all we know, the Insider could be one of us."

"You think one of us is freelancing as the Insider?" That thought had occurred to Andrea as well. She forced herself to appear casual as she glanced up and down the media row. Her gaze hesitated on the *New York Horn*'s Kirk West. She noticed the reporter looking back at her.

"She's not an ex-wife or an ex-girlfriend." Frederick spoke from his seat between Andrea and Jenna. "She's an ex-employee."

Andrea blinked at Frederick. "But the Monarchs haven't fired anyone in years. Why would an ex-employee start a blog to blast the team now?"

Sean snorted. "Because this is the first time the Monarchs have made it to the postseason in years.

They're in the spotlight again. That makes them more vulnerable to negative publicity."

Frederick shrugged. "Sounds plausible, but the Monarchs *have* fired someone recently. Troy Marshall."

Andrea's shoulders stiffened. "The *Insider* postings started before that. Troy isn't the blogger."

Sean leaned forward, waiting until he had the other reporters' attention. "Speaking of Troy and gossip, word on the street is that Gerry's calling around to the other franchises in the city. Knicks, Yankees, Mets, Jets, Giants—"

Jenna interrupted him. "We get the idea, Sean. All of the franchises. Why is he calling them?"

"He's *advising* them not to hire Troy. He's blackballing his ex-marketing veep."

Andrea's stomach muscles knotted. Her head spun. Déjà vu. "Who told you this?"

Sean's brows flew under his bangs. He barked a laugh. "You know I can't give up my sources."

Jenna glanced from Andrea to Sean. "How are the other franchises responding?"

Sean shrugged. "I don't know." There was a sense of excitement around the reporter. His eyes gleamed as though the scent of the hot news story intoxicated him.

Jenna slid another look toward Andrea. Her hazel green eyes were dark with concern. "For all we know, no one's taking his calls."

Frederick spoke without lifting his attention from his computer monitor. "Gerry isn't well liked in the city. It got worse after Andrea's story."

Sean straightened in his chair. "Still, Troy got in front of a camera and called his boss a liar and a fraud." He shrugged again. "That was a really dumb move."

"He was trying to protect his team." Andrea watched the Cleveland Cavaliers and Brooklyn Monarchs return to the court. But her thoughts remained with Troy. His impulsive act had cost him much more than he realized. Gerald was trying to destroy him. She had to find a way to help him, but would he even let her?

"We need to talk." Andrea sat in her car in the parking lot of the Empire Arena after the Monarchs third loss of the best-of-seven series. Her cell phone was pressed to her ear as she tried to force her way into the traffic exiting the parking garage. It was a very delicate modern-day game of chicken.

"About what?" Troy's voice was puzzled and perhaps a little sad. Had he watched the game?

"It's about Gerry." She nudged her Ford compact a little farther into the traffic pattern.

"What about him?" Troy's voice had tensed.

Eureka! Someone let her join the traffic stream in front of his car. Andrea pulled out, then waved her gratitude. "Can we meet in person?"

"We can talk at my place." He gave her the address to his condominium building. "Take Utica Avenue. It's faster."

"I'll be there as soon as I can." Andrea ended the call. She dropped her cell phone back into her purse. She couldn't afford a ticket if New York's finest caught her using her cellular in traffic.

Forty minutes later, she was standing beside the security desk in the posh lobby of a building she'd only ever admired from outside. Troy arrived to escort her to his condo. Her breath still caught each time she saw him in casual clothes. The silver jersey sculpted his broad, well-defined chest and shoulders. The jersey and black warm-up pants gave Troy a relaxed and approachable look, much more in her league than his designer business suits. He smiled at her, and her heart jumped once in her chest.

Troy nodded at the older security guard before once again capturing her gaze. "Come on up."

He led her to the elevator and pressed the button for his floor. The doors closed and they began the slow, silent ascent to his condo on the twentieth floor. Andrea could feel his warmth beside her. She smelled his subtle scent, citrus and cinnamon. She swallowed.

Several floors into their journey, Troy shifted toward her. "You're going to make me wait, aren't you?"

Andrea's gaze shot to his face. "For what?"

His ebony eyes were puzzled. "To talk about Gerry. Isn't that why you're here?"

Andrea tried to nod, but her neck felt stiff. "Yes. I was just thinking about the game. Did you see it?"

Troy leaned against the back of the elevator. "Yes. It's even harder to watch them lose on TV. Between the Insider's blog about my being fired and the team's loss, it hasn't been a great day."

"I'm sorry."

He shrugged. "How was the postgame press conference?"

Andrea managed a wry smile. "Marc didn't make any new fans tonight. He's taken saying nothing to an art form."

A mixed expression of admiration and frustration settled on Troy's features. "He's a media executive's worst nightmare."

Andrea laughed with him. The sparkle in his dark

eyes, the sexy curve of his full lips framed by his goatee, made the elevator seem even warmer. She looked away, willing the conveyance to move faster.

They finished the ride in silence. When the doors finally opened, Andrea walked with Troy down a wide, thickly carpeted hallway. He led her into his spotless and spacious condo. The layout was open, made to appear even more so by the bright white walls and warm wood flooring. She hesitated outside of the large, white-tiled kitchen with its modern, stainless steel appliances. Her low-heeled shoes tapped against the hardwood as she hurried to catch up with Troy.

His combination living/dining room was at least two-and-a-half times the size of the one she shared with Faith, Constance, and Tiffany. Bronze curtains were pulled open over windows that afforded a breathtaking night scene of the lights around the Prospect Heights neighborhood.

The room housed the latest technology tucked away on modern, black lacquer shelving: a stereo surround-sound compact disc player, huge flat-screen television mounted to the wall above a Blu-ray digital video disc player.

Andrea stood beside the black leather sofa. "Your home is beautiful."

Troy was an arm's length from her. "Thank you."

Andrea's eyes circled the picture-perfect black and bronze room before settling on her host. "Your office in the Empire had more personality, though. Why is that?"

He gave her a crooked smile. "Is that what you *needed* to talk with me about?"

It wasn't. But now that she was here, Andrea found herself distracted from her mission by her unwise urge to know as much about the marketing executive as she could. She walked the room's perimeter but discovered more questions than answers.

The modern art displayed on the walls said more about the artist than the man who'd made the purchases. The black lacquer surfaces of the corner tables were bare of telling trinkets and knickknacks. However, the wall-mounted shelves held a treasure trove of family photos. In one, an attractive older couple stood in Troy's living room. They were hugging each other while laughing at the camera. In another, a young boy and toddler girl entertained the same couple as they sat playing on the porch of a wood and brick home.

Andrea gestured toward the photos. "Are these your parents?"

"Yes, with my niece and nephew."

She glanced at him over her shoulder. He couldn't possibly see the image from where he stood. Had he memorized the pictures? Since he didn't appear in any of them, Andrea assumed Troy had been the photographer at each event.

She inclined her head toward a picture of a much younger couple posing with the same girl and boy. "Who's this couple?"

His stance relaxed. His mouth eased into a smile. "My sister and her husband with their children. But you didn't come here to look through my family photos, either."

Andrea circled back and settled onto the sofa. "Could you sit down, please?"

Troy hesitated before joining her. "Spit it out, Andy."

She ignored the nickname. It was starting to grow on her. "Gerry's blackballing you with the city's other franchises." She sensed the shock shoot through him before he stilled beside her.

"How do you know that? Did Gerry tell you?" His voice was eerily calm.

"One of the other reporters told me, but he wouldn't tell me his source."

Troy stood and crossed to the window. "Gerry can say what he wants. No one's going to listen to him."

"You don't know that."

It was as though he hadn't heard her. "It doesn't matter anyway because I'm going to get my job back."

"You don't know that, either, Troy."

He turned to her. His eyes burned with conviction. "Yes, I do. Once I prove Gerry's the Insider, I can go back to the Monarchs."

Frustration pushed Andrea to her feet. "Troy, you made a mistake. Face it and do something before the situation gets worse."

"I lost my job. How can it get any worse?"

Andrea spread her arms to draw his attention to their surroundings. "You can lose everything. That's how it can get worse. I know because that's what happened to me."

12

The anger in Troy's eyes was replaced with concern. "Why do other reporters ignore you?"

Andrea swallowed to ease the dryness in her throat. "A couple of years ago, I made a rash decision. It cost me my job. And then I lost everything I had."

"What happened?"

Troy focused his intense gaze completely on her. It seemed as though he was trying to read her mind. Did she want to give him access to her thoughts? She admired him because of his control. She found his confidence attractive. Did she want to reveal to him a part of herself that was less than commendable? She had to. How else could she convince him of the risk he was taking? He had to understand why it was so important to stay in control.

Andrea held Troy's gaze despite the shame slowly crushing her. Confession was good for the soul. Or so she'd heard. But it took a lot of courage to make yourself this vulnerable to another person. "I made up a story about a successful professional basketball player whose family was well known and well loved in the community. I was sure the team was giving the player preferential treatment."

Troy's eyebrows leaped almost to his hairline. "What made you think that?"

"Jealousy." She responded without emotion. She wouldn't dress up or excuse her behavior. "I couldn't believe someone my age could have so much. I was certain someone somewhere was breaking the rules."

Troy prompted her. "And were they?"

"Of course not." Her courage stumbled. She forced herself to continue. "The day the story ran, the player's family complained to my editor. I admitted I'd made it up. My editor fired me on the spot, of course. And because the player was from a prominent family in the community, no one would hire me."

"The player's family had you blackballed?"

Andrea's cheeks heated. "I deserved it."

There was an extended silence as Andrea relived her mistakes. What must Troy think of her? How much harder would it be to earn his trust now?

He broke the silence first. "Did you ever apologize?"

"I tried to."

"What did he say?"

"She." Andrea took another breath. "Jackie Jones saw me at the Morning Glory Chapel's soup kitchen."

Troy's eyes widened. "Jackie?"

Willpower kept her standing when her knees wanted to give way. "She said I'd suffered enough. In the eight months since I'd been fired, I'd lost my car and my apartment." And her mother.

"So she forgave you."

"And she got me an interview with *Sports* when no one else would give me a chance."

Troy paced back to her. "If she's forgiven you, why can't you forgive yourself?"

Andrea blinked. "What makes you think I haven't?"

Troy gave her a curious smile. "You mean you *want* to work for *Sports*?" He spread his arms. "It's a fine paper, but you could do a lot better, Andy. I mean *a lot*."

His compliment took her off guard. She didn't know how to respond. "You've never said that before."

"I should have. Why haven't you left *Sports*?"

She combed her fingers through her hair. "You were in D.C. when this happened. It wasn't a big deal there. But in New York, it was huge. Jackie's grandfather made sure no editor would talk to me."

"I'm sorry."

"Don't be. I brought it on myself." It was difficult remembering that time in her life. She'd accepted responsibility for her actions, but that didn't ease the guilt or the shame. "And now I'm concerned Gerry's trying to hurt your job search. I don't want you to go through what I went through."

Troy crossed to his telephone beside the sofa. "I'll talk to Gerry and tell him to stop trying to jeopardize my career."

Andrea rushed to the phone before he could pick it up. She covered his broad hand with her own. His skin was warm to her touch. "Slow down, Troy. You can't keep leaping before you look. We don't have proof Gerry's calling franchises."

He looked at their hands together on the phone before raising his eyes to hers. "A reporter told you he was."

His face was so close. She felt his heat. She wanted to stroke her hand over his impossibly sexy goatee.

Smooth his furrowed brow. Cup his stubborn chin. "We have to verify his story. You can't keep acting on impulse. I know you *think* everything will work out. But people don't always bounce back that easily."

He turned his hand over to take hold of hers. His touch was strong, firm, and a little rough. A working man's hands on a desk jockey. Andrea shivered.

Troy straightened away from the phone and turned to her. "You said I can't sit around hoping no one will pay attention to anything Gerry says." His tone was low and husky, sliding into her system.

It was a struggle to stay in their conversation while their bodies were speaking a different language. "We need a plan, one that doesn't involve further antagonizing your former boss."

His ebony eyes twinkled at her. "OK. You work on that plan. I'll work on another."

He stepped closer to her and wrapped an arm loosely around her waist. Andrea's muscles trembled as Troy's gaze slid from her eyes to her parted lips. Her breath caught as he lowered his head to hers. Slowly. He hesitated as though giving her time to back out of his embrace. His scent carried to her again. Warmth, citrus, and cinnamon. Andrea sighed. She lowered her eyelids and rose on her toes to meet his mouth.

His taste was intoxicating, full, and rich. It shot straight into her system and made her head spin. The thick, hard muscles of his chest moved beneath her palms. Her skin tingled as she slipped her hands up to grip his broad, sculpted shoulders. She held on tight as his lips moved over hers, sipping them, shaping them.

The feel of his lips. The taste of his mouth. The smell of his skin. She was dizzy. Andrea wrapped her arms around his neck and drew even closer to him, the only stable force in her shaking world. Troy tightened both of his arms around her. The feel of his hot, hard body pressed to hers made her nipples tighten. She gasped into his mouth.

Troy's heart raced in his chest. He pressed his tongue between Andrea's lips and deeper into her mouth. Sweet. She was so sweet. Her scent. Her taste. Her touch. He stroked his left palm down her slender back to her hips. His right palm cupped the side of her breast. The warm weight was precious in his hand. Almost since the day he'd met her more than three years ago, he'd wondered how the cool and captivating reporter would feel in his arms. She was sweet as a memory, soft as a dream.

He tested the weight of her breast in his palm. Andrea moaned softly. The sound added fuel to his desire. Troy deepened their kiss. Andrea met his tongue with her own, stroking and teasing him. She explored his mouth the way he wanted to explore her. Deeply. Thoroughly. Over and over again.

Troy brought his hands up to take Andrea's blazer from her. She lowered her arms to help him. The material dropped to the floor in a muted swoosh. He tugged her thin, cotton blouse free of the waistband of her pants and slipped his right palm beneath her top to caress her warm, naked back. Her skin was smooth and firm. His muscles tightened with the need to touch more of her, to taste more of her. He cupped her bottom with his left hand, pressing her against him as he slid his right up her back. Troy palmed her breast inside her lacy bra. Her nipple grazed his hand.

Andrea's body shivered in his embrace. She broke off their kiss. She arched her back, pressing her hips against his. Troy followed her, planting kisses along the long, elegant curve of her throat. He hesitated above the rise and fall of her breasts beneath her blouse before leaning in. He grazed her right nipple with his teeth through the fabric.

She gasped and pressed her small hands against his shoulders. "Troy, wait."

His body protested, but he managed to pull away from her. "Too much?"

She swayed as she stepped back. "Too soon. I'm not ready. I'm not ready to lose control this way."

Troy frowned his confusion. "What are you afraid will happen?"

She took another step away and another, then turned from him. "The last time I lost control, I ended up living in the street."

He couldn't understand her. His body was still heated. His mind was sluggish. "Are you afraid you'll lose your job if we sleep together?"

"It's not that." She faced him as she tucked her blouse into her pants.

"I would never take advantage of you."

"I'm not worried about you. I'm worried about me." Andrea picked up her blazer from the floor.

He masked his sudden fear beneath a smile. "That sounds like a brush-off."

She spun toward him. Her bright eyes were wide and surprised. "It's not." Three hurried strides brought her back to him. Andrea stroked his goatee. Her gentle touch soothed him. "It's definitely not. I just need to move a little more slowly. Is that all right?"

He nodded. "Of course."

"Thank you." She kissed him, then turned away.

He wasn't ready to let her go. "I'll ride down with you."

Troy shoved his hands into the front pockets of his warm-up pants. He'd been attracted to her forever. And, after tonight, he wanted her even more. But how could he be certain her passion was for him and not some story?

"Thanks for meeting with me away from the arena." Troy looked at Jaclyn seated across the table in the little neighborhood café.

"You're welcome." Jaclyn looked up as the server returned with their drinks. "I don't think either you or Gerry is ready to see the other yet."

"You're right." Troy scanned the Friday lunch crowd as he drank his soda.

He and Jaclyn already had placed their orders. They'd both requested the soup of the day and a half sandwich. The young woman had assured them their food would be ready soon.

Jaclyn met Troy's gaze. "What's on your mind?"

Direct as always. He thought about Jaclyn forgiving Andrea for the libelous article the reporter had written about her. He'd never once sensed tension between the two women. And, because of Jaclyn's generosity, Andrea had been able to start putting her life back together. Would Jaclyn also be able to help him?

"Gerry's telling the other New York sports franchises to blackball me."

Jaclyn closed her eyes briefly with a sigh. "That shouldn't surprise us. Gerry is spiteful."

Troy tightened his hold on his glass. It was cold and damp in his grip. "Can you stop him?"

Jaclyn sipped her soda. "Most team owners don't respect Gerry."

He couldn't blame them. "Why not?"

"New York teams are loyal to their fans and the fans are loyal to their teams. When the public found out Gerry was trying to move the Monarchs out of Brooklyn, they realized he didn't have any loyalty."

Troy wasn't comforted. "You think because of that the other owners aren't listening to what he's saying about me?"

"I don't think Gerry has any credibility with the other owners." She pinned him with her gaze. "But, Troy, most employers expect loyalty from their employees. You went on ESPN to call your boss a liar. Don't worry about Gerry attacking your character. You've done enough damage on your own."

He didn't look away. "Gerry hasn't given up on his plan to ruin the franchise. If he isn't the Insider, he knows who is. That blog is his M.O."

"*Knowing* Gerry's involved with that blog and *proving* it are two different things."

Troy leaned forward. "If I can prove it, will you give me my job back?"

"Of course." Jaclyn's prompt response was gratifying. "It was Gerry's decision to fire you, not mine. But you'd have to prove that Gerry lied."

"That shouldn't be hard." Troy spoke with more confidence than he felt.

Judging by the look she gave him, Jaclyn had her own doubts. "Until we're able to rehire you, I'll be happy to give you references."

Troy tried a smile. "Thanks, but I'm coming back to the Monarchs."

"Then you'd better find proof that Gerry's still targeting us." Jaclyn paused to thank the young woman serving their lunch. "Every major sports owner in New York as well as several NBA owners all over the country have told me they're watching Gerry like a hawk and hoping he'll do something to get tossed out of the league."

Fierce satisfaction gave Troy an adrenaline rush. "Does Gerry know about his fan club?"

Jaclyn shrugged. "I'm sure he's noticed the cool reception he gets from other owners, but he doesn't care. He's more focused on destroying what my grandfather built."

"Even though he's destroying his family's legacy as well?"

"As long as he gets his way, he doesn't care who he runs over."

Troy picked up his chicken sandwich. "I'm not going to be Gerry Bimm's roadkill."

Andrea squinted at her work computer monitor. Her eyes were dry and scratchy. It had been a long Friday after a long and sleepless Thursday. Troy. He was on her mind and in her blood. The problem was, she couldn't afford another addiction.

She looked up as Willis walked into the newsroom and stood surveying the cramped, cluttered space. His green gaze met hers. Something in his eyes made her muscles tense.

Willis raised his deep graveled voice to be heard above the typing, talking, and telephones. "Can I have everyone's attention? I have an announcement to make." He had to repeat himself before the cub reporters heard him. "Let's step into the conference room."

Andrea and her fellow reporters exchanged concerned looks before two of the five followed their publisher and the administrative assistant, Vella, into the large meeting room. From the anxious expressions on the faces of the three reporters on the telephone, they would be ending their calls quickly to join the group.

Peter Story, who covered New York's hockey teams—the Islanders and Rangers—leaned his hips against the room's far wall. "What's going on, Will?"

Willis waited until the staff had filed into the room, circling the large, battered rectangular conference table. No one opted to sit.

Henry Chin, the baseball reporter, rushed into the room. He must have hung up on the person with whom he'd been speaking. "What did I miss?"

"Nothing." Willis shoved his hands into the pockets of his faded brown pants. "Where are John and Alice?"

Henry jerked a thumb over his shoulder. "They're still on the phone. Sounds like Alice's talking to one of the Red Bulls' coaches and John's interviewing Eli Manning."

"I'll speak with them later, then." Willis scanned the room, which was teaming with boxes, dust, and edgy reporters. "There's no easy way to say this. *Sports* has been struggling for several years now. I'd hoped we would make it to the end of this year, but I don't know if we'll make it to the summer."

The air sucked out of the office. A couple of Andrea's colleagues seemed to check their balance. Andrea's shoulders slumped under the weight of another uncertain future.

Henry's jaw dropped. "What?"

"The paper's folding?" John Adai, the football reporter, had just joined them.

"How long have you known?"

Andrea winced at the accusation in Peter's tone. "The signs have been here for a while." She just hadn't been brave enough to see them. The message was carved on Willis's face. His hollowed green eyes and grayish pallor told the story of the strain he bore.

Peter turned on her. "He told you?"

Andrea shook her head. "He didn't have to. Why do you think the freelance budget went away?"

Vella nodded. "The holiday party was cancelled, too."

"How long do we have?" Alice Ramirez's question came from the conference room doorway. The soccer reporter looked resigned.

Willis pulled his fingers through what remained of his lank, gray hair. "I'm not sure yet."

Peter heaved a frustrated sigh. "At least give us an idea."

"A few months. June or July." Willis shared his gaze with the rest of his staff. "I'll give everyone here a letter of recommendation. You've all earned it."

Peter snorted. "A fat lot of good that'll do us. We don't need your letter of recommendation. We need jobs."

Willis nodded. "And I'll do everything I can to help you find jobs as soon as possible."

Vella wrung her hands. "Maybe we could take pay cuts, at least until the paper's finances are stable again."

Peter turned his scowl on the assistant. "Are you kidding me? He's barely paying us anything now. I've got bills to cover."

Andrea clenched her teeth. "Everyone in this room is going to be devastated if this paper folds, including Will. Vella is trying to come up with a solution."

Willis held up one hand, palm out. "Cutting the payroll isn't an option. I realize I don't pay you what you deserve. But I pay you as much as I can."

John frowned. "Will there be any cutbacks? Training camp's going to start soon. Will our expenses be covered?"

Willis lowered his hand. "Yes, just try to keep expenses down." He looked at Andrea. "You can travel for the play-off away games, too." His gaze took in the rest of the room. "As soon as I work out more of the details, I'll let everyone know what's going to happen when. I'm sorry. More sorry than I can tell you."

Andrea watched her editor and publisher leave the room. His gait was slow, his shoulders stooped. He loved the paper. She could tell he was dying with it.

Peter's harsh tone broke the silence. "He's sorry? He's sorry? Is that supposed to make us feel better?"

Alice glared across the scarred conference table toward the agitated hockey reporter. "Your ranting isn't helping. Pull yourself together."

Henry nodded. "Why don't you chill, man? This isn't easy for him, either."

Peter swung an arm toward the door. "His financial mismanagement got us into this mess."

"With a little help from the failing economy." John's tone was dry. "Or haven't you noticed what's been going on outside of your own little world?"

Peter scowled. "Oh, I've noticed all right. I've noticed all of my bills going up."

Andrea crossed her arms. "We've all got bills to pay, Pete. That's why we need to come up with a solution. Are you going to help us or just continue to attack everyone?"

Peter narrowed his eyes. "You must be pretty scared about all this. Do you think three years has been long enough for other papers to forget your stunt with that Jackie Jones story?"

Andrea stared at the angry young man. In all the time they'd worked together—almost a year—he'd never brought up her past. Her gaze circled the room. Had Willis's announcement changed the rules? Would her coworkers ostracize her now, too?

She returned her attention to Peter. "I guess I'll find out. But don't worry about me, Pete. I've landed on my feet before. I can do it again."

Peter spread his arms wide. "You call this landing on your feet?"

"Since we're *both* standing here, what would you call it?" Andrea left the conference room. Peter's question followed her.

What would she do if the industry hadn't forgiven her past transgressions?

What would she do if she'd run out of chances?

13

Something's wrong.

Troy found Andrea standing beside the security desk of his condominium's marble and mirrored lobby. She seemed nervous as she shifted her weight from one leg to another.

Troy glanced at the young security guard. "Thanks, Ted."

Ted nodded. "You're welcome, Mr. Marshall."

Her gaze was uncertain as she stood clutching her purse strap. "Sorry for the surprise visit."

"No problem. Come on up." Troy followed her into the elevator. The doors closed, and they climbed to his condo on the twentieth floor.

Unable to take the awkward silence, Troy closed the distance between them. He placed his fingers under Andrea's chin. Her skin was smooth and warm. Just as it had been last night.

He tipped her face to his. This way, she couldn't avoid his gaze. "What's wrong?"

Her eyes were worried. "*Sports* is folding."

The news wasn't surprising. The company practically advertised its financial troubles. But he was disappointed for her sake. They were in similar situations now, with uncertain employment futures. Was she experiencing the same anger, fear, and frustration?

"I'm sorry." Troy lowered his hand.

Andrea stared at the liquid crystal display tracking their progress to his condo. "So am I." She expelled a tired breath.

Troy leaned a shoulder against the elevator's back wall. His eyes traced her profile, from her smooth forehead and high cheekbones to her stubborn chin. His heart contracted knowing she'd come to him first after receiving the bad news. What did that say about him? About them? He couldn't get last night out of his mind. Could she?

The elevator doors opened. Troy escorted her to his condo. "How much notice did Will give you?"

She shrugged as she preceded him into his home. "Two or three months. He's not sure."

Her voice was tense. How much of her emotions was she keeping inside? He'd run for miles after Gerald had fired him. How did Andrea deal with stress?

Troy walked with her to his living room. "How do you feel?"

Andrea stopped beside his sofa. "The numbness is starting to thaw. I think I'm heading toward panic."

"Is there anything I can do for you?"

"I just needed someone to talk to." She sounded surprised.

"I'm glad you came to me." He couldn't describe the feeling. It was too strong, too special. "Do you want a drink?"

"No, thank you." Her response was slow in coming.

He started toward the cupboard where he kept his wine rack. "It'll take the edge off your panic."

Andrea caught his arm before he passed her. "As much as I want a drink, I can't have one. I'm a recovering alcoholic."

Shock ricocheted through Troy. "I didn't know."

"How would you?" She released his arm and gave him a proud, if unsteady, smile. "I've been sober for three years."

"Congratulations." Troy studied her, trying to piece together this new information with what he knew—or thought he knew—of Andrea Benson.

"Thank you." Andrea settled onto his sofa. "I started drinking—a lot—when my mother got ill. She was my best friend. My everything. I know it sounds like an excuse, but my judgment was impaired when I decided to write that article on Jackie. Self-pity and alcohol make for a dangerous combination."

Troy sat beside her. "It doesn't sound like an excuse. You went through a difficult time."

Andrea rose to wander the living room. "Stress is the trigger. If I'm not careful, I could lose control again."

Her words were familiar. She'd said something similar the night before. "You're afraid of losing control because you're a recovering alcoholic?"

Andrea paused in front of his display of family photographs. "I can't afford to fall off the wagon. I have enough strikes against me without resurrecting my drinking problem."

Troy leaned forward, bracing his forearms on his thighs. He couldn't imagine the calm, disciplined woman in front of him ever losing control. "This is the push you've needed to get a better job. You're a good reporter, Andy. Don't sell yourself short."

She turned to him in surprise. "You've never told me that before."

Perhaps he'd been unfair, but the team had to come first. "We're on opposite sides. You're the reporter who wants to uncover the news. I'm the marketing executive who wants to control the message."

Andrea folded her arms. "I'm not worried about your messaging. I'm concerned about my readers. I want to give them information they can use to better understand the sport they enjoy."

Troy stood. This part of their disagreement always made him impatient. "What family wants a spotlight on their dysfunction?" He thought of his own family and the disputes he'd had with them over the years. "You do a more balanced job with our faults than other papers, but those articles still hurt our image."

Andrea blinked. Had Troy finally admitted she'd been balanced in her coverage of the Monarchs? She'd needed those words, especially now. They had been a long time coming. What had changed his mind?

She continued her trek around his spacious living room, pausing to study his family photos again. "I don't expect other papers to forget my poor judgment with the article on Jackie." She looked at him over her shoulder. "But is three years long enough for them to give me another chance?"

"You got a lot of positive buzz with your exclusive on Gerry's attempt to move the Monarchs out of Brooklyn." Troy shoved his hands into the front pockets of his khaki pants. "Why didn't you use that article to get another job?"

Andrea shifted her shoulders in a restless movement and turned away from him. "I should have."

She sensed Troy's approach. His hand on her shoulder was such a simple touch, so light she barely felt it. So warm, it seeped into her bones.

"You'll get another job, Andy." His words pulled her from the edge of her pity party.

His hand fell away from her shoulder as she turned to him. Troy replaced the touch of his hand with the warmth of his gaze.

Andrea stared into his ebony eyes. The concern was still there, joined by curiosity. But there wasn't any pity, thank goodness. "Thank you for believing in me. I needed that."

The right corner of Troy's lips kicked up. Andrea's cheeks heated as she read admiration in his gaze.

"We can use the buddy system for our job searches."

Andrea exhaled a laugh. "You'll get your job back with the Monarchs."

Troy chuckled low in his throat, a rumbling sound that reverberated in her abdomen. "Our being on the same side feels strange, but I like it."

Andrea arched a brow. "You said you've been my secret admirer for a while."

He stroked her cheek with the tips of his fingers. "Then it's not a secret anymore, is it?" He dropped his hand.

Andrea's skin tingled where his fingers touched her. "It's strange that it took both of us losing our jobs before we let down our guards."

"Have we let down our guards?"

His voice was as mesmerizing as a magician's spell. It wrapped around her until all she saw was him. Desire glowed like burning coals in his dark gaze and tightened his chiseled features. The heat mirrored the urgency stirring inside her.

Andrea's heart beat hard against her chest. "I'm afraid to lose control."

"Then take control instead." He came closer, offering himself to her.

Andrea's eyes widened with understanding—and excitement. She scanned his body, from his model good looks to his athlete's build—broad shoulders, slim waist, taut hips, and long legs. He was putting all of that under her control? She closed her eyes briefly as images overwhelmed her.

She stepped forward. Standing on her toes, Andrea raised her hand to cup the back of his head. She brought him closer and whispered against his mouth, "I accept your offer."

Their lips touched and a shiver moved through her body, from head to toe. She was light-headed, lost in the taste and texture of him, like a fine liqueur. Strong. Full. Addicting. She touched the tip of her tongue to his lips. He opened his mouth, giving her more of himself. She slipped inside and swept the moist cavern, seeking more of his flavor.

Troy groaned deep in his throat. Andrea answered his call, rising higher on her toes to press against him. Her fingertips pressed into the corded muscles of his shoulders beneath his jersey. His arms wrapped around her, holding her close. His hard body against her. His taste on her tongue. His scent, citrus and cinnamon, in her head. Andrea's nipples tightened with need.

She broke the kiss. "Your bedroom."

She sought his gaze. His eyes were even darker than before. His cheeks were flushed. She was the one managing the pace, where they were going and how they would get there. But an urgency was directing her, and she was eager to answer it.

Troy swung her into his arms. "You're still in control. It's just quicker this way."

He crossed his living room and strode down a hallway. He stopped at the first room on his left and pushed the door open with his foot.

Andrea pressed her hand against his chest. His heart was strong, swift, and steady beneath her palm. "Do you have protection?" This sense of urgency wasn't going to push her into being stupid.

"In the nightstand."

Her thigh stroked against his erection as her feet touched the floor. Her skin burned through the soft material of her brown pants. All that power under her control. Her stomach muscles clenched in anticipation. She'd been denying her attraction to the Monarchs' marketing czar for some time. She'd feared a relationship with him could have spelled professional as well as personal disaster. But tonight, with his invitation, her want had overcome her fear, and she would realize a fantasy she hadn't even known she'd harbored.

"I'm in control?" Even whispering the words made her feel strong, powerful—feelings she'd never had before.

"Yes." His sexy lips curved just a bit. His heated gaze was a challenge and an invitation.

Andrea swallowed a groan. She stepped closer until she could feel his warmth, breathe his scent. She slipped her hands beneath his jersey. It rose as she stroked over his abdomen. His muscles were tight and flat. They quivered under her touch. Andrea kept her eyes on his, eager to see his reaction to her touch. His smile faded. His eyes burned her.

She traced the line of hair from his navel. She spread her palms on his chest hair that fanned over his pectorals. Abruptly, Troy pulled the jersey over his head, exposing his sculpted torso. Andrea's mouth went dry. While his arms were tangled in his clothes, she stepped forward to trace his right nipple with her tongue. Troy jerked. She smiled against his chest.

Troy tossed his jersey across the room. "Sneak attacks? I'd have thought that was beneath you." His grin removed any hint of chastisement.

She turned him so she could walk him backward to his bed. "That's where I want you."

"I can't think of a better place to be with you." His voice was a rough caress.

Troy toed off his loafers and shed his khaki pants. As she removed her clothing, Andrea studied his form-fitting white briefs. She wanted to pull them off with her teeth. She walked to him, wearing only her bra and underwear, and pressed his shoulders to encourage him onto the bed.

Andrea straddled his thighs, following him onto the mattress as he shifted to lie across its width. The look in his eyes made her feel sexy, attractive, and powerful. In this moment, she believed she was all those things.

She moved in, lowering her head to inhale his scent again. Her body dampened with arousal. She felt Troy brush her hair behind her shoulder. Andrea turned her head to kiss him. She caressed his mouth, nibbling it and sucking on his lower lip. Troy tunneled his fingers into her hair, holding her steady to deepen their contact. She felt his other hand moving toward her bra.

Andrea rose away. "Uh-uh. I'm in control." Her smile spread as she reached back to stroke his erection. He was hot and hard. "And I'm really going to enjoy this."

Troy lowered his arms. "Just promise you'll respect me in the morning."

She leaned forward again to kiss him hard. "I promise."

She worked her way back down, drawing her fingertips through the fine hair covering his muscled chest. She followed the trail as the hair narrowed down his abdomen and disappeared beneath the waistband of his sinfully sexy briefs. Andrea scattered kisses across his torso, licking his taut, hot skin, until she once again arrived at his underwear.

Her gaze rose over his torso, pausing at his rapidly rising and falling chest. Andrea met his heated eyes. Holding his attention, she tucked her fingertips under his waistband and peeled away his last remaining article of clothing. His body was stiff with need. She was the cause of that. Her own body was almost drenched with desire.

She climbed back onto the bed, once again straddling Troy. Andrea hovered above his arousal to stroke his length with her tongue. She heard his groan, watched his body move. For so long, she'd been attracted to and admired his self-assurance. Only a very confident man would give control over completely to a woman to ensure her pleasure. Andrea's excitement built to a breaking point.

She moved farther up his body. "Can I look inside your nightstand?"

Troy exhaled with relief. "Yes." He nodded toward the nightstand behind her, then watched her stretch to reach the top drawer.

His eyes followed the slender line of her toned body. Even during his inappropriate fantasies, Troy had never considered that, beneath her conservative clothes, the tenacious reporter wore lace demi-cup bras and bikini underwear. Her breasts would perfectly fill his hands. His palms itched to cup her rounded derriere. His mouth went dry imaging the taste and feel of her naked skin.

She turned back to him, tearing the condom packet open with her teeth. Troy peeled his tongue from the roof of his mouth. "Do you need help?"

Andrea shook her head. Her hair danced around her narrow shoulders, bare but for the thin, dark blue bra straps. She wiggled past his hips to his thighs. He felt her lips on his arousal again before she applied the condom. He squeezed his eyes shut and focused on breathing while her touch, soft and quick, rolled the condom over him.

He opened his eyes as she stood away from the bed to remove her underwear. His heart was pounding in his chest. His blood was rushing through his veins.

Troy found Andrea's hungry gaze. "I'm going to touch you now."

"Please." She came to him, placing her slender arms on either side of his face.

Troy lifted his head slightly and suckled her nipples into his mouth. She was so sweet. Andrea groaned and pressed her hips against his waist. Her hair swung forward, brushing against his face. He smelled her shampoo. Troy released her left breast to take her right nipple into his mouth.

He slid his hands down her back from her shoulder to her hips. Her skin was as smooth and soft as silk beneath his touch. He cupped her bottom with his left hand and shifted his right hand between their bodies. She was damp against his palm. Troy slipped his index finger into her. Andrea made a sound between a scream and a groan. She tightened around his finger. Her body moved faster. Her arms trembled.

Troy released her breast and whispered in her ear. "Sit up, honey. Sit up and take me inside you. You're in control."

Andrea rose and Troy positioned himself so she could have him. He clenched his teeth as she lowered to him slowly. Andrea moaned as she took more and more of him. Troy tightened his hold on her thighs, lifting himself to meet her. He struggled not to come as he watched Andrea seated on him. Her slender body arched, her nipples puckered, and her breasts bounced with their movements. This image was light-years from the tightly controlled reporter. He slid his hands up to touch her breasts. He stroked them, caressed them, rubbed his palms over her nipples. Andrea pressed his hands against her as she moved with him.

Troy freed his hands and drew them back down her body. Touching her waist, dipping into her navel, cupping her hips, and making his way to the juncture of her thighs. He watched Andrea for her reaction. Her eyes were closed. She caught her lower lip with her teeth. He touched her with his thumb. She gasped. Her body bowed. She pressed herself harder against his caress. Troy deepened his touch as he picked up his rhythm between her legs. He raised his left hand to knead her breast, rolling and pinching first her right nipple, then her left. Andrea's gasps became pants. Her body tightened around him. Her muscles squeezed him harder and harder. As she screamed her climax, her body trembled against him, pulling him with her.

She collapsed onto him. Troy held her tight as his own body shuddered with his release.

Andrea stilled in his arms. Why had it been so easy to put himself under someone else's control? Or rather, why had it been so easy to give up control to Andrea?

"Oh, my word." Andrea stared blindly at the ceiling of Troy's bedroom. Her pulse had slowed and she'd finally caught her breath.

"Ditto." His voice was muffled against his pillow.

Andrea chuckled. "Actually, it would take several words, and yet I find myself speechless." She was feeling pretty smug, too.

Troy rolled onto his side to face her. "Me too."

"You need confidence to allow someone to have that much control over you." It had been incredible to be in control of such a large, well-made man. Her body was still pleasantly buzzing. And tomorrow, she wouldn't have a hangover.

"You're welcome." Troy's expression was uncertain. "I think."

Andrea rolled her head on the pillow to look at him. "Your self-confidence is the first thing that attracted me to you. You always know what to do and how to do it."

His expression clouded. "Except when it comes to Gerry."

She winced in empathy. "You have to work on your impulse control."

"So I've been told." Troy rolled onto his back.

Andrea felt his regret in her gut. She didn't want to lose the afterglow of their intimacy, but she had to know who'd first warned him about his recklessness. It was more than curiosity. She wanted to know everything about Troy Marshall. She needed to know.

"What's your story, Troy? What event in your past do you most regret?"

"Getting married."

If Mindy hadn't told her Troy had an ex-wife, Andrea would have tumbled off the bed and fallen to the floor. Still, she was startled by his certainty that his marriage was his greatest regret. "What happened?"

Troy sat up, allowing the bedsheets to settle low on his hips. "She was a liar."

Andrea dragged her eyes away from his six-pack abs and sculpted pecs. She pushed herself to sit beside him, tucking the sheets under her arms to keep her breasts covered. "What did she lie about?"

Troy glared at the wall across the room. "Being pregnant."

Andrea's thoughts disappeared, like a blackboard being erased. "Your wife told you she was pregnant when she wasn't?"

"No. My girlfriend told me she was pregnant so I'd marry her." Troy looked at Andrea. "I was a sophomore at Georgetown on a full basketball scholarship. I wanted to graduate. She wanted me to enter the NBA draft."

"She pretended to be pregnant so you'd marry her and quit school?" Andrea was outraged.

"Except I married her and stayed in school." Troy tossed off the sheets and climbed out of bed. He wandered naked across the room. His movements were restless, as though the emotions from the past had come back to him.

The sight of his firm gluts and long, muscled

thighs distracted Andrea for several heartbeats. "So you left Georgetown with a degree and a divorce."

"Not what I had in mind. My parents, either. The worst part is that I suspected she was lying."

Andrea blinked. "How?"

"She was on the pill. She said she'd missed a couple of days when she was cramming for her finals. When I questioned her, she made me feel guilty for not believing her. So I introduced her to my family." The slump of his shoulders told the rest of Troy's story.

"Your parents were disappointed."

"Very." He turned toward her, oblivious to his nudity. "It turned out to be a no-win situation. They were disappointed when we thought she was pregnant. They were disappointed again when we found out she'd lied."

Andrea stood, pulling the sheet off the bed and wrapping it around her. She went to Troy and laid a hand on his shoulder. His muscles were tight. "Your parents should have been proud of you for accepting responsibility."

"Instead, my girlfriend caused a rift in our relationship that took years to fix. She also ended my basketball career."

Andrea frowned. "What do you mean?"

"I thought I was going to be a father, so I quit the team and got a job. By the time she told me she'd lied about the pregnancy, I'd lost my spot on the team."

Andrea lowered her arm. "I'm so sorry, Troy. You must have been devastated."

"So were my parents." Troy crossed his arms over his chest. "My ex-wife went on to marry one of my teammates. He left early for the draft."

His bitterness was still fresh. She could hear it.

"Now I understand why it's difficult for you to trust people."

Troy looked at her. "What?"

"It's been fifteen years. You've repaired your relationship with your parents. You have a successful career with a well-respected organization. But you can't let go of your anger toward your ex-wife."

He scowled. "No, I can't."

She pulled the sheet tighter around her. "Are you still in love with her?"

"God, no." His tone more than his words helped her breathe again.

She considered his stiff stance and furrowed brow. "Then why can't you let go of the past?"

"I have." Troy passed her to enter his large, adjoining bathroom. The muscles in his back, butt, and legs flexed and relaxed with each stride.

Andrea shivered, still clutching the bedsheet. He may think he'd let go of his past, but he hadn't. Her eyes strayed toward the rumpled bed. Being with Troy had been wonderful, even knowing the risks. Professionally, if he returned to the Monarchs, their intimacy could affect their working relationship. Personally, she knew she'd need more than a one-night stand. But would his lack of trust destroy any chance of their having a long-term relationship?

14

"Did you get me to come over here so I could thank you for letting me stay at your place Tuesday night?" Barron stared at a wedge of his dry wheat toast with tired, red eyes.

Troy watched in amusement as Barron studiously avoided looking across the table at him or his breakfast.

"Bling, it's Saturday morning. If your gratitude were that important to me, I'd have asked you four days ago." Troy scooped his fluffy scrambled eggs.

"Then why am I here?" Barron bit into the crispy slice of toast. His movements were sluggish and careful.

Troy scanned the restaurant. The weekend crowd was thin. That's why Troy had asked Barron to meet him at eight o'clock. Most people were either still in bed or eating breakfast at home. He was surprised Barron had agreed to the early call. From the window on his left, Troy could see the Empire Arena two blocks away.

"The Monarchs could be swept out of the play-offs in the first series." He lifted the eggs to his lips.

Barron paled and looked away. He took a shaky breath. "We've only played three of the seven games."

"And you've lost all of them. It's the best of seven, Barron. Tomorrow night, you have your second home game of the series."

"I know how the play-offs work." Barron swallowed more toast.

Troy lowered his fork. "Then you know if you don't win, you're done for the season."

Barron sighed, rubbing his forehead. "What's your point?"

"Are you going to play *any* of those games without a hangover?"

Barron pushed aside the plate with what remained of his toast and glared at Troy. "You're blaming *me* for our losses? There are twelve other guys on that team."

Troy ignored the rest of his scrambled eggs and turkey bacon. "You're the only one drinking your way through the play-offs. Are you doing drugs, too?"

"I'm not." Barron looked indignant.

Troy studied Barron's bloodshot eyes and drawn features. The other man was drinking himself into oblivion even on his off nights. "Your drinking's affecting your game. Have you noticed?"

"I'm entitled to an off game."

"No. You're not." He thought back to what Andrea had said about her drinking problem. "What's bugging you, Bling?"

Barron gulped his second mug of coffee. "There's nothing wrong with me."

Troy knew the other man was lying. His body language screamed *I have a hangover*. His lack of eye contact said he had a secret. "Then why are you getting drunk every night of the week?"

Someone stopped beside their table. "Troy Marshall.

Imagine running into you here." The silky female voice filled him with dread.

Troy stood to greet his former administrative assistant. "How are you, Mindy?"

The tall redhead tilted her head to one side. "It's good to see you, Troy."

From the corner of his eye, he saw Barron get to his feet. "How've you been, Mindy?" The baller gave her a smooth once-over.

"Hello, Barron." Mindy gave the NBA player a cool look before turning her attention back to Troy. Her voice warmed. "I've heard through the grapevine that you're no longer with the Monarchs."

"That's right." He swallowed his resentment. Did his voice sound strained?

Mindy smiled. "Sounds like we have something in common. I'm still between jobs myself. But if I hear of anything for you, I'll be sure to let you know."

At what cost? "Thanks."

Mindy shrugged one shoulder. "What are friends for?" Before he could react, she leaned forward and kissed his lips. "I hope to see you again. Soon." With a toss of her hair, Mindy left the restaurant.

"What's with you and Mindy?" There was laughter in Barron's voice.

"Nothing." Troy reclaimed his seat.

Barron sat again also. "Man, that didn't look like 'nothing' to me."

"We were talking about you."

"I don't want to talk about me." Barron gave him a disgusted look. "You're not my mother. What makes you think you can tell me what I can and can't do?"

"That's not an answer, Bling."

Barron sat back in his seat. "I don't answer to you,

Troy. You're not my coach. You don't even work for the team anymore." He started to stand.

Troy grabbed Barron's left wrist from across the table and held on tight. "Sit down, Barron." His gaze bore into the younger man, willing him to return to his seat.

Barron pulled his wrist free and sat. "Make it quick, man. I've got practice."

"In three hours." Troy's tone was dry. "But it's up to you how quickly we get out of here."

Barron glowered at him. "What do you want from me?"

"I want you to ease up on your drinking. You still have to play the postseason. You've got a shot at a ring." Troy leaned forward to emphasize his words. "The team needs your best game now. You can't keep playing with a hangover."

Barron's lips curled. "I can handle my alcohol."

"What are you looking for in those bottles? Courage?"

Barron's eyes glowed with anger. "Are you calling me a coward?"

Troy held his gaze. "Is there something you're afraid of?"

Barron stood. He threw some bills on the table, then caught Troy's eyes. "The next time you want to see me, buy a ticket to the game."

Troy watched the Monarchs' team captain walk out of the restaurant. His steps were careful and hesitant and unsure. Did he really believe people couldn't tell something was wrong with him? Barron was running from everything and everyone, including himself.

* * *

From her perch at her mother's side on the tan love seat, Tiffany turned her head toward Andrea. "My jersey is green."

Andrea accepted the mug of tea Faith handed her as her roommate settled onto the sofa beside her. "Yes, it is. And it's as pretty as your eyes."

The little girl giggled and pressed her face into her mother's side.

Cupping her own mug, Faith shifted to face Andrea. "This is the kick in the pants you needed to find a better job. You were wasting your talent at *Sports.*"

Andrea sipped her tea, Faith's cure for whatever ails you. "In this economy, it doesn't matter how much talent you have. It's going to take a while for me to find a new job."

Faith crossed her legs and drank some tea. "We won't let you starve."

Andrea offered a weak smile. "Thank you. I have some savings, but it will go pretty fast."

Constance shared a look between the other two women. "Speaking of food, are we all home for dinner tonight?"

Andrea avoided Faith's knowing look. "I am."

A knock on the door interrupted their Saturday evening dinner discussions.

Faith rose from the sofa, steadying her mug. "I'll get it."

Andrea stood and waited for Constance to help Tiffany to her feet. The other woman was young and pretty in knee-length denim shorts and a white cotton blouse. Once Tiffany stood steady, Andrea followed mother and daughter to the doorway.

Faith checked the peephole. "Who is it?"

"Wade Street. I've come for my *wife.*"

The angry male voice on the other side of the door froze Andrea's blood in her veins. Her eyes shot to Constance. The young mother gripped her daughter's shoulders, holding her close against her legs. Constance's skin was paper white; even her lips were pale. Her green eyes, the only color remaining in her face, were stretched as wide as saucers. So were Tiffany's.

"Open the door." Constance's voice was thin. She shifted Tiffany to stand behind her despite the little girl's protests.

"Are you sure?" Andrea bit her lips to keep from screaming, "No!"

Faith looked from Andrea to Constance. "We should call the police."

Constance straightened, squaring her shoulders. "Let me talk with him first. Open the door."

Andrea stepped forward to release the security lock. She took a steadying breath before pulling open the door. Constance's soon-to-be ex-husband reminded Andrea of a concrete wall. He was tall, maybe six feet, and broad, perhaps more than two hundred pounds. He was clean-shaven with neatly trimmed, wavy brown hair and beady blue eyes.

Andrea kept her grip on the doorknob and forced a cool greeting. "May I help you?"

"It's about damn time." Wade Street looked past Andrea to Constance. "Get your stuff. You're coming home."

Constance stood tall. Her hand remained on Tiffany's arm to keep the little girl behind her. "How did you find me?"

Wade smirked. "Your mother told me you were working for the Monarchs. I followed you here from the arena."

The malice in Wade's expression gave Andrea chills. He'd followed his estranged wife from her place of work to her home. He'd probably told her to frighten her. Andrea looked at Constance and saw her roommate swallow hard. She willed the young mother to remain strong.

Faith moved closer to Constance's side. "This is our home and we don't want you here."

Wade gave Faith a dismissive look. "Get your stuff, Connie. And the girl's. I don't have all day."

Constance didn't waver. "Tiff and I aren't leaving. This is our home."

Faith settled her hands on her hips. "You heard her. Now leave."

"Faith." Andrea tried a soft, warning tone. Her friend's temper wouldn't help the deteriorating situation.

Wade's narrowed eyes shifted from Constance to Tiffany and back. "If you want to stay here, the hell with you. But you can't have the girl." Wade spoke to Tiffany. "Come here. Now."

Tiffany stood with her mother. Her lips thinned. "No."

Andrea saw the promise of a stubborn personality. She started to close the door. "You have your answer. Now, we'd like you to leave."

Wade slammed his hand against the door. Andrea felt the impact shoot from her palm all the way to her elbow. It reverberated in her shoulder. She held on despite the pain.

"Get your things. *Now.*" Wade's tone was just short of a roar.

Several of the surrounding apartment doors opened in response to the noise. Andrea's cheeks heated with embarrassment, but the additional witnesses increased their protection.

In her peripheral vision, Andrea saw Faith step forward. "Faith, take Tiff to her room."

Faith hesitated. "But—"

"Please." Andrea kept her attention on Wade. He pushed against the door, trying to force his way in without her neighbors noticing.

The elderly lady across the hall called out to them. "Is everything all right, Andrea?"

Andrea locked eyes with Wade. "We have the situation under control, Mrs. Garrard. He's *not* coming in."

Faith scooped the little girl into her arms. "Come on, baby."

Tiffany reached for her mother, wiggling in Faith's arms. "I want to stay with my mommy."

Faith sighed as she carried Tiffany to her room. "So do I, baby. So do I."

Constance stepped forward. She grabbed the doorknob from Andrea's hold and confronted her bully. She pitched her voice so the neighbors could hear her. "We don't want any part of you. Sign the divorce papers and get out of our lives."

Andrea blinked. Now that her cub was out of harm's way, the tigress had unsheathed her claws. Andrea stood beside Constance, preparing herself for Wade's response. She could only hope it wouldn't be a physical one.

"Young man." Mrs. Garrard's voice carried from across the hall again. "I've called the police. Get away from that door."

Andrea clenched her fists. The situation was spinning out of control. When she didn't think it could get any worse, two tall, broad shadows settled in front of her door. Troy and Serge stood in the hallway outside of her apartment. They were burdened with paper grocery bags.

Serge looked from Wade to Constance. "What's going on?"

Wade glanced over his shoulder, raising his chin to meet Serge's eyes. "Who are you?" His tone wasn't quite as belligerent now.

Serge arched his brow. "Serge Gateau. Who are you?"

"Wade Street. Connie is my *wife.*"

Andrea watched the ice collect in Serge's gaze. His arms flexed around the grocery bags. Constance must have spoken to Serge about the circumstances of her failed marriage.

"I've filed for divorce." Constance's tone was firm. "Wade's leaving. *Now.*"

Troy stepped closer. "You heard the lady. Don't let us keep you."

Wade's gaze traveled from Troy to Serge. He wouldn't be able to bully them. He looked at Mrs. Garrard and the other neighbors watching from their doorway.

He returned his attention to Constance and Andrea. "This isn't over."

Serge moved closer to Wade. "Make no mistake. This is indeed over." His voice was low, but the threat was clear.

Wade glared a moment longer at Serge. There was uncertainty in his blue eyes. He was a big man, but the NBA player had almost a foot on him and was in much better shape. Perhaps that's what convinced the bully to turn and stomp away.

Constance pulled the door wider. Troy and Serge crossed into the apartment as doors shut up and down the hall.

Troy's gaze touched both women with concern. "Are you all right?"

Constance gave him a shaky smile. "Yes, thank you."

Andrea stepped into the hallway. "Thank you, Mrs. Garrard."

The elderly lady clasped her hands in front of her rounded hips. "You're welcome, dear. I didn't really call the police. They would have taken too long to get here, and I thought we could handle him on our own."

Andrea was relieved. "You were right."

Mrs. Garrard nodded once. Her gray bob swung around her chin. She glanced toward Andrea's guests before meeting her eyes again. "Good evening, dear." She closed and locked her door.

Andrea returned to her apartment. Her eyes took in Troy's slim brown sweater. It molded the muscles of his arms, which flexed as he unpacked the shopping bags. Above the V-shaped neckline was a tempting display of chest hair. Last night, those arms had held her close against his chest. She remembered the sound of his heart.

Andrea took a moment to pack those memories away. "What are you guys doing here?"

Troy looked up from the bags. His dark eyes were clouded with concern. His sexy smile was forced. "We're cooking dinner for you."

Serge kept glancing toward the kitchen doorway as he unpacked his bags onto the counter. From his vantage point, he could see the bedroom doors. "It's our way of thanking you for inviting us to dinner Tuesday."

Andrea blinked. "That wasn't necessary."

She followed Serge's gaze to her roommates. Faith had emerged from Tiffany's room. She stood with mother and daughter as Constance comforted Tiffany. Or maybe it was the other way around. The toddler had an old soul.

Andrea crossed to Constance and laid her hand on her friend's shoulder. She could feel the young mother trembling. "You were incredible."

"Yeah?" Constance blinked away tears and cuddled Tiffany closer. The little girl clung to her mother like a monkey. "I don't know where I found the courage to defy Wade. I've never done that before." She glanced from Faith to Andrea. "Maybe it's because I knew I was surrounded by people who would support me."

Andrea looked up as Serge entered the dining area. He stopped in front of Constance and wrapped her and Tiffany in his arms.

The little girl giggled. "You're squeezing me."

Andrea exchanged a look with Faith. She and her roommate joined Troy in the kitchen to give Serge, Constance, and Tiffany privacy. "What are you making?"

"Salmon, rice, and salad for the adults. Fish sticks, tater tots, and corn for Tiffany." Troy's features were tight with strain.

She walked up behind him to massage his shoulders. The bunched muscles relaxed beneath her fingers.

He turned and crushed her in his embrace. "If Wade had touched you—" He bit off the rest of his threat.

Andrea's eyes widened with surprise. She caressed his back. "We're OK."

Faith sighed. "All right, you two. I'm running out of rooms to go to."

Troy pulled back, but his eyes remained on Andrea. "Sorry."

Andrea cupped the side of his face, moved by the caring she saw there. "I'm not."

Faith gestured toward the food on the counters. "We fed you spaghetti. You're repaying us with salmon? Can we keep the change?"

Troy laughed, easing the atmosphere in the kitchen. He turned to Faith. "This is our thank-you. Whether it's with salmon or burgers, it's sincere."

Andrea patted Troy's back. She needed to touch him. "We appreciate it. Or should I say, you're very welcome. I'll get the pans and bowls for you."

It was a tight squeeze, but Andrea, Faith, and Constance managed to help Troy and Serge cook dinner while Tiffany entertained them with running if disjoined commentary. Serge supplied chardonnay. Andrea was touched that Troy had bought white grape juice, which he shared with her and Tiffany.

At first, the dinner frivolity seemed forced. It was obvious everyone was trying to recover from Wade's unexpected and undesired visit. But the good food and friendship finally eased the tension. Andrea couldn't miss the newfound confidence in Constance or the sense of relief surrounding mother and daughter.

Faith leaned back in her chair and sighed. "I ate way too much."

Constance chuckled. "So did I."

Tiffany grinned. "I ate the whole thing."

Serge leaned forward to look at the little girl. "If you'd eaten even one more tater tot, you would have turned into one."

Tiffany's giggles spread to the rest of the group.

Andrea pushed to her feet. "That was delicious, gentlemen. Thank you very much."

Troy wrapped his long, warm fingers around her wrist. "What are you doing?"

Andrea gave him a puzzled smile. "Clearing the table."

Troy stood, taking her dishes from her and adding them to his own. "Serge and I will take care of that. Dinner's our responsibility today."

Faith gave the two men a hopeful look. "Only for today?"

Serge pushed away from the table. "I'm afraid so."

Andrea joined her roommates in the living room while Troy and Serge cleared the table and cleaned the dishes. Faith and Andrea took their customary seat on the sofa. Constance settled Tiffany beside her on the love seat.

Constance glanced toward the kitchen before leaning forward. She lowered her voice. "What do you think this means? I've never had wealthy men cook me a meal much less clean up afterward." She frowned. "Actually, I've never had *any* man cook me a meal or clean up after."

Faith crossed her legs. "It means either we've died and gone to heaven or we're being punked and any minute Ashton Kutcher is going to jump out of a closet with a camera."

Andrea chuckled. "I don't know what it means, but I'm enjoying it."

It didn't take long for the men to complete their kitchen duty. But when they rejoined Andrea and her roommates, their serious expressions drained the joy from the room.

Andrea tensed. "What's wrong?"

Troy glanced at Serge before answering. "Serge

needs to leave now. He's got to get some rest for game four tomorrow. But he and I discussed it, and I'd like to stay over in case Wade comes back tonight."

Faith shifted on the sofa to face the two men. "Thank you for offering, but we can take care of ourselves."

Andrea stood. "Troy, that's very generous of you. But we'll be fine. If Wade returns, we'll call the police."

Serge looked at Constance. "You handled Wade very well this evening. But this isn't about you. It's about us." The Monarchs player gestured between himself and Troy. "We're worried about all of you."

Constance spread her arms. "You don't need to be. There are three of us." She smiled at her roommates. "I'm certain I'll be OK because I'm not alone anymore."

Troy inclined his head. "Make that four. I'll go home to get an overnight bag, then I'll come back and sleep on the couch."

Andrea, Faith, and Constance exchanged horrified looks. Andrea touched the cushion beneath her. "This sofa's not that comfortable."

Troy winked at her. "One night won't kill me."

She couldn't say the same. Just thinking of him sleeping outside her bedroom door made her stomach muscles dance. It was going to be a long night.

15

"We need to talk." Troy's eyes were as hard as his tone.

Andrea's smile of welcome wavered, then disappeared as they stood in the doorway of her apartment Sunday morning. Where was the man who'd shared waffles with her this morning? What happened to the lover who'd kissed her good-bye before leaving her apartment?

Andrea noticed the printouts gripped in Troy's hand. "Sure. Come in."

She turned to lead him through her apartment. Along the way, he exchanged much more pleasant greetings with Faith, Constance, and Tiffany. Andrea pushed open the window and climbed onto the fire escape.

She waited for Troy to join her before closing the window partway. "What's wrong—"

"What the hell is this?"

Andrea took the printout Troy thrust at her. It was the latest *Monarchs Insider* blog dated that morning. The heading was MARSHALL'S SECRET MARRIAGE. Andrea's lips parted. Her grip tightened on the sheet. *How did the anonymous blogger get this information?*

She scanned the entry. It was written as though the blogger had interviewed someone with knowledge of Troy's divorce. Andrea's frown cleared. The *Insider* had tried this format before with Jamal and Warrick. But Jamal had denied ever meeting the blogger. Instead, information from the "interview" must have been compiled from the blogger's eavesdropping.

Who does that remind me of?

She saw the accusation in Troy's furious gaze. "You think *I'm* the Insider's source?"

"You're the only one outside of my family and college teammates who knows anything about my divorce."

Andrea lowered her hand still clutching the printout. A brisk spring breeze combed through her hair and pushed at the paper. "Actually, I'm not. Mindy Sneal told me about your divorce a week ago."

Surprise replaced the anger in Troy's gaze. "I've never talked to Mindy about my personal life."

Andrea thought back to her conversation with the former Monarchs administrative assistant. "You didn't have to. Mindy eavesdrops."

"How do you know?"

"She told me." Could Mindy Sneal be the Monarchs Insider? If so, was Troy right? Was Gerald involved? "Was Mindy fired or did she quit?"

Troy leaned into a corner of the fire escape. "She quit."

Andrea heard his reluctance. "Why?"

Troy shoved his hands into the front pockets of his black Dockers. "Our working relationship had become strained."

Andrea frowned. "What happened?"

He flexed his broad shoulders with a restless movement. "Why are you asking? What does it matter why Mindy left?"

Her curiosity increased. "Humor me."

Troy rubbed the back of his neck. "She was coming on to me."

Andrea blinked. "What?" Mindy Sneal had tried to seduce Troy. Why did that revelation make her want to slap Mindy? Really hard.

Troy looked away almost as though he were embarrassed. "You don't think men are ever harassed in the workplace?"

"I didn't say that. I was just surprised. She was coming on to you?" She was definitely jealous. They'd spent one night together and now she was a possessive lover. Andrea wasn't proud of that.

"She stood too close. She was always touching me. Her offers to work late were becoming more suggestive." He faced her again. "When I realized she was reading my e-mails and listening to my phone conversations, I'd had enough."

"If she was reading your e-mails and listening to your phone calls, she knows a lot more about you than you think."

"Probably." Troy looked highly irritated.

"And she didn't quit. You fired her."

Troy shook his head. "I didn't want to fire her. Mindy was good at her job. She just wouldn't take no for an answer. I asked Jackie if we could reassign her."

Andrea's eyebrows jumped. "Jackie knows what happened?"

Troy rubbed his right hand over his eyes as though wiping away an unpleasant memory. "I had to tell her. But that's one conversation I wouldn't want to relive. Uncomfortable is an understatement."

Andrea crossed to Troy and rested her hand on his shoulder. "The situation wasn't your fault."

His gaze held frustration as well as regret. "I wish it hadn't happened."

So did she. Andrea squeezed his shoulder, then dropped her hand. "Did you offer Mindy another position in the organization?"

Troy crossed his arms over his chest. "Yes, but she refused to take it. She said if she couldn't work for me, she'd quit."

Andrea imagined that wasn't a conversation Troy would want to repeat, either. "I take it she was angry."

"Very." Troy paused. "Do you think she's the Insider?"

Andrea felt the excitement sweeping over him. "She could be. And I think I know how to get her to admit to it."

Troy smelled the potpourri as soon as he entered Mindy Sneal's apartment Sunday afternoon. Her living room was over-the-top feminine. Frills, lace, pastels, and furniture he was afraid to sit on.

He cautiously lowered himself onto one of her spindly, padded armchairs. He braced his elbows on the chair's carved maple arms. "Thanks for letting me stop by."

Mindy made herself comfortable on her flowered pink sofa. She crossed her legs, smoothing the hem of her dark yellow skirt at her knee. "When you said it was about a possible job opportunity, how could I say no? As you know, I'm currently unemployed."

The look in her eyes was more amused than accusing. Or maybe Troy was reading into it. "Actually, I think you may already have this job."

She lifted her eyebrows. "What job is that?"

"It's with the *Horn*. You're the Insider."

She didn't flinch. She didn't blink. She didn't protest. Mindy just smiled. "You said Gerry was the Insider."

Troy searched her eyes. She was a cool one. "Gerry doesn't know about my divorce."

Mindy cocked her head to the left. Her red hair swung behind her shoulders. "What makes you think I do?"

"Andy said you told her I was divorced."

"So you *are* sleeping with her." Mindy's eyes glittered. Her features hardened. Was it anger, jealousy, or both?

Troy ignored the blood pounding in his ears. "Did Gerry put you up to this?"

Mindy's smile was forced. "Why are you always accusing Gerry?"

Troy stood. He couldn't take another second in the spindly chair. Even Andrea's secondhand furnishings were more comfortable than Mindy's doll fixtures. "You couldn't land an opportunity like that on your own. You don't have the connections. No one knows you. You would've needed help."

Her mask melted. Anger heated her eyes and her tone. "I didn't need anyone's help. They were excited to publish my copy."

Troy stared down at his ex-administrative assistant. "You approached the *Horn* on your own?"

Mindy's eyes widened with surprise and dismay. Her gaze shifted left, then right. Finally, she sighed, her shoulders falling with resignation. "Yes."

Andrea had been right. He'd attacked Mindy's ego and she'd spilled her guts. "Why?"

Mindy glared up at him. "I wanted to be with you. But you fired me."

His puzzlement increased. "You quit."

Mindy stood, closing in on him. "*I* worked for the franchise. Andy Benson's a reporter. She's the enemy. But you were more interested in her than me."

Troy couldn't make sense of Mindy's answers. "You betrayed the franchise because you thought I was attracted to Andy?"

Mindy threw up her hands and spun away from him. "You were always talking about protecting the Monarchs' image. But then you gave your precious Andy an exclusive claiming Gerry was going to move the Monarchs out of Brooklyn. Which of us committed a bigger betrayal?"

"Did Gerry convince you to do the blog?"

"Why do you think Gerry's responsible for everything?"

Troy crossed his arms. "Not everything, just every *bad* thing that's ever happened to this team."

"That's not fair."

"No, it's not. So tell me the truth. Did Gerry give you the idea of writing the blog?"

Mindy's smile grew smug again. "No, he didn't."

Troy tensed. He studied Mindy's posture, her features, and her eyes. "I don't believe you."

"Of course you don't. It would be a lot more convenient for you if you could link Gerry to the blog. Then you wouldn't be known as the marketing executive who slandered his boss on ESPN, of all things."

Troy dropped his arms. "You're right. It would be. But I'll have to be satisfied with identifying you as the Insider and saying you acted alone."

Mindy threw back her head and laughed. She was more than confident. She was arrogant and genuinely amused. "And who will believe you? First you accused your boss on television and now you're accusing your ex-administrative assistant who quit because you were sexually harassing her."

He fisted his hands to hold on to his temper. "I never harassed you."

"Of course you didn't. But I can be very convincing. In the end, it will be just your word against mine."

Troy pulled the audio recorder from his inside jacket pocket. "Not exactly." He rewound the device and played the last ten seconds of the recording.

"I never harassed you."

"Of course you didn't. But I can be very convincing. In the end, it will be just your word against mine."

Mindy gaped at him. "You can't use that tape."

"I will if I have to." He tucked the recorder back into his pocket. "Andy's going to submit her article about your being the Insider for Monday's edition of the paper as well as post it on the *Sports* website today. Kind of ironic. By tomorrow, your anonymity will be over."

Mindy's glare was lethal. "It will still be just your word against mine."

Troy shook his head. "I don't think so. If you continue the blog, the next time I go on ESPN, I'll share this tape on air." He stepped around her on his way to her front door. "Don't bother to show me out. I know my way."

He'd have to thank Andrea again. Sending him with the audio recorder had been part of her plan in case Mindy denied being involved with the blog. It also had been Andrea's idea to attack Mindy's ego. It was good to have a plan. Who would have thought he and Andrea Benson would make a good team?

Troy pressed the elevator's button and waited for his ride to the lobby. He'd been so certain Gerald was involved with the *Monarchs Insider* blog, if he weren't the actual blogger. Being wrong disappointed him more than he could measure.

How could he return to the Monarchs now?

Andrea sat beside him on his black leather sofa. Her sherry brown eyes were dark with concern. "I'm sorry things didn't work out the way you'd hoped they would with the blogger."

So was he. But he was glad she was here. He could use the company to help him get through the disappointment. "The important thing is we've given Mindy an incentive to take down the *Insider*."

"Will's going to run the story in tomorrow's paper. It's on our website now. Needless to say, he's thrilled. One last hurrah before the paper folds." Andrea had come straight to his condo after filing her exposé on the Monarchs Insider with *Sports*.

Troy linked his fingers with hers. She was wearing her reporter's uniform: blazer and slacks in neutral colors and a pale blouse. "Removing the blog will be one less worry for the team. Now if they could just keep from being swept out of the play-offs."

It was almost four hours before game four of the Cleveland Cavaliers versus Brooklyn Monarchs best-of-seven-games series.

"I thought playing in the Empire would give them an advantage for games three and four." Andrea looked at their joined hands before raising her gaze to his. "You've said all the right things. Now tell me how you feel."

"Frustrated. Scared." Troy stood to cross his living

room. He needed to distance himself from those words. He stopped in front of his picture window and let the view of his Prospect Heights neighborhood sooth him. "I want my job back."

"How are you going to change Gerry's mind?"

He clenched his teeth. "I still want him as far away from the Monarchs as possible."

"But he hasn't caused any more problems. Maybe he's given up his plans for revenge."

Troy faced Andrea. His eyes widened with surprise. "Do you believe that?"

She spread her arms. "He wasn't involved with the blog."

"If you believe Mindy."

"He's not pushing negative stories about the team."

"That we know of." He turned back to the window. The scene didn't calm him anymore.

Andrea's shoes tapped against his hardwood floor as she came to him. She laid her head between his shoulder blades. "Troy, leave Gerry to Jackie. She can handle him. Focus on what *you* can control."

"I don't have control over anything anymore."

"Yes, you do. Finding another job is in your control. Jackie will provide you with a good reference. I'm also sure she'll use her contacts to help you get another position."

He didn't want to think about Jaclyn giving him a reference for another job. He wanted *his* job back. He wanted the *Insider* blog gone. He wanted Gerald away from the franchise, and he wanted the Monarchs to win tonight. But he didn't have control over any of that.

He couldn't even control his feelings for Andrea. They were more than want, stronger than need. How had she gone from being a threat to being his friend? His lover?

Troy turned to take her into his arms. "Talking about control, do you want it?"

Her eyes heated. She raised her hand and cupped his cheek. "Why don't we share it?"

The temptation of her smile. The sexy promise of her words. The knowledge that she trusted him enough to share control with him. All of these things combined to set Troy on fire. He bent his head to kiss her deeply, showing her with action the feelings he wasn't ready to put into words.

Andrea wrapped her arms around his neck and moved closer to him. She parted her lips and let him inside. Troy's blood heated. His pulse raced. He released her to tug the blazer from her shoulders. Without breaking their kiss, Andrea lowered her arms to let him. Troy felt her warmth through her thin pink blouse, her slender curves beneath his palms, her full breasts against his chest.

Troy pulled away from her to close the living room's bronze curtains, leaving only the faint hallway light behind them. In the shadows, he saw Andrea's wicked smile. She held her arms out to him. Troy joined her.

He lowered his head to resume their kiss. Troy stroked his tongue along the seam of Andrea's mouth, coaxing her to open for him. She did, and Troy pressed inside. Her taste was intoxicating, like fine wine. His thoughts spun. He caressed her tongue with his own, stroking it and suckling it as he undressed her. In her arms, he was as confident as she thought him to be.

Cool air rushed against Andrea's skin as Troy tugged her blouse from her. She trembled from the chill and the desire building inside her. She felt his nimble fingers at the belt and waistband of her pants. He stepped away as her trousers fell to the floor. He claimed her gaze, then, without a word, dropped to his knees before her. He pulled down her underwear. Andrea stepped out of her shoes and nudged the pile of clothing aside. She took off her bra and stood naked in front of him.

Troy pressed his face against her abdomen. He kissed her navel, then twirled his tongue inside. Andrea's breath hitched. His right hand moved up her calf to her knee, then slid between her thighs. Her body tightened with excitement as she anticipated his touch. Troy palmed her as he continued to kiss her stomach. He teased her navel and nipped her hip bone. Slowly, he moved his hand back and forth against her, nurturing her need, making her crazy.

Andrea closed her eyes. Her knees began to shake. She felt the familiar hunger building for this man. She braced her hands on his shoulders.

"Troy, please." Her voice was thin, so thin she could barely hear it.

"Soon, honey. Soon."

He stroked two fingers between her folds, and Andrea jumped. She parted her legs farther to encourage him. "Please, Troy."

"Yes, honey." Troy slipped his index finger inside her and stroked her with his thumb.

Andrea sucked in a breath. Her hips moved back and forth with the rhythm of his touch. She tightened her grip on the muscles of his shoulders. Her body began to shake. Her nipples tightened. Every nerve ending in her body felt his touch. Troy removed his hand, and her body sagged with disappointment. She opened her eyes.

He took her wrist and pulled her toward him. "Come here."

She went down on her knees in front of him. Troy kissed her as he lowered her to the plush Oriental rug. His right hand molded her breasts, moved down to her waist, and cupped her hips. Troy worked his way down her body, kissing her nipples and suckling her breasts. His soft jersey brushed against her skin. Andrea's body began to buzz again. She heard the blood rushing in her ears. He kissed and licked her navel, nipped her hip bone, then pulled her knees over his shoulders.

Andrea's eyes popped open. "Troy—"

He kissed her deeply, intimately. Andrea sucked in a breath, arched her back, and pressed her head against the rug. Electricity flooded her. Her nipples beaded painfully. Troy kissed her again and licked her, stroking his tongue over and around her. Andrea's hips lifted for his next caress. Her body yearned for it. Begged for it. She gasped. She moaned. She pressed her forearm against her mouth to keep from screaming. And then she shattered against his tongue.

Troy kissed her there one last time, then pressed his hand between her legs. He rose to kiss her lips. He rubbed her with his palm until she calmed, then he caressed her until her hips began to move again.

Troy stood and removed his clothes quickly, pulling a condom from his pants pocket. He could still taste her. He smelled her on him. Her scent made his pulse beat even faster. As he moved toward Andrea, she rose to her knees and licked his arousal with one long, slow stroke of her hot, wet tongue. Troy shook. His body hurt with his arousal.

Andrea lay back down and watched him. Her eyes were sharp and intense. Troy covered his erection with the condom, then joined her. He needed to slow his pace. He ached for her too much. But he didn't want her to think he was an animal without control. He didn't want her to turn away from him.

Troy drew Andrea into his embrace and kissed her, slowly, thoroughly. She shifted closer to him. Her body was soft and hot to his touch. He slid his hand down her smooth back, loving its curves and the toned muscle beneath her silky skin. He tangled his fingers in her thick, dark hair.

"You feel so good," he murmured against her lips.

"I want you," she said against his.

Troy closed his eyes. Her words strained his self-control. He rose away from her, then watched as Andrea rolled onto her back. She raised her arms, encouraging him to come to her. Troy settled between her legs, lowering himself gently onto her. Andrea wrapped her arms around his neck and he lost himself in her kiss.

He lifted his hips to enter her. Troy squeezed his eyes shut and groaned into Andrea's mouth at the pleasure of being in her. She was tight, hot, and wet. He stilled to catch his breath. Andrea wrapped her legs around his hips and rubbed herself against him. Troy had to move. He pressed into her. Deeper. Wanting to get even closer to her. She arched her back, lifting her breasts. They were an offering he couldn't refuse. Troy dipped his head to kiss and suckle her nipples. Her restless movements beneath him made his body burn. The spell of desire wove around him until it was just the two of them and their hunger for each other. Their breaths gasping. Their blood rushing.

Their muscles straining. He needed their release now. He never wanted this feeling to end.

Andrea threw back her head and screamed his name. Troy covered her mouth with his own, then leaped over the edge with her.

16

"Why didn't you tell us you were having problems with your job?" Charles Marshall's voice commanded his son's respect from the other end of the long-distance telephone line.

His father's attack stole the satisfaction he'd felt in the wake of his afternoon with Andrea. Minutes ago he'd kissed her good-bye before she left for the Empire Arena to cover game four of the Cavaliers versus Monarchs series. "Shelley told you?"

"No, she didn't." His mother was on the other extension. "We guessed."

"How?" Troy hadn't really believed Michelle had told their parents he'd been fired. She was a know-it-all younger sibling, but she wasn't a tattletale.

Danielle Marshall's patience sounded forced. "When we asked her when she'd last spoken to you, she sounded concerned. And, since all you ever do is work, we thought that was it."

His father interrupted. "Why didn't *you* tell us?"

"I didn't want you to worry." Troy pinched the bridge of his nose. That had been a lame response.

But it also was the truth. He hadn't wanted them to think less of him, either.

"What happened?" His mother made it sound like all his woes were skinned knees and all his cures could be found in Neosporin and a hug.

Troy hesitated. How much had they figured out? "I had a difference of opinion with Gerry Bimm. He's one of the team's owners."

"You argued with your boss and got yourself fired?" His father sounded as though his head were going to pop off. Troy was twelve years old again.

In the background, probably in the room from which his father spoke, Troy could hear the television. "The situation sounds worse than it is."

Charles spoke over him. "Were you fired?"

Troy's temples throbbed as muscle memory kicked in. "Yes."

"Then it's as bad as it sounds." Charles's tone didn't leave room for debate. "What were you thinking?"

"What about your other boss, Jackie? Can she help you?" Danielle seemed to realize Troy would need more than Neosporin and a hug.

He sank into his armchair. "It's complicated, Mom."

"We aren't nitwits. Explain it to us." Charles made it a command.

Was there any way out of this conversation? He stared around his living room and imagined his parents in the home where he'd grown up. His father must be in the living room watching the Washington Wizards on the big-screen television. His mother was using the extension in the master bedroom, perched on the edge of the mattress.

Troy stood and wandered to his picture window. "I went on TV and accused Gerry of writing a damaging column about the team. Unfortunately, he wasn't the anonymous columnist. Gerry demanded my resignation."

"Oh, my word." Danielle whispered the words.

His father's response was stronger. "Are you kidding me?"

Troy pushed his fisted right hand into the front pockets of his sweatpants. "Dad, I wanted to—"

Charles interrupted again. "What were you thinking?"

"That Gerry is a coward who hides behind other people." Troy raised his voice to be heard above his father's condemnation. "I thought if I exposed him, he wouldn't be able to hurt the team."

"But you were *wrong* and now you're out of a *job*." Charles's pronouncement was another punch in the gut.

"Charles." Danielle's exclamation demanded attention. "His intention was in the right place. He was trying to help his company."

"His *intensions* are always in the right place." His father was implacable. "His actions are the problem. He's still behaving like an unruly teenager."

Troy stiffened, hearing the reference to his failed marriage in his father's words. "Calling out Gerry was a risk I was willing to take."

"But you didn't have to." Charles paused as though searching for patience. "You don't think things through. Your impulses were great when you were a kid working on your basketball skills, stealing passes and making rebounds. But you're an adult. Be responsible."

"This isn't the time for this lecture, Charlie." Danielle's tone was a warning. "Troy, there's no need to limit your job search. Why don't you come home?"

Because I don't want to be within easy access of Dad's lectures. "Mom, this isn't over."

Charles's voice sharpened. "What does that mean?"

"It means I want my job back." Troy paced back to his armchair.

"How are you going to do that if Gerry's still there?"

Troy dropped into the chair. Yes, how? "I'm working on that."

"Congratulations on exposing the Insider, Benson." Jenna Madison shifted in her seat at the Empire Arena Sunday night.

Andrea hesitated as she made her way to the empty seat beside Frederick Pritchard. Jenna's warm greeting was still unfamiliar to her. "Thanks."

Game four of the Cleveland Cavaliers series against the Brooklyn Monarchs was less than an hour away. The seats were filling quickly. Tonight, the Monarchs would either win or go home. Kevin Rudolf's "I Made It" filled the arena with a hopeful note.

Andrea unpacked her laptop. The smell of the chicken strips, hot dogs, and pretzels fans purchased from the concession stands overlaid the arena's basic gym scent.

Sean Wolf leaned forward. "Yeah. How'd you know it was Mindy Sneal?"

Andrea glanced at the *Post* reporter as she set up her laptop. "Troy's divorce was the subject of her last post."

Jenna propped her elbows on the media desk. "I didn't know Troy'd been married. Did you?"

Andrea ignored the question. She powered her computer, trying not to think about the woman who'd been Troy's first wife and whose lies had left permanent scars. "I knew Mindy was one of the few people who'd learned of it. As I wrote in my article, she admitted to being the anonymous blogger." Her colleagues didn't need to know about Troy's involvement.

Jenna inclined her head. "You're good."

"Or lucky." Sean tapped his pen against the long laminate desk.

Jenna looked at Sean. "*You* would need luck. Other people have talent." She returned her attention to Andrea without giving Sean a chance to respond. "Your phone will be ringing off the hook with other newspapers interested in adding you to their staff."

Andrea could only stare at Jenna. It had been a long time since the other reporters had held a conversation with her. Now it seemed as though the chilly period of their relationship was over. The knot of nerves in her stomach relaxed.

Andrea tried a smile. "I hope you're right. I could use some good news."

Frederick Pritchard glanced at her before returning to his Internet searches. "Is it true that *Sports* is going under?"

Andrea logged on to her computer to avoid facing her colleagues. "Yes. Will made the announcement last week. Unless something drastic happens, the paper will probably fold this summer."

"I wouldn't worry about it." Frederick spoke with almost stunning insensitivity. "It's time you moved on.

It's been four years since your Jackie Jones story ruined your career. You're ready for a fresh start."

Andrea blinked her surprise. "Thank you, Fred." *I think.*

"I agree with Fred," Jenna added. "You're good. You'll get another newspaper job, and quickly. I'll let you know if I hear of anything."

Andrea was breathless with surprise. "I'd appreciate that."

"So will I." Sean sounded grudging, but Andrea would take even that type of help.

Silence settled over the group as they prepared to cover the game. The Monarchs cheerleaders came out to entertain the audience with dance routines to various pop songs, including B.o.B.'s "I Am the Champion."

The arena lights went down and Andrea's pulse picked up. The laser light show glowed above the fans and danced around the ceiling. The announcer called the names of the Cleveland Cavaliers' players. Then his booming voice introduced the Monarchs' starting lineup—Serge Gateau, Vincent Jardine, Anthony Chambers, Jamal Ward, and Barron Douglas.

The game started, and Andrea tuned out everything else.

Win or go home. Postseason was on the line.

A stressful hour later for Monarchs fans, the team emerged from their locker room to start the third quarter and face their 21-point deficit to the Cavaliers. Their fans had booed them off the court at halftime in response to the 68-to-47 score. Many of those fans had left the arena in anger. The rest sat in silent disgust.

DeMarcus Guinn joined the players. His hand rested on Warrick's shoulder as he motioned the other players to him. Though his expressionless mask was firmly in place, he delivered last-minute instructions with an intensity Andrea felt eight rows up in the stands. If only she could hear his words.

The buzzer sounded the start of the third quarter. DeMarcus stepped back. Andrea watched Serge, Anthony Chambers, Vincent Jardine, Jamal Ward, and Warrick Evans jog to the court. Her eyes widened as she realized Barron remained behind. On the bench, the team captain sat with his head cupped in his hands. On the court, the team had renewed energy.

Warrick positioned his teammates with gestures and words Andrea couldn't hear. But she knew his directions accounted for more talking than the Monarchs had done all game. Seeing Warrick on the court revived Andrea's optimism. If you weren't talking, you weren't winning. She'd heard athletes say that often.

Over the next twelve minutes, she sat mesmerized as the Monarchs challenged the Cavaliers' lead. Warrick provided the strongest defense the team had seen all series. He kept the Cavaliers' point guard from shooting from the outside or driving in the paint. He blocked passing lanes and stole rebounds, opening opportunities for his teammates to score.

Serge, Vincent, and Anthony had hot hands in the post and the perimeter. And, for the first time during the game, the players worked Jamal into the offense. The rookie's participation helped keep the Cavaliers' defense off balance. By the end of the third quarter, the Monarchs had cut the Cavaliers lead by more than half, finishing 77 to 69. The fans were back in the game, whipped into a frenzy by their team's resurgence. Andrea felt the electricity in the arena.

The fourth and final quarter began. Twelve more minutes. Andrea sat straighter in her chair.

The Monarchs returned to the court. The effort of their third quarter showed in their legs. Immediately, the Cavaliers sped past the older, more winded team, adding 6 points to their lead, 83 to 69. Warrick clapped his hands and called to his teammates. Andrea couldn't make out his words above the crowd noise, but the Monarchs seemed to dig deep to pick up their pace. Andrea pressed her left fist against her lips as she watched her Brooklyn team make their stand to remain in the play-offs.

Nine minutes later, the score stood at 103 to 98. The arena shook with excitement as fans dared to hope their beloved Monarchs would take the win. Andrea couldn't hear herself think. Her shoulders tensed with suspense. Would the Monarchs survive?

Her gaze shot to DeMarcus, who prowled the side-line in his black suit and silver tie. His attention bounced between the court and the game clock. Three minutes remained in game four. The Monarchs needed a miracle.

On the court, Anthony Parker, one of the Cavaliers' stars, inbounded the ball past Warrick to his Cavaliers teammate Antawn Jamison. Serge moved up to defend Jamison as the Cavalier worked his way into the paint. The six-foot-ten Monarch shut down the six-foot-nine Cavalier, forcing Jamison to pass the ball back to Anthony Parker. Warrick leaned into the open lane and stole the pass, sending the Monarchs back to their basket, the Cavaliers in heavy pursuit. Midway down the court, Warrick jettisoned the ball to Anthony, who stood at the perimeter and took a leap of faith for a three-point shot.

Andrea held her breath until the ball swooshed

through the net. The daring play had cut the Cavaliers lead further, 103 to 101. The game clock showed two minutes and ten seconds remaining. Andrea fisted her palm beneath the media desk. The Monarchs had to win. They just *had* to.

The Cavaliers' Ramon Sessions caught the rebound and hustled his team back down the court. Vincent caught Sessions across the court, defending him close. Sessions tried a quick spin around the Monarchs center, but Anthony moved in to close off access. Double-teamed, Sessions stepped back to try to match the Monarchs three-point shot. The shot traveled past the fingertips of Vincent and Anthony and over Jamal's head. A foot from the basket, Serge leaped. He blocked the ball from its goal and held on to it.

Andrea swallowed her heart. She watched as Serge dribbled three steps before lobbing the ball to Vincent. Vincent sped straight for the basket. Two points. The Monarchs had tied the game at 103. The game clock ticked down to fifty-five seconds.

The Cavaliers head coach, Byron Scott, called for a timeout. Andrea breathed a sigh of relief. She needed the break.

Frederick leaned closer to Andrea and raised his voice above the fan frenzy. "Even if the Monarchs win this game, they'll probably still lose the series. In the history of the play-offs, ninety-eight teams have been down three and oh, and all ninety-eight teams have gone on to lose the series."

Frederick was bringing up the odds now? Really?

Andrea controlled her irritation. "I'll take this win."

The timeout ended. The Cavaliers moved into position. The Monarchs circled like predators assessing their prey. The Cavaliers' Antawn Jamison inbounded the ball to Anthony Parker. Warrick moved in to defend. Parker passed the ball to the Cavaliers' Anderson Varejao. Anthony stepped closer to Varejao.

Fifty-three seconds remained in the game. Monarchs fans surged to their feet like the sixth man rallying their team. They chanted, "Defense!" Andrea pressed her fist against her lips as faith and tension blanketed the arena. With the score tied at 103, it was a whole new ball game. A lot could happen in fifty-three seconds.

Serge defended Jamison. Warrick guarded Parker. Anthony had Varejao. Vincent was assigned to Ramon Sessions, and Jamal took Daniel Gibson. The Cavaliers played a wicked game of keep-away as they passed the ball from Jamison to Parker, Varejao, Sessions, and then Gibson without anyone taking a shot.

The game clock showed thirty-seven seconds. The shot clock wound down to eight seconds. Andrea watched the action on the court. Were the Cavaliers trying for a shot clock violation by exceeding the twenty-four-second limit? How would that benefit them?

Five seconds on the shot clock.

The Cavaliers' Gibson dribbled twice before pulling up to take the shot. Jamal rushed forward to block him and ran into the point guard. A referee blew his whistle and charged Jamal with a personal foul. It was the rookie's fifth foul of the game. The crowd let out a collective gasp and went silent with disappointment.

Gibson made both of his free throws, giving the Cavaliers the lead, 105 to 103. Thirty-four seconds left to the game.

Warrick grabbed the rebound. He sent the ball to Vincent, who advanced it to Anthony. Anthony set his feet and went for the easy layup. But Parker was waiting and slapped the ball straight into Varejao's hands.

Twenty-seven seconds on the game clock. A fresh twenty-four on the shot clock. Andrea's heart turned to ice. Beneath the media desk, her nails bit into her palms.

Varejao raced to the other end of the court, where Warrick stood alone to defend the basket. His arms were spread. His knees were bent. His stance was wide. The clock was ticking. Varejao charged toward him, at the last moment spinning left. Warrick danced with him. Varejao pressed forward. Warrick held ground.

Twenty seconds. The shot clock turned off.

Nineteen.

Eighteen.

The Monarchs were out of timeouts. They'd need to foul the Cavaliers—and soon—to save precious seconds.

The rest of the Cavaliers circled the paint. The Monarchs took their defensive positions. Varejao passed the ball to Gibson. Instead of letting more time drain from the game clock, the Cavalier aimed at the wide-open basket . . . and missed the shot.

The fans roared their relief.

Fifteen seconds and counting.

The Cavaliers' Parker caught the rebound as the ball bounced from the basket rim. He tried to set up for another attempt. The Monarchs swarmed him. Parker lost the ball. Vincent came up with it. The tension in the arena was dense. Vincent threw the ball to the Monarch closest to their basket, the rookie Jamal Ward.

Five seconds.

Jamal sprinted up the court, dribbling the ball.

Antawn Jamison hustled after him. Andrea wanted to close her eyes. Jamison stretched his right hand forward and tipped the ball from under Jamal's palm. The ball rolled to Warrick's feet. The game clock drained to two seconds. Andrea willed the Monarchs' point guard to take the shot. He'd been passing the ball most of the night. There wasn't time for that now.

Take the shot!

Warrick spun from Jamison. He lined up behind the three-point line. He centered his body, leaped into the air, and released the ball an instant before the end-game buzzer sounded. The shot would still count if it went through the basket. Silence crashed into the arena. The air was sucked out of the space. Andrea's eyes followed the ball's trajectory up, up, over, over. And through the net. Three points, Monarchs 106, Cavaliers 105.

Monarchs win!

Andrea wanted to jump from her seat and throw her arms in the air. But she couldn't. No cheering in the press box—or the press row. With great concentration, she finished her news article.

"Well, who'd have thought it?" Sean stood from the table and stuffed his laptop into his carrier. "The Monarchs survived getting swept out of the play-offs. Their Cinderella season continues."

Jenna sounded shocked as well. "Forget Cinderella. The Monarchs owe this win to Rick Evans. DeMarcus Guinn should have made that starting lineup change four games ago."

Frederick grunted. "They won tonight, but they won't win the series. No team has ever come back to win a seven-game play-off series after losing the first three games."

Andrea was well aware of the odds. But tonight,

anything was possible. She tossed Frederick, the human basketball encyclopedia, a cheeky smile. "Don't count out the Monarchs."

She shrugged her laptop case onto her shoulder. Andrea hurried down from the press section through the underground passage toward the postgame press conference. She caught snippets of conversations as she wove through the crush of stunned and exhilarated fans.

"Evans was epic."

"I'm glad I didn't leave at the half."

"The Monarchs are back, baby! I can feel it!"

"Andrea! Andrea Benson!"

The sound of her name being hailed with urgency stopped Andrea's forward momentum. She spun to find a game referee closing in on her. Or rather a former referee. "Mario, exciting game tonight."

With his hand on her elbow, the retired official guided Andrea out of the pedestrian traffic. "That was a good article you wrote on the Insider."

The strange tension she sensed in the older man puzzled Andrea. "Is something wrong, Mario?"

"You do a lot of investigative reporting." His dark gaze was intent on hers. His Spanish accent made the English words longer. "First the article on Gerry Bimm and now this article on the blogger."

"Mario, what's on your mind?" Her concern grew as the former referee glanced around them. Why was he behaving so strangely?

"My nephew is in trouble." Mario grabbed her gaze.

"Otto? What kind of trouble?"

Mario's expression briefly softened. "He's very excited to have been chosen to referee the play-offs. Otto has always worked hard. He's smart, and he's a good boy."

Hearing Mario refer to his thirty-something-year-old nephew as a boy almost brought Andrea's smile back. "If he's anything like you, he's the best. What kind of trouble is he in?"

Mario escorted her farther from the thinning crowd. Andrea glanced at her wristwatch. She didn't have much time to get to the postgame press conference.

He finally came to a stop. "My nephew's being black-mailed to throw play-off games."

Andrea's muscles froze in shock. Her legs stopped moving, bringing Mario up short. "By whom?"

Mario hesitated. He glanced around again, then came closer to Andrea. "Gerald Bimm."

17

Andrea's mind went blank before spinning into overdrive. "Gerry's blackmailing your nephew? With what?"

Shame thickened his Spanish accent. "He went to Otto and said he wanted to make sure the Monarchs didn't advance in the play-offs."

Incredible. Mario had no reason to lie, but Andrea couldn't believe this could be true. "The Monarchs have been losing on their own. I've watched the games. No one can say Otto or the other refs have made bad calls."

"Gerry wanted insurance. He wanted Otto to throw the games if it looked like the Monarchs would win the series. Otto said no. Our family has too much honor to get involved with this. But Gerry said if the Monarchs win the series, he'll say Otto took bribes."

Andrea was sick with disgust. Once again, Gerald was making someone else do his dirty work and take the fall, leaving him able to walk away from the mess with complete deniability.

"When the Monarchs won tonight, Otto panicked."

She made it a statement. Mario nodded. "Contact the commissioner's office. Tell them—"

Mario was shaking his head as soon as Andrea mentioned the league. "No, Otto doesn't want to go to the commissioner. He's afraid David Stern will believe Gerry instead of him. It's the word of an owner over a referee. Who would you believe?"

In this instance, she would definitely believe Mario's nephew over Gerald. No question about it. But that was her. David Stern and the league might view things differently. "I understand Otto's concern."

"I came to you because I thought you could investigate the situation quietly, like the first time you reported on Gerry and today, with the Insider story."

Andrea squirmed under Mario's regard. He looked at her as though she were some sort of superhero. It was a surreal experience. For years, people didn't want to talk to her because they were afraid of what she would do with their information. Now a former NBA official was coming to her for help. She didn't have superpowers. Still, could she find a solution to his problem? She had to try, for the Monarchs' sake.

She put a hand on his upper arm. "I'll work on this. It may take a while, though."

Mario's eyes widened. His voice was strained. "Game five of the series is Tuesday in Cleveland. What if the Monarchs win again?"

She hoped they did. But two days didn't give her much time to pull together a plan. She'd have to work fast. Andrea squeezed Mario's arm. "I'm not going to let Gerry cause problems for your nephew. I promise."

Mario looked marginally less anxious as she turned to leave. She couldn't blame him. Andrea wasn't certain of her course of action, but she knew she'd figure something out—with Troy and Jaclyn's help.

"Gerry's doing *what*?"

Troy winced as Jaclyn's incredulous words climbed several octaves. Andrea sat in the black guest chair beside him in Jaclyn's arena office. It was Monday morning. The team would be flying back to Cleveland tonight for game five of the series.

Troy rested his forearms on his thighs. "He's blackmailing Mario Nunez's nephew, Otto, to convince him to throw games to make sure the Monarchs don't advance in the play-offs."

Jaclyn's wide-eyed gaze swung from Andrea back to Troy. "When did Gerry first speak with Otto about his plan?"

"Around the same time the play-offs started." Troy glanced at Andrea for confirmation. She nodded. Troy returned his attention to his boss.

Jaclyn leaned into her black executive chair. She crossed her legs. "At the risk of sounding disloyal to my man and my team, the Monarchs have shown they can lose on their own. Gerry doesn't need to go to the lengths of bribing a ref for that outcome."

Andrea spread her hands. "Gerry's not taking their losses for granted. Frankly, Jackie, last night's win proves you should never count out your man or your team."

A ghost of a smile flickered across Jaclyn's lips. "Why would Mario go to a reporter rather than the league?"

Troy drummed the fingers of his right hand on the arm of the cushioned chair. He couldn't understand Mario's motives, either.

Andrea shrugged one slender shoulder beneath her tan blazer and light blue blouse. "Otto doesn't want to risk an NBA investigation. Something like that can follow him his whole career."

Jaclyn nodded slowly. "I understand."

There was a subtle tone in Jaclyn's response that made Troy glance between the two women. Were they thinking of Andrea's past?

He stood, propelled by impatience to pace his boss's office. "I knew Gerry wasn't done antagonizing the team. I was looking in the wrong place." He put his hands on his hips. "If Mario is right and Gerry *is* trying to force Otto to throw the games, Gerry will be banned from the NBA for life."

"Probably." Andrea's soft caution drew his attention. "But if we don't have indisputable proof of Mario's claims, Gerry will sue us for libel. He'll try to take away everything we value."

Like the Monarchs, Troy thought. He wouldn't put that past Gerald.

Jaclyn held up both palms. "Let me think. We don't have proof because Gerry spoke to Otto. He didn't put anything in writing."

Troy circled the room. "That's right."

Jaclyn lowered her arms. "And no one overheard the conversation. It's Otto's word against Gerry's."

Troy paused. "This has Gerry Bimm, Puppet Master, written all over it. We know it's him."

Andrea looked at Troy with concern. "*Knowing* it to be true and *proving* it are two different things."

His impatience was growing. Troy kneaded the muscles at the back of his neck. "He hides behind other people, newspaper reporters, fake drug dealers, and now referees. He's too much of a coward to do his dirty work himself."

Andrea stood and walked to him. She put her hand on his arm and held his gaze. "All of what you're saying is true, Troy. We're not arguing that. But what happened the last time you went after Gerry without proof?"

Troy's muscles relaxed. He glanced at Jaclyn, who watched them with open interest. He returned his attention to Andrea. "He fired me."

"This time, we need a plan—a well-thought-out plan." Andrea gave him a pointed look.

Jaclyn stood. "Righteous indignation isn't a plan."

Troy broke eye contact with Andrea. "I understand."

Jaclyn continued. "No one wants Gerry out of the franchise more than I do. Working with him isn't my idea of a dream job. Nor do I like doing my job and your job while watching my back."

Troy sighed. "All right. What's the plan?"

Jaclyn's curious eyes touched on Andrea again before answering Troy. "It won't be easy. Gerry's right to be cautious. If he's caught, he could go to jail."

Andrea hugged her elbows. "We have to be careful. If Gerry knows we're on to him, he might blame everything on Otto."

Troy frowned. "Then what are we going to do?"

Jaclyn tapped her pen on the surface of her desk. "We'll have to catch Gerry in the act."

Troy shook his head. "That would be next to impossible. He's too cautious."

Jaclyn's smile was slow. "No, it's not. We're going to set up a sting."

He straightened in his chair. "I like the idea. How do we pull it off?"

Jaclyn crossed her arms. "I'll work out the details."

Troy nodded. "Should we have someone from the commissioner's office there?"

Andrea shook her head. "No. If Gerry doesn't offer Otto a bribe or try to blackmail him, we'll have wasted the commissioner's time. It will seem as though we're trying to cause trouble for Gerry rather than trying to protect the league and the franchise from more scandal."

Jaclyn touched the Monarchs lapel pin fastened to her bright green blouse. "We'll also make ourselves look stupid or paranoid—or both. But I wish we could have an independent party there to verify our story."

Andrea turned to Jaclyn. "I'd like to cover the sting for *Sports.*"

Jaclyn inclined her head. "Of course. I appreciate your bringing this problem to my attention. Once again, you've given us advance warning of a potentially damaging situation."

Troy took Andrea's hand, entwining her fingers with his own. "Yes, thanks again." He smiled as her cheeks flushed from his gratitude.

Andrea looked to Jaclyn. "Telling you about this rumor is giving me a better story. Besides, I'm helping Mario Nunez, who was a friend when I didn't have many."

Troy pulled his attention from Andrea to Jaclyn. "What can I do to help?"

Jaclyn drew her hand through her hair. "Right now, nothing. I'll update you as things progress."

Troy stood. "Then we'll get going."

Andrea collected her purse as she rose. "Thanks for letting us interrupt your morning."

Jaclyn escorted them to her office door. "No, thank *you* for telling us what Mario told you. The

Monarchs name will be associated with this scandal. There's no way around that if Gerry's trying to blackmail Otto. But at least this way we can minimize the damage."

Andrea said good-bye to Jaclyn, then waited while Troy took a few minutes to ask Jaclyn for an update on the team's "The Monarchs Return" campaign. His expression hardened as Jaclyn explained Gerald had put the project on hold.

When they reached his silver Lexus parked in the arena's lot, Troy held the passenger door open for Andrea. She thanked him, then watched as he settled his long, lean body behind the steering wheel.

Troy turned the ignition and the engine started with a purr. Andrea sighed with envy. Why didn't her car's engine start like that? With more than twenty years and almost two hundred thousand miles on it, she was happy when her car started at all.

Troy checked his car mirrors before merging into traffic. The silence in the luxury vehicle was thick but comfortable as he drove them from the Empire Arena to her apartment building in the Williamsburg area. Andrea mentally developed story angles and leads for this update on Gerald's activities. She imagined Troy was planning how to spin this event to minimize the long-term fallout for the Monarchs.

His voice startled her. "It's probably going to take a while for Jackie to arrange the sting."

Andrea studied his profile. His eyes were glued to the traffic. A frown knitted his brow. Was he regretting their decision to let Jaclyn take the lead on their response? "It's better to take our time with this problem. There's a lot at stake, for the franchise, for Otto, and for Gerry."

He navigated the Lexus around a double-parked

car. "I realize that. But I want to be there whenever she's able to pull it off."

Relief eased her muscles. "That's a good idea."

His shrug was self-deprecating. "I'm finally learning the value of having a plan."

"You're exerting impulse control. Impressive."

"With some things." He stopped at a red light before giving her a sexy wink.

Andrea chuckled. "It looks like we're both making progress. I've sent out some resumes."

"That's great. It's about time."

Her laughter faded to a smile. "You sound like Faith." She turned to look through the passenger window. "There's nothing like pending unemployment to light a fire under your job search."

Troy eased the car into the intersection once the traffic light turned green. "Look, I know things are hard everywhere now. But don't say yes to your first job offer, unless it's for a really good company. You're a good reporter. Don't settle."

Andrea stared at him, wide-eyed and speechless. A knot grew in her throat. It was difficult to swallow, difficult to breathe. "Thank you for saying that."

"It's the truth." Troy studied the street. Illegally parked cars and jaywalking pedestrians further snarled the traffic flow.

"It means a lot coming from you. You used to call me the enemy."

His grin was unrepentant. "If you weren't a good reporter, I wouldn't have considered you the enemy. You wouldn't have been a threat to the team."

Andrea laughed. "That's a backhanded compliment. I don't know whether to thank you or take your number out of my cell phone."

Troy's laughter joined hers. "We're always going

to be on different sides of the issues. Take this situation with Gerry. I'd rather the Monarchs were kept out of the story. But, if anyone's going to cover it, I'm glad it's you. At least that way, I know the Monarchs will get a fair shake."

"Thank you." Andrea sobered, still drinking in his words. They were definitely better for her confidence than the alcohol she'd been addicted to.

"But I do have a question for you."

A glance out the windshield showed they were blocks from her apartment building. Andrea's gaze dipped to his white-knuckled grip on the steering wheel. "What's that?"

"Am I one of your redemption projects?" Troy slowed as he crossed onto her street and began searching for a space to park.

Her eyes lowered again to his hands. Did the answer matter to him that much? Andrea opened her heart. "It started that way. I understood what you were going through since I'd gone through it myself."

Troy directed his car into an open space a few yards down the block from her apartment. "I don't want to be someone's special project, Andy."

"You stopped being my special project once I got to know you."

He put the car in park and turned to face her. "What does that mean?"

Her heart was racing. "You're a different person away from your executive image. You're not the arrogant, jerk executive who tries to tell me how to do my job. You're actually a nice guy."

Troy gave her the crooked smile that made her pulse trip. "I've been telling you that for years."

Andrea thought of the players rallying around him when he lost his job. It was a reaction worthy of a respected colleague and friend. The way he'd helped convince Constance's ex-husband to leave their apartment building showed he was a good person. And his attention to her needs when they were intimate was the sign of a caring lover.

She took a steadying breath. Still her voice was a thin whisper. "Seeing is believing. And I believe I'm falling in love with you."

Troy's expression cleared with surprise, knitted with confusion, then sharpened with desire. He leaned forward over the gear-shift console toward her and settled his lips against hers. Andrea leaned into him. His lips were firm but gentle as they moved over hers. There was a message in his kiss, something he was trying to convey. But she was too lost in his taste and touch to figure it out.

Andrea closed her eyes with a sigh, then breathed in to let his scent seduce her. She melted into him and parted her lips to kiss him more deeply. His touch was tender as his large, lean hand moved up her right arm to her shoulder.

She raised her hand to cup the back of his head. Andrea moaned as his tongue stroked hers. She gave chase, twining her tongue around his. She tried to move even closer. Troy's hand slid over her shoulder, pressing her torso to his. Her heart pounded in her chest, shortening her breath. She opened her mouth wider, wanting more of him. The restless feeling inside her was growing to a painful level.

Troy raised his head, releasing her mouth. "I—" He cleared his throat.

Andrea held her breath, waiting for his words.

Troy straightened away from her. "I'll walk with you to your apartment."

She watched Troy get out of the car. She hustled to

gather her scattered thoughts before he opened her door for her. His smile as he helped her out of the sedan and his touch on her elbow jumbled her mind again.

What did that kiss mean? How did he feel about what she'd told him? Had she spoken too soon? She wasn't going to ask him. She didn't want to be *that* woman.

But she was desperate to know.

Troy held the door open for her to walk into her apartment building's lobby. His hand on her shoulder stopped her from walking to the elevator. His ebony eyes were dark and glittering with unquenched desire as he looked down at her.

His kiss was a brief tribute that stole her breath. "I'm falling for you, too, Andrea Benson."

Her lips parted in surprise. A smile spread over her face as she watched him leave before she floated toward the elevators.

He was falling for her, too. Now, what did *that* mean?

Five days later, Troy sat in a rear, tall-backed booth in a dimly lit sports bar watching Gerald Bimm talk with Otto Nunez. The two men sat at one of the front tables. Saturday's off-hour lunchtime crowd was thin. Still, it provided enough cover for him, Andrea, and Jaclyn as they made themselves inconspicuous.

Gerald's back was to them. But, by leaning closer to Andrea seated beside him, Troy could see Otto clearly. The referee's features were tight with controlled anger.

Andrea pinched him, and Troy settled back into the booth.

"Between the suspense of tonight's game seven against the Cavs and this meeting, I might have a heart attack." Jaclyn sat on the inside of the booth across the table from Troy.

"Me too." Troy was only slightly exaggerating. The Monarchs had managed to tie the series with the Cleveland Cavaliers, three games each. Although he was hoping for a miracle, the basketball pundits didn't think Brooklyn's team would win.

"This meeting between Gerry and Otto shouldn't last much longer." Andrea sat beside Troy on the outside of the booth facing Otto's table. She was hard to recognize in a baggy brown sweatsuit with her silky dark hair tucked under a black baseball cap. At least Troy hoped Gerald didn't recognize her.

He checked his watch. Again. "It's already been thirty minutes."

"The longest thirty minutes of my life." Jaclyn finished her second glass of iced tea. "The worst part is not being able to see what's going on." Jaclyn had wanted to sit facing Otto and Gerald, but Troy was afraid her partner would spot Jaclyn as soon as he walked into the sports bar. She was hard to miss, dressed in a silver and black sheath dress in a Cleveland sports bar.

Troy considered his unsweetened iced tea. Had he already added the sugar? "We can't risk Gerry turning around and seeing you."

Andrea stiffened in her seat. "Otto just adjusted his baseball cap. That's our signal."

Finally! Relief and excitement surged through Troy as he followed Andrea from the booth. "Now, let's hope Gerry goes quietly." He grabbed the restaurant bill from the table and waited for Jaclyn and Andrea to precede him from the booth.

Gerald's beady brown eyes widened with recognition as he saw the group appear beside him. His expression gave Troy a sense of deep satisfaction. Well worth waiting for.

Jaclyn put her hand on the referee's shoulder. "Hello, Gerry. Hi, Otto. How are you?"

Otto's expression was a picture of relief. "I'm well. Thank you, Ms. Jones."

"Jackie." Gerald's cool gaze swept over each of them. "What are you all doing here?"

Jaclyn glanced at Troy and Andrea as they stood beside her. "Funny thing, Gerry. We heard a rumor that you're blackmailing referees in an effort to get them to throw play-off games."

Gerald shot a venomous look at Otto, who sat silent and impassive in the seat across the table from him. "That's absurd." He returned his attention to Jaclyn. "Where did you hear that?"

"I thought it was pretty absurd, too." Jaclyn shifted her hand from Otto's shoulder. Troy saw her white-knuckled grip on the back of the referee's chair. "After all, blackmailing officials, bribes, and tampering with the outcome of games are all against league rules. I was certain you knew that."

"Of course I do."

Troy almost believed Gerald's affronted tone. He stepped closer to Otto's table to give a server more room to walk past. "Then where did the rumors come from, Gerry?"

Gerald shrugged his shoulders beneath his dark blue jersey. "Maybe *you* started them, Troy. You've been more paranoid than usual lately. After all, you slandered me on ESPN."

Troy fought the discomfort of Gerald's comment. No one wanted to be reminded of mistakes from their past. Behind him, Andrea's hand settled on the small of his back. It was an encouraging gesture, a supportive touch, and he leaned into it. "Where there's smoke, there's fire, Gerry. I made the wrong call with the *Insider* blog. But I don't make the same mistake twice."

Gerald narrowed his eyes on Troy. "I'm happy for you."

Jaclyn settled her right hand on her hip. "So the rumors of you blackmailing refs aren't true, Gerry?"

Gerald looked directly at Jaclyn. "No, they're not."

Troy thought Jaclyn's left hand tightened on the back of Otto's chair as she continued to question her business partner. "And you have no idea where the rumors came from?"

Gerald didn't blink. "No, I don't."

Several silent moments passed as the two partners seemed to take each other's measure. Troy's impatience stirred. What was Jaclyn waiting for? Surely she hadn't changed her mind about reporting Gerald to the NBA's front office. He started to prompt her when Jaclyn held out her hand, palm up, in front of Otto. The referee unbuttoned the chest pocket of his tan corduroy shirt and withdrew a digital audio recorder. It was the same device Andrea had loaned Troy for his meeting with Mindy Sneal, the Monarchs Insider. Otto placed it in Jaclyn's palm.

Jaclyn held up the recorder so Gerald could see it. "Then tell me, Gerry, what will I hear when I listen to this recording?"

Otto removed his ball cap and dragged his blunt fingers through his thick hair. "Now, it's no longer your word against mine. It's been recorded."

All semblance of civility drained from Gerald's features. He pinned Otto with his glare. "You can't use that recording against me. This was a private conversation. You had no right to record it without my knowledge."

Troy arched a brow. "But it's OK for you to black-mail him?"

"Wait, Troy." Andrea pressed her hand into the center of his back again.

Jaclyn dropped the recorder into her oversized silver purse. "We can debate morality all day. The fact is, Gerry, you're violating league rules, and you were doing it to hurt your own team."

Troy heard the pain of betrayal in Jaclyn's voice.

Gerald's eyes shifted from Jaclyn's purse back to her face. "What are you going to do with that?"

Jaclyn adjusted her purse on her shoulder. "Give it to the commissioner. He'll determine what happens to you. But it doesn't look good, Gerry. You know what a stickler the commissioner is for the rules." She looked at the referee. "Care to join us, Otto? I'm sure Gerry can handle the bill."

Gerald sprang to his feet. Troy stepped forward, putting himself between Gerald and Jaclyn. Gerald shifted his attention to the marketing executive. "This isn't over."

Troy narrowed his eyes. "Somehow, Gerry, I think it is." He gestured for Andrea, Jaclyn, and Otto to precede him from the bar's dining area.

Troy hoped Gerald's chapter with the Monarchs

was indeed over. Would that clear the way for Troy to start over with the franchise?

That night, Troy joined Jaclyn in Quicken Loans Arena's visiting owner's suite to watch the final game of the Brooklyn Monarchs versus Cleveland Cavaliers seven-game play-off series. Win or go home.

Jaclyn welcomed him with a drink and gestured toward the older man by her side. "Troy, you remember Julian Guinn, Marc's father, don't you?"

Troy shook Julian's hand. "Yes. It's nice to see you again, Mr. Guinn."

Julian grinned. "Call me Julian. I'm too nervous to answer to anything else."

Ignoring the television monitors hanging around the suite's ceiling, Julian turned to view the basketball court below through the room's large window. Althea Gentry, Jaclyn's administrative assistant, joined him.

With her gaze on the couple, Jaclyn leaned closer to Troy. "They've just started dating."

Troy smiled. Jaclyn sounded almost smug. Did she have a hand in the budding romance?

The game was half an hour away. On the court, television crews were taking pregame footage. Players were warming up. Fans were filling the arena. Troy spotted Andrea taking her seat with the other reporters to record the game.

Jaclyn interrupted his thoughts. "Andrea helped me save the audio recording as a computer file. I e-mailed it to the commissioner."

Troy gave Jaclyn his attention. "Do you think Stern will ban Gerry from the NBA?"

Jaclyn sipped from her glass of iced cola. "I hope

so. What Gerry did isn't just bad for the team. It's bad for the league. But even if the commissioner doesn't ban him, Gerry can't come back to the Monarchs."

"Why not?"

Jaclyn's smile was bitter. "The morality clause in the partners contract states that if any partner violates NBA rules, he or she must immediately sell his or her shares equally to the remaining partners. The moment Gerry tried to affect the outcome of the play-offs, he broke our contract."

Troy arched a brow. "Gerry's no longer with the Monarchs?"

Jaclyn nodded. "Do you know what that means?"

Troy sighed his relief. "That Gerry won't have access to insider Monarchs information any longer."

Jaclyn gestured toward him with her glass. "And you have your job back."

Troy grinned. "That's the best news I've heard in a while."

Jaclyn nodded toward the court below them. "Let's hope we get some more good news tonight."

18

Andrea's palms were sweating. On the court five rows beneath the media section, the Brooklyn Monarchs and Cleveland Cavaliers were in the final game of their seven-game series. The winner would move to the next round of the play-offs. The game clock counted down the remaining two minutes and thirty-seven seconds of the game. The Monarchs had ended the first half with a tenuous 7-point lead. During the last twenty-one minutes, Cleveland had cut their bank in half, Monarchs 87, Cleveland 83.

In the seat in front of her, the *Cleveland Plain Dealer* reporter had lost his jaded expression. The middle-aged man no longer seemed confident of the game's outcome. Frankly, neither was Andrea.

Daniel Gibson, a Cleveland point guard, caught Jamal flatfooted at the post and grabbed the Monarchs' rebound. Andrea's gaze flew to DeMarcus coaching from the sideline. His sphinx-like mask dropped. She read his lips as he yelled one word, *Jamal*. The cocky point guard still had trouble on defense.

Gibson sped past Jamal and down the court to Cleveland's basket. The Monarchs gave chase, but

Gibson was a blur. His rapid reflexes and lightning speed kept the Cavaliers' hopes alive. Behind Andrea, Cleveland fans leapt to their feet in thunderous approval.

Gibson drove the ball to the basket for an easy layup. Cleveland closed in on the Monarchs lead, 87 to 85 with two minutes and thirty-three seconds left to the game. Serge snatched the ball midair and lobbed it forward to Vincent. The Monarchs center jogged back up the court, dribbling the ball with him. The veteran role player managed the clock and controlled the speed. The sudden molasses-like pace made Andrea tense. But she understood the older Monarchs couldn't allow the Cavaliers to force a faster tempo.

Behind Vincent, Warrick shared a few words with Jamal. The rookie point guard seemed uncomfortable even as he nodded his understanding. Had Warrick taken Jamal to task for his sloppy defense? The veteran had a gift for coaching on the court.

DeMarcus signaled for a twenty-second time-out. Andrea used the time to catch up with her copy. She sensed the reporters around her doing the same. Her fingers flew over the computer keys as she recapped the Cleveland plays and playmakers who were challenging the Monarchs' lead as well as the team's response as they fought back. She'd check for typos later.

The time-out ended. Andrea watched Jamal step up to defend Cleveland's Gibson. She wondered what DeMarcus had said to inspire the rookie. Warrick jogged past Vincent as the center kicked the ball out to him. He positioned his teammates with words and gestures. Andrea read the game clock. With two minutes and twenty-seven seconds left to the game, the Monarchs' lead stood at 2 points.

For the next seventy-five seconds, the lead went back and forth between the Cavaliers and the Monarchs. Gibson caught an easy shot from behind the perimeter for a three-point basket. The Cavaliers led the game, 101 to the Monarchs' 98. Their fans went wild. One minute and twelve seconds left in the game.

Anthony pulled in the ball for the Monarchs, drawing it away from the basket before tossing it to Vincent. The Monarchs' center hustled up court as Cleveland's Ramon Sessions shadowed him. Antawn Jamison guarded Serge at the post. Gibson kept Jamal from the perimeter. Anderson Varejao, the Cavaliers' forward, pressured Anthony on the right. Cleveland's Anthony Parker shadowed Warrick on the left. The crowd chanted "Defense!" in one thunderous and insistent voice.

Vincent feinted forward, pushing the Cavaliers back before passing the ball to Anthony. Nineteen seconds on the shot clock. Anthony stepped away from Varejao, luring the Cavaliers' defense toward him. Without a clear shot, he handed off to Warrick. Warrick caught the ball. Fifteen seconds on the shot clock. He spun toward the post, dribbling right. The Cavaliers followed him like the Pied Piper. Jamal remained unguarded just outside the perimeter. Warrick threw the ball behind him. Jamal claimed it on the bounce. He danced to the arc and leaped for the three-point swoosh. The game was tied at 101.

Forty-two seconds on the game clock. Gibson dribbled the ball back down court. Jamal hurried after him. The Monarchs defended their assignments in and around the paint. Anthony stood with Varejao.

Vincent stayed with Sessions. Serge blocked Jamison. Warrick defended Parker. In her mind, Andrea screamed "Defense!"

Thirty-eight seconds on the clock. The Monarchs covered the Cavaliers' offense like cheap suits. Jamal stepped up as Gibson surged forward—and drew the foul. Otto Nunez, the head referee, blew his whistle. The game clock stopped. The Cavaliers and Monarchs lined up on either side of the paint, waiting for Gibson to take his two free throws. Andrea's hopes remained high. Gibson was only forty-one percent at the line. Surely, he wouldn't make both baskets.

The first shot rode the rim before diving through. The second shot sank cleanly. Cavaliers, 103; Monarchs 101. Andrea was disgusted. *Now* Gibson decided to improve his free-throw percentage? *Now?*

Anthony jumped for the ball. He heaved it up to Vincent. The game clock started counting down from thirty-eight.

DeMarcus shouted instructions from the sidelines. Warrick directed his teammates on the court. Andrea felt the tension from five rows up. Was it from the players or from her? Less than a minute remained. The Cavaliers were up by 2. The Monarchs could go for the tie and send the game into overtime. But Andrea sensed the players' fatigue. If they didn't win in regulation, could they keep up with the younger team in overtime?

The game clock showed thirty-four seconds. The shot clock read twenty. Vincent advanced the ball to Anthony, who sent a rainbow to the basket. The shot fell short. Varejao jumped for the rebound. Serge slapped it away. Sessions reached for the loose ball. Vincent grabbed it from him, keeping the ball for the Monarchs.

Twenty-four seconds and counting. The shot clock turned off. Andrea's heart was beating too fast. She felt light-headed. Vincent hit Serge near the post. Serge passed the ball to Anthony. Nineteen seconds. Anthony faked a three. The Cavaliers surged forward, then shifted back. Anthony sent the ball back to Serge. Seventeen seconds. Serge stepped back and went for the tie. Jamison tipped the ball. The shot slapped the rim. Fourteen seconds. Serge grabbed his own rebound and hooked the ball to Jamal. Jamal went for the three. The shot came up short. Warrick leaped and tipped the ball in. The game was tied at 103. Overtime seemed inevitable.

Ten seconds on the game clock. The Cavaliers charged back down the court. Past half-court, Gibson sent the ball forward to Parker. Warrick stepped into the open lane and grabbed the ball in the air. He spun on a dime and sprinted back up court. Cavaliers' fans screamed their dismay.

Eight seconds. Seven seconds. Gibson was gaining on him. Six seconds. Five seconds. Warrick leaped for the rim and stuffed the basket. Monarchs 105, Cavaliers 103.

Andrea blinked at the score. The Monarchs had won. They'd beaten the odds. After losing the first three games in the best-of-seven-games series, they'd swept the Cavaliers to advance in the play-offs. She didn't think she'd ever stop smiling.

Monday morning, Troy got to the office early. He was determined to get the promotional campaign he and Jaclyn had approved back on track. Steam poured from his ears when he realized just how much damage Gerald had done to the schedule and the ads he'd had designed. Troy loosened his tie and freed the top button of his shirt.

The knock on his open door put a break on his rising temper. He looked up from his desk and found Constance smiling in his doorway.

She crossed his threshold. "Welcome back, Mr. Marshall."

Troy put down the pen he was using to update the advertising schedule and stood. "I thought we'd agreed on Troy." He gestured toward the three black guest chairs in front of his desk.

"Troy." Constance settled into one of the cushioned seats. "Faith, Tiffany, and I watched the game Saturday night. It was so exciting."

Troy sat again. "The Monarchs defied the odds when they won the Cavs series."

Constance's gaze dropped to his desk. Her glow faded. "You're updating the Monarchs' new image campaign."

"We've missed several deadlines."

Constance gave him an earnest look. "I'm really sorry about that, Mr.—Troy. I didn't think you'd like the changes Mr. Bimm made to the design, so I brought the files to Ms. Jones. She agreed that the redesigns weren't any good."

Troy picked up the customer order form for one of the ad changes Gerald had made. "You're right. We can't announce 'The Monarchs Return' with a quarter-page, black-and-white ad. That's not the tone we're looking for."

Constance relaxed. "I thought it would be better to run the ads late. They say you only get one chance to make a good first impression."

What happened to the timid woman he'd hired? Constance had changed a lot in the three weeks since he'd met her. The woman sitting before him was much more relaxed and, more important, confident.

"You made the right call, Connie. Thank you."

Constance's cheeks bloomed with color. "Thank you, Mr.—Troy." She gestured toward the folder on his desk. "Would you like me to call the publications to reschedule the ads?"

Troy collected the ad forms. "Not yet." He was still pissed over Gerald's sabotage, but Constance was correct. He only had one chance to launch this campaign. It had to be right. "I'm going to review the ad dates again. Once I'm done, I'd like you to contact the publications."

"Of course. Did you want me to put together a list of giveaways for—"

Another knock on his door interrupted them. Warrick Evans gave him a mock scowl. "Vacation time's over, slacker. Get to work."

Constance's surprised laughter made Troy's lips twitch. He stood as he laughingly admonished. "Don't encourage him."

"I don't need encouragement." Warrick strode into Troy's office with his hand outstretched. "Welcome home, man. Good to see you."

Troy noted the point guard was wearing a black T-shirt with his baggy black shorts. Warrick was back on the starting lineup. What did that mean for Barron?

"Thanks, Rick." Troy shook the guard's hand and slapped him on the back. "It's good to be home. Congratulations again on Saturday night's win."

Warrick stepped back. "So, what's the word on Gerry?"

Constance stood. "I'd better get to work."

Warrick turned to her. "I didn't mean to interrupt."

Troy spoke at the same time. "There's no need to

leave. You can hear this, too. The NBA has barred Gerry from team offices and all NBA arenas, pending an investigation into the blackmail allegations."

Warrick frowned. "But Andrea's story said Gerry's conversation with Otto had been recorded."

Troy slid his hands into the front pockets of his pants. "The commissioner still wants to talk to Gerry and Otto personally."

Warrick shrugged. "There's no way Gerry can explain that recording. This is probably a formality."

Constance nodded. "And hopefully, it won't take too long."

Troy looked at Warrick. "In the meantime, I hope it's not a distraction to the team."

Warrick shook his head. "Stop worrying, man. We've got this."

Constance took a step backward. "Everything will work out. I'll leave you gentlemen to talk alone now and get some work done."

As Constance left the office, Troy gestured toward the visitors' chairs. "Do you have a few minutes?"

Warrick took a seat. "Sure. Practice doesn't start for another couple of hours. I was just coming to see you before hitting the weight room."

"Thanks." Troy gave him a searching look. "How's the team feeling about playing the Knicks?"

Warrick rested his right ankle on his left knee. "We're excited to start the series tonight. We know it's not going to be easy. But, hey, the Cavs series wasn't a walk in the park, either."

Troy nodded toward Warrick's black T-shirt. "I'm glad you're starting. What's going on with Barron?"

"Do you mean, is he still drinking?" Warrick nodded. "I think so. We took a risk with him. Some of us weren't sure we should have let it go so long. But in the end, Bling made the decision for us. He wouldn't change, so we had to."

Troy knew it must have been a difficult decision for DeMarcus to change the starting lineup and for Warrick to take over Barron's spot. "I don't know what it will take to get Barron to clean up his act."

"Let's hope it's nothing drastic."

"Have you talked with Mary?"

A cloud settled over Warrick's expression at the mention of his wife. A moment passed before he answered. "Not since game one of the Cavs series."

Troy's eyebrows lifted. "That's more than two weeks ago."

Warrick straightened in his seat and put both feet on the floor. "I know. She won't return my calls. She left me a note instead."

"What did it say?" Was he prying? It seemed that Warrick wanted to talk.

"She needs time."

"How much time?"

"I don't know. She didn't say."

That couldn't be good. "I'm sorry, Rick."

Warrick stood. His movements were much slower than when he'd entered the room. "I'd better get to the weight room."

Troy rose with him. His friend was hurting. He didn't know what to say or do to help him. He circled his desk to lay his hand on Warrick's shoulder. "Good luck. With everything."

"I'll need it."

Troy watched the other man leave his office. His curved shoulders and dragging steps indicated the pain Warrick carried, and not just in his body. Troy hoped he never experienced that kind of hurt. He didn't know if he'd survive it.

* * *

"I saw you through the window." Jenna stopped beside Andrea's table in the little sandwich shop. They were a couple of blocks from Madison Square Garden, home of the New York Knicks. Game one of the Monarchs versus Knicks series was almost an hour away—and counting.

Jenna angled her chin toward the window beside Andrea. It was the front of the eatery, which was made of glass. The *Times* sports reporter rested her palm on the back of the empty chair on the other side of Andrea's table. "Mind if I join you?"

Andrea tried to cover her surprise. She swallowed a mouthful of her roasted turkey wheat wrap. "Of course not."

"Thanks." Jenna removed her laptop case from her shoulder and settled it beside her seat out of customer traffic. She placed her tray of chicken salad and bottled water on the table before folding her model-thin body into the dark wood chair. "I haven't seen you since that miraculous Monarchs win in Cleveland Saturday. Good job on getting the scoop about Gerald Bimm and the blackmail rumor. You're the original intrepid reporter."

Andrea listened hard but didn't hear any of the meanness that had tainted the tone of reporters when they'd spoken to her in the past. "Thank you."

Jenna looked puzzled. "That was a big deal. You were the first with the story that an owner could be banned from the NBA for life. Why aren't you excited?"

Andrea sipped the cup of coffee she'd ordered with her turkey wrap. Old fears and uncertainties tried to take hold of her. "I got another job rejection today. *Sports* is closing in less than two months and I'm running out of places to apply."

Jenna lowered her forkful of salad. "Where are you sending your resumes?"

"I sent one to the *Horn*." Andrea watched her companion chew and swallow a mouthful of salad. Was that bowl of lettuce with pieces of chicken actually filling?

"They can't afford you."

Andrea rushed to swallow her coffee before she choked on it. "I work for *Sports*. I'm sure the starting salary of every other paper in the city is almost twice what I'm making now."

Jenna held Andrea's gaze. "And you're worth more than that. You're aiming too low."

Andrea ignored the wrap in her hands and stared at the veteran reporter. "You think those other papers rejected me because they thought they couldn't afford me?" That was absurd.

Jenna swallowed her ice water. "You sent them your resume with clippings of your exclusive interview with Jackie Jones, your expose on the Insider's identity, and your breaking news that Gerry Bimm may be banned from the NBA, right?"

"I didn't include the article about Gerry. It hadn't run at the time."

Jenna waved her fork. "It doesn't matter. The other two clips are strong. Those editors took one look at your work and knew they couldn't afford you. And, even if they did hire you, a bigger paper would come along and steal you away in a matter of months."

Andrea laughed as she picked up her coffee. "I love your fantasy world. It's very pretty there."

Jenna didn't even crack a smile. "I'm serious." She

stabbed some more lettuce and the last cube of chicken. "You think the papers aren't giving you the time of day because of that Jackie Jones incident four years ago, don't you?"

Andrea stiffened. Her turkey wrap turned to cardboard in her mouth. She washed it down with coffee. "What other reason could it be?"

"I just gave you the other reason. And I'm right."

Andrea frowned at her. "You think the newspapers don't think they can afford me. So what am I supposed to do about that?"

"Aim higher." Jenna pushed her salad plate away from her.

The plate still had several lettuce leaves and slices of cucumber and green peppers. Jenna would probably be able to finish them off if she had some nice blue cheese dressing. She considered the other woman's delicate frame. The dressing probably would be too many calories.

Andrea lifted her coffee cup. "Do you think I should send my resume to the *Times*?"

"Yes." Jenna drained her water.

Andrea finished her coffee. She'd fantasized about working for *The New York Times* one day. She'd packed that dream away three years ago. "I'm not sure."

Jenna sighed as though she cared. "The industry isn't holding your past against you anymore. *You're* the one who can't move on."

"After I lost my job because of the Jackie Jones article, it took me more than a year to get another one. Every paper slammed the door in my face."

"Jackie's grandfather asked them to. That won't happen again." Jenna leaned toward her. "Be bold, Andrea. Take a chance on yourself."

Andrea gave Jenna a hesitant nod. "All right. What

could it hurt?" She watched Jenna's intense frown ease into an encouraging smile.

She couldn't believe how nervous she was at the thought of sending a resume to *The New York Times*. Before this conversation with Jenna, Andrea thought she'd forgiven herself for her past missteps. Now she realized she had lingering doubts and uncertainties. What would it take for her to find the courage to truly start over?

19

"My name is Barron 'Bling' Douglas and I'm an alcoholic."

Andrea blinked at Barron seated beside her in the *New York Sports*'s cluttered, stained, and musty conference room Tuesday morning. "Barron, I'm—"

"That's what you want me to say, isn't it?" Barron glared at her.

Andrea sank farther into her chair, weighted by disappointment. When Barron had shown up at the newspaper, she thought he was ready to accept her help. "Only if you believe it's true."

"And then you'd print it in your paper, right?"

She refused to give up hope. Just as she still hoped the Monarchs could win even one of their games against the Knicks despite their convincing loss the night before. "Only if you told me I could."

"Why should I tell you anything?" His words slapped at her.

Andrea slapped back. "Because I've been where you are now. And, if you don't get yourself together, you're going to end up where I was. I can assure you, it's not a pretty fall. It's an even uglier landing."

His surprised expression diffused her temper. "You're an alcoholic?"

"I'm a *recovering* alcoholic." It didn't shame her to admit that as it had in the past. "I lost everything— my job, my home, my reputation—before I convinced myself to stop drinking. You've lost your starting spot. How much more are you going to give up before you take control of your life?"

Barron ran his palm over his thick, black braids. They were longer now than they had been at the beginning of the season. He looked away from her to stare across the room, but Andrea didn't think he saw the dented and dusty boxes piled against the opposite wall. His eyes were focused on a spot farther away.

"Why are you here, Barron?"

He didn't answer right away, but Andrea knew he'd heard her. She could tell by the stillness in his posture and the awareness in his eyes.

Barron leaned his elbows on the conference table and dropped his forehead into his palms. "I think I need help."

"Why?" Andrea clenched her fists. She wouldn't push him. No matter how much she wanted to. She would not push him.

Barron raised his head. He folded his hands together on the table. "I've wanted an NBA championship ring since I was eleven years old. Now I'm in the play-offs after thirteen seasons. I'm finally in the play-offs. And I'm blowing it."

He glanced at her as if to see whether she was listening to him. In silence, he looked away.

"Why do you think you're blowing it?" She knew the answer. Did he?

Again, he didn't answer right away. Barron arched

his back as though easing the tension building there. "Because I'm scared."

Andrea's own muscles began to relax. She exhaled in quiet relief. "Of what?"

"That I'm not good enough. That I don't belong."

"So you're sabotaging yourself by not practicing and not working out. And you're getting drunk every day."

Barron hunched his shoulders. "I drink because it makes me feel better."

"Do you want to get drunk or do you want a ring?"

Barron met her gaze. "I want a ring."

"What are you willing to do for it?"

He propped his elbows on the table and dropped his head into his hands again. "I don't know."

So close. Andrea leaned forward. "Does the next drink matter more to you than playing in the NBA? Than earning a championship ring?"

Barron hesitated. "No. I need to stop drinking. I know I'm ruining my career. But I don't think I *can* stop."

She wouldn't tell him that if she could do it, he could, too. She wouldn't minimize his fears that way. But she had to help him face them. "It isn't easy, but you don't have to do this on your own. The NBA will find a program to help you."

Seconds ticked by, growing into minutes. Andrea watched Barron stare down the table. Finally, he nodded. He settled deeper into his seat and let his head fall back. "I'll try."

Andrea swallowed a sigh of relief. "Only one percent of college basketball players make it to the NBA. You've beaten the odds before, Barron."

A slow smile vanquished the tension across his

face. "Yeah, I did." He turned to her. "What about your article?"

Andrea stood. She was almost giddy with success. "I wasn't after a story. I wanted to help you. I didn't want you to go through what I went through."

Barron rose and offered his hand. "Thank you."

With the warmth in his voice and the sincerity in his eyes, Andrea felt as though she'd won the Pulitzer Prize for Best Human Being. Or at least gotten a better paying job.

She took his hand. "You're welcome."

He let her hand drop. "I'd be willing to give you that interview."

Andrea caught her breath. "Are you sure?"

He shrugged. "Maybe it will help other people who are in the same boat I'm in."

She sat again. "It will."

Troy stood after hearing Jaclyn's knock on his door Tuesday afternoon. His boss's somber expression made the muscles on the back of Troy's neck tighten. "The Monarchs had a bad loss against the Knicks last night, but we have six more games."

Jaclyn crossed his office and sat in one of the seats in front of Troy's desk. "This isn't about the series. Not exactly."

Troy sat. "What's wrong?"

"I just met with Marc and Barron. Barron's entered a substance abuse program."

Relief swept over him. "That's great news, isn't it?"

"It *is* great news. Marc and I are very happy for Barron. We know he'll succeed because he wants to." Jaclyn crossed her legs, adjusting the skirt of her bold blue dress over her knee. "He's asked to be put on IL for the rest of the play-offs."

Troy's thoughts scattered in shock. "The Inactive List? Can't he play *and* do the program?"

Jaclyn touched her Monarchs lapel pin, fastened near the shoulder of her dress. "The stress of the play-offs escalated his addiction."

Troy's thoughts raced. How could he keep the team together? "He doesn't have to start. He can come off the bench."

"Barron doesn't believe he can help the team in his current condition. He's right, Troy. If he comes off the court now, he can start getting stronger, mentally and physically, for next season."

Troy failed. Again. "I know he and Marc have butted heads. And Barron's had some problems on and off the court. I just wish there was a way for him to be part of our play-off run."

Jaclyn held his gaze. "Is that the reason you didn't tell us Barron's drinking was getting worse?"

Troy forced himself to meet her eyes. "Yes."

Jaclyn nodded. "How did *you* know about it?"

Troy lowered his eyes. "I follow him on Twitter. He started sending messages, inviting people to drink with him."

Jaclyn sat straighter in her chair. "In the future, don't keep information like that from Marc or me. You're not helping anyone by keeping secrets."

Troy felt his face heat. "I'm sorry."

Jaclyn folded her hands in her lap. "Barron's a part of the team, whether he's on the court or the sideline. We won't leave him out of the play-offs."

Troy sat back in his seat. "How is he?"

Jaclyn appeared to consider her answer. "He seemed relieved."

Troy supposed that made sense. The pressure was off. Barron could take care of himself now. "And Marc?"

Jaclyn gripped the arms of the cushioned chair. "Our play-off run has just gotten harder. We're down to twelve men in the rotation. The Knicks have fifteen. Let's hope everyone else stays healthy." She stood. "Prepare a statement for the media. I don't want the press speculating about the reason Barron's on IL. Let's get in front of this."

Troy rose to his feet. "Are you sure you want to tell the media Barron's going into rehab?"

Jaclyn seemed puzzled. "They're going to wonder why our team captain is standing on the sidelines in a suit. I'd rather be upfront with them than have them come up with reasons on their own."

He shook his head, staring at his desk. "I wish the press and the public could respect Barron's privacy."

She rested her hands on her hips. "The fans have a right to know what's going on with their players."

"It could be a distraction."

"Only if we let it."

Troy nodded despite his continued misgivings. "I'll have something for your review within the hour."

Jaclyn stopped at the door. "Barron said Andrea played a big part in convincing him to get help for his drinking."

Her words gave Troy pause. "I knew she was concerned about him."

"She's a very special lady. She's been through a lot. And, instead of breaking her, it's made her stronger."

Troy slid his hands into the front pockets of his pants. This was the opening he'd been hoping for. "Andy told me what you did for her after she lost her job."

Jaclyn crossed her arms and rested her shoulder against the doorjamb. "She'd suffered enough."

"But she wrote an article full of lies that showed you in a bad light."

Jaclyn shrugged her left shoulder. "I knew it wasn't true. The people who mattered knew it wasn't true. She'd paid for her mistake. It was time for both of us to move on."

Troy shook his head in amazement. "Not a lot of people would have seen things that way."

"She's a good reporter."

Troy narrowed his gaze. "You weren't tempted to hold a grudge against her after that article?"

Jaclyn shook her head. "Not at all."

"Why not?"

"What good would that do?" Jaclyn straightened away from the door. "Even though she says our history together doesn't have anything to do with the way she treats us, her style of getting the whole story and not just the sound bites Gerry fed her has worked to our benefit."

"Her last tip helped us move Gerry out of the franchise."

"And for that, I will be eternally grateful." Jaclyn dropped her arms. "The two of you are good together. She keeps you from acting on impulse. She's been a good influence on you—and Barron. Have you stopped seeing her as the enemy?"

Troy forced himself not to squirm under Jaclyn's teasing regard. "Yes. I've realized she's not out to get the team."

She smiled. "Good. I hope you're both very happy together." Jaclyn left his office.

Troy sat, spinning his chair back to his computer. He hoped they'd be happy, too. His career was back on track. His love life was looking up, and the Monarchs had advanced in the play-offs. What more could a person ask for?

"You *are* a good cook." Andrea's taste buds were still singing from the seafood platter Troy had prepared for their dinner.

"I'm not just a pretty face." He led the way into his kitchen as they cleared the table together.

Andrea chuckled. "I suspected that when you and Serge made dinner for us the other day. But I'm even more impressed now that I've witnessed your skills without Serge's assistance."

Troy turned from the sink, took Andrea into his arms, and gave her a deep, lingering kiss that curled her toes inside her stockings.

He raised his head, keeping his eyes on her lips. "I'm not just good in the kitchen."

Andrea licked her lips and felt his arms tighten around her waist. "I know. You're also very good in the office." She grinned, wiggling out of his embrace. With a bounce in her step, she left the kitchen to continue clearing the dining room table.

"Very funny." His voice followed her.

She laughed. "I thought so."

Troy grabbed the serving tray and utensils. "Has Connie's ex-husband come back?"

Andrea balanced their empty glasses and the pitcher of what remained of their iced tea. "No, thank goodness. Connie's lawyer thinks he's gone back to Iowa. At least, his response to the divorce filing has an Iowa return address. It looks like he's going to fight it."

Troy moved to the kitchen sink. "I'm sorry about that. I hope he reconsiders."

"We all do." Andrea studied the play of muscles beneath Troy's navy blue jersey as he lifted dishes from the sink to place them in the dishwasher. Her eyes were drawn to his tight glutes. Her hands itched to stroke them. "But, in the meantime, even our neighbors are keeping watch for Wade. We don't want anything to happen to Connie or Tiff."

Troy looked up from the dishwasher to capture Andrea's gaze. "And I don't want anything to happen to you. Be careful if he does come back."

His words added to the warmth she already felt from watching him. "You're the one who acts impulsively, remember?"

Troy grunted. "Just promise to be careful."

"I promise." Andrea rested a hip against his kitchen counter. "I got your statement today about Barron going on IL to start his treatment."

Troy added detergent to the machine's reserve. "I wish he didn't have to come off the court, but it's his call. And Jackie and Marc support him."

"I do, too." Andrea recalled Barron's tension. "I spoke with him this morning about his decision to enter the program. He needs to put distance between himself and the fears that cause him to drink. At least until he can learn how to resist those triggers."

Troy locked the dishwasher's door as he straightened. "You called him after I sent the press release? I guess I should have expected that." He sounded disappointed.

Andrea corrected him. "Barron came to the *Sports* office *before* you issued the statement. He agreed to let me interview him."

Troy gave her a sharp look. "You're doing a story

on Barron's addiction?" He didn't seem as excited at the prospect as she was.

"Barron can help readers understand why people fight against admitting they have a problem. His story could convince people who are under similar pressure to get help. It could help prevent them from making the same mistakes he made."

Troy rubbed the back of his neck. "Don't you think Barron deserves his privacy?"

Confused, Andrea searched Troy's features. "He *offered* to let me interview him."

"With a little persuasion?" The skepticism in Troy's eyes hurt.

"I'm telling you the truth. I didn't talk him into this interview. He asked if the only reason I'd been after him to talk about his alcoholism was because I wanted to write about it—"

"There, you see?"

She raised her voice over his interruption. "And I told him no. I'm concerned about his welfare because I know what he's going through."

"Use your own story if you want to help people."

Her irritation was straining at its leash. Why was he attacking her? She'd thought they'd come further than this. "Come on, Troy. You know public figures bring more attention to issues."

Troy crossed his arms. "I also know stories about sex, drugs, and athletes sell more papers than articles about the good they do in the community."

She was numb. How could he claim to love her but know so little about her? "That's not the kind of reporter I am. I don't exploit people to help Will sell papers."

"You expect me to believe he's never asked you to?"

Willis was excited this morning when she'd told

him about her interview with Barron. She pushed the memory from her mind. That wasn't the reason she'd interviewed the NBA player. "I expect you to believe I never would. I've covered the Monarchs' food drives and clothing drives. I've written about their work at the Morning Glory Chapel, including donating money so the chapel could expand its homeless shelter."

Troy inclined his head. "Those were good articles—"

"I don't have to prove anything to you. I know I'm doing the right thing. I'm trying to help people."

"I don't see how this article helps Barron."

She took a breath to stave her rising temper. "Obviously, *he* does, otherwise he wouldn't have allowed me to interview him."

Troy uncrossed his arms and left the kitchen. "I have a problem believing Barron agreed to the interview."

Andrea followed him, afraid to even ask the question. "Do you think I'm lying?"

"I think you did more persuading than you're admitting."

His words were a punch to her heart. "Why don't you trust me? Why am I back to being the enemy?"

Troy spun toward her. "The team has had to cope with Barron's erratic behavior, the Insider, and then finding out one of the franchise owners was willing to blackmail a referee to have them lose in the play-offs. It's enough, Andy. Give Barron his space."

Andrea's shoulders dropped. "Is that what you think about me?" She cleared her throat. "I'm not out to get Barron or the team. I'm writing this article to help as many people as I can."

Troy sighed. "You're always looking for ways for

atonement. That's why you invited a homeless woman and her child to move in with you."

"It's worked out well." Andrea crossed her arms and angled her chin.

"It's also the reason you convinced a professional athlete to enter a substance abuse program."

"What's wrong with that?"

"When will it be enough?"

"Why does it have to be?"

Troy spread his arms. "You're a sports reporter. Write about the game."

Andrea shook her head. "I have a platform that allows me to help people, and I want to use it."

Troy paced across the room, massaging the back of his neck. "I don't want you to write that piece."

"This will not be a negative article." She felt like a broken record. "Why won't you believe me?"

"You may not mean for it to show the Monarchs in a bad light, but a lot of readers will interpret it that way." He spoke with his back to her.

"Not the way I intend to write it."

"That's a gamble, and this isn't a good time for it. It will pull the team's attention from the play-offs."

Andrea hooked her hands onto her hips. "In your mind, I don't think there will ever be a good time to run a story that doesn't glorify the Monarchs."

Troy looked over his shoulder toward her. "You're probably right. I'm asking you not to run this one."

Andrea's muscles went slack with shock. "You're telling me what to write?"

He faced her. "I'm asking you."

"You can't do that."

"I am."

Andrea struggled to pull her thoughts back together. "You're my lover, not my editor."

His expression was sad, almost tormented. "Are we always going to butt heads?"

Andrea's eyes stung. "I'm in love with you. But I won't change who I am. I wouldn't ask you to change, either."

"I'm in love with you, too, Andy. But I have a responsibility to the team. Don't ask me to choose between you."

Andrea's legs were heavy as they carried her to his sofa. She lifted her large brown purse to her shoulder and slipped her feet into her shoes. "Maybe this relationship wasn't a good idea." She waited a beat, but he didn't respond. "It looks like we both have a lot to think over."

Troy didn't move. "Maybe we do."

Stop me. Don't let me leave. Tell me that you trust me. You've already said you love me.

Silence continued. Andrea left his condo and crossed to the elevator doors.

How can you break up with someone after you tell her you love her? She swiped away the tears that rolled down her cheeks. She'd given him her heart. Did she have to give up her career, too? She'd fought so hard to reclaim it. Why wasn't her love enough?

20

A gentle knock on Troy's office door Thursday morning distracted him from his regrets. He looked up to find Constance in his doorway. The concern in her eyes drew his full attention.

"Mr. Bimm is here to see you." She stepped aside.

Gerald appeared in the threshold. He watched Constance leave before giving Troy a wry smile. "'Mr. Bimm'? Mindy used to say, 'Gerry's here.'"

"Connie isn't Mindy." *Thank God.* Troy got to his feet with reluctance. "What do you want, Gerry?"

"I came to say good-bye."

Music to his ears. Maybe now the franchise could focus on rebuilding. But if the other man only wanted to give his regards, why was he taking one of the seats in front of Troy's desk?

"Good-bye." Troy returned to his chair.

The former Monarchs co-owner settled into the center visitor seat. Even as he was preparing to leave the franchise, Gerald was still getting in Troy's face— literally and figuratively.

Gerald had the air of someone who may have had a setback but refused to be counted out. He crossed his legs, then adjusted the crease of his navy trousers. "I've got some opportunities in Reno."

"Good luck." Troy didn't care whether Gerald was going to Nevada or the moon. He'd savor the knowledge that the Monarchs' nemesis was leaving New York.

Gerald studied Troy for several silent seconds. "You think you beat me. But it wasn't you. It was Jackie and Andrea."

The other man was baiting him. Troy wouldn't react. That was something else he'd learned from Andrea. He breathed through the pain in his heart at the thought of her. *Why did she have to run Barron's article?* "It was a team effort."

Anger flickered in Gerald's eyes. "How do you feel knowing that by trying to protect the team you caused it more trouble than I ever did?"

It was harder to resist reacting to that. But coming from his former boss, the charge didn't sting as much as it had when Jaclyn had made it. "It all worked out in the end." Troy pulled his chair under his desk and folded his hands on its surface. "I want to know why you risked everything to destroy the team your uncle helped create."

Temper burned brighter in Gerald's brown eyes. His skin flushed, almost matching his dark red shirt. His gaze traveled around Troy's office. What was the former partner thinking as he viewed the news clippings that decorated the walls with details of successes from the Monarchs' recent past?

Gerald returned his attention to Troy. "My uncle was an equal partner with Gene Mannion, Cedrick Tipton, and Jackie's grandfather. But he never received any credit for his role in the Monarchs' success. Instead, Frank Jones conspired to push my uncle out."

"What?" The word was a sigh of impatience.

"When Mannion died, he left his twenty-five percent of the franchise to Frank, making Jackie's grandfather a majority owner. Frank gave one percent of his shares to Cedrick. That left my uncle as the minority shareholder."

Troy heard the resentment in Gerald's voice but knew the other man had revised history. "Your uncle was more interested in making money than he was in building the team. That's why Mannion left his shares to Frank."

"Did Jackie tell you that?"

"It's common knowledge."

Gerald's voice rose with his anger. "It's a lie the Jones family spread about my uncle."

Troy knew that wasn't true. "You got yourself banned from the NBA for life to punish Jackie's family for not giving your uncle credit for the Monarchs' success?" Did Gerald hear how insane that was?

Gerald cocked his head. "Sound familiar?"

"No." What was Gerald implying?

"You'll take any risk to protect the Monarchs, just as I'll go to any length to avenge my family."

Troy's stomach turned. "I'm nothing like you."

Gerald laughed. "You got yourself fired trying to protect the Monarchs."

Troy's face burned. "A lot of people were hurt by the Insider."

Gerald smirked. "Whenever the media runs a story that you don't like about the team, you punish them. How can you blame me for punishing Jackie for the way her family treated my uncle?"

Troy stiffened. "It's my job to protect the team's image."

"You alienated the media because they didn't always

write positive stories about the Monarchs." Gerald's lips stretched into a wide, mocking smile. "How does that old saying go? 'There's no such thing as bad press.'"

Troy leaned back in his chair. "The fact is, you're blaming Jackie and her family for your uncle's mistakes."

"And who are you blaming when you strike out at the media for taking potshots at your team?" Gerald stood. "We're alike. We both have something to protect and we're willing to do whatever it takes to accomplish our goal."

Troy watched Gerald leave his office. The former Monarchs co-owner was wrong. They were nothing alike. Gerald was the one deluding himself about his uncle. Popular opinion was that Quinton Bimm had been a drunk and a philanderer. He'd have bled the franchise dry.

Troy wasn't blaming other people for his mistakes. He wasn't out for revenge. He was hard on the media because the media were hard on his team. This was about the team. It had nothing to do with him.

The screeching telephone interrupted Andrea as she second-guessed herself Thursday morning. *Thank goodness.* She rubbed an area on the left side of her chest, cleared her throat, then lifted the receiver. "*Sports.* Andrea Benson."

"You made me sound good." Barron sounded surprised.

Andrea was surprised as well. She'd only given Barron the draft of the feature she'd written about his personal and professional struggles that morning after working on it Tuesday evening and all day Wednesday. "You've already read the story?"

"Twice."

Andrea checked her wristwatch. It was barely eleven o'clock. "I just sent it to you an hour ago."

"It was a fast read."

That was a good start. But was the story worth it? Which should she choose, her lover or her career?

Andrea tapped out the computer key commands that pulled the electronic version of the feature onto her monitor. "Are you comfortable with it?" Did she want him to take the decision out of her hands? Andrea blushed. She didn't know.

"Like I said, you made me sound good."

Andrea heard papers shuffling in the background as though Barron was reviewing the draft for a third time as they talked on the phone. "Did you think I'd make you sound like the villain?"

"Well, yeah." His voice deepened with regrets. "I let my teammates down. I let my coaches down. I let everybody down. The fans. Myself."

Andrea hurt for him. "You're not a bad person, Bling. You just need help working through some things. Like I did."

Barron grunted. "You didn't turn out too bad."

Andrea chuckled at the stingy praise. "And you'll be fine, too. But in the meantime, are you sure you want to go with this article? You don't have to. I'll understand if you want me to pull it."

Barron didn't hesitate. "Let's go with it. I mean, this article will help people. And, you know, after all the people I hurt, I want to help some. You know what I mean?"

"I understand." That's what she'd been trying to do for the past four years, help people. If she backed off now, she'd be breaking a promise she'd made to herself. Was she willing to do that? Could she compromise herself, even for Troy?

Barron was still talking. "Thanks for not giving up on me. I mean, when I didn't want to listen, you got in my face. And when I didn't want to do the article, you said it wasn't about me. It was about other people who needed me. I owe you."

Andrea blinked. The feature wasn't about Barron. It wasn't about her or Troy, either. It was about all the people who were struggling with the same personal demons she and Barron were fighting. It was about the kids who thought they'd be set for life if they could just make it to the NBA. Because even more than covering professional sports, she wanted to write articles that made a difference in people's lives. If Troy couldn't understand that, then maybe he wasn't Mr. Right For Her after all.

She took a breath to ease the constriction in her chest. "You can repay me by not giving up on yourself."

"I won't." His voice was determined. "When will the story run?"

"Sunday." Andrea glanced toward Willis's office. He'd planned a prominent spot for the feature. At the time, she hadn't cared. Now it was important to her.

"Two days after the Monarchs' game three against the Knicks." Barron's observation reclaimed Andrea's attention.

She smiled. Athletes tended to interpret things in terms of their sports calendars. "Maybe the article will inspire them for Tuesday's game four."

Barron's chuckle was dry. "They split the first

two games with the Knicks. They're playing better without me."

Andrea sensed his uncertainty. It was important for Barron to remain confident and positive. "Focus on getting healthy. You'll help them with their run for the championship next season."

Barron exhaled a deep breath. "That's right. Back-to-back championship titles. You heard it here first."

Andrea chuckled. "I'll write that down. See you at Friday's game."

Barron and Andrea wrapped up their conversation before she recradled the phone. With her hand still on the receiver, she gathered courage for her next conversation. She suspected it wouldn't progress nearly as well.

Forty minutes later, she faced Troy behind his closed office door. There was more than his desk between them. They hadn't spoken in almost two days. Even the memory of their last conversation hurt. How had things gotten so bad so quickly?

She crossed her right leg over her left as she settled into the black cushioned visitor's chair. "We're running Barron's story in the Sunday edition. I thought you'd want to know."

Troy leaned back in his seat. "And it doesn't matter that I don't want you to."

Did he know the effect his gentle tone had on her? Probably not. He'd used it often enough without getting the results he'd wanted. Still, resistance wasn't ever easy. "This story has value. It's accurate and it's newsworthy. There's no reason to kill it."

Troy folded his hands on top of the pile of papers on his desk. His gaze moved over each of her features as though memorizing her. "The franchise is still reeling from all the news coverage of Gerry trying to blackmail a league official. We can't handle your releasing a story about our team captain being an alcoholic on top of that."

She studied his determined features. "It sounds as though this article is just what the team needs. It's a good piece, and it shows the Monarchs in a positive light."

He gave her a skeptical look. "This season we've taken one black eye after another. We can't risk any more bad press. We've just launched a new image campaign."

Andrea tightened her grip on the padded arms of her chair and absorbed the blow. "This isn't bad press. Barron's comfortable with the article. He sees it as an opportunity to help other people who may be going through the same thing he's facing right now. I understand how important that is for him."

Troy's dark eyes sharpened. "Barron read the draft? Can I read it?"

His request took her breath away. First he wanted to tell her what she could and couldn't write. Now he wanted to review her article? "No. You cannot. You'll have to take my word for it that the feature is a solid human interest piece that won't bring shame to your franchise."

"You let Barron read the article in advance."

"It's important that he's comfortable with the way he's portrayed in the article. You're a different situation. I'm not sending you the draft for approval, Troy."

"Then why are you here?" Troy pushed himself back into his chair with an air of defeat.

"To tell you when the article's running." Andrea's

shoulders rose and fell in a useless sigh. "I'd hoped you'd reconsidered your decision."

"I'd hoped you had." His disappointment hurt, but not enough to make her change her mind.

Andrea saw her own regrets reflected in Troy's ebony eyes. "Why won't you trust me, Troy?"

"An exclusive interview with an NBA star admitting he's an alcoholic will raise your profile. We're obviously going to see that article differently."

"You trusted me when you were on this side of that desk." She nodded toward the desk between them. "Now that you're back in that chair, I'm the enemy again."

"It's my job to protect the team."

She heard Troy's frustration. Well, she was frustrated, too. Even more so once she'd realized he was making her pay for another woman's actions. "If the team gets bad press, it's not the players' fault. It's not your fault. It's the media's fault. Is that a holdover from your experience at Georgetown?"

Troy frowned his confusion. "What?"

"When your college girlfriend told you she was pregnant, you blamed *her* for your quitting the basketball team."

Andrea's attack stunned him. "That's because she'd lied. I'd never have quit the team if I didn't think I was going to have a family to take care of."

"And when you went on television to accuse Gerry of being the Insider, you blamed *him* when he fired you."

Troy's voice was tense enough to crack. "The *Insider* blog sounded like something Gerry would do."

Andrea pinned him with an unwavering gaze. "What happened at Georgetown and with ESPN are examples of you blaming others for your behavior.

No one did those things to you, Troy. Those were decisions you made yourself. Take responsibility."

Troy froze as Andrea's words echoed around him. He'd accused Gerald of blaming others for his uncle's behavior. His former boss had said they were alike. That couldn't be true.

His throat was dry. "I take responsibility for my mistakes."

Andrea wouldn't allow him an easy out. "Then why haven't you forgiven your ex-wife for lying to you about the pregnancy?"

Troy pushed out of his executive chair and prowled his office. "Why should I forgive her? She lied to get what she wanted, and her lie cost me a place on the team and my scholarship."

Andrea's words chased him across the room. "If you'd wanted to play basketball, you could have stayed on the team. Or you could have left early for the draft."

Troy paced back toward his desk. "What about my college degree?"

"You could have gone back for that." Andrea shrugged one slim shoulder. "Vince Carter did."

Troy knew the Phoenix Suns player had returned to college for his degree. "I didn't want to do that."

Andrea spread her hands. "That was your decision, too. And, by the way, protecting the team from Gerry was Jackie's job."

Troy's brow knitted. Was she questioning his job performance as well? "I'm the media and marketing executive."

"And you've designed a great image campaign for the Monarchs. But there was nothing you could have done to change Gerry's attitude. You can only manage your own."

"Is that on a greeting card?" Troy regretted his flippancy as soon as the question left him.

"You're holding on to past grudges that are affecting your actions today."

"That's not true."

"Fifteen years later, you still blame your ex-wife for ending your basketball career. She's the reason for your rash reactions whenever you even imagine someone's threatening the Monarchs. It's time to accept responsibility for your actions and move on."

"Are you done?" Troy stared out at the marina behind the Empire Arena. She expected him to forgive his ex-wife for lying to him and forget that Gerald had fired him. It was easy for Andrea to pass judgment from the outside looking in.

"You can't work with me or any member of the media if you don't trust us. And until you come to terms with your past, you won't be the media and marketing executive the Monarchs need to rebuild their franchise."

Troy heard Andrea leave. Her parting comment had shaken Troy more than he wanted to admit.

21

Constance knocked on Troy's door. "I've e-mailed the new advertising specifications to all the publications on your list. If there's nothing else you need today, I'll say good night."

Startled, Troy glanced at his watch. It was after five o'clock. It had been a long and unproductive Thursday. "Good night, Connie, and thanks."

"You're welcome."

As she started to turn away, Troy gave in and stopped her. "Connie, do you have a minute?"

She turned back. Her brows raised in question. "Is there something you needed?"

Troy stood. His question was awkward. It might even be out of line, but he had to ask. "How do you like living with Andy and Faith?"

Her smile was answer enough. "It's great. I was hesitant at first. I didn't know whether Andrea was planning to ask me about the team."

"Does she?" It was a struggle to sound casual.

Constance adjusted her tan purse strap on her shoulder. "She never asks anything beyond, 'How was your day?' It's like she's going out of her way to avoid asking me about the team."

"I see." Images of Andrea with Constance and her daughter played through his mind. She seemed to genuinely care about them.

"Faith and I talk more about work."

And what did Faith tell Andrea? "What does Faith do?"

"She's an accountant with a firm. Her boss sounds like a real jerk. She's thinking about looking for another job, but with the economy, she's not sure she'll find anything better."

Was he jumping to conclusions? Maybe Faith didn't tell Andrea anything. Maybe he should take Andrea's actions at face value. "I wish her luck."

Constance leaned her shoulder against the doorjamb. "It meant a lot that you trusted my judgment about moving in with them." She lowered her gaze as her cheeks bloomed with color. "I'm not used to that."

Troy frowned. His gaze dropped to his desk before returning it to his assistant. "I knew you wouldn't give Andrea any inappropriate information about the team."

Constance tipped her head to the right. "How did you know that? I mean, you hadn't known me long. How could you be so sure that you could trust me that way?"

Why had he been able to trust Constance, a woman he'd just met, while he was still suspicious of Andrea's motives? He'd known the reporter a lot longer and they'd been through much more together. Was Andrea right? Was his past experience affecting the way he did his job today?

He moved his shoulders restlessly. "This job is important to you. You wouldn't risk it by leaking internal information to the press." And Andrea wouldn't put Constance in that position. He was sure of that now, even if he hadn't been before.

Constance nodded. "It does mean a lot. It's helped Tiff and me get back on our feet. So has living with Andrea and Faith."

Troy's brows knitted. "I'm sure you're both more comfortable being out of the shelter."

She shook her head. "It's more than that. I'm grateful to Andrea for convincing me to take a chance and move in with them. It hasn't been a month yet. Who knows? In a couple of weeks, we may be driving each other crazy. But Andrea and Faith are really welcoming people."

"Yes, they are." They'd invited him and Serge to stay for dinner even though they hadn't had much. It was the company more than the menu that had made it special.

Constance smiled. "Even the neighbors are kind. I know they're watching out for Tiff and me after that episode with Wade." She hesitated. "Wade's fighting the divorce, but I'm not changing my mind. I want to start over. Tiff deserves for me to start over."

Troy saw the new Constance Street again. A confident, strong woman who was stepping out of the shadows. "I'm proud of you, Connie."

She blushed again. "Thank you. But I think a lot of it is because of Andrea and Faith. This is the environment Tiff and I needed to complete the healing process."

"I'm sure you're right."

She laughed. "Listen to me. I'm not telling you anything you don't already know. I think you and Andrea are good together. You make her happy."

Maybe he had. Troy didn't want to be the one to tell

Constance that he and Andrea had broken up. Andrea
could explain in her own time.

"I'm glad things are working out for you at the
apartment."

Constance's smile was embarrassed. "I'm sorry. I
didn't mean to get so personal."

Troy held up a hand, palm out. "No, you're fine."

She didn't seem convinced. "OK. Well, good night,
Troy."

He watched her leave. In the morning, would he
join Faith's employer as The Jerk Boss?

Faith stared down at Andrea as she lay curled on
the sofa. "What's going on?"

"Nothing. What's new with you?" She didn't have
a prayer of distracting Faith. Her friend was as tenacious as a bulldog.

Faith lowered herself to the armchair cattycorner
to the sofa. Her tan V-neck top and brown crew
pants looked incongruous with her big, fuzzy
orange slippers. "This is the third night in a row that
you've spent at home. It's not that we don't enjoy
your company—"

"I'm glad you said that. I was beginning to wonder."

"—but you have a fine-looking man. No one would
blame you for making as much time as possible with
him. So what gives?"

Andrea shook her head. Misery was a weight pressing on her chest. She couldn't speak. She couldn't
move. She could barely breathe.

Faith leaned forward in the armchair. Her forehead creased with concern. "Andrea, what's wrong?"

She swallowed. The lump in her throat stung. "Troy
and I broke up."

Faith gaped. "What happened?"

Andrea blinked once, twice. Then the tears came. She couldn't wipe them away fast enough. They flooded her cheeks. Faith appeared in front of the sofa with a box of tissues.

Andrea swung her legs off the sofa and sat up. "Thanks." Her voice was thick with sobs.

"Do you want to talk about it?" Faith sat beside her. She put her right arm around Andrea's shoulders.

Andrea dried her eyes. "Troy doesn't trust me."

"Why do you think that?"

Andrea swallowed again. The lump in her throat still didn't move. "He accused me of writing negative stories about the Monarchs to advance my career."

"You write for *Sports*. Either the stories you're writing aren't negative or you're doing something wrong." Faith sounded confused.

Andrea blew her nose. "I'm serious."

"So am I."

Andrea placed the box of tissues on her jeans-clad lap. "Barron gave me an interview. The feature focuses on the reasons for his alcohol abuse and his decision to enter the rehab program. It's a good piece."

"I'm sure it is. You're a great reporter."

Andrea scowled. "Not according to Troy. First, he asked me not to write the article. Then he asked to review it before it's published."

Faith's eyebrows shot up again. "Are you going to let him see it?"

"No." She was surprised Faith would even ask.

"Maybe he'd feel better if he saw it first, though." Her friend's tone was pensive.

Andrea angled herself toward Faith. "Do you think I was wrong to refuse to show him the article?"

Faith's arm fell away from Andrea's shoulders. "I don't know."

Andrea pulled a fresh tissue from the box and dabbed at her eyes. "I don't review his marketing campaigns before he launches them."

"But this is different. He's afraid that your story will hurt the Monarchs."

Andrea pulled her fingers through her hair, cupping her head between her hands. "I'm tired of the team coming between us. Everything was fine before he got his job back."

Faith spread her hands. "With the man comes his job."

Andrea pushed off the sofa. She stalked to the window overlooking the fire escape. "I come with a job, too. He didn't have any problem with it when he wanted my help stopping the Insider and Gerry. He loved my job then."

"What do you want him to do?"

Andrea folded her arms, consoling herself as she thought of what she couldn't have. The words came haltingly. "I want him to want all of me. The woman he comes to when he needs help. The friend to whom he confides his secrets. The lover he holds in his arms." She turned from the window. "And the reporter who writes about the Monarchs. Am I wrong to want that?"

"I want one of those, too."

Andrea returned to the sofa. She dropped beside Faith. "Should I have shown him Barron's feature?"

Faith put her arm around Andrea's shoulders. "You have two choices. You can either show him the feature before it's printed on Sunday or you can ask him to trust you."

"I already asked him to trust me. He said no."

"Is this issue worth breaking up your relationship?"

Another lump formed in Andrea's throat making her voice husky. "Without trust, we don't have a relationship."

"Then you have your answer."

Andrea pulled a tissue from the box to dry her tears. "I hate it when you do your Yoda impersonation. Why can't you ever give a straight answer? 'Yes, you did the right thing.' Or 'No, you didn't.'"

Faith gave Andrea's shoulders a squeeze before releasing her. "Only you know what's right for you. No one else can answer that."

Tiffany hopped into the living room, bathed and dressed for bed in a butter yellow cotton gown. Constance, wearing dark gray sweatpants and a silver Monarchs jersey, followed her daughter. Her honey blond hair was pinned on top of her head. Loose locks floated around her face.

When Tiffany saw Andrea, she slowed to a walk. The little girl placed her small, warm hand on Andrea's cheek. The gesture was similar to her mother's. "You sad?"

Andrea's expression softened. "A little."

"Want Bear?"

Andrea smiled at the offer of the little girl's stuffed toy. She pulled Tiffany onto her lap. "No, I'll just hug you."

Tiffany giggled as Andrea cuddled her tight.

Constance lowered herself to the love seat across from her roommates. Her eyes were wide with concern. "What's wrong?"

Andrea loosened her hold on Tiffany and squared her shoulders. "Troy and I broke up."

Constance's eyes widened. "I'm so sorry. That

explains why he looked sad when I mentioned your name."

Andrea's lips parted with surprise—and hope. She squelched both. "I'm sorry, too." She looked down at Tiffany. The toddler seemed drowsy. "We need to find more positive relationships so this little one doesn't think all men are D-O-G-S."

Tiffany perked up. "D-O-G spells dog."

Andrea stiffened. Constance smothered her laughter behind her right palm.

Faith arched a brow. "Next time, spell Rottweiler."

Constance's laughter broke free.

Tiffany sat straighter. "And the dog goes 'woof, woof, woof.'"

Andrea shook her head with a smile. "Tiff, I wish you'd told me that sooner."

Jaclyn walked into Troy's office Monday morning, waving the *New York Sports*'s Features section in one hand and cradling a cup of coffee in the other. Some of her energy came from the caffeine. But Troy was sure his boss was still riding the excitement from the Monarchs' win Friday night. The team now led the series with two games to one over the New York Knicks.

"This is the article you warned me about Friday." She laid the paper faceup on Troy's desk before settling into one of the visitor's armchairs. "I told you everything would be fine."

Troy glanced at the photo of Barron standing in the middle of the street outside his Prospect Park condo, staring pensively back at him. He'd read the article—twice—Sunday and studied the photo at length. The team captain wore a silver Monarchs warm-up suit. The photo reinforced the article's message, which was that Barron "Bling" Douglas had traveled a tough and lonely road. However, he was ready to recover, make amends, and become a positive role model in the community. It was a good article. Troy would readily admit he'd been wrong.

He looked at Jaclyn. "The article's terrific. It shows Barron in a strong, positive light."

Jaclyn sipped her coffee with reverence. "It will also inspire other people to get help with their addictions, which I think was Andrea's goal."

"I called her yesterday to thank her for the article, but she wasn't there. I left a message." Actually, he'd left several messages on her cell phone, including one this morning. She still hadn't returned his call. *Please don't let it be too late to say, "I'm sorry."*

Jaclyn leaned into the chair. "I have a feeling you should have called to apologize as well."

Troy studied his boss. "What do you mean?"

Jaclyn drank more coffee. "You're too hard on the media."

His discomfort increased at his boss's criticism. "I'm only as tough as I need to be to protect the team's image."

"Protecting the team's image is my job. We've talked about that before." Jaclyn crossed her legs, adjusting the skirt of her gold dress over her right knee. "I've always been impressed with your marketing campaigns. They're strong and memorable."

"Thank you." Troy heard a "but."

"But you treat the media like our opponents."

Troy struggled against a rising sense of defensiveness. "I'm cautious with the press because I want to avoid bad publicity."

"As a result, you're alienating them. I want the Monarchs to have a good relationship with the press.

We can't grow our fan base without media coverage. That's Marketing 101."

Troy drummed his fingertips on his desk. "I have good reason to be suspicious of the press. If reporters sense any negativity in a story, they'll exploit it."

She gestured with her mug toward the newspaper on Troy's desk. "Andrea didn't exploit Barron, and she certainly could have."

"We got lucky." Troy remembered the disappointment in Andrea's eyes.

"This wasn't luck. We can't dictate what reporters write. If they give us positive stories, we'll thank them. If they write something negative, we'll deal with it."

Troy spread his hands. "With all due respect, Jackie, I'd rather be proactive than reactive."

Jaclyn's tone was dry. "Your idea of being proactive got you fired. Remember?"

Heat rose into Troy's cheeks. Dammit. He was a grown man. Why was he blushing? "I've learned from that experience. I know I need to plan before I react."

Jaclyn arched a brow. "Was that Andrea's influence?"

Troy's throat muscles worked as he struggled with his regrets. "Yes."

Jaclyn's gaze dropped to the paper laying untouched on Troy's desk. When she raised her eyes, Troy saw the curiosity in them. "You've seemed preoccupied lately and a little sad. Did you and Andrea have a falling out because of this story?"

Troy sank back into his chair. He was reluctant to admit just how wrong he'd been. "I thought it would cause trouble for Barron and the team. I asked her not to write it."

Jaclyn briefly closed her eyes. "I thought you were past that, at least with her."

He sat up and rubbed the back of his neck. "I called Sunday to apologize, but she won't return my messages."

Jaclyn sighed. "Troy, you've got to make some changes."

Troy stared blindly at his desk. "How can I when she won't talk to me?"

"I'm not talking about Andrea. I'm talking about here."

Panic made him cold. He'd just gotten his job back. Was he about to lose it again? "What changes?"

Jaclyn uncrossed her legs and sat forward, cupping the coffee mug between her palms. "Your blind loyalty to the team has been the greatest threat to the Monarchs all season. You withheld your knowledge of Barron's addiction and challenged Gerald in the press."

Troy held Jaclyn's gaze with difficulty. "I'm sorry."

"I'm sure you won't make the same mistakes again. But I don't want you making similar ones, either."

"I won't."

She glanced again at the feature. "What about your reaction to Andrea's story? Asking her not to run it was over the top."

"I know. I should have realized she'd do a good job with it."

Jaclyn nodded. "Andrea has been very fair in her coverage of the franchise over the years. If it weren't for her, Marc's reputation would have been ruined."

That possibility gave Troy pause. Where would the team be without DeMarcus as its head coach? More than likely watching the postseason games from their sofas. "And Gerry would still be co-owner."

"Stop. You'll give me nightmares."

Troy sent her a reluctant smile. "I'll work on

improving my relationship with the press. I'll reach out to them more and not give them such a hard time when they're working on a story."

"Good." Jaclyn rose from her chair. "I hope things work out for you and Andrea, too. I think she's just what you need."

Troy stood, too. "I know. But am I what she needs?" The answer scared him.

Jaclyn tipped her head to the side. A slight smile curved her lips. "I think you are."

"Why?" Troy's pulse raced with renewed hope.

"I've seen the two of you together."

Troy watched his boss leave after making that cryptic comment. What had Jaclyn meant? What had she seen? And how could he convince Andrea to give him another chance?

22

Andrea walked into the *Sports*'s reception area Monday afternoon. She should have known Troy wouldn't go away just because she wasn't returning his calls. Her knees grew weak at the sight of him in a gunmetal gray, slim-cut suit and sapphire tie. He turned and caught her gaze. Andrea's heart tripped.

"Hello, Troy. What can I do for you?" She kept her voice and expression cool even as the muscles in her stomach quivered like Jell-O.

"Have lunch with me."

Andrea didn't trust his invitation or his crooked smile. Did he intend to take away her home court advantage so he could rake her over the coals about her feature on Barron? She was proud of that piece, and nothing he could say would change her mind.

She raised her chin. "No, thank you."

His smile wavered. Uncertainty winked in his ebony eyes. "Andy, I'd really like to talk with you."

Andrea angled her head, no longer sure of his intent. "I'm listening."

Troy glanced toward Vella, who sat at her receptionist's desk, before reclaiming Andrea's gaze. "In private."

"Fine." Andrea spun on her heel and led him to the newspaper's conference room.

He was walking too close to her. Andrea's body wanted to lean into his. She wanted to bury her face in his neck and breathe his citrus and cinnamon scent. She fisted her hands and increased her pace.

As they crossed the newsroom, she was battered by curious stares from the other reporters. Andrea did her best to ignore them. She just wanted to get through this confrontation. It was too bad they were meeting in the cramped, stale-smelling conference room. But she didn't want him to tear out her heart in a crowded restaurant.

At the doorway, Andrea stepped aside so Troy could precede her into the room. She shut the door. "Let's have it, Troy. I've been preparing for this conversation all weekend."

"I doubt that." He rested his hips against the edge of the conference table. His hands gripped the scarred wood on either side of him. "You did a great job with the story on Barron."

Andrea blinked. Was she imagining his compliment? She moved farther into the room to put space between them. "You *liked* the story?"

Troy shifted on the table to face her. "So did Jackie. If you'd returned any one of my messages, I'd have told you."

They weren't going to have a confrontation. Relief eased her strained muscles. But then regret made its presence known. "Thanks for coming by to tell me." *Why hadn't he sent her an e-mail?* Andrea started toward the door.

Troy's brows knitted in confusion. "Everything's OK. The article didn't hurt the team."

Andrea paused with her hand on the doorknob. Disappointment was a bitter taste in her mouth. "I told you it wouldn't."

"You were right. It showed Barron in a positive light, and it was an encouraging story."

Was it her imagination or was Troy tripping over himself to praise her work? "I want the story to inspire other people who're struggling with fears or negative feelings to get help."

"Your story will do that."

Was that pride in his voice? Was he actually proud of her article? Andrea gave him a hard stare. Could she trust that his new attitude toward her work was permanent and not a temporary aberration?

Andrea released the doorknob and crossed the room. She needed the space between them. "If I can help even one person with this story, I'll be satisfied. Barron would be, too."

"I'm sure you'll help a lot of people." Troy stood from the table. His arms hung loosely at his sides. "Are we OK, you and I?"

It was tempting to pretend not to understand his question, but Andrea didn't want to prolong this pain. Every minute in his company weakened her resolve. But she had to do what was best for her in the long term.

Andrea stood in front of the stack of old and dusty storage boxes. She gathered her courage and a breath, inhaling the musty stench of the files behind her. "No, Troy. We're not OK."

Pain flashed in his eyes. "Why not?"

The emotions flickering over his features tore at her heart. Would these cuts now protect her from heartbreak later? "I told you I wasn't writing a negative article about Barron."

"And I told you I realized you were right."

"Why didn't you trust me *before* the article was printed?"

Troy smoothed his goatee. "I have trouble completely trusting the press."

Andrea wouldn't let him get away with that one. "I can't imagine you asking Jenna, Fred, or even Sean to review their articles before publication. Why am I different?"

"Because you mean more." His voice was strained.

Unfair! "What's that supposed to mean?"

Troy spread his arms. "I wasn't in a relationship with Jenna, Fred, or Sean. But with you, if things had turned out differently, it would have hurt more."

"Because we were in a relationship, you should have trusted me."

Troy smoothed his hand over his wavy hair. "I'm sorry. I made a mistake."

Andrea looked away. With Troy in front of her and the boxes at her back, she felt trapped. "But it's your job to protect the team, isn't it? And, since you don't trust me, you saw my article as a threat."

Troy narrowed his eyes. "That's not fair."

"I agree."

Andrea could tell by his tight features that Troy realized she referred to his treatment of her.

Frustration oozed from every angle of his long, leanly muscled form. "I said I was sorry."

"I forgive you."

"But you won't take me back."

God, she wanted to. "I can't."

"I'm in love with you, Andy." He still wasn't playing fair. His husky whisper stole into her heart.

"There can't be love without trust. And this lack of trust isn't between you and me. It's between you and your ex-wife."

Troy felt as though Andrea had knocked him on his butt. "What are you talking about?"

"You have an overdeveloped need to protect the team because no one protected you from your ex-wife's lies."

Was she serious? Troy searched her face. She looked serious. "That's ridiculous. I haven't even seen her in fifteen years."

"And you've never forgiven her. Until you let go of your past, everything you do will be affected by it."

Troy shook his head in disbelief. "That sounds like bad pop psychology."

Andrea shrugged, but she still seemed tense. "I had a lot of counseling and read a lot of self-help books to deal with my alcoholism."

Troy turned to pace the length of the narrow, crowded conference room. How could he make her understand? "I don't have feelings for my ex-wife anymore."

"Yes, you do." Andrea sounded certain. "They're negative feelings, but they're very strong."

Troy turned to study Andrea's expression, trying to read her thoughts. "Are you jealous?"

"Of a woman you hate?" She actually laughed. "It bothers me that you won't trust me because of something she did."

Frustration whirled inside him. "I do trust you."

"You trust me today. What happens the next time I want to write an in-depth article on the Monarchs?"

"Now who doesn't trust who? I admitted I was wrong. I told you I was sorry."

"I want to write a story on the original Monarchs' owners and the end of their partnership."

Troy's head spun at her apparent change of topic. "Is this a test?"

"Is that a wide-eyed look of hope or horror?" Her tone was wry.

Troy spread his arms. "Why do you want to write that story?"

"Are you afraid I'd play up the sensationalism, the greed, and jealousy that spanned generations?"

He shoved his hands into his pockets and forced a casual shrug. "It would sell a lot of papers."

"And look good in my portfolio. I'd raise my profile and get ahead by hurting other people. Isn't that what your ex-wife tried to do to you?"

Troy's skin grew cold. "Isn't that what you tried to do with Jackie?"

Andrea stiffened, but she didn't look away. "Is that the reason you don't trust me?"

Troy resumed his pacing. He kneaded the muscles at the back of his neck, but the tension wouldn't ease. "I'm sorry. That was a stupid thing to say."

"No, it wasn't. It's the truth. I wrote a damaging article about Jackie. It was full of lies that I created from petty jealousy. Is that the reason you don't trust me?"

Troy exhaled an impatient breath. The room was hot and stuffy. "I do trust you. You're not the same person you were four years ago." *How many times would he have to repeat himself before she'd believe him?*

"Maybe that's why your ex-wife and I are connected in your mind."

Troy turned and paced back toward the front of the room. He took off his suit jacket and hooked it on the back of a chair. "You two couldn't be more different."

Andrea sank into one of the chairs crowded between the storage boxes and the conference table. "Jackie was able to forgive me. I'm not saying I deserved it. But her generosity helped me to be a better person, and I think it helped her to move forward after what I did."

Troy loosened his tie. Anger heated his skin and caused his heart to race. "My ex-wife cost me my basketball scholarship, my parents' respect, and my chance at the NBA. You expect me to forgive her?"

Andrea spread her hands. "I'm sorry for everything she cost you. But you earned your degree. You have a job you love working for a well-respected organization. And I'm certain your parents are proud of you. How does it benefit you to hold onto your resentment?"

Troy hooked his hands on his hips. "Why do I have to forgive her?"

Andrea stood. She pressed her palms against her thighs. "Jackie not only forgave me, but she helped me restart my career. She saved my life."

Troy's temper cooled as he gave silent thanks to Jaclyn's huge heart. "I know."

"If you had been in her place, would you have been able to forgive me?" Her voice was breathless.

Her question rocked him back on his heels. She stood as still as a statue. Troy sensed her trying to read his mind.

Troy lowered his arms. What could he say to keep her with him? "You're talking in hypotheticals. You've never written anything about me."

"Humor me. Would you have been able to forgive me?" She was relentless.

Troy's chest hurt. His shoulders slumped. "I don't think I could have."

"Not even for your own sake?"

He shook his head. "I don't think so."

Andrea nodded. "Neither do I." Her voice was low.

Troy tried a last-minute rally. "Why is this important? It's all make-believe."

Andrea lowered her eyes. "It means you wouldn't have given me a chance to change. I'm not saying I deserved a second chance, but I'm glad I got one."

"So am I." Troy fisted his hands to keep from reaching for her. Would she want his touch? He didn't know, but he couldn't bear for her to flinch from him.

Andrea looked up to meet his gaze. "By holding on to the past, you aren't allowing yourself a chance to change, either."

His irritation stirred. "I wasn't the one who needed to change. She was."

"It's not too late to give her that chance."

Did she know what she was asking of him? How could he forgive someone who had taken so much from him?

"I don't know whether I can change that much, not even for you." Troy collected his jacket. Leaving Andrea was one of the hardest things he'd ever done.

"Nice shot, Trademark." Warrick added applause to his praise.

Troy grabbed his own rebound, then turned to face the Monarchs' point guard on the court of the team's practice facility.

He checked the clock on the facility's far wall. It

was after six-thirty on Wednesday evening. "What are you doing here so late?" Troy flung the ball toward Warrick.

Warrick caught the pass, considered the basket, hopped, then sunk a jumper from beyond the perimeter ring. "No one to rush home to. I thought I'd come here to work off some extra energy before I went home."

Troy collected the basketball from the court as it bounced toward him. He wasn't anxious to spend the rest of the evening in his own company, either. Like Warrick, he'd come to the practice facility to work out.

"When last did you hear from Mary?" *If only he'd been able to stop the Monarchs Insider sooner.*

"She finally answered my call this morning. She said she needed more time." Warrick dragged his right hand over his clean-shaven head. "It's been a month."

It was closer to three weeks, but Troy knew how Warrick felt. He hadn't spoken to Andrea in two days; it felt like a week. "More time for what?"

Warrick shrugged. "To think things through. How much time does she need?"

Troy knew the question wasn't directed at him. "I'm sorry, man." He plucked his silver Monarchs T-shirt, damp with perspiration, from his torso and rubbed his sweaty forearm across his brow. "I'm sorry about the loss last night, too." Now the Monarchs were tied with the New York Knicks at two games a piece in the seven-game series.

Warrick turned. He wandered off the court to the bleachers. "Another reason I'm not eager to sit alone at home. As company, my own thoughts would suck."

Troy tossed the ball into a black wire cart filled

with other basketballs before following his friend across the court. "The team is playing better since you've worked Jamal into the games." Troy sat beside the other man. "You're playing more like a team. Barron wouldn't do that."

Warrick shrugged. "Barron brought a different chemistry to the game."

Troy studied the other man, puzzling his relationship with the rookie. "Jamal looks up to Barron, but you're the one who's helping him."

Warrick frowned at a spot across the court. "Barron leads by example. Jamal needs more help finding his way."

"But you're helping him even though he talks trash about you in the media. And to your face. How can you overlook that?"

"Consider the source. Jamal's insecure." Warrick chuckled. "He's also impatient. He thinks he can build his NBA legacy overnight."

Troy stood to pace. "But he's trying to build it by attacking yours. How can you forgive him?"

Warrick leaned forward, resting his elbows on his thighs. The intensity in his brown eyes made Troy pause. "Jamal isn't in control of my game. I am. What matters to me at the end of my day are my stats. Am I winning or am I losing? Everything else is noise."

Troy adjusted the waistband of his baggy black shorts before sitting back down. "Jamal's lucky he chose to target you instead of Barron."

Warrick laughed. "That's true."

Troy stared across the court, considering Warrick's words. His body began to cool and his skin was starting to dry.

The point guard was right. Warrick was in control of his game. That's why Jamal's criticisms didn't affect him. Just as Jaclyn was confident of her basketball skills, which is the reason she recovered from Andrea's damaging article. Did Troy have the confidence to put the past and his ex-wife's offenses behind him?

Warrick's words interrupted Troy's thoughts. "I liked the article Andrea wrote about Barron going into rehab. It was really good."

"Yes, it was." Troy sensed Warrick looking at him.

"That wasn't exactly a ringing endorsement. What's wrong?"

Troy took a breath, drawing in the sharp scent of polished wood. "She broke up with me."

"Over the story about Barron?"

Troy nodded. "I asked her not to write it. She said I should have trusted her."

"She's right."

Troy glanced at Warrick, then away. "I know. I apologized, but she doesn't believe I've learned my lesson. She thinks, in a similar situation, I still won't trust her."

Warrick shifted on the bleacher. "Would you?"

Troy hesitated. "I don't know."

Warrick grunted. "Then she's right not to believe you."

Troy dragged his right hand over his hair. "She said if I can't trust her, then I don't love her. Well, this sure feels like love to me."

"How do you know?"

"I just do." Did he sound insane?

Warrick patted Troy's shoulder. "Do you want to know if you're in love?"

Troy looked at the embattled husband. "Yeah."

"Ask yourself if you're better with her than you are without her. If the answer's yes, then you're in love."

"Is that how you feel about Mary?" Troy saw the flash of pain in Warrick's eyes.

"Yes."

Troy sighed. "Then what do we do?"

Warrick hesitated. "We ask ourselves if they're better with us than they are without us. If the answer's yes, we have to find a way to convince them."

Troy's stomach muscles knotted. "What if the answer's no?"

Warrick looked bleak. "Then we're screwed."

Were the odds in his favor? Andrea gave him confidence. She'd taught him patience. But what had she gotten from their relationship? Maybe she was better off without him.

But maybe he could change.

23

Andrea hustled to keep up with the *New York Horn*'s managing editor, Bruce Donnelly, as he led her through the newsroom to his office Thursday. His brown, cuffed pants were a little long for his short, stocky frame. His blue, white, and brown striped shirt was wrinkled and stained with newsprint—and it was only eight-thirty in the morning.

She dodged a couple of storage boxes and circled stacks of old newspapers as she examined her surroundings. The competition didn't appear to believe in reinvesting in their product either. Computers and printers were outdated. Workspace was overcrowded. Office furniture was bruised and battered. The air stank of aging newsprint and burned coffee. If it weren't for the unfamiliar cast of characters speed walking past her and shouting across the room, she'd think she was still at *Sports*.

Kirk West, the *Horn*'s basketball reporter, glared as she passed his desk. She wouldn't receive a warm welcome there. Andrea nodded at the other reporter as she adjusted the strap of her brown purse on her shoulder. She inconspicuously wiped her sweating palms on the skirt of her light gray business suit. Why did this feel like a mistake?

She entered Bruce's office. The older man shared the space with several boxes. Was he moving?

"Thanks for coming." Bruce lowered himself into his seat behind his desk.

Andrea settled into the sole guest chair. It squeaked. "What made you change your mind about the interview? You rejected my initial application."

"We've been following your work for a long time." Bruce smoothed back what was left of his iron gray hair and leaned back in his chair. It wailed in protest. "You're good."

"Thank you." Andrea waited for Bruce to continue. She gripped her purse in her lap.

"What do you know about hockey?" Bruce's narrowed hazel eyes pinned her.

Andrea played along. "There are thirty teams, six divisions. The season starts in September. It runs through April, when the Stanley Cup play-offs begin."

"Who won the 2010 cup?"

"The Chicago Blackhawks." She hoped Bruce didn't ask the team captain's name. That she didn't remember. "Why are you asking all of these questions?"

Bruce sat forward. He folded his hands on the flood of papers on his desk. "Our hockey reporter gave two weeks' notice. That's why I called you yesterday. The job is yours if you want it."

Andrea blinked. This was a one-hundred-and-eighty-degree switch from her last job-hunting experience. "In two weeks."

Bruce nodded. "That's right. I hear *Sports* will fold in a month, give or take."

The ticking time clock. Andrea was too aware of how long she had before she had to reach into her meager savings. It grew warmer in the room. She tugged a little at the high collar of her white polyester blouse.

Andrea looked at the stained and cluttered walls. She wasn't a big hockey fan, but that would help her remain objective as she covered the season. She could learn the sport. Who was the New York Rangers team captain? She knew the New York Islanders hadn't done well last season.

She returned her attention to Bruce. The editor's sharp gaze seemed to sift through her thoughts. She wished she could do that to him.

"What's the benefits package?" Not that she had much of a package with *Sports*.

"Medical. Dental. Five vacation and seven sick days after a year."

That was identical to *Sports*'s benefits package. Five vacation days a year. That was disappointing. "And the salary?"

The starting salary Bruce named was exactly the same as she made now. Andrea swallowed a groan. "Is that negotiable?"

Bruce shook his head. "That salary is in line with what we pay all of our reporters with similar experience to yours."

That was hard to believe. "What's the salary range for those years of experience?"

"The salary we're offering you is on the high side of that range." Bruce's eyes and expression gave nothing away. His chair whined as he sat back.

Andrea wished he'd sit still. "That salary is quite a bit less than I was hoping for."

"I understand. But in a few weeks, you won't have *any* income."

The clock's ticking grew louder. Andrea swallowed a sigh. "How soon do you need a response?"

"As soon as possible."

Andrea's brow furrowed. "But I thought your reporter gave two weeks' notice yesterday? Why do you need a replacement so quickly?"

Bruce shrugged. "I want him to train you. Introduce you to his contacts. That kind of thing. It's easier to do that if the two of you can work together for a few days."

The pressure was building. She looked over her shoulder at the newsroom behind her. The newsroom that was interchangeable with the one in which she'd spent the past three years. She would argue that she'd grown during that time. The offer the *New York Horn* had made would be a step back. She was desperately in need of a step forward.

Bruce prompted her. "Isn't something better than nothing?"

Andrea lifted her hand to rub the back of her neck. She paused midmotion. She'd picked up Troy's mannerisms. His voice whispered in her ears. *You're a good reporter. Don't settle.*

She raised her head. "No, it's not."

Surprise flickered in his hazel eyes. "In this economy, you shouldn't make rash decisions."

"You're right." Andrea slipped her purse strap onto her shoulder and stood. "And taking this job would be a rash decision."

Bruce rose as well. "Are you sure? Because there are other candidates I'm scheduled to see."

Andrea recognized Bruce's game. "You should hire one of them." She offered him a smile and her hand. "Thank you for this opportunity."

Bruce shook her hand. "Thanks for coming in. Let me know if you change your mind."

Andrea walked out of his office and past Kirk West's desk. The NBA reporter glared at her again. Andrea winked at him before continuing out of the newsroom.

She was nervous. Who wasn't afraid of the unknown? But she'd finally stopped punishing herself. She deserved more. This time, she was leaving herself open to better opportunities. She hoped they wouldn't take too long to come knocking.

Thursday morning, Troy rode the Amtrak express train from Manhattan's Penn Station to Union Station in Washington, D.C. He arrived in time to have lunch with his parents. The home-cooked meal brought warm memories. But even those were tainted by the reason he'd returned.

Troy settled into the overstuffed, rose-patterned armchair. "Thanks again for lunch, Mom."

Danielle Marshall lowered herself onto the matching love seat beside his father. She adjusted the skirt of her pink coatdress. "It wasn't any trouble. You so rarely come home anymore."

Troy struggled against a smile at his mother's not-so-subtle attempt to make him feel guilty. "I was just home for Easter."

"You arrived Friday night and left after church Sunday morning. That wasn't a visit. That was a drive-by." Danielle sniffed and crossed her slender legs.

Charles Marshall squeezed his wife's hand and linked their fingers. "He had to work, Dani. The Monarchs had a game that night."

Danielle remained stubborn. "They have a game tonight, too."

Game five versus the New York Knicks at Madison Square Garden. The Monarchs had split the series with their hometown rivals at two games a piece. Tonight's tiebreaker was critical. Troy checked the clock above the fireplace. He needed to make the five o'clock Amtrak express back to New York for the nine o'clock tip-off.

"He's here now, Dani." His father's ebony eyes met Troy's. "What's wrong, son?"

Was he ready to answer that question? It didn't matter. Troy straightened in his chair and took a breath. "I need to know if you've both forgiven me for marrying Susan."

His parents exchanged a look before Charles responded. "That was fifteen years ago."

Troy's gaze shifted between his parents. They were both in their sixties. Their dark brown hair was peppered with gray. They'd collected more laugh lines around their eyes and mouths. But otherwise they hadn't changed much since he was a child. Their active, healthy lifestyle had always inspired him.

"I know it's been a long time, Dad. But I also know I disappointed you and Mom." The words weren't spoken easily. They pulled him back to a dark place.

Charles still looked baffled. "But that was *fifteen* years ago."

Danielle patted her husband's thigh. Her hands were slim with neatly manicured pink nails against the tan material of Charles's khaki pants. "That's not the point, Charlie. We were so busy dealing with the situation that we never stopped to talk about it."

Troy squared his shoulders. "You never said it, but I sensed you were disappointed."

Danielle shook her head. Her brown curls bobbed around her softly rounded features. "We were never disappointed *in* you. We were disappointed *for* you."

Charles grunted. "No, I was disappointed in you. I'd taught you about condoms and safe sex."

Troy dragged his hand over his hair. "She said she was on the pill."

Danielle glared at her husband before looking at Troy. "We should have done a better job preparing you to know when people are trying to take advantage of you."

Charles grunted again. He smoothed the blunt fingers of his right hand over his wavy salt-and-pepper hair. "That lesson wouldn't have stuck any better than the condom lesson."

"That's not fair, Dad." Maybe this hadn't been a good idea.

Charles ignored the interruption. "We also tried to teach you patience. That didn't stick, either. By the time you told us about the situation, you were already married. You'd given up your scholarship, quit the team, and gotten a job. Obviously, you didn't learn anything."

Danielle shook her head as though she'd mentally traveled back to that frustrating time. "Troy has always been impulsive. Most first babies are late. He was early."

Troy had heard that story before. "I'd made a mistake and was trying to fix it."

"Instead you made additional mistakes." Charles's voice was more contemplative than angry or disappointed.

Danielle freed her hand from her husband's hold and smoothed her dress again. "Son, we weren't upset because you thought you'd gotten your girlfriend pregnant—"

Charles raised his hand. "I was."

Danielle patted her husband's knee. "All right. We were upset about that. I also was upset that instead of coming to us, you rushed to take care of the situation by yourself. Only to have it turn out that Susan wasn't even pregnant."

Charles shifted on the love seat. "It's been fifteen years. Why do you want to discuss this now?"

Why do I? Troy stood. He rubbed the back of his neck as he circled the armchair. "Yeah, Dad, it's been a long time. And I need to let go of the past. I can be impatient, although I've learned the benefits of planning. I'm still impulsive, but I've seen the value of talking things over with other people." Specifically Andrea. Troy turned to pace back across the Oriental rug to his chair.

Danielle tilted her head. "Recognizing those things about yourself is a good sign."

Troy stilled. He hooked his hands on his hips. "But it's only the first step. I need to talk with Susan."

His parents again exchanged a look before Charles spoke. "Why?"

He frowned at his father. "I need to put the past to rest, and she's an important part of that past."

His father grunted. "That sounds like pop psychology crap."

Danielle scowled at her husband. "Troy has a point, Charlie. The reason we're still talking about this now is that we didn't talk about it before."

Charles shrugged. "You have."

Troy frowned at his mother's wide-eyed expression. "Who've you been talking with, Mom?"

Danielle's slender shoulders rose and fell with a deep breath. "Susan. And I only spoke with her twice."

Troy's skin chilled. "Why didn't you tell me?"

Danielle shot a glare at an unrepentant Charles before answering Troy. "Every time we mentioned Susan's name, you'd clam up. We didn't think you'd want to talk with her."

Troy sank onto the armchair. "When did you speak with her?"

Danielle frowned as though trying to remember. "She called us about ten years ago, after she divorced her first husband."

Charles interrupted. "Troy was her first husband."

Danielle's sigh was impatient. "Her second husband, then. She called me again a couple of months ago. She's getting ready to marry Howard."

Charles held up three fingers. "Her third."

Danielle continued. "She wanted to apologize for the trouble she'd caused in the past."

Troy leaned forward, bracing his elbows on his thighs. "How can I get in touch with her?"

"How'd your interview with the *Horn* go this morning?" Willis leaned back in the chair behind his desk. It squeaked.

Andrea rested a shoulder against his doorjamb. "Bruce Donnelly offered me the job."

Willis's face lit with pleasure. "Congratulations."

Andrea shook her head. "I turned him down."

Willis sat up, causing his chair to squeak again. His green eyes widened. "Why? You're going to be out of work in a month."

"I know, Will."

"Then why didn't you take the job?"

Andrea's gaze swept her editor's office. She glanced over her shoulder. What was the difference between *Sports* and *Horn?* Not much that she could see.

She turned back to Willis. "Someone once told me not to accept my first job offer unless it's for a really good company. *Horn* wasn't the right fit for me."

Willis shook his head in disbelief. "Is this person going to help you pay your bills?"

Andrea crossed her arms and returned her editor's incredulous gaze. "If I'd taken the job at the *Horn,* I would have been going backward. I want a job that will advance my career."

Willis gestured to the newsroom. "Most of the other reporters already have another job lined up."

Was he trying to make her nervous? "I'm happy for them. I truly am. But I have to do what's best for me." It felt good to say that.

Willis smoothed his lank gray hair. "I sure hope you know what you're doing."

Not exactly a ringing endorsement. Four years ago, if someone had said those words to her, she may have gone running for her phone to beg Bruce Donnelly to give her a job. But that was three years ago.

Strain had dug deep furrows across Willis's forehead. The bags under his eyes were more pronounced. With *New York Sports* preparing to close, leaving Willis with a lot of outstanding debt, he had enough to worry about without adding her future to his list.

She straightened away from the doorjamb. "I do know what I'm doing. But what about you? What will you do once the paper closes?"

Willis propped his elbows on the table and balanced his head in his hands. "I don't know. I put a lot of people in a tough financial spot. I feel really bad about that."

"Bill Cosby once said, 'People can be a lot more forgiving than you can imagine. But you have to forgive yourself.' He's right."

Willis looked up. "Is this what it felt like for you after your Jackie Jones story?"

She couldn't answer that because she didn't know what it felt like for him. "Everyone's journey is different. My point is, you hired reporters fresh out of college or, in my case, from a bad situation. Because you gave us a chance, we'll be able to find other jobs. Focus on that."

Willis nodded once. "Thanks, Benson."

She shrugged. "I don't have any illusions that you hired us for altruistic reasons. No one in their right mind would work for the pittance you paid. Still, it was an opportunity. And, most of the time, we could pay our bills."

He gave her an embarrassed smile. "*Sports* was a start-up company. I didn't have a lot of money." His smile faded. "And now it's folding."

"*Sports* has been around for eight years. It was a good run, Will." Andrea turned to leave.

Back at her desk, she noticed the message light blinking on her phone. She punched in her voice mail code, grabbed a nearby pad of paper, and pulled a pencil from behind her ear. The recording started and a male voice identified himself as a sports editor for *The New York Times*. He was calling to invite her for a job interview.

Andrea's knees gave way. She fell into her seat.

24

Troy was going to forgive Susan, then ask Andrea for another chance. But as his ex-wife walked into his office Friday afternoon, his mind went blank except for one question, "Why'd you do it?"

Susan stopped just inside his doorway. "I was stupid."

This was going to take a lot longer than he'd thought. Troy closed his door, then followed Susan across his office. He circled his desk, waiting for her to take one of the guest seats before lowering himself to his chair.

Troy considered the woman he'd married and divorced. The years had been kind to her. She was still slim. But her glossy, dark brown hair swung in a shorter style above her shoulders. More subtle makeup highlighted her cocoa features. He sensed a difference in her beyond these surface changes, but the anger snaking inside him made it hard to identify.

He pulled his chair farther under his desk. "We were both juniors. We probably would have gotten married after graduation. Why couldn't you have waited?"

"I was also impatient."

Troy unclenched his jaw. "Are you being flippant?"

Susan gripped the arms of the black cushioned chair. "No, Troy. I'm trying to apologize. I've wanted to for so long, but I don't know how to start."

Troy's heart pounded in his chest like a breakaway offense with seconds on the clock. He was almost light-headed. "You can start by explaining why you lied to me. You cost me my scholarship and a shot at the NBA. Worst of all, you hurt my relationship with my parents."

"None of that was supposed to happen." Susan's gaze wavered before returning to his. She blew out a deep breath. "You were my ticket to the glamorous life."

"Funny. I thought I was your boyfriend." His words were sour in his mouth.

Susan bit her lower lip. "I thought that if I told you I was pregnant, you'd enter the NBA draft. I never imagined you'd quit the team and get a job."

"I told you I wanted my degree."

Her voice dropped to a whisper. "I know. I thought you wanted to play basketball more."

Years of anger blurred his vision. "So you gambled with my future and I lost."

Susan breathed in and out again. "I'm truly sorry, Troy. I know that what I did was wrong. It was selfish. I regret hurting you."

Troy stood and paced away from his desk. Away from Susan. "You did more than hurt me. You made a decision that changed my future." He hooked his hands on his hips and glared through his office window at the cool waves of the marina and the full bloom of spring on the trees below.

Susan's voice carried tentatively across the room. "I never should have lied to you. I was wrong. But, Troy, it was your decision to quit the team. And you

were the one who said we should get married before
we talked to your parents."

Troy turned back to her. "You told me I was going
to have a family to take care of. I couldn't continue
to play basketball. I had to earn a paycheck."

Susan stood, clutching her rose handbag, which
perfectly matched her linen pants suit. "You didn't
tell me you were going to give up your scholarship.
You just did it."

Troy ran his hand over his hair. "It seemed like a
logical decision."

"But it was *your* decision, not mine." Susan spread
her arms to encompass his office. "And it seems
everything turned out fine for you. Your mother said
you were happy."

Troy scanned his office, lingering over the familiar
awards and commendations. He was a successful executive working for an organization that was well regarded
in the community. He hadn't needed Andrea to tell him
that. But she'd been right to insist he take responsibility for his actions. The realization shamed him.

He shoved his hands into the front pockets of his
suit pants. "Yes, I'm very happy."

"And I'm very sorry. What more can I say?" Susan's
gaze appealed to him.

Now that he could think clearly, Troy realized he
was verbally striking out at a college coed who no
longer existed. She'd grown into a mature woman
whose sincerity he couldn't doubt. He heard it in her
words and saw it in her expression. Troy returned to
his desk.

"Please." He gestured toward her chair. They both
sat. "Why was it so important to you to apologize after
all this time?"

A blush rose into her cheeks. "I've wanted to apologize to you for a while."

"Why didn't you?" Troy picked up his pen from his desk and rolled it between his right thumb and index finger. "You could have reached me through the Monarchs. The number's listed."

Susan crossed her legs and folded her hands on her right thigh. "After my second marriage fell apart, I took a hard look at my life."

"It must have been easier with the divorce settlement. I heard you made out like a bandit." He regretted the dig almost as soon as it was out of his mouth.

Susan inclined her head. "The decision was very generous. I asked the court to stop the payments ten years ago."

Troy did the math. She'd ended her alimony one year after her divorce. "Why?"

"I wasn't in love with Sam when I married him. But the divorce still left me with a lot of regrets, on top of the ones I had from our breakup. I wanted to start over."

"Why didn't you call me then?"

Susan shrugged. "I was ashamed, so I put the past behind me. It worked at first. I was building my consulting company and taking care of myself. And then I met someone. A couple of months ago, he asked me to marry him."

"Oh, yeah?" Troy's surprised gaze dropped to her ringless fingers.

Susan's smile was unsteady. "I told him what I'd done and that I needed to at least apologize to you before I could plan for my future. I've already apologized to Sam."

He heard Andrea telling him that with forgiveness came second chances. He wasn't going to deny Susan a second chance at happiness. It's what he wanted, too, with Andrea.

"You were right. I made my own decisions. Things didn't turn out the way I'd planned, but I'm very happy. And I hope you will be, too." Troy's heart felt lighter than it had in more than a decade. He hadn't realized how much of a burden it had been to carry that much hatred and resentment.

Susan's smile bloomed into a grin. Her eyes shone like dark marbles. "Thank you, Troy. You don't know how much your words mean to me."

He dropped his pen. "I think I do."

The sensation of freedom stole his breath. All this time he'd been too stupid to realize he'd been chained to his past. Now he could move forward toward his own future. His blood chilled. But, dear God, was he too late?

"Did you get the job?"

Andrea's key was still in her apartment door Friday afternoon when Faith appeared out of thin air demanding answers. Her roommate had changed out of her business clothes and into baggy green sweatpants and an oversized white jersey displaying a red exclamation point.

Andrea freed her key from the lock. She squeezed past her roommate into the apartment and secured the door. "They offered it to me."

Faith's brown features lit like a firecracker on Independence Day. "Congratulations! That's wonderful!"

Andrea observed her friend. She should be the one jumping up and down and screaming. She'd just secured a dream job with *The New York Times* weeks before *New York Sports* closed for good. She should be babbling with excitement. Instead she was numb.

"Thank you." Andrea dropped her keys into her purse. Why didn't she feel anything?

Faith's enthusiasm stuttered and died. "Did you take the job?"

She started toward the living room. "I haven't decided yet."

"What? Are you nuts?"

Andrea winced at Faith's shriek. "I don't want to make a mistake." She dropped onto the sofa, still wearing her blazer and clutching her purse.

Faith sat beside her. Her brown eyes were wide with incredulity. "How could accepting your dream job be a mistake?"

Andrea stared across the room. Through the window was the fire escape where she and Troy had started the uneasy alliance that had grown into the greatest love affair of her life. "I don't know whether I'm qualified for what they want me to write."

Faith folded her arms and crossed her legs. "This is *The New York Times,* not a student newspaper. They wouldn't hire you if they didn't think you were qualified."

Andrea started to feel again. Her fingers drilled into her purse while panic battered her like tsunami waves. "They want me to write human interest features."

"They don't want you to write sports?" Faith sounded confused.

"I'll cover some sports, but my focus will be the personality pieces." She pulled her fingers through her hair. "They want me to 'get into the mind of high-profile people in the community.' Their words."

Faith frowned. "You mean like the stories you wrote about Barron and Gerry?"

"That's right."

"You've done it before. So what's the problem?" Faith's voice was as dry as dust.

Andrea bent forward. She steadied her elbows on her lap and pressed her forehead against her fists. She was swamped with emotions—edgy, restless feelings that made it difficult to think. "Suppose those stories are the only personality pieces I have? Those stories came to me."

"No, they didn't. You found them because you dug deeper than other people were willing to look." Faith stood. "When that anonymous source called you with a tip about the Monarchs' head coach, you went to the coach to check it out."

Andrea raised her head. "So?"

Faith threw her arms up. "And when other people dismissed Barron's drinking and careless behavior as just the same old, same old from Mr. Bling, you nagged him until he faced his fears."

She hadn't nagged Barron. "That's because I'd been where he was going."

"That's why you're able to write these stories." Faith sat again. "You're sensitive to the subject matter and willing to take the time to dig a little deeper. You went through a bad situation after that Jackie Jones article, but it's made you an even better reporter."

Andrea pulled her handbag off her shoulder. "I don't know about that."

"I do." Faith's tone was adamant. "I'm not a newspaper reporter. I write comic books. But I know talent when I read it. You have to believe in yourself."

Andrea breathed deeply to steady her nerves. She caught the spicy scent of the chicken Faith was cooking for dinner. "I believe I can cover sports. I don't know if I have a series of in-depth personality profiles in me."

"Do you want to find out?"

Her stomach muscles knotted. "Part of me does. It would be a new challenge. And, although I like covering sports, those profiles impacted people beyond the game." She dropped her gaze to her white-knuckled grip on her purse. "But the other part of me is scared witless."

Faith spread her hands. "Why? You've already proven you can do it."

"I've proven I can write two." Andrea shrugged out of her blazer and folded it over the back of the sofa.

Faith's brows knitted. "Is this the same insecurity you told me about from your past? The one that led you to write that story about Jackie Jones in the first place?"

Andrea stood from the sofa and hooked her hands on her navy blue pants. Troy had advised her against taking the first job offer—unless it was for a good company. Well, this offer was from a good company, so why was she hesitating?

Because she was afraid.

Her dream company wanted her to write the type of stories she hadn't even realized she wanted to write. Stories that would make a difference in the community, comfort some and inspire others.

Your story will do that. She heard again the pride in Troy's voice when he'd said those words.

Faith prompted her. "Are you going to let your insecurities defeat you again?"

Andrea dropped her arms. "No, I'm not."

"Do you want the job or not?"

Andrea checked her wristwatch. It was almost six o'clock. Constance and Tiffany would be home soon, but she was certain *The New York Times* sports editor was still at his desk.

"Yes, I do." She strode to the sofa and dug through her purse for the editor's business card. She turned to the telephone on the corner table. "Please let him still be there."

Andrea lifted the receiver and pressed the direct dial numbers for the editor's desk. The final steps on her personal journey for redemption. She'd finally and fully forgiven herself for her past. She could do this job. She wanted the position and she deserved this opportunity. She closed her eyes and thought of Troy. The journey's end would have been much more satisfying if he'd been there to meet her.

Andrea arrived at Madison Square Garden half an hour before game seven of the Brooklyn Monarchs versus New York Knicks series Monday evening. The sound system had boosted Lenny Kravitz's "Come On Get It." The JumboTron suspended from the rafters was telecasting highlights from previous games in the series.

Was the excitement pulsing through her veins coming from her? Or was she picking up the tension from the fans pouring into the arena? It was hard to tell since the outcome of the game was so important to her. With their win in the Empire Arena Saturday, the Monarchs had tied the series at three all. A win would send them to the Eastern Conference Championship. A loss would finish their Cinderella season. Andrea didn't want the magic to end.

She stopped beside Jenna Madison's chair and pitched her voice above Lenny Kravitz's latest rock anthem. "Thank you for recommending me to your editor."

Jenna shook her head. "It wasn't me. It was your writing. I'm looking forward to working with you."

Andrea glowed on the inside. "I'm looking forward to working with you, too."

Jenna jerked her chin toward the court before turning back to Andrea. "Will you miss covering the games?"

Andrea watched the Monarchs going through their shooting drills and stretches on the far side of the court. DeMarcus and the other coaches were studying sheets Andrea assumed were the plays and scouting reports. Troy was probably in the visiting owners' booth above them. She tensed her muscles so she didn't look up.

She met Jenna's green gaze. "A little. But I'll enjoy just watching them. I'll be able to cheer out loud."

Jenna chuckled. "There is that."

Andrea continued her search for an empty chair in the media row. She settled into a seat and booted up her laptop, strenuously avoiding even glancing at the luxury boxes above her.

Two hours later, Andrea wanted to scream, "Time-out!" The game clock counted down the remaining twenty-eight seconds of the game. The Monarchs had more turnovers than the neighborhood bakery, and the lead had changed six times in the last twenty minutes. Andrea sensed the Monarchs slowing down. This was their second series playing all seven games. They had the oldest roster in the NBA, and it was beginning to show. Andrea fought to hold on to hope.

Twenty-seven seconds. Twenty-six. Twenty-five. The shot clock shut off.

For now, the Knicks had the lead—109 to 107—as well as possession. Ronny Turiaf was almost at half-court dribbling the ball forward and gesturing his teammates into position. In a panic, Andrea realized the Knicks' forward was slowing the pace of the game and using up the clock. Twenty-four seconds. Twenty-three. She was going to lose her mind.

Warrick defended Amar'e Stoudemire. Serge blocked Carmelo Anthony at the post. The Monarchs' Anthony guarded Turiaf at the left perimeter. Jamal covered Renaldo Balkman on the right. Vincent defended Chauncey Billups in the paint. Twenty-two seconds. Twenty-one. Andrea's mind screamed, "Somebody *do* something!"

As though hearing her thoughts above the shouts of the crowd, Vincent moved up to help Warrick pressure Stoudemire. Anthony shifted right to split his defense between Turiaf and Billups.

Stoudemire took a chance and sent a rainbow toward the basket. Serge and Carmelo leaped for the ball, grabbing it together and falling back to the court in a tangle of limbs. The referee blew his whistle. Jump ball. Andrea hated that, but she'd hate a loss even more.

With the game clock frozen at fifteen seconds, the referee took his position between Serge and Carmelo. He held the ball above his head. As he blew his whistle again, he hoisted the ball up and stepped back. Serge leaped, and Andrea almost rose with him. He punched the ball toward Vincent, who snatched it out of the air and sprinted down court. The crowd rocked the Garden with their roars of "Defense! Defense!"

Vincent bounced the ball hard, advancing it to Anthony with eleven seconds on the clock. Ten. Nine. Eight. The Knicks' Carmelo dove into the open lane for the steal. Andrea's heart lodged in her throat as she watched him hustle up court with Anthony and

Vincent giving chase. She wanted to close her eyes, but she couldn't. Seven seconds. Six. Five.

Warrick glided into Carmelo's path. With a move as graceful as a modern dancer, he spun around Carmelo, scooping the ball with him. Andrea blinked. *How had he done that?*

As Warrick flew past Anthony and Vincent, his teammates defended his back against the Knicks. Under her breath, Andrea chanted, "Hurry! Hurry! Hurry!" The game clock drained. Four. Three. Warrick pulled up at the perimeter. Two. He leaped into the air. One. And released the ball.

Three points. The Monarchs stole the win, 110 to 109, and advanced to the Eastern Conference Championship.

Andrea was drained.

Troy looked up as Andrea opened the door to her apartment Sunday afternoon. His gaze moved from her bare feet with their bright yellow toenails, up her long legs in slender blue jeans. She wore a pale yellow jersey with a black-and-white sketch of the Underdog superhero cartoon. Her long dark hair was tussled around her heart-shaped face. Her sherry eyes were wary.

"Troy?" She stood with her left hand on the doorknob.

"I've changed." That wasn't the greeting he'd practiced last night after the Monarchs had beaten the Knicks. But it seemed to work.

Andrea stepped back to let him in. "As much as I like Mrs. Garrard, I'd rather she didn't overhear our conversation."

She locked the door behind them, then led him

through her small apartment. In the living room, he paused to greet her roommates.

Faith sat curled on the sofa. She lowered her sketchbook. Her startled eyes dodged from him to Andrea and back. "Troy, how've you been?"

He offered her a smile. "Fine, thanks. And you?"

Faith nodded. "Great. Great."

Troy looked to Constance, seated on the love seat with her daughter. "Hi, Connie."

Constance gave him a warm smile. "Hi, Troy."

Tiffany hopped off the love seat. "D-O-G spells dog. Woof! Woof!"

Troy chuckled at the little girl's antics. His humor faded as he considered Andrea's and her roommates' frozen expressions. He crossed his arms over his black cotton shirt as he struggled with a grin. "I take it she wasn't supposed to perform that for me?"

Andrea grabbed his upper arm. "Why don't we step out onto the fire escape?"

He hated the fire escape, but he let her lead him there anyway. "At least it's warmer today."

"I thought you said you'd changed." Andrea muscled open the window, then climbed onto the fire escape.

Troy contorted his frame to fit through the tiny opening, stepping gingerly onto the red metal structure. "I have, Andy. I took your advice and met with my ex-wife."

Andrea's eyebrows jumped toward her hairline. "When?"

He pushed his hands into the back pockets of his blue jeans. "Friday."

Her eyes darkened with concern. "How do you feel?"

He gave a startled laugh. Troy hadn't expected her to ask that question. "I feel free. You were right. I carried a lot of baggage with me from that experience. And I put a lot of blame on her for things that were my fault. I've accepted responsibility for my own poor decisions."

Andrea blinked a couple of times before speaking. "Troy, I'm so happy for you."

He wanted more than that. "I'm not saying Susan and I are friends now. But I've forgiven her for lying to me, and I don't resent her for the choices I made anymore."

Andrea nodded. Her eyes shimmered with happy tears. "That's what I'd wanted for you."

Troy pulled his hands from his pockets and let his arms fall to his sides. "While I was talking with Susan, I realized my life may not have turned out the way I'd planned, but I'm happy. I'm where I'm supposed to be. But I don't want to be here without you."

Troy's words were so similar to the thought that had echoed in her mind when she'd accepted *The New York Times*'s job offer Friday night. They sent a sweet ache through Andrea's body. She closed her eyes against the draw of his ebony gaze.

A soft breeze feathered her cheek. Andrea opened her eyes as Troy lowered his hand from her face. She stepped back, startled to find him so close. He'd moved so quietly.

He caught her hand to keep her near. "You asked me to change, Andy. I didn't think I could, but I wanted to try. And you were right. I needed to clear the past with Susan. Now I want a future with you. Give me another chance. I love you so much."

She'd played this game before. She didn't want to lose again. "Suppose I wanted to write that article about the Monarchs' founding partners." She didn't, but she had to test him again.

Troy stayed silent for so long. Every second chipped away at her hope. His dark gaze hovered inches above her face. "I can't think of a reporter who'd do a better job with that story."

Andrea narrowed her eyes on his too-handsome face. She needed a harder question, a bigger lie. "I want to interview Rick Evans about the strain his NBA career has had on his marriage."

Surprise shifted in Troy's eyes. "I can't force Rick to talk with you, but I promise not to get in your way."

Her lips parted in surprise. "Really?" Could she believe him?

"Andy, your questions are sensitive and your stories are fair. You proved that when you interviewed Jackie about Gerry's meddling and Barron about his drinking. It's Rick and Mary's decision if they want to talk with you."

Andrea crossed her arms. "Suppose I told you those stories would appear in the *Times*, which has a much larger circulation than *Sports*?"

A broad grin brightened Troy's classic good looks. "You're working for the *Times* now?"

Andrea laughed. "Yes." She enjoyed sharing the good news with him. "So what would you say if I wrote those articles for the *Times*?"

Troy swept her into his arms and held her tight. "I'd say they were lucky to have you."

Andrea blinked her surprise. She pulled back to look at him. "You really *have* changed."

His lips hovered inches above her own. "I was highly motivated and had a game plan to win you back."

Andrea smiled. "I do love a man with a plan."

She rose onto her toes and sealed his lips with a kiss.

If you enjoyed *Smooth Play,*
don't miss Regina Hart's

Fast Break

Available wherever books are sold.

Prologue

"Clock's ticking, Guinn."

DeMarcus Guinn, shooting guard for the National Basketball Association's Miami Waves, looked at his head coach, then at the game clock. Thirteen seconds remained in game seven of the NBA finals. The Waves and Sacramento Kings were tied at 101. His coach had just called a time-out. DeMarcus stood on the sidelines surrounded by his teammates. He wiped the sweat from his forehead and drained his sports drink. It didn't help.

He looked into the stands and found his father standing in the bleachers. He saw the empty seat beside him. His mother's seat. DeMarcus rubbed his chest above his heart.

"Guinn! You need to step it up out there." His coach's tone was urgent.

Why? What did it matter now?

His coach grabbed his arm. "Do you have this, Guinn?"

The buzzer sounded to end the twenty-second time-out.

DeMarcus pulled his arm free of his coach's grasp. "I've got this."

He joined his teammates on the court, walking through a wall of tension thick enough to hammer. Waves' fans had been cheering, stomping and chanting nonstop throughout the fourth quarter. DeMarcus looked up again at the crowd and the empty seat.

"Are you with us, Marc?" Marlon Burress, his teammate for the past thirteen years, looked at him with concern.

"I'm good." *Was he?*

DeMarcus saw the intensity of the four other Waves on the court. He looked at his teammates and coaches on the sideline. He saw his father in the stands. He had to find a way to play past the pain, if not for his team or his father, then for his mother's memory.

DeMarcus took his position near midcourt. The Waves' Walter Millbank stood ready to inbound the ball. Marlon shifted closer to the basket.

The referee tossed Walter the ball. The Kings' Carl Landry defended him, waving his arms and leaping to distract him from the play. Marlon balanced on his toes and extended his arms for the ball. Thirteen seconds on the game clock. The referee blew his whistle to signal the play.

Ignoring the Kings' defender, Walter hurled the ball to Marlon. With the ball an arm's length from Marlon's fingers, the Kings' Samuel Dalembert leaped into the lane. Turnover. The crowd screamed its disappointment.

Eleven seconds on the game clock.

Dalembert spun and charged down court. Marlon and Walter gave chase.

Ten seconds on the game clock.

DeMarcus saw Dalembert racing toward him. The

action on the court slowed to a ballroom dance. The crowd's chants of "Defense!" faded into the background.

DeMarcus's vision narrowed to Dalembert, the ball and the game clock. From midcourt, he stepped into Dalembert's path. His concentration remained on the ball. He smacked it from Dalembert, reclaiming possession. Waves fans roared. The arena shook.

Seven seconds on the game clock.

DeMarcus's vision widened to include his teammates and the Kings' defenders. With Marlon, Walter and the other Waves guarding the Kings, DeMarcus charged back up court. His goal—the net, two points and the win. He felt Dalembert closing in on him from behind.

Five seconds. Four seconds. Three seconds.

DeMarcus leaped for the basket, extending his body and his arm, stretching for the rim.

One second.

Slam!

Miami Waves, 103. Sacramento Kings, 101.

The crowd roared. Balloons and confetti rained from the rafters. The Waves' bench cleared. The team had survived the last-minute challenge from the Kings to claim the win and the NBA championship title.

DeMarcus looked into the stands and found his father. He was cheering and waving his fists with the other Waves fans. Beside him, the seat remained empty. His mother would never cheer from the stands again.

Less than an hour later, showered and changed from his Waves uniform into a black, Italian-cut suit, DeMarcus entered the team's media room. Reporters waited for the post-finals press conference. They lobbed questions at him before he'd taken his seat.

"What does this championship mean to you?"

"Why did you seem dazed during the fourth quarter?"

"You made the winning basket. What are you going to do now?"

He latched on to the last question. "I'm retiring from the NBA."

DeMarcus stood and left the room.

1

Two years later

"Cut the crap, Guinn."

DeMarcus Guinn felt the sting of the honey-and-whiskey voice. It slapped him from the doorway of his newly acquired office in the Empire Arena. He looked up from his National Basketball Association paperwork and across the room's silver-carpeted expanse.

Standing in the polished oak threshold, Jaclyn Jones radiated anger. It vibrated along every curve of her well-toned figure. Contempt hardened her long cinnamon eyes. The media had nicknamed the former Women's National Basketball Association shooting guard the Lady Assassin. Her moniker was a tribute to her holding the fewest number of fouls yet one of the highest scoring records in the league.

As of today, DeMarcus called her boss.

DeMarcus pushed his heavy, black executive chair back from his massive oak desk and stood. He didn't understand Jaclyn's accusatory tone or her hostility, but confusion didn't justify poor manners. "Excuse me?"

"You took the Monarchs' head coach position."
She threw the words at him.

DeMarcus's confusion multiplied. "Why wouldn't
I? You offered it."

Jaclyn strode into his office. Her blood red skirt
suit cut a wave of heat across the silver carpet, white
walls and black furniture. Her fitted jacket highlighted the rose undertone of her golden brown skin.
Slender hips swayed under the narrow, mid-calf skirt.
Three-inch red stilettos boosted her six-foot-plus
height.

She stopped behind one of the three black-cushioned guest chairs facing his desk and dropped her
large gray purse onto its seat. Her red-tipped nails
dug into the fat chair cushion. "That was my partners' decision. Gerry and Bert extended the offer.
I was against it."

Her admission surprised him. DeMarcus shoved
his hands into the soft pockets of his brown khaki
pants. Why was she telling him this? Whatever the
reason, it couldn't be good. "I didn't ask to interview
for the Brooklyn Monarchs' head coach job. *You*
came to *me*."

Jaclyn shook her head. Her curly, dark brown hair
swung around her shoulders. It drew his attention
to the silver and black Brooklyn Monarchs lapel pin
fastened to her collar. "Not me. Gerry and Bert." Her
enunciation was crisp and clear.

So was her meaning. *You don't have what it takes. Stop
wasting our time.*

Confusion made a blind pass to bitterness. De-
Marcus swallowed it back. "Why don't you want me as
your coach?"

"The Monarchs need a winning season. We need

this season. You don't have the experience to make that happen."

"I don't have coaching experience, but I've been in the league for fifteen years—"

Jaclyn raised her right hand, palm out, cutting him off. "And in that time, you won two NBA championship rings, three MVP titles and an Olympic gold medal. I saw the games and read the sports reports."

"Then you know I know how to win."

She quirked a sleek, arched brow. "You can *play* to win, but can you *coach?*"

"Winning is important to me."

"It's important to me, too. That's why I want an *experienced* head coach."

DeMarcus clenched his teeth. Jaclyn Jones was a pleasure to look at and her voice turned him on. But it had been a long, draining day, and he didn't have time for this shit.

He circled his desk and took a position an arm's length from her. "If you didn't want to hire me, why am I here?"

She moved in closer to him. "Majority rule. Gerry and Bert wanted you. I'd hoped, after the interview, you'd realize you were out of your element."

DeMarcus's right temple throbbed each time he remembered the way she'd interrogated him a month ago. He should have realized she'd been driven by more than thoroughness. Gerald Bimm and Albert Tipton had tried to run interference, but the Lady Assassin had blocked their efforts.

DeMarcus shook his head. "I'm not out of my element. I know the game. I know the league, and I know what it takes to win."

Jaclyn scowled up at him. A soft floral fragrance—lilac?—floated toward him. He could see the darker flecks in her cinnamon eyes. His gaze dipped to her full red lips

"But you don't know how to coach." Her expression dared him to disagree. "When you were with the Miami Waves, you led by example, picking up the pace when your teammates weren't producing. You were amazing. But I don't need another player. I need a coach."

DeMarcus crossed his arms. "We went over this during my interview. I wouldn't have taken this job if I couldn't perform."

Jaclyn blinked. Her gaze swept his white shirt, green tie and brown pants before she pivoted to pace his cavernous office. "We're talking about coaching."

"I know." DeMarcus tracked her movements from the black lacquered coffee service set against his far left wall and back to his desk. Her red outfit complimented the office's silver and black décor, the Monarchs's team colors.

The only things filling the void of his office were furniture—his oak desk, a conversation table, several chairs and a bookcase. The tall, showy plant in the corner was fake.

Jaclyn paced away from him again. Her voice carried over her shoulder. "The Monarchs finished last season with nineteen wins and sixty-three losses."

DeMarcus heard her frustration. "They finished at the bottom of the Eastern Conference."

"We were at the bottom of the *league*." Jaclyn turned to approach him. Her eyes were tired, her expression strained. "What are you going to do to turn the team around?"

He shrugged. "Win."

She was close enough to smell the soft lilac fragrance on her skin, feel the warmth of her body and hear the grinding of her teeth. "You sound so confident, so self-assured. It will take more than the strength of the Mighty Guinn's personality to pull the team out of its tailspin."

"I'm aware of that." He hated the nickname the media had given him.

"Then how are you planning to win? What's your strategy?"

As majority owner of the Brooklyn Monarchs, Jaclyn was his boss. DeMarcus had to remember that, even as her antagonism pressed him to respond in kind.

He took a deep breath, calling on the same techniques he'd used to center himself before making his free throws. "I'm going to work on increasing their speed and improving their defense. Your players can earn style points, but they do everything in slow motion." Jaclyn stared at him as though expecting something more. "I can give you more details after I've studied their game film."

He glanced at the tower of digital video discs waiting for him to carry them home. It was late September. Training camp had started under the interim head coach, and preseason was two weeks away. He didn't have a lot of time to turn the team around.

Jaclyn settled her long, slender hands on her slim hips and cocked her right knee. The angle of her stance signaled her intent to amp up their confrontation. DeMarcus narrowed his eyes, trying to read her next move.

"Maybe I should have been more specific." Her voice had cooled. "The players no longer think they're capable of winning. How are you going to change their attitudes?"

"By giving them the skills they need to win."

"These aren't a bunch of high school kids. They're NBA players. They already have the skills to win."

"Then why aren't they winning?"

Jaclyn dragged her hand through her thick, curly hair. "Winning builds confidence. Losing breeds doubt. I'm certain you've heard that before."

"Yes." But why was she bringing it up now?

"Even with the skills, they won't win unless they believe they *can* win. How do you plan to make them believe?"

DeMarcus snorted. "You don't want a coach. You want Dr. Phil."

Jaclyn sighed. "And you're neither. I'd like your resignation, please."

DeMarcus stared. He couldn't have heard her correctly. "What?"

"It would save both of us a great deal of embarrassment and disappointment."

His mind went blank. His skin grew cold. Jaclyn had landed a sucker punch without laying a finger on him. "You want my resignation? I've only been here one day."

"Think of your reputation. Everyone remembers you as a winner. You're jeopardizing your legacy by taking a position you're not qualified for."

Blood flooded his veins again, making his skin burn. "I disagree. I have what it takes to lead this team."

Jaclyn didn't appear to be listening. She dropped her hands from her hips and paced his spacious office. "You can keep the signing bonus."

"It's not about the money." The vein above his right temple had started to throb. He heard the anger in his voice but didn't care. He was through playing nice with his new boss. She was threatening his goal and maligning his character.

Jaclyn frowned at him. "Then what *is* it about?"

DeMarcus doubted she was interested in his motives for wanting to be the head coach of the Brooklyn Monarchs. "I'm not a quitter."

"You're not a coach."

DeMarcus studied the elegant features of her golden brown face—her high cheekbones, pointed chin and long-lidded eyes—searching for a clue to her thoughts. What was her game? "Do you have someone else in mind for my job?"

Her full, moist lips tightened. "We interviewed several candidates I consider much more qualified to lead this team."

"Gerry and Bert hired me. Your partners don't respect your opinion."

Jaclyn made an irritated sound. "I've realized my business partners don't have the team's best interests at heart."

"Careful, or you'll hurt my feelings."

Jaclyn's eyes narrowed. "Are you helping them destroy the team?"

"What are you talking about?" Was Jaclyn Jones unbalanced?

"Why would you stay where you're not wanted?"

He gave her a wry smile. "But I *am* wanted. I have the letter offering me this job to prove it."

"I didn't sign that letter."

DeMarcus turned to reclaim his seat behind his desk. "Two out of three isn't bad."

Jaclyn followed him, stopping on the other side of his desk. "You should be more careful of the company you keep. Gerry and Bert don't care about the team. They don't care about you, either."

"I don't need your help picking my friends." DeMarcus pulled his seat under his desk before giving

Jaclyn a cool stare. "Now, you'll have to excuse me. I have work to do."

Jaclyn straightened. "I want your resignation. Now."

DeMarcus dropped his mask and let her see all the anger he'd been hiding. "No."

"Then you're not getting my support."

"Lady, you don't scare me." He leaned back in his seat. "You're convinced I don't have what it takes to coach your team, but you haven't given me one damn reason why you've made that call."

"I've given you several."

DeMarcus held up one finger. "You want someone who'll get in touch with your players' emotions. Look, if they don't want to win, they don't belong on your team."

"You don't have the authority to fire players." There was apprehension in her eyes.

He raised a second finger. "You think your partners aren't looking out for the team. That's only because you didn't get your way."

"That's not true."

He lifted a third finger. "You don't think I can coach." DeMarcus stood. "How do you know that? Have you seen me coach?"

"Have *you* seen you coach?" Jaclyn clamped her hands onto her hips.

DeMarcus jerked his chin, indicating his office. "This is what I want, an opportunity to lead the Brooklyn Monarchs to a winning season. And, in a few years, bring home the championship. We have to be realistic. That won't happen this season. But it will happen. That's my goal. And I'll be damned if I'm going to let anyone deny me."

Jaclyn's gaze wavered. But then she raised her chin

and squared her shoulders. "That's a very moving speech, Guinn. Can you back it up?"

"Watch me." DeMarcus settled back into his seat and nodded toward his doorway. "But do it from the other side of the door."

The heat of her anger battered his cold control. DeMarcus held her gaze and his silence. Finally, Jaclyn inclined her head. She grabbed her purse from the guest chair and left.

DeMarcus scrubbed his face with both hands, hoping to ease his temper. The Lady Assassin had charged him like a lead-footed defender at the post.

Why?

They shared the same goal—a winning season for the Monarchs. Then why was she determined to get rid of him?

Cold air cut into Jaclyn's skirt suit as she exited the Empire Arena. Leaving her coat at home during autumn in Brooklyn hadn't been a good idea. But at least the chilled breeze was cooling her temper.

She shivered as she hustled toward the curb. "Thanks for waiting, Herb." Jaclyn gave the liveried limousine driver a grateful smile.

Yes, she was angry about the Mighty Guinn's galactic stubbornness and mammoth ego. But she wouldn't project her wrath onto Herbert Trasker. The quiet older gentleman from the limo service she retained had been driving her around the city for years.

Herbert straightened away from the silver Bentley sedan. The black suit and tie made his wiry frame seem taller. "You're welcome, Ms. Jones."

Herbert's emerald eyes twinkled at her. With a

familiar gesture, the driver touched the brim of the black leather hat covering his iron gray hair. He opened the back passenger-side door and waited while Jaclyn thanked him before settling in. Their routine eased some of her tension.

Herbert slid behind the wheel. "The Bonner and Taylor office, Ms. Jones?"

"Yes, thank you, Herb." She'd stopped trying to get him to call her Jaclyn.

Herbert muscled the Bentley into the crowded, chaotic streets and set it on a course toward the downtown law firm. Bonner & Taylor represented the owners of the Empire Arena, which had been the home of the Brooklyn Monarchs since the franchise's birth in 1956.

Herbert maneuvered them past the neighborhoods of the borough in which she'd been born and raised—the congested city sidewalks, packed bodegas and busy storefronts. Framing these streets were trees, young and old, their brilliant autumn colors vying for attention.

The glass and metal corporate building that housed Bonner & Taylor rose into view. Jaclyn beat back her cresting nervousness. Could she convince the arena owners' lawyers to extend the franchise's opt-out clause?

Herbert double-parked beside a delivery van and activated the Bentley's hazard lights. He climbed from the driver's seat and circled the sedan to hand Jaclyn from the car. Stepping onto the street, Jaclyn felt as though she were moving in slow motion.

"I'll meet you right here, Ms. Jones."

She smiled with more confidence than she felt. "Thank you."

Jaclyn strode to the offices. Revolving doors swung

her into the tall, thin building. Her stilettos clicked against the stone floor as she crossed the lobby. The business directory mounted to the marbled teal wall listed Bonner & Taylor's offices on the twenty-eighth floor of the thirty-floor structure.

Jaclyn wove through the hustling crowd toward the express elevators. The lobby reeked of wealth, prestige and self-importance. As she waited for the elevators, Jaclyn straightened the jacket of her power suit. Hopefully, it would prove more effective with Bonner & Taylor than it had with the Mighty Guinn.

Despite its claim to express service, the elevator ride gave her plenty of time to settle her nerves. It wasn't until its doors opened to the firm's offices that she realized she hadn't been successful.

A thin-faced, blond receptionist looked up as Jaclyn approached. "Good afternoon. May I help you?"

Jaclyn tried another confident smile. "Jaclyn Jones to see Misters Bonner and Taylor."

The receptionist's expression warmed to a polite welcome. "Yes, Ms. Jones. They're expecting you." She gestured toward a grouping of beige armchairs to the left of her desk. "Please make yourself comfortable. I'll let them know you're here."

She'd just settled into the chair, which was as comfortable as her sofa, when a tall, middle-aged gentleman in a double-breasted, navy pin-striped suit strode toward her. "Ms. Jones, I'm Greg Bonner. It's a pleasure to meet you."

Jaclyn stood and accepted Gregory's outstretched hand. "Thank you for meeting with me, Mr. Bonner."

"Greg, please." The firm's senior partner studied her with sharp, gray eyes. His salon-styled chestnut hair grew back from his forehead.

"And I'm Jackie."

"Denny's waiting for us in the conference room."

Jaclyn recognized the name of his law partner, Dennis Taylor. She fell into step beside Gregory. Her stilettos sank into the plush teal carpet that led to a wood-paneled conference room at the end of the wide hallway.

Another tall, stylish middle-aged man stepped around an impressive glass conference table to greet her.

He gave her right hand a firm shake. "I'm Denny Taylor, Ms. Jones. It's very nice to meet you."

"The pleasure's mine, Denny. And please call me Jackie."

Jaclyn sat, waiting for the law partners to join her before beginning. She assumed the inscrutable expression she wore when negotiating contracts for her firm's corporate clients. "Gentlemen, you know why I'm here."

Gregory shifted to face her across the glass table. "This season is the Monarchs' final opportunity to earn a profit. If it doesn't, our client can break your contract without either party incurring a penalty."

Jaclyn corrected the senior partner. "Earn a profit or break even."

"That's right." Dennis nodded, his dark blond hair catching the light.

The lawyers' blank expressions were unnerving. Jaclyn folded her shaking hands together. "We have several programs we're implementing this season to increase attendance and ticket sales. We're offering discounts on multiple ticket purchases, and hosting fan contests and theme games." The beat of silence lingered. Jaclyn resisted the urge to chatter nervously.

Gregory picked up his platinum Cross pen and

rolled it between his thumb and forefinger. "You reduced ticket prices last season. Sales didn't increase."

Dennis's concerned frown was disheartening. "If you reduce the price again, you'll have to sell even more tickets just to break even."

Jaclyn hid her own misgivings. "We've planned a more aggressive marketing campaign to increase sales."

Gregory shifted again in his maroon, straight back chair. "The Monarchs' fan base has eroded."

Dennis looked doubtful. "You'll have to do more than lower ticket prices to lure your fans back. Because of low attendance during the past three seasons, the Monarchs' games were blacked out of television more often than not. Without being able to see the games, a lot of your fans switched their loyalty to the New York Knicks. And the Knicks are winning."

Gregory nodded. "You'll have to win."

Dennis's smile was wry. "But that might not be so far-fetched now that you've hired Marc Guinn. He's a winner. He'll help revive the Monarchs' winning tradition."

Gregory brushed his hair back from his forehead. "And with his reputation, people will attend the games just to see him."

Jaclyn kept her own counsel. The Empire owners' lawyers didn't need to know she was hoping the media's NBA darling would pack his bags and leave. "That's a possibility." Her vague answer appeared to satisfy them.

Gregory rolled his pen again. "Even that bump in sales won't be enough to get the Monarchs out of the red. Have you considered asking the mayor to support a levy? The revenue from the tax increase could save your organization."

Jaclyn stiffened. "That's not an option. My grandfather started the Monarchs to give something back to his community. I'm not going to dishonor his legacy by going to the community with my hand out."

Dennis glanced at Gregory before returning his attention to Jaclyn. "What do Gerry and Bert think?"

"We've only briefly discussed the contract deadline, but I assume they agree with me." Jaclyn had no reason to believe otherwise. "Why are you asking?"

Gregory sat back in his chair. His sharp gaze scanned her features. "They called a couple of days ago to discuss options for getting out of the contract and moving the team."

Jaclyn blinked. "They never mentioned this to me."

Gregory and Dennis exchanged looks again before Dennis spoke. "We'd assumed this was the reason you wanted to meet. But without access to your accounting records, we don't know what kind of an offer you can expect from markets looking for NBA teams."

Jaclyn's heart stuttered. Gerald and Albert wanted to relocate the team? They knew she would never agree to move the Monarchs out of Brooklyn. Gregory had unknowingly confirmed her suspicions about her partners' intent toward the Monarchs. Some of their business decisions—such as hiring an inexperienced coach to save a struggling team—had struck her as irresponsible.

Why would Gerald and Albert discuss their plans with outsiders before talking with her? When she'd invited them to this meeting, they must have known the lawyers would mention their conversation. Had they intended she learn of their plans this way?

Jaclyn swallowed her dismay. "We're determined to turn the team around and generate more revenue." Or at least *she* was. "Is it possible to get another year on the opt-out clause in our arena contract?"

Gregory's tone was sympathetic. "I'm afraid not. Your grandfather agreed four years was a fair amount of time to allow the team to recover in the event of financial difficulties."

But when her grandfather had passed away almost two years ago, he probably had never dreamed his beloved Monarchs would fair so poorly.

Jaclyn straightened her shoulders and rose to her feet. There was nothing left to say. For now. The law partners stood with her. "Gentlemen, thank you for your time."

Dennis extended his hand to her. She winced at the pity in his pale blue eyes. "Good luck, Jackie. We hope you're able to rebuild the team."

Gregory escorted her back to the lobby. "The Monarchs have been good for the community. The franchise brought a lot of jobs in addition to excitement to Brooklyn. I hope you're able to keep it here."

She considered the senior partner. Her employer, Jonas & Prather Legal Associates, had negotiated with Bonner & Taylor on behalf of their clients in the past. Bonner & Taylor had always been diligent in protecting their clients' interests but fair in their dealings. "Do you have any advice for me?"

"We care about what happens to the community. But our client's interests have to come first." Gregory gave her a sympathetic smile. "Make the playoffs."

"I'll do my best." But it wouldn't be easy with her partners working against her. The weight on her shoulders was steadily increasing.